HOLY FOOLS

Joanne Harris

CHIVERS PRESS
BATH

First published 2003
by
Transworld Publishers Ltd
This Large Print edition published 2003
by
Chivers Press
by arrangement with
Transworld Publishers Ltd

ISBN 0 7540 9308 5

British Library Cataloguing in Publication Data available

Printed and bound in Great Britain by
Antony Rowe Ltd., Chippenham, Wiltshire

To Serafina

PART ONE
JULIETTE

CHAPTER ONE

♥

July 5th, 1610

It begins with the players. Seven of them, six men and a girl, she in sequins and ragged lace, they in leathers and silk. All of them masked, wigged, powdered, painted; Arlequin and Scaramouche and the long-nosed Plague Doctor, demure Isabelle and the lecherous Géronte, their gilded toenails bright beneath the dust of the road, their smiles whitened with chalk, their voices so harsh and so sweet that from the first they tore at my heart.

They arrived unannounced in a green and gold caravan, its panels scratched and scarred, but the scarlet inscription still legible for those who could read it.

Lazarillo's World Players!
Tragedy and Comedy!
Beasts and Marvels!

And all around the script paraded nymphs and satyrs, tigers and olifants in crimson, rose and violet. Beneath, in gold, sprawled the proud words:

Players to the King

I didn't believe it myself, though they say old Henri had a commoner's tastes, preferring a wild-beast show or a *comédie-ballet* to the most exquisite

3

of tragedies. Why, I danced for him myself on the day of his wedding, under the austere gaze of his Marie. It was my finest hour.

Lazarillo's troupe was nothing in comparison, and yet I found the display nostalgic, moving to a degree far beyond the skill of the players themselves. Perhaps a premonition; perhaps a fleeting vision of what once was, before the spoilers of the new Inquisition sent us into enforced sobriety, but as they danced, their purples and scarlets and greens ablaze in the sun's glare, I seemed to see the brave, bright pennants of ancient armies moving out across the battlefield, a defiant gesture to the sheet-shakers and apostates of the new order.

The Beasts and Marvels of the inscription consisted of nothing more marvellous than a monkey in a red coat and a small black bear, but there was, besides the singing and the masquerade, a fire-eater, jugglers, musicians, acrobats and even a rope-dancer, so that the courtyard was aflame with their presence and Fleur laughed and squealed with delight, hugging me through the brown weave of my habit.

The dancer was dark and curly-haired, with gold rings on her feet. As we watched she sprang onto a taut rope held on one side by Géronte and on the other by Arlequin. At the tambourin's sharp command they tossed her into the air, she turned a somersault and landed back on the rope as neatly as I might once have done. Almost as neatly, in any case; for I was with the *Théâtre des Cieux*, and I was l'Ailée, the Winged One, the Sky-dancer, the Flying Harpy. When I took to the high rope on my day of triumph, there was a gasp and a silence and the audience—soft ladies, powdered men, bishops, tradesmen, servants, courtiers, even the King himself—blanched and stared. Even now I remember his face—his powdered curls, his eager eyes—and the deafening surge of applause. Pride's a sin, of course, though personally I've never understood why. And some would say it's pride brought me where I am today—brought low, if you like, though they say I'll rise higher in the end. Oh, when Judgement Day comes I'll dance with the angels, Soeur Marguerite tells me, but she's a crazy, poor, twitching, tic-ridden thing, turning water into wine with the mixture from a bottle hidden beneath her mattress. She thinks I don't know, but in our dorter, with only a thin partition between each narrow bed, no one keeps their secrets for long. No one, that is, but me.

The Abbey of Sainte Marie-de-la-mer stands on the western side of the half-island of Noirs Moustiers. It is a sprawling building set around a central courtyard, with wooden outbuildings to the side and around the back. For the past five years it has been my home; by far the longest time I have ever stayed in any place. I am Soeur Auguste—who I was does not concern us; not yet, anyway. The abbey is perhaps the only refuge where the past may be left behind. But the past is a sly sickness. It may be carried on a breath of wind; in the sound of a flute; on the feet of a dancer. Too late, as always, I see this now; but there is nowhere for me to go but forward. It begins with the players. Who knows where it may end?

*　　　*　　　*

5

The rope-dancer's act was over. Now came juggling and music, while the leader of the troupe—Lazarillo himself, I presumed—announced the show's finale.

'And now, good sisters!' His voice, trained in theatres, rolled across the courtyard. 'For your pleasure and edification, for your amusement and delight—Lazarillo's World Players are proud to perform a Comedy of Manners, a most uproarious tale! I give you'—he paused dramatically, doffing his long-plumed tricorne—'*Les Amours de l'Hermite!*'

A crow, black bird of misfortune, flew overhead. For a second I felt the cool flicker of its shadow across my face and, with my fingers, forked the sign against malchance. *Tsk-tsk, begone!*

The crow seemed unmoved. He fluttered, ungainly, to the head of the well in the courtyard's centre, and I caught an impudent gleam of yellow from his eye. Below him, Lazarillo's troupe proceeded, undisturbed. The crow cocked his head quickly, greasily, in my direction.

Tsk-tsk, begone! I once saw my mother banish a swarm of wild bees with nothing more than that cantrip; but the crow simply opened his beak at me in silence, exposing a blue sliver of tongue. I suppressed the urge to throw a stone.

Besides, the play was already beginning: an evil cleric wished to seduce a beautiful girl. She took refuge in a convent, while her lover, a clown, tried to rescue her, disguised as a nun. They were discovered by the evil suitor, who swore that if he could not have the girl then no one would, only to be foiled by the sudden appearance of a monkey, which leaped onto the villain's head, allowing the

6

lovers to make good their escape.

The play was indifferent; the players themselves all but exhausted by the heat. Business must have been very bad, I thought, for the players to come to us. An island convent can offer little more than food and board—not even that, if rules are strictly applied. Maybe there had been trouble on the mainland. Times were hard for itinerants of all kinds. But Fleur loved the performance, clapping her hands and shouting encouragement to the squealing monkey. Next to her Perette, our youngest novice, looking rather like a monkey herself with her small vivid face and fluffy head, hooted with excitement.

The act was nearing its end. The lovers were reunited. The evil priest was unmasked. I felt slightly dizzy, as if the sun had turned my head, and in that moment I thought I saw someone else behind the players, standing against the light. I knew him at once; there was no mistaking the tilt of his head, or the way he stood, or the long shadow cast against the hard white ground. Knew him, though I saw him for no more than a second: Guy LeMerle, my very own black bird of ill-omen. Then he was gone.

*　　　*　　　*

This is how it begins: with the players, LeMerle, and the bird of malchance. *Luck turns like the tide*, my mother used to say. Maybe it was just our time to turn, as some heretics say the world turns, bringing creeping shadow to the places where once there was light. Maybe it was nothing. But even as the dancers capered and sang, spat fire from reddened lips, smirked from behind their masks, tumbled and rollicked and simpered and stamped the dirt with their gilded feet to the tune of tambour and flute, I seemed to perceive the shadow as it crept closer, covering scarlet petticoats and jingling tambourin, screaming monkey, motley, masks, Isabelle and Scaramouche with its long dark wing. I felt a shiver, even here in the midday sunlight with the whitewashed abbey walls buzzing with heat. The inexorable beginnings of momentum. The slow procession of our Last Days.

I'm not supposed to believe in signs and auguries. All that's in the past now, with the *Théâtre des Cieux*. But why see LeMerle, of all people, and after all these years? What could it mean? The shadow across my eyes had already passed and the players were coming to the end of their masque, bowing, sweating, smiling, flinging rose petals over our heads. They had more than earned their board for the night, and supplies for their journey.

Beside me, fat Soeur Antoine clapped her meaty hands, her face mottled with exertion. I was suddenly aware of the smell of her sweat, of the dust in my nostrils. Someone clawed my back; it was Soeur Marguerite, her pinched face halfway between pleasure and pain, mouth drawn down in a trembling bow of excitement. The reek of bodies intensified. And from the sisters lined against the heat-crackling walls of the abbey came a cry both shrill and oddly savage, an *aiiii!* of pleasure and release, as if natural energies, loosened by the heat, had brought a kind of insanity to their applause. *Aii! Encore! Aii! Encore!*

Then I heard it; a single raised discordant voice,

almost lost in a fury of acclamations. *Mère Marie,* I
heard. *Reverend Mother is . . .* then once again the
distracted buzzing of heat and voices, then the one
voice again, higher than the rest.

I looked around for the source of the cry and
saw Soeur Alfonsine, the consumptive nun,
standing high upon the chapel steps, arms spread,
her face white and exalted. Few of the sisters paid
her any attention. Lazarillo's troupe was taking a
last bow: the actors went round once more with
flowers and bonbons, the fire-eater gave a final
spurt of flame, the monkey turned a somersault.
Arlequin's face was running with greasepaint.
Isabelle—too old for the part, and with a visible
paunch—was melting away in the heat, her scarlet
mouth smeared halfway to her ears.

Soeur Alfonsine was still shouting, straining to
be heard above the voices of the nuns. 'It's a
judgement on us!' I thought she said. 'A terrible
judgement!'

Now some of the nuns looked exasperated;
Alfonsine was never happier than when she was
doing penance for something. 'For pity's sake,
Alfonsine, what now?'

She fixed us with her martyr's eyes. 'My sisters!'
she said, more in accusation than grief. 'The
Reverend Mother is dead!'

And at those words a silence fell over all of us.
The players looked guilty and confused, as if aware
that their welcome had been suddenly withdrawn.
The tambourin player let his arm drop to his side
in a harsh jangle of bells.

'Dead?' As if it could not be real in this iron
heat, beneath this sledgehammer sky.

Alfonsine nodded; behind me, Soeur Marguerite

was already beginning to keen. *Miserere nobis, miserere nobis . . .*

Fleur looked up at me, puzzled, and I caught her in my arms with sudden fierceness. 'Is it finished?' she asked me. 'Will the monkey dance again?'

I shook my head. 'I don't think so.'

'Why not? Was it the black bird?'

I looked at her, startled. Five years old and she sees everything. Her eyes are like pieces of mirror reflecting the sky—today blue, tomorrow the purple-grey of a storm cloud's belly.

'The black bird,' she repeated impatiently. 'He's gone now.'

I glanced back over my shoulder and saw that she was right. The crow had gone, his message delivered, and I knew then for certain that my premonition was true. Our time in the sunlight had finally come to an end. The masquerade was over.

CHAPTER TWO
♥

July 6th, 1610

We sent the players into town. They left with an air of hurt reproach, as if we had accused them of something. But it would not have been decent to keep them in the abbey, not in the presence of death. I brought their supplies myself—hay for the horses, bread, goat's cheese rolled in cinders and a bottle of good wine, for the sake of travelling theatres everywhere—and bade them good-bye.

Lazarillo gave me a keen look as he turned to

go. 'You look familiar, *ma soeur*. Could it be that we have met before?'

'I don't think so. I've been here since I was a child.'

He shrugged. 'Too many towns. Faces begin to look the same.'

I knew the feeling, although I did not say so.

'Times are hard, *ma soeur*. Remember us in your prayers.'

'Always.'

* * *

The Reverend Mother was lying on her narrow bed, looking even smaller and more desiccated than she had in life. Her eyes were closed, and Soeur Alfonsine had already replaced her *quichenotte* with the starched wimple, which the old woman had always refused.

'The *quichenotte* was good enough for us,' she used to say. '*Kiss not, kiss not*, we told the English soldiers, and wore the bonnet with the boned lappets to make sure they got the message. Who knows'—and here her eyes would light with sudden mischief—'maybe those English plunderers are hiding here still, and how then would I keep my virtue?'

She had collapsed in the field as she was digging potatoes, so Alfonsine told me. A minute later she was gone.

It was a good death, I tell myself. No pain; no priests; no fuss. And Reverend Mother was seventy-three—an unthinkable age—and had already been frail when I joined the convent five years ago. But it was she who first made me welcome here, she who delivered Fleur, and once more, grief surprises me like an unexpected friend. She had seemed immortal, you see: an immovable landmark on this small horizon. Kindly, simple Mère Marie, walking the potato fields with her apron gathered up peasant-fashion over her skirt.

The potatoes were her pride, for though little else grows well in this bitter soil, these fruit are highly prized on the mainland, and their sale—along with that of our salt and the jars of pickled *salicorne*—ensures us enough revenue to maintain our little independence. That and the tithes bring us a prosperous enough life, even for one who has been used to the freedom of the roads, for at my age it's time to have done with the dangers and the thrills, and in any case, I remind myself, even with the *Théâtre des Cieux* there were as many flung stones as sweetmeats, twice as many lean times as good, and as for the drunkards, the gossips, the lechers, the men . . . Besides, there was Fleur to think of, then as always.

One of my blasphemies—my many, many blasphemies—is the refusal to believe in sin. Conceived in sin, I should have given birth to my daughter in sorrow and contrition; exposed her, perhaps, on a hillside, as our ancestors once abandoned their unwanted young. But Fleur was a joy from the beginning. For her, I wear the red cross of the Bernardines, I work the fields instead of the high rope, I devote my days to a God for whom I have little affection and less understanding. But with her at my side, this life is far from unpleasant. The cloister at least is safe. I have my garden. My books. My friends. Sixty-five of us, a family larger and closer in some ways than any I

12

ever had.

I told them I was a widow. It seemed the simplest solution. A wealthy young widow, now with child, fleeing persecution from a dead husband's creditors. Jewellery salvaged from the wreck of my caravan at Epinal gave me what I needed to bargain with. My years in the theatre served me well—in any case, I was convincing enough for a provincial Abbess who had never ventured out of sight of her native coast. And as time passed I realized my subterfuge was unnecessary. Few of us were impelled by holy vocation. We shared little except a need for privacy, a mistrust of men, an instinctive solidarity, which outweighed differences of upbringing and belief. Each one of us fleeing something we could not quite see. As I said, we all have our secrets.

Soeur Marguerite, scrawny as a skinned rabbit and eternally twitching with nerves and anxieties, comes to me for a tisane to banish dreams in which, she says, a man with fiery hands torments her. I brew her tinctures of chamomile and valerian sweetened with honey, she purges herself daily with salt water and castor oil, but I can see from the feverish look in her eyes that the dreams plague her still.

Then we have Soeur Antoine, plump and redfaced, hands perpetually greasy from her cookpots, mother of a dead child at fourteen. Some say she killed it herself; others blamed her father in his rage and shame. She certainly eats well for all her guilt; her stomach is perpetually swollen beneath the seam of her wimple, her helpless, moony face bracketed by half a dozen quivering chins. She holds her pies and pastries to her bosom

13

like children; difficult to tell, in these shadows, who is feeding whom.

Soeur Alfonsine: white as bone but for the red spot on either cheek, who sometimes coughs blood into her palm and who lives in a state of perpetual exaltation. Someone has told her that the afflicted have special gifts, denied to those who are sound in body. As a result she cultivates an otherworldly air and has seen the Devil many times in the form of a great black dog.

And Perette: Soeur Anne to you, but always Perette at heart. The wild girl who never speaks, aged thirteen or a little older, found naked on the seashore a year ago last November. For the first three days she would not eat but sat motionless on the floor of her cell, face turned to the wall. Then came the rages, the smeared excrement, the food flung at the sisters who tended her, the animal cries. She flatly refused to wear the clothes we gave her, strutting naked about the freezing cell, occasionally giving voice to the tongueless hooting sounds that signalled her frenzies, her strange sorrows, her triumphs.

Now, one might almost take her for a normal child. In her novice's whites she is almost pretty, singing our hymns in her high wordless voice, but happiest in the garden and the fields, wimple discarded on a bramble bush, skirts flying. She still never speaks. Some wonder if she ever did. Her eyes are gold-ringed, unreadable as a bird's. Her pale hair, shorn to rid her of lice, has begun to grow back and stands out around her small face. She loves Fleur, often warbling to her in that high birdy voice and making toys for her from the reeds and grasses of the seashore with quick, clever fingers. I too am a special friend, and she often comes with me to the fields, watching me as I work and singing to herself.

Yes, I have a family once again. All refugees in our different ways: Perette, Antoine, Marguerite, Alfonsine and I; and with us, prim Piété; Bénédicte, the gossip; Tomasine, with the lazy eye; Germaine of the flaxen hair and ruined face; Clémente, the troubling beauty who shares her bed, and senile Rosamonde, closer to God than any of the saner ones, innocent of memory or sin.

Life is simple here—or was. Food is plentiful and good. Our comforts are not denied us— Marguerite her bottle and her daily purges, Antoine her pastries. Mine is Fleur, who sleeps alongside my bed in a cot of her own and comes with me to prayer and fieldwork. A lax regime, some might say, more like a country girls' outing than a sisterhood brought together in contrition, but this is not the mainland. An island has a life of its own; even Le Devin across the water is another world to us. A priest may come once a year to celebrate Mass and I'm told the last time the Bishop visited was sixteen years ago, when the old Henri was crowned. Since then, the good King too has been murdered—it was he who declared that each home in France should have a broiled fowl every week, and, thanks to Soeur Antoine, we followed his command with more than religious zeal—his successor a boy not out of short coats.

So many changes. I mistrust them; outside in the world there are tides at work which may tear the land apart. Better to be here, with Fleur, while all around us the dissolution rages, and above us, the birds of malchance gather like clouds.

Here, where it's safe.

CHAPTER THREE
♥

July 7th, 1610

An abbey without an Abbess. A country without a
King. For two days now we have shared France's
restlessness. Louis Dieudonné—the God-given—a
fine, strong name for a child brought to the throne
beneath the shadow of assassination. As if the
name itself might lift the curse and blind the
people to the corruptions of Church and Court and
the ever-growing ambitions of the Régente Marie.
The old King was a soldier, a seasoned man of
government. With Henri, we knew where we stood.
But this little Louis is only nine years old. Already,
barely two months after his father's death, the
rumours have begun. De Sully, the King's adviser,
has been replaced by a favourite of the Médicis
woman. The Condés have returned. I need no
oracle to foresee uneasy times ahead. Normally,
these things do not concern us, here at Noirs
Moustiers. But, like France, we need the security of
leadership. Like France, we fear the unknown.

Without the Reverend Mother we remain in
flux, left to our own devices, while a message is sent
to the Bishop in Rennes. But our holiday
atmosphere is tainted by uncertainty. The corpse
lies in the chapel with candles burning and myrrh
in a censer, for it is high summer and the air is foul
and ripe. We hear nothing from the mainland, but

16

we know the journey to Rennes should take four days at least. Meanwhile, we drift anchorless. And we need our anchor: the laxity of our former régime has become stretched still further until it is shapeless and without meaning. We barely worship. Duties are forgotten. Each nun turns to what gives her most comfort: Antoine to food, Marguerite to drink, Alfonsine to the scrubbing of the cloisters over and over on her knees until her skin breaks and she has to be carried to her cell with the scrubbing brush still clutched in her trembling hand. Some weep without knowing why. Some have sought out the players who have remained in the village, two miles away. I heard them coming back late to the dorter last night and caught laughter and a hot reek of wine and sex from the opened window.

Outwardly, little has changed. I carry on much as usual. I tend my herbs, I write my journal, I walk to the harbour with Fleur, I change the candles by the poor corpse in the chapel. This morning I said a prayer of my own, without recourse to the gilded Saints in their niches, alone and in silence. But the trouble within me grows daily. I have not forgotten my premonition on the day of the players.

Last night in the silence of my cubicle, I read the cards. But there was no comfort for me there. As Fleur slept, heedless, in her cot at my bedside, again and again I drew the same combination. The Tower. The Hermit. Death. And my dreams were uneasy.

17

CHAPTER FOUR

♥

July 8th, 1610

The abbey of Sainte Marie-de-la-mer stands in a piece of reclaimed marshland some two miles from the sea. To the left, marshes which flood regularly in winter, bringing the brackish waters less than a stone's throw from our doorway and occasionally seeping through into the cellarium where our food is stored. To the right, the road leading into town, where carts and horses pass and every Thursday a procession of vendors, moving from one market to another with their assortments of cloths, baskets, leather and foodstuffs. It is an old abbey, founded some two hundred years ago by a community of black friars and paid for in the only true coin the Church accepts: the fear of damnation.

In those days of indulgences and corruption a noble family ensured its succession to the Kingdom by giving its name to an abbey, but the friars were dogged by misfortune from the start. Plague wiped them out sixty years after the abbey's completion, and the buildings were abandoned until two generations later, when the Bernardines took them over. There must have been far more of them than there are of us, however, for the abbey could house twice as many as we have here, but time and the weather have done their work on the once-fine architecture and many of the buildings are now unusable.

Yet, there must have been wealth enough

lavished upon it once, for there is good marble flooring in the chapel and the one unbroken window is of marvellous design, but since then the winds across the flats have eroded the stone and tumbled arches on the west side so that in that wing barely any of the remaining buildings are habitable. On the east side we still have the dorter, the cloister, infirmary and warming room, but the lay quarters are a shambles, with so many tiles missing from the roof that birds have taken to nesting there. The scriptorium, too, is in sad disrepair, although so few of our number can read, and we have so few books in any case, that it hardly matters. A chaos of smaller buildings, mostly of wood, has sprung up around the chapel and the cloister: bakehouse, tannery, barns and a smokehouse for drying fish, so that instead of the grandiose place of the black friars' intention the abbey now appears more like a rough shanty town.

The lay folk do much of the common work. It is a privilege they pay for in goods and services as well as tithes, and we repay our side of the bargain in prayers and indulgences. Sainte Marie-de-la-mer herself is a stone effigy, now standing at the chapel doorway on a pedestal of rough sandstone. She was discovered ninety years ago in the marshes by a boy searching for a lost sheep: a three-foot lump of blackened basalt crudely carved into the semblance of a woman. Her breasts are bare and her tapering feet are tucked beneath a long featureless robe, which in the old days led folk to call her the Mermaid.

Since her discovery and laborious transportation into the abbey grounds forty years ago, there have been several miraculous healings of folk who have appealed to her, and she is popular amongst fishermen, who often pray to Marie-de-la-mer for protection from storms.

For myself, I think she looks very old. Not a Virgin but a crone, head lowered in weariness, her bowed shoulders glazed from almost a century of reverent handling. Her sagging breasts, too, are noticeably burnished. Barren women or those wishing to conceive still touch them for luck as they pass, paying for the blessing with a fowl, a cask of wine or a basket of fish.

And yet in spite of the reverence shown by these islanders, she has little in common with the Holy Mother. She is too ancient, to begin with. Older than the abbey itself, the basalt looks as if it might be a thousand years old or more, speckled with shards of mica like fragments of bone. And there is nothing to prove that the figure was ever supposed to represent the Holy Mother. Indeed, her bared breasts seem strangely immodest, like those of some pagan deity of long ago. Some of the locals still call her by the old name—though her miracles should long since have established her identity as well as her holiness. But fisherfolk are a superstitious lot. We co-exist with them, but we remain as alien to them as were the black friars of old, a race apart, to be placated with tithes and gifts.

*　　　*　　　*

The abbey of Sainte Marie-de-la-mer was an ideal retreat for me. Old as it is, isolated and in disrepair, it is the safest haven I have ever known. Far enough from the mainland, the only Church official a parish priest who could barely read Latin himself, I found myself in a position as humorous as it was absurd. I began as a lay sister, one of only a dozen. But out of sixty-five sisters, barely half could read at all; less than a tenth knew any Latin. I began by reading at Chapter. Then I was included in the services, my daily tasks reduced to allow me to read from the big old Bible on the lectern. Then Reverend Mother approached me with unusual—almost timid—reserve.

The novices, you understand . . . We had twelve, aged thirteen to eighteen. It was unseemly for them—for any of us—to be so ignorant. If I could teach them—just a little. We had books hidden away in the old scriptorium, which few were able to study. If I could only show them what to do . . .

I understood quickly enough. Our Reverend Mother, kind as she was, practical as she was in her shrewd, simple fashion, had kept a secret from us. Had hidden it for fifty years or more, learning long passages from the Bible by heart to conceal her ignorance, feigning weak eyesight in order to avoid the ordeal. Reverend Mother could not read Latin. Could not, I suspected, read at all.

She supervised my lessons to the novices with care, standing at the back of the refectory—our improvised schoolroom—with head to one side as if she understood every word. I never referred to her deficiency in private or in public, deferring to her on minor points upon which I had previously briefed her, and she showed her gratitude in small, secret ways.

After a year I took vows at her request, and my new status permitted me to take full participation in all aspects of abbey life.

I miss her. Good Mère Marie. Her faith was as simple and honest as the land she worked. She rarely punished—not that there was much to punish in any case—seeing sin as proof of unhappiness. If a sister offended, she spoke to her kindly, repaying the transgression with its opposite: for theft, gifts; for laziness, respite from daily tasks. Few failed to be shamed by her unfailing generosity. And yet she was a heretic like myself. Her faith skated perilously close to the pantheism against which Giordano, my old teacher, used to warn me. And yet it was sincere. Careless of the more complex theological issues, her philosophy could be summed up in a single word: love. For Mère Marie, love overrode everything.

Love not often, but for ever. It's one of my mother's sayings, and all my life it has been the story of my heart. Before I came to the abbey I thought I understood. Love for my mother; love for my friends; the dark and complex love of a woman for a man. But when Fleur was born, everything changed. A man who has never seen it may *think* he understands the ocean, but he thinks only of what he knows; imagines a large body of water, bigger than a millpond, bigger than a lake. The reality, however, is beyond imagining: the scents, the sounds, the anguish and the joy of it beyond any comparison with previous experience. That was Fleur. Never, since my thirteenth summer, had there been such an awakening. From the first instant, when Mère Marie gave her to me to suckle, I knew that the world had changed. I had been alone and had never known it; had travelled, fought, suffered, danced, fornicated, loved, hated, grieved and triumphed all alone, living like an

22

animal from day to day, caring for nothing, desiring nothing, fearing nothing. Suddenly now everything was different: Fleur was in the world. I was a mother.

It is a perilous joy, however. I knew, of course, that children often died young—I had seen it happen many times on my travels, of sickness, accident or hunger—but I had never before imagined the pain of it, or the terrible loss. Now I am afraid of everything. The reckless Ailée, who danced on the rope and flew the high trapeze, has become a timid creature, a clucking hen; clinging to safety for the sake of her child, where once she would have ached for adventure. LeMerle, the eternal gamester, would have scorned that weakness. *Stake nothing that you would not lose.* And yet I can pity him, wherever he is. His world has no oceans.

This morning, Prime was barely observed; Matins and Lauds, not at all. I am alone in the church as dawn breaks, a milky light brimming through the roof above the pulpitum, where the slates are fewest. A thin rain is falling and the overspill chimes a little three-note scale against the broken gutter. We sold most of the lead the year we built the bakehouse; exchanged bad stone for good metal, bread for the heart of the South Transept, the belly for the soul. We replaced the lead by clay and plaster mortar, but only lead lasts.

Sainte Marie-de-la-mer looks down with round expressionless eyes. Her other features are blunted with time; a huge stone woman, squatting effortfully as do the gypsies in childbirth. I can hear the sea borne across the flats and the cries of birds through the open door. Gulls, no doubt. There are no blackbirds here. I wonder if Mère Marie can see me now. I wonder if the Saint hears my silent prayer.

Perhaps it is only the shriek of the seagulls that makes me uneasy. Perhaps the scent of freedom sweeping across the flats.

There are no blackbirds here.

But it is too late. Once invoked, my incubus is not so easily banished. His image seems tattooed across my eyelids so that, open or closed, I see him. I feel that I have never ceased to see him, my Blackbird of misfortune. Awake or asleep, he has never been truly out of mind. Five years of peace was more than I expected—more, perhaps, than I deserved. But everything returns, as the islanders say. And the past rushes in like the tide.

CHAPTER FIVE
♥

July 9th, 1610

My earliest memory was of our caravan, which was painted orange with a tiger on one side and a pastoral scene with lambs and shepherdesses on the other. When I was good I played opposite the lambs. When I was disobedient I was given the tiger for company. Secretly I loved the tiger best.

Born into a family of gypsies, I had many mothers, many fathers, many homes. There was Isabelle, my true mother, strong and tall and beautiful. There was Gabriel the acrobat, and Princess Farandole, who had no arms and used her toes as if they were fingers; dark-eyed Janette, who told fortunes, the cards flickering like flames between her clever old hands, and there was Giordano, a Jew from southern Italy who could read and write. Not just French, but Latin, Greek and Hebrew. He was no relation of mine as far as I knew, but he cared for me best of all—loved me, in his pedantic way. The gypsies named me Juliette; I had no other name, nor needed one.

It was Giordano who taught me my letters, reading to me from the books that he kept in a secret compartment in the body of the caravan. It was he who told me about Copernicus, taught me that the Nine Heavens do not revolve around the earth, but that the earth and planets circle the sun. There was more, not all of which I understood, about the properties of metals and the elements. He showed me how to make black burning-powder with a mixture of saltpetre, sulphur and charcoal and how to light it using a length of twine. The others nicknamed him *Le Philosophe*, and made merry of his books and his experiments, but from him I learned to read, to watch the stars and to mistrust the Church.

From Gabriel I learned to juggle, to turn somersaults, to dance on the rope. From Janette, the cards, bones and the use of plants and herbs. From Farandole, pride and self-reliance. From my mother, the lore of colours, the speech of birds and the cantrips to keep evil at bay. Elsewhere, I learned to pick pockets and to handle a knife, to use my fists in a fight or to flick my hips at a drunken man on a street corner and lure him into shadows where eager hands waited to strip him of purse and poke.

We toured the coastal cities and towns, never staying in one place long enough to attract unwelcome attention. We were often hungry, shunned by all but the poorest and the most desperate, denounced from pulpits across the country and blamed for every misfortune from drought to apple-rot, but we took our happiness where we could, and we all helped each other according to our skills.

When I was fourteen we scattered, our caravans burnt by zealots in Flanders amidst accusations of theft and sorcery. Giordano fled south, Gabriel made for the border, and my mother left me in the care of a little group of Carmelites, promising to return for me when the danger was past. I stayed there for almost eight weeks. The sisters were kind, but poor—almost as poor as we ourselves had been—and they were for the most part frightened old women, unable to face the world outside their order. I hated it. I missed my mother and my friends; I missed Giordano and his books; most of all I missed the freedom of the roads. No word had come from Isabelle, for good or for ill. My cards showed me nothing but a confusion of cups and swords. I itched from the crown of my cropped head to the soles of my feet, and I longed more than anything to be away from the smell of old women. One night I ran away, walked the six miles into Flanders and lay low for a couple of weeks, living on scraps, hoping to hear news of our company. But by then the trail was cold; talk of war had eclipsed everything else and few people remembered one group of gypsies among all the rest. In despair I returned to the convent, but found it shut, and a plague sign on the door. Well, that was the end of it. With or without Isabelle, I no longer had a choice: I had to move on.

And so it was that I found myself alone and destitute, living perilously and poorly from theft and scavenging as I made my way towards the capital. For a time I travelled with a group of Italian performers, where I learned their tongue and the rudiments of the *commedia dell'arte.* But the Italianate trend was already losing its popularity. For two years we lived indifferently until my comrades, discouraged and homesick for the orange groves and the warm blue mountains of their native land, decided to return home. I would have followed them. But maybe it was my demon prompted me to remain, or maybe the need to stay on the move. I made my farewells and, alone, though with money enough now for my needs, I turned my face again towards Paris.

It was there that I first met the Blackbird. Named *LeMerle* for the colour of his unpowdered hair, he was a firebrand amongst the languid gentlemen of the Court, never at rest, never quite in disfavour, but always on the brink of social disgrace. He was unremarkable to look at, favouring unadorned clothing and the simplest of jewellery, but his eyes were as full of light and shadow as trees in a forest, and his smile was the most engaging I had ever seen, the smile of a man who finds his world delightful, but absurd. Everything was a game to him. He was indifferent to matters of rank or status. He lived on perpetual credit and never went to church.

It was a carelessness to which I responded eagerly, seeing in it some reflection of myself; but we were nothing alike, he and I. I was a little savage of sixteen; LeMerle was ten years older, perverse, irreverent, irrepressible. Naturally, I fell in love.

A chick, hatching from the egg, will take as its mother the first object that moves. LeMerle pulled me from the street, gave me a position; most of all, he gave me back my pride. Of course I loved him, and with the unquestioning adoration of the new-hatched chick. *Love not often, but for ever.* More fool me.

He had a troupe of player-dancers, the *Théâtre du Flambeau,* under the protectorship of Maximilien de Béthune, later to become the Duc de Sully, who was an admirer of the ballet. Other performances too could be arranged, these not so public, and unsponsored—though not unattended—by the Court. LeMerle trod a discreet, perilous line of blackmail and intrigue, skating the parameters of fashionable society without ever quite falling for the lures cast to him there. Though no one seemed to know his real name I took him for a nobleman—certainly he was acknowledged by most. His *Ballet des Gueux*—the Beggar's ballet that had been such a success at Court—had been an immediate success, though condemned by some as impious. Unabashed by his critics, his audacity even went as far as to include members of the Court in his *Ballet du Grand Pastoral*—with the Duc de Cramail dressed as a woman—and was planning even as I joined his troupe the *Ballet Travesti,* which was to prove the final straw with his respectable patron.

It flattered him at first, to have me at his feet; and it amused him to see how hungrily men watched me as I danced on stage. We performed,

28

LeMerle's troupe and I, in *salons* and theatres all over the city. By then, *comédie-ballets* were becoming fashionable: popular romances from classical themes, interspersed with long interludes of dance and acrobatics. LeMerle wrote the dialogue and choreographed the routines— adapting the script to allow for the tastes of each audience. There were heroic speeches for the dress circle, flimsily clad dancers for the ballet enthusiasts, and dwarves, tumblers and clowns for the general public who would otherwise have become restless, and who greeted our act with loud cheers and laughter.

Paris—and LeMerle—had improved me almost beyond recognition: my hair was clean and glossy, my skin glowed, and for the first time in my life I wore silks and velvets, lace and fur; I danced in slippers embroidered with gold; I hid my smiles behind fans of ivory and chickenskin. I was young; intoxicated, to be sure, by my new life, but Isabelle's daughter was not to be blinded by frills and fripperies. No, it was love that blinded me, and when our ship of dreams struck aground, it was love that kept me at his side.

The Blackbird's fall from grace was as abrupt as his ascendancy. I was never quite sure how it happened. One day our *Ballet Travesti* was all the rage, and then the next, disaster: de Béthune's protectorship withdrawn overnight, players and dancers scattered. Creditors who had held back now moved in like flies. All at once, the name of Guy LeMerle was no longer spoken; friends were suddenly never at home. Finally, LeMerle narrowly escaped a beating at the hands of lackeys sent by the famously austere Bishop of Evreux and fled

Paris in haste, having called in the few favours still outstanding and taking with him what wealth he could. I followed. Call it what you will. He was a plausible rogue, with ten years more experience than I, and with a fine coat of Court polish over his villainy. I followed; it was inevitable. I would have followed him to hell.

He was quick to adapt to the traveller's life. So quick, in fact, that I wondered to what extent he was not, like myself, a soldier of fortune. I had expected him to be humiliated by his disgrace; at the very least, a little chastened. He was neither. From Court gentleman he transformed overnight to itinerant performer, shedding his silk for a journeyman's leathers. He acquired an accent midway between the refined speech of the city and the provinces' rough burr, changing weekly to suit whichever province we happened to be visiting.

I realized that he was enjoying himself; that the whole game—for this is how he recalled our flight from Paris—had excited him. He had escaped the city unharmed, having caused a series of impressive scandals. He had insulted a satisfactory number of influential people. Above all, I understood, he had goaded the Bishop of Evreux—a man of legendary self-control—into an undignified response, and as far as LeMerle was concerned, that alone was a significant victory. As a result, far from being in any way humbled, he remained as irrepressible as ever, and almost at once set about the plans for his next venture.

Of our original troupe only seven now remained, including myself. Two dancers—Ghislaine, a country girl from Lorraine, and Hermine, a courtesan past her prime—with four dwarves, Rico,

Bazuel, Cateau and Le Borgne. Dwarves come in many shapes. Rico and Cateau were of childlike build, with small heads and piping voices; Bazuel was plump and cherubic, and Le Borgne, who had only one eye, was of normal proportions, with a sound chest and strong, well-muscled arms—or would have been, but for his absurdly short-ended legs. He was a strange and bitter little half-man, fiercely contemptuous of the Tall People, as he called us, but for some reason he tolerated me—perhaps because I did not pity him—and he had a grudging respect—if not a genuine liking—for LeMerle.

'In my grandfather's day it was worth your while to be a dwarf,' he would often grumble. 'You'd never be short of food, at least; you could always join a circus or a travelling troupe. And as for the church . . .'

Church people had changed since his grandfather's day. Nowadays there was suspicion where once there might have been pity, with everyone trying to find someone to blame for their bad times and misfortune. A dwarf or a cripple was always fair game, said Le Borgne, and such undesirables as gypsies and performers made good scapegoats.

'There was a time,' he said, 'when every troupe had a dwarf or an idiot, for luck. Holy fools, they called us. God's innocents. Nowadays they're just as likely to throw stones as to spare a crust for a poor unfortunate. There's no virtue in it any more. And as for LeMerle and his *comédie-ballets*—well!' He grinned savagely. 'Laughter sits poorly on an empty stomach. Come winter, he'll know that with the rest of us.'

Be that as it may, in the weeks that followed, we attracted three more players, members of a disbanded troupe in Aix. Caboche was a flautist, Demiselle a reasonable dancer and Bouffon, a one-time clown lately turned pickpocket. We travelled under the name of *Théâtre du Grand Carnaval*, performing mostly burlesque plays and short ballets, with tumbling and juggling from the dwarves, but though the entertainments were well received, they were for the most part indifferently paid, and for a while our purses were thin.

It was nearing harvest-time, and for some weeks we would arrive at a village in the morning, earn a little money helping a local farmer mow the hay or pick fruit, then in the evening we would perform in the courtyard of the nearest alehouse for what coins we could glean. At first LeMerle's soft hands bled from the fieldwork, but he did not complain. I moved into his caravan wordlessly one night, he accepting my presence without surprise or comment, as if I were his due.

He was a strange lover. Aloof, cautious, abstracted, as silent in passion as an incubus. Women found him attractive, but he seemed mostly indifferent to their advances. This was not from any loyalty to me. He was simply a man who, already having one coat, sees no reason to go to the trouble of buying another. Later I saw him for what he was: selfish, shallow, cruel. But for a time I was taken in; and, hungry for affection, was content—for a time—with such small scraps as he was able to give me.

In exchange, I shared with him what I could. I showed him how to trap thrushes and rabbits when food was scarce. I showed him herbs to cure fevers

32

and heal wounds. I taught him my mother's cantrips; I even repeated some of Giordano's teachings, and in that especially LeMerle showed a keen interest.

In fact, I told him more about myself than I had intended—much more, indeed, than was safe. But he was clever, and charming, and I was flattered at his attention. Much of what I said was heretical, a mixture of gypsy lore and Giordano's teachings. An earth—planets—moving about a central sun. A Goddess of grain and pleasure, older than the Church, her people unfettered by sin or contrition. Men and women as equals—at this he smiled, for it was beyond outrageous, but knew better than to comment. I assumed, in the years that passed, that he had forgotten. Only much later did I realize that with Guy LeMerle nothing is forgotten; everything is set aside for the winter, every scrap of information added to his store. I was a fool. I make no apologies. And in spite of what happened I'll swear he had begun to care for me a little. Enough to cost him a pang or two. But not enough for me, when the time came. Not nearly enough.

I never learned his true name. He hinted it was a noble one—certainly he was not of the people—although even at the height of my infatuation I believed less than half of what he told me. He had been an actor and a playwright, he said, a poet in the style of the classics; spoke of misfortune, of ruin; grew elated at the memory of thronged theatres.

That he had been an actor I did not doubt. He had the gift of mimicry, a broad and winning smile, a certain flourish in his way of walking, of carrying his head, which spoke of the stage. His skills served

33

him well—be it selling fake cures or bartering a winded horse, his powers of persuasion were little short of magical. But he had not begun his career as a performer. He must have studied; he could read Latin and Greek, and was familiar with several of Giordano's philosophers. He could ride a horse as well as any circus equestrienne. He could pick pockets like a professional, and he excelled at all games of chance. He seemed able to adapt to any circumstance, acquiring new skills as he went, and however much I tried, I was unable to pierce the layers of fiction, fancy and outright lies with which he surrounded himself. His secrets, whatever they were, remained his own.

There was one thing, however. An old brand high up on his left arm, a fleur-de-lys faded almost to silver over the years, which, when I questioned him, he dismissed with a smile and a claim of forgetfulness. But I noticed that he took care always to cover the mark after that, and I drew my own conclusions. My Blackbird had lost feathers in that encounter, and did not care to be reminded of it.

CHAPTER SIX
♥

July 11th, 1610

I have never believed in God. Not in *your* God anyway, the one who looks down onto his chessboard and moves the pieces according to his pleasure, occasionally glancing up at the face of

34

his Adversary with the smile of one who already knows the outcome. It seems to me that there must be something horribly flawed in a Creator who persists in testing his creatures to destruction, in providing a world well stocked with pleasures only to announce that all pleasure is sin, in creating mankind imperfect, then expecting us to aspire to perfection. The devil at least plays fair. We know where he stands. But even he, the Lord of Deceit, works for the Almighty in secret. Like master, like man.

Giordano called me pagan. To him this was no compliment, for he was a devout Jew, believing in a heavenly reward for his earthly sufferings. To him, to be pagan was to be immoral, ungodly, to indulge freely in the pleasures of the flesh, to delight too frequently in the other hazards encountered on the road. My old teacher ate sparingly, fasted regularly, prayed often, immersing himself for the rest of the time in his studies. He was a good companion—our only grievance was that on his Sabbath he refused to help with the work around the camp, preferring to go without a fire, even on a winter's night, than to take the trouble to light one. Apart from this peculiarity, he was just like the rest of us; and I never saw him eat the flesh of children, as the Church claims his people do. In fact he rarely ate any kind of flesh at all. Which simply goes to show how misguided the Church can be.

Perhaps Giordano was misguided too, I told myself, as I strove dutifully to be more like my mentor. His Jewish God seemed so very like the Catholic God—which One True Religion seemed to me almost indistinguishable from that of the Huguenots or the Protestant heretics in England.

There must be something else, I told myself repeatedly; something beyond sin and solemnity, dust and devotions; something which loved life as indiscriminately as I did.

My thirteenth birthday brought a kind of awakening. All that summer was a languorous procession of delights: a new awareness, a boundless energy, a heightened sense of taste and smell. For the first time, or so it seemed, I really noticed the flowers along the roadside; the scent of night falling by the seashore; the taste of my mother's new bread, baked black in the coals but tender inside the crust of ash. I noticed, too, the delicious friction of my clothes against my skin, the icy splash of stream water as I bathed . . . If this was to be pagan, then I wanted more of it. The world had become maternal almost overnight, and her mysteries were boundless. I opened myself to her initiations. Every shoot, every flower, tree, bird, creature filled me with tenderness and joy. I lost my maidenhead to a fisherman in Le Havre and the world exploded in a revelation no less momentous to me than that of Saint John.

Giordano shook his head sourly and called me shameless. For a while he taught me nothing but theology so that my head span and I rebelled, demanding the return of my history lessons, my astronomy, my Latin, my poetry. For a while he resisted me. I was a savage, he told me with disapproval, little better than the natives of newly discovered Quebec. I stole his books and pored over Latin erotica, my fingers following the script with agonizing slowness. When winter came my senses froze and my teacher forgave me, resuming our studies with his habitual sour shake of the head. But secretly, pagan I remained. Even in the abbey I am happier in the fields than in the chapel, the burn of my working muscles a kind of remembrance of that summer when I was thirteen and ungodly.

*   *   *

Today I worked until my back ached. When no more could be done amongst the herbs and vegetables, I moved to the salt flats, regardless of the sun's glare, my skirt kilted to my knees, ankles mired in rime and mud. At the abbey we have lay folk to do the heavy work, the fishing, slaughtering of cattle, curing of leathers and work in the salt fields, but I've never been shy of hard labour, and it keeps the fear at bay.

There is no word yet from Rennes and last night my dreams were terrible, a nightmare hand of flung cards with LeMerle's face on every one. I wonder whether I have brought these visions upon myself by writing so much about him in my journal, but the tale, now begun, is a runaway colt beneath my hands. Hopeless to try to break it now; better to hang on and let it run itself to exhaustion.

Janette taught me to value my dreams. They are like waves, she told me, of the tides which bear us, from which strange jetsam may be gathered, strange eddies from the deeps for those to read who can. I must use my dreams, not fear them. Only a fool fears knowledge.

*   *   *

Our first winter was the worst. For two months the

Théâtre du Grand Carnaval was forced to a standstill just outside Vitré, a small town on the Vilaine. It had snowed throughout December, our money was almost gone, our food was running low, one of our caravans had lost a wheel and there could be no hope of moving on until spring.

I think we all took it for granted that LeMerle would not beg. He was, he told us, writing a tragedy which, when performed, would prove to be the solution to all our problems. Meanwhile we scavenged, scrounged, danced, juggled and tumbled ankle-deep in the frozen refuse of the streets. The girls earned more than the men—at times we rivalled even the dwarves, once their novelty had worn off. Le Borgne grumbled, as ever, and seemed to take this as a personal affront. LeMerle accepted what money we brought him as if he expected no less.

One day, as January thawed to rain and mud, a fine carriage swept past our camp and beyond towards the town, and later LeMerle gathered us together and told us to prepare ourselves for a special performance at the castle. We arrived freshly bathed and in the dancers' costumes we had salvaged in our flight from Paris to find half a dozen gentlemen assembled in the large dining hall, where a game seemed to be under way. There were cards on the table, and I caught the glint of gold in the candlelight. There was a scent of mulled wine and woodsmoke and tobacco, and LeMerle was sitting in their midst in his Court finery, a cup of punch in one hand. He seemed on excellent terms with the little company; we might almost have been in Paris again. I sensed danger, and knew that LeMerle sensed it too. But he was clearly enjoying himself.

A plump young gentleman in rose-coloured silk leaned forward and peered at me through a lorgnette. 'But she's charming,' he said. 'Come closer, my dear. I don't bite.'

I moved forwards, my satin shoes whispering over the polished floorboards, and made my courtesy. 'My card, sweetheart. Come on, take it; don't be shy.'

I was feeling vaguely uncomfortable. I had grown since we left Paris, and my skirt was shorter, my bodice tighter than I remembered. I regretted now not taking the time to make the necessary adjustments. The rose-pink gentleman smirked and handed me a playing card between finger and thumb. I saw that it was the Queen of Hearts.

LeMerle winked at me and I was reassured. If this was one of his games, I thought, then I could play it with the best of them; certainly it looked as though the others were familiar with the rules. The Three of Spades fell to Hermine, to Cateau the Jack of Clubs and to Demiselle the Ace of Diamonds, until at last each of us had been given the name of a playing card—even the dwarves—and this to ribald laughter, though I was far from understanding why. We danced then: first some comic acrobatics and then a simplified version of the *Ballet des Gueux*.

From time to time I was aware as I danced of playing-cards being tossed into the centre of the table, but the dance was a strenuous one and my attention could not be spared. It was only when it came to an end and four winners rose to claim their prizes that I realized the purpose of the game—and the stakes. Comic cursing from the remaining players, left with the dwarves. As I was led up the broad stairway towards the bedchambers, feeling trapped and stupid, I heard LeMerle behind me calmly suggesting a rubber of piquet.

I half turned at the sound of his voice. Hermine caught my eye and frowned—she alone of the four dancers understood what was going on. In the golden light from the sconce I thought she looked old, her painted cheekbones shining with grease. Her eyes were hard and blue and very patient. Their expression told me everything I needed to know.

The rose-pink gentleman seemed to notice my hesitation. 'Fair's fair, sweetheart,' he said. 'I won, didn't I?'

LeMerle knew I was watching him. He'd gambled on my reaction as well as on the turn of the card, and for a second I was an unknown quantity to him, a thing of passing interest. Then he turned away, already intent upon the new game, and I hated him. Oh, not for the brief moment of inconvenience on the couch. I'd had worse; and the lordling was quickly spent. No, it was the *game*, as if I, and the others, had been nothing more to him than the cards in his hand, to be played or set aside as the game allowed.

Of course, I would forgive him. 'But Juliette, do you think I *wanted* to do it? I did it for you. For all of you. Do you think I would have let you starve to safeguard my own delicacy?'

I had taken out my knife, its dark blade sharpened to a sliver. My fingers throbbed with the urge to bleed him. 'It didn't have to be that way,' I said. 'If only you'd told me.' It was true; if he had told me of his plans I would have accepted, for his

40

sake.

His eyes fixed mine and I saw the knowledge there. 'You could have refused,' he said. 'I wouldn't have forced you, Juliette.'

'You *sold* us.' My voice was trembling. 'You tricked us and you sold us for money!' He knew I could not have refused. If we had withheld our favours that night it would have been to see LeMerle in the pillory—or worse—the following morning. 'You used us, Guy. You used *me*.'

I could see him measuring the situation. I was a little overwrought, but my anger wouldn't last. It wasn't as if I had been a virgin, after all. Nothing was really lost. Gold clinked between his fingers. 'Juliette, listen to me . . .'

It was the wrong time for cajolery. As he reached out towards me I slashed at him with the knife. I only meant to keep him at a distance, but my movement was too quick for him to evade and my blade sliced cruelly across his outstretched palms.

'Next time, LeMerle.' I was shaking, but the knife was steady. 'Next time I'll take your face right off.'

Any other man would have glanced at his wounded hands—instinct demands it—but not LeMerle. There was no fear at all in his eyes, no pain. Instead, there was surprise, fascination, delight, as if at some unexpected discovery. It was a look I had seen on his face before, at the card table, or in front of an angry mob, or flushed with triumph in the gleam of the footlights. I held his gaze defiantly. Blood dripped from his fists onto the ground between us, and neither of us looked down.

'Why, sweetheart,' he said. 'I believe you would.'
'Try me.'

Now blood was the only colour about him; against his black coat, his face was ashen. He took a step towards me and stumbled; without thinking, I caught him as he collapsed. 'You're right, Juliette,' he said. 'I should have told you.'

That disarmed me, as he had known it would. Then, still smiling, he passed out.

I bandaged his hands myself with betony and fresh linen. Then I found him brandy and stood over him while he drank it, mentally replaying the scene as I did so until it seemed to me almost as if he had sacrificed himself for us instead of the other way around. The greatest risk *had* been his, of course. Besides the gold paid for the performance—public and private—LeMerle fleeced the young card players with shameless expertise whilst Bouffon and Le Borgne searched the house for valuables, standing up fully five hundred *livres* richer than when he arrived.

When his victims finally understood the imposture he had perpetrated upon them, it was too late. The troupe had already left town, although reports and rumours of LeMerle's deception followed us all the way to La Rochelle and beyond. It was the beginning of a long chain of impostures and deceits, and for the next six months we travelled under many colours, many names. Our notoriety dogged us for longer than we had expected, but in spite of the risks and the continued efforts for our capture, we felt little anxiety. LeMerle had begun to take on an almost supernatural character in our minds. He seemed invulnerable—and so, by association, were we all.

If they had caught him, they would certainly have hanged him, and probably the rest of us for good measure. But travelling players were not uncommon in the west, and by then we were the *Théâtre de la Poule au Pot*, a group of jongleurs from Aquitaine. As far as anyone could tell, the *Théâtre du Grand Carnaval* had vanished into smoke. And so we escaped from the encounter—and others of the same kind—and I forgave LeMerle for a time, because I was young, and because I believed in those innocent days that there was good in everyone, and that one day perhaps even he could be redeemed.

It has been more than five years since I saw him last. Too long, to be sure, for me to be so deeply troubled at these recollections. He may even be dead by now—after Epinal, there's reason enough to believe it. But I do not. All these years I have dragged the memory and the pain of him behind me like a dog with a stone tied to its tail, and I would know if I were free of him.

Today we must bury the Reverend Mother. It has to be today. The sky is pitiless in its clarity, promising wide blue spaces, scorching sun. No one wants to take responsibility, I know, but the corpse in the chapel is already overripe, liquefying in its bath of spices. No one wants to bury her before her successor arrives. But someone has to make the decision.

I have not slept since yesterday night. My herbs are no comfort: neither geranium nor rosemary brings me any respite, and lavender fails to clear my head. Belladonna, brewed strong, might show me something worth seeing, but I have had enough of visions for the present. What I need is rest. From

43

the high window I can see the first sliver of dawn as it opens up the sky like an oyster. Fleur sleeps beside me, her doll tucked under her arm and a thumb lodged comfortingly in her mouth, but for me, in spite of my exhaustion, sleep is a distant land. I put out my hand to touch her. I do this often, for my own comfort as well as hers, and she responds sleepily, curling into the half-circle of my body with a blurry sigh. She smells of biscuit and warm bread dough. I put my nose into the baby hair at the nape of her neck, which is sweetness and joy and, now, a kind of anguish, as if at the anticipation of some unimaginable future loss.

Arms around my daughter, I close my eyes again. But my peace is gone. Five years of peace dispelled like smoke in an instant—and for what? A bird, a memory, a glimpse of something from the corner of my eye? And yet the Reverend Mother died. What of it? She was old. Her life was over. There is no reason to believe that *he* is in any way linked to this. And yet, Giordano taught me that *all* life is linked, that all terrestrial things are made from the same elemental clay: man, woman, stone, water, tree, bird. It was heresy. But Giordano believed it. One day he would find it, he told me. The Philosopher's Stone that would prove his theory right, the recipe for all matter, the elixir of the Nine Worlds. Everything is linked: the world is in motion around the sun, everything returns, and every act, however small, has a thousand repercussions. I can feel them now, coming at me like ripples from a stone flung into a lake.

And the Blackbird? We too are linked, he and I; I need no philosophy to tell me that. Well, let him come. If he has a part to play, let him play it soon,

44

and quickly, because if ever I see him again in flesh, he knows that this time I will kill him.

CHAPTER SEVEN
♥

July 12th, 1610

We buried her in the herb garden. It was a quiet affair—I planted lavender and rosemary to sweeten her body's corruption and everyone said a little prayer. We sang the *Kyrie eleison*, but badly, for some were overcome with grief. This outpouring of grief surprises me—more than a dozen sisters have died since my arrival here, some of them young, and not one was mourned with such fierce despair—and yet it should not. We have lost more than one of our own. Even the murder of King Henri in Paris, only two months ago, had less impact on our lives.

That being so, it seems wrong to bury her with such little ceremony. She should have had a priest, a proper service. But we could wait no longer; the news from Rennes is slow in coming, and corruption spreads fastest in summer, bringing disease. Most of the sisters have no idea of this, preferring to trust to the power of prayer, but a lifetime on the roads has taught me the value of caution. There may well be demons, my mother used to say, but foul water, bad meat and tainted air are the real killers, and her wisdom has served me well.

Anyway, I talked them round to my way of

thinking in the end. I always do, and besides, this simple burial was what the Reverend Mother would have wanted: no stone vaulting, but a linen sheet already marbled with mould, then the raw white earth, upon which our potatoes thrive so sweetly.

Perhaps I'll plant potatoes above her grave, their flesh mingling with hers in the soil so that every joint nurtures a tuber, every bone a shoot, the salt of her flesh combining with the salt earth to nurse the roots to pallid life. A pagan thought, strangely lacking in solemnity in this place of mournful secrets. And yet my gods have never been theirs. The master of the world is surely not this stern, stony face, this pointless sacrifice, this life without joy, this endless fixation upon sin . . . Better to nourish potatoes than fleshless heaven, hopeless hell. But still word does not come.

Seven days. The Creation of the world took less time. Our world remains in limbo, suspended in the clear indifference of these summer days, a rose under glass. And yet the world outside moves on without us; growth, decay, life, death moving on at their usual pace, tide in, tide out, as if God has his own agenda. The scent of the sea blows through the window, already tinted with shades of autumn; the leaves bleached grey by the sun, the grass burnt blonde. The land is an anvil for summer's strike, flat and shimmering.

At least I have my work in the salt field, the wooden *ételle* in my hands skimming the crust of rime from the mud onto the heap by my side. It is simple work, requiring little thought, and I can watch Fleur and Perette playing nearby, splashing noisily through the warm brown water. These days in the fields—such a burden to the others—are my secret pleasure, with the sun on my back and my daughter at my side. Here I can be myself again, or as much of myself as I care to recall. I can smell the sea, the hot reek of the salt flat, feel the sharp wind coming over from the west, hear the birds. I am not one of these soft sisters, hiding in their darkness for fear of the world. Nor am I an ecstatic like Soeur Alfonsine, driving my poor flesh into a passion of mortification. No, the work pleases me. The long muscles in my thighs tense and stretch, I feel the tautening of my biceps like oiled rope. My arms are bare; my skirt hitched up to the waist, my wimple discarded on the mud bank.

Other than Fleur, my hair is my only extravagance. I cut it when I arrived at the abbey, but it has grown back, thick and red as a fox's brush and gleaming. It is my only beauty. Otherwise I am too tall, too hard, my skin burnt brown by the sun of many summer roads. If Lazarillo had seen my hair, then he might have remembered me. But one wimple is very like another. Here in the fields, I can discard the coiffe. There is no one to see my unbound hair or my strong bare shoulders. I can be myself; and although I know I can never be l'Ailée again, for a short time I can at least be Juliette.

*   *   *

For six more years I was to remain with the troupe that became the *Théâtre des Cieux*. After Vitré I moved out of LeMerle's caravan. I loved him still— there was no escaping that—but my pride forbade me to stay. By then I had a caravan of my own, and when he came to me, as I knew he would, I made

47

him wait to be admitted, like a penitent. It was a small enough vengeance, but it changed the balance between us, and for the time I was satisfied.

We travelled along the coast, targeting markets and fairs where there was money to be had. When business was bad we sold sickness cures and love charms, or LeMerle fleeced the unwary at cards or dice. Most often we performed; snatches of ballets, masquerades or carnival but with the occasional play growing gradually more frequent as time passed. I developed a rope-dancing act with the dwarves—a child's game, no more, but it was popular with village audiences—and I taught my fellow dancers the simpler moves. The act grew more ambitious as we developed it, but it was my idea to take it to the high rope, and that was the beginning of our success.

At first we performed over a sheet with a dwarf at each corner, in case of accident. As our daring increased, however, we dispensed with the sheet and took to the air, not content merely to walk the rope, but dancing, tumbling and finally *flying* from one rope to another by means of a series of interlinked rings. Thus, l'Ailée was fledged.

I have never been afraid of heights. In fact, I enjoy them. From a certain height, everyone looks the same—men, women, villains, kings—as if rank and fortune were simply an accident of perspective and not something ordained by God. On the ropes I became something more than human; at every performance more people came to watch. My costume was silver and green, my cloak a sweep of coloured feathers, and on my head I wore a cockade of plumes, which exaggerated my height still further. I have always been tall for a woman—already I overtopped everyone in the *Théâtre des Cieux* except LeMerle—but in my dancer's costume I passed six feet, and when I left the gilded cage from which I began my act, children in the crowd would murmur and point, and their parents would wonder aloud that such a creature could even mount the climbing pole, let alone fly.

The rope was stretched thirty feet above their heads; below, cobbles, earth, grass. I risked broken limbs or death if I made a mistake. But l'Ailée made no mistakes. My ankle was fastened to a thin gilt chain—as if without it I might take wing and fly away. Rico and Bazuel held onto the other end, taking care to stay as far away from me as possible. Sometimes I growled and pretended to lash out, making the children scream. Then the dwarves released the chain, and I was free.

I made it effortless. Of course it was not; the smallest move takes a thousand hours of practice. But in those moments I was no longer myself. I danced on silken cords so thin they were barely visible from the ground, using the linked rings to travel from one to the other, as Gabriel once taught me, a lifetime ago, by the orange caravan with the tiger and the lambs. Sometimes I sang, or made wild sounds in my throat. People looked up at me in superstitious awe and whispered that I must indeed be of another breed, that perhaps somewhere beyond the oceans just such a race of fox-haired harpies swooped and soared over the endless blue acres. Needless to say, LeMerle did nothing to discourage this kind of thinking. Nor did I.

As months passed, and years, our act grew in

49

popularity until we were courted from Paris to province. It made me bold; there was nothing I would not dare. I devised wilder leaps, more breathtaking flights between the poles, leaving the others far below me. I added more levels of cord to the act: swings, a trapeze, a suspended platform. I performed in trees and over water. I never fell.

Audiences loved me. Many believed LeMerle's fiction: that I was of another race. There were rumours of witchcraft, and a few times we were forced to leave a town in haste. But those times were few; our fame spread, and at LeMerle's orders we moved north again towards Paris.

Two and a half years had passed since our flight from the city. Time enough, said the Blackbird, for our little *contretemps* to have been forgotten. Besides, he had no ambition to re-enter society; the King was getting married, and we were not alone in making for the celebrations. Every troupe in the country was doing the same: actors, jugglers, musicians, dancers. There was money to be made, said LeMerle, and with a little imagination, a little initiative, we could make a fortune.

But by this time I knew him too well to believe the simple explanation. That look was back in his eyes—the look of dangerous enjoyment he wore when planning an outrageous venture—and I was wary from the first.

'He's hunting a tiger with a pointed stick,' Le Borgne was wont to say. 'Finding it's the easy part, but God help us all if he runs it to ground.'

LeMerle, of course, denied any such intent. 'No mischief, I promise you, my Harpy,' he said, but with so much suppressed laughter in his voice that I did not believe him. 'What, are you afraid?'

'Of course not.'

'Good. This is no time to start suffering from nerves.'

CHAPTER EIGHT
♥

July 13th, 1610

It was the height of l'Ailée's career. We had money, fame; crowds adored us, and we were coming home. With the approach of the King's wedding, Paris was in perpetual carnival; spirits were high, drinking deep, purses loose, and you could smell the hope and the money and, behind that, the fear. A wedding, like a coronation, is a time of uncertainty. Rules are suspended. New alliances are made and broken. For the most part, they mean little to us. We watch the big players on France's stage, simply hoping that they will not crush us. A whim could do it; a king's finger is heavy enough to wipe out an army. Even a bishop's hand, cleverly wielded, may crush a man. But we at the *Théâtre des Cieux* did not consider these things. We could have read the signs if we had chosen to, but we were drunk on our success; LeMerle was hunting his tigers and I was perfecting a new—and increasingly dangerous—routine. Even Le Borgne was uncharacteristically cheery, and when we received word on entering Paris that His Majesty had expressed an interest in watching us perform, our elation knew no bounds.

The days that followed passed in a blur. I've

seen kings come and go, but I've always had a soft spot for King Henri. Perhaps because he cheered so heartily on that day; perhaps because his face was kind. This new Louis is different, this little boy. You can buy his portrait in any market, crowned with a sun halo and flanked by kneeling saints, but he makes me fearful with his wan face and heart-shaped mouth. What can such a little boy know of anything? How can he rule France? But all that was to come; when l'Ailée performed at the Palais-Royal, we had more security, more happiness than we had enjoyed since before the wars. This marriage—this alliance with the Médicis proved it; we saw it as a sign that our luck had turned.

It had—but not for the better. The night of our performance we celebrated with wine and meat and sweet pastries, and then Rico and Bazuel went to watch a wild beast show near the Palais-Royal while the others got even more drunk and LeMerle went off on his own towards the river. Later that night, I heard him return, and when I passed his caravan I saw blood on the steps and I was afraid.

I tapped at the door, and, receiving no answer, went inside. LeMerle was sitting with his back to me on the floor, with his shirt wadded against his left side. I ran to him with a cry of dismay; there was blood all over him. More blood, in fact, than real hurt, as I discovered to my relief. A short, sharp blade—not unlike my own—had glanced off his ribs, leaving a shallow, messy gash about nine inches long. At first I assumed he had been attacked and robbed—a man in Paris by night needs more than luck to protect him—but he still had his purse, and besides, only a very inept footpad would have dealt him such a clumsy blow.

52

As LeMerle refused to tell me what had happened, I could only conclude that this mischief was somehow of his own making, and dismiss it as an isolated case of ill fortune.

But there was more bad luck to come. The following night, one of our caravans was set on fire as we slept, and only chance saved the rest. As it was, Cateau got up for a piss and smelt smoke. We lost two horses, the bulk of our costumes, the caravan itself, of course, and one of our number: little Rico, who had got blind drunk during the evening and failed to awaken to our cries. His friend Bazuel tried to go in after him, though we could see it was hopeless from the start, and he was overcome by smoke before he even got close.

It cost him his voice. When he recovered, he was unable to speak in anything above a whisper. Even after that, I think, his heart was broken. He drank like a sponge, picked fights with anything that moved and performed so badly in his act that in the end we had to leave him out altogether. When, some months later, he chose to stay behind, no one was surprised. And anyway, as Le Borgne said, it wasn't as if we had lost a rope-dancer. Dwarves could always be replaced.

We left Paris furtively and in sombre mood. The celebrations were far from over, but now LeMerle was eager for us to be gone. Rico's death had affected him more than I expected; he ate little, slept less, snapped at anyone who dared speak to him. It was the first time I had ever seen him truly angry. It was not for Rico, I soon realized—nor even for the damaged equipment—but for his own humiliation, the spoiling of our triumph. He had lost the game, and, more than anything else, the

Blackbird hated to lose.

No one had noticed anything on the night of the burning. LeMerle, however, had his suspicions, though he would not speak of them. Instead, he sank into a dangerous silence, and not even the news that his old enemy, the Bishop of Evreux, had been waylaid by footpads a few days before was enough to brighten his spirits.

After Paris, we made our way south. Bazuel left us in Anjou, but we gained two more people in the months that followed: Bécquot, a one-legged fiddle-player, and his ten-year-old son, Philbert. The boy was a natural on the high rope, but he was too reckless; he took a bad fall later that year and was useless for months. All the same, LeMerle kept him with us through the following winter and, although the boy was never fit for the flying act again, fed him and found him useful work to do. Bécquot was grateful, and I was surprised, for business had taken a bad turn and money was short. But Le Borgne simply shrugged and muttered something about tigers. Nothing came of it, however; the boy remained with us for another eight months, after which LeMerle left him with a group of Franciscans on their way to Paris who, he said, would care for him.

We moved on. We worked markets and fairs throughout Anjou and down into Gascony, sometimes helping with harvests as we had done in the early days, staying in one place over winter. The second winter, Demiselle died of a fever, leaving us with only two dancers—at thirty, Hermine was getting too old for the high rope, and it was painful to watch her. Ghislaine tried her best, but never mastered the jumps. Once more, l'Ailée flew alone.

Undaunted, LeMerle returned to playwriting. His farces had always been popular, but his plays became gradually more satirical as we journeyed across France. His favourite subject was the Church, and several times we were forced to pack up in haste as some zealous official took offence. The public, for the most part, enjoyed them. Evil bishops, lecherous friars and religious hypocrites had always attracted excellent audiences, and when there were also dwarves and a Winged Woman, the show never failed to bring in money.

LeMerle played the clerical roles himself—he had somehow acquired a variety of religious garments and a heavy silver cross, which must have been valuable, but which he never tried to sell, even when times were poor. It was a gift, he said when I questioned him, from an old friend in Paris. But his eyes were hard as he said it, and his smile was all teeth. I did not pursue the matter, however; LeMerle could be sentimental about the strangest things, and if he wanted a thing kept secret, then no amount of questioning would loosen his tongue. All the same, I wondered a little—especially when I was hungry and food was scarce. Then, after a while, I put it out of mind.

Now began our drifting time. We travelled south in winter, north in summer, always following markets and fairs. We changed our colours in the more hostile regions, but for the most part we were still the *Théâtre des Cieux*, and l'Ailée danced the high rope, and people cheered and threw flowers. Even so I sensed that my heyday was coming to an end—one year a torn tendon kept me in agony for a whole summer—but we knew we could always fall back on LeMerle's plays. They were more hazardous than the rope act, certainly; but they earned us good coin, especially in Huguenot country.

Five more times we made the journey south. I learned to recognize the roads, the good places, the dangerous places. I took lovers where and when I chose, without hindrance from LeMerle. He still shared my bed when I wanted him to; but I had grown up a little, and my slavish adoration of him had turned to a more comfortable affection. I knew him now. I knew his rages, his triumphs, his joys. I knew him, and I accepted what he was.

I knew, too, that there was much in him to hate, much to mistrust. Twice, to my knowledge, he had murdered—once a drunkard who struggled too violently to retrieve a stolen purse, once a farmer who stoned us near Rouen—both deeds committed in stealth and darkness, only to be discovered long after we had gone.

I asked him once how he reconciled such things with his conscience.

'Conscience?' He raised an eyebrow. 'You mean God, Judgement Day, and that kind of thing?'

I shrugged. He knew that wasn't quite what I meant, but rarely passed over an opportunity to tease me over my heretical beliefs.

LeMerle smiled. 'Dear Juliette,' he said. 'If God is really up there—and, if we are to believe your Copernicus, that must be a very, *very* long way up—then I don't trust his perspectives. To him, I'm a speck. Down here, from where I'm standing, things are different.'

I didn't understand, and I said so.

'I mean that I'd rather be something more than a

gambling chip in a game of unlimited stakes.'

'Even so, to kill a man . . .'

'People kill each other all the time. At least I'm honest. I don't do it in God's name.'

Knowing him for good or ill—or so I thought—I could still love him; believing as I did that in spite of his sins, the essential heart of the man was good, was faithful to itself, a thieving blackbird singing a mocking song . . . But that was the man's talent. He could make people see what they wanted to see, reflections of themselves as vain as shadows in a pond. I saw my foolish self in him, that was all. I was twenty-two, and I had not grown up half as much as I believed.

Until Epinal.

CHAPTER NINE
♥

July 14th, 1610

It is a pleasant little town on the Moselle, in Lorraine. It was the first time we had come that way, concentrating as we did mostly on the coastal regions, and we arrived in a small village called Bruyère a few miles out of the town. A quiet place: half a dozen farms, a church, orchards of apple and pear trees half eaten by mistletoe. If I felt anything unusual I cannot recall it now; maybe a sharp glance from a woman by the roadside, a sly forking of the fingers from a child at the crossroads. I read the cards, as I did at any new spot, but I drew only a harmless Fool, a Six of Staves and a Deuce of

Cups. If there was a warning there, I did not see it.

It was August; parched summer dragging into a premature autumn turning dank and sweet with rot. Hailstorms a month earlier had crushed the ripe barley, and the fields lay spoiling in an alehouse stench. The sudden heat in the wake of the storms was overwhelming, and the people seemed dazed by the sun, blinking foolishly at our caravans as they passed. Nevertheless, we managed to negotiate a field for our camp, and that night we performed a short burlesque around our campfire, to the sound of crickets and frogs.

Our audience was sparse, however. Even the dwarves barely brought a smile to the mirthless faces made bloody in the firelight, and few seemed inclined to stay afterwards. The only regular entertainments in that region were hangings and burnings, said the talk in the alehouse: a sow had been hanged a few days earlier for eating her young, a pair of nuns in a nearby convent had set themselves on fire in imitation of Saint Christina Mirabilis, and there was always at least one person in the pillory, so the villagers of Bruyère, inured to strong entertainments, were unlikely to be much moved by the arrival of a troupe of players.

At this LeMerle shrugged philosophically. There were good days and bad, he said, and these small villages were unused to culture. Epinal would be better.

We arrived there on the morning of the Festival of the Virgin to find the town in carnival mood. We had expected as much; after the procession and the Mass the populace would retire to the alehouses and the streets where already the celebrations were under way. This was no time for one of LeMerle's

58

satires—Epinal had a reputation for piety—but there might be good takings for a rope-dancer and a troupe of jongleurs. I could already see a tabor-player and a flautist beneath the portals of the church, plus a masked Fool with his wand and bells and, strangely out of place, the Plague Doctor, black long-nosed mask over whitened face, his dark cloak flapping. Other than that slight note of discord, things seemed much as normal. Perhaps there was another troupe in town, I told myself, with which we might have to share the takings. I know I thought no more about them. And yet I should have recognized the signs. The black Doctor in his crow's garb. The sounds of excitement—almost of fear—as we passed. The look in a woman's eye as I smiled at her from my caravan, the sly fork of the hand repeated over and over ...

LeMerle scented trouble from the first. I should have known—there was a reckless gleam in his eyes as he scanned the crowd, a broadness to his smile which should have checked me. It was our custom at times like this to send out the dwarves amongst the revellers, giving out sweetmeats and invitations to the performance, but this day he signalled for the dwarves to keep close, Le Borgne occasionally spitting fire from the tail of my caravan like a comet, Cateau calling out in his piping voice: 'Players! See the players today! See the Winged Woman!'

Today, however, I could see that the crowd's attention lay elsewhere. The procession of the Holy Mother was about to begin, and there was already a great glut of people outside the church. People lined the street on either side, some carrying

59

images and flowers, votives or flags. There were vendors, too: sellers of pasties and cooked meats and ale and fruit. The air was thick with the smells of candle smoke and sweat, roasting meat, dust and incense, leather and onions and refuse and horses. The noise was almost unendurable. Cripples and children stood near the front, but already there were too many people, and the crowd pressed against the sides of our caravans, some looking up curiously at the painted signs and bright pennants, others shouting at us for being in their way.

I was already beginning to feel dazed; the cries of the vendors, the heat of the sun, the many stenches were too much for me, and I tried to turn back into some quieter street, but it was too late. Urged forward by the mass of worshippers, our caravans had reached the steps of the church almost at the same time as the Virgin's Day procession was due to leave. Unable to retreat or go forward I watched, curious, as the great platform carrying the Holy Mother emerged from the main door of the church and into the light.

There must have been fifty people underneath. Another fifty along the sides, shoulders straining against the long poles that supported it. It was heavy, and swayed as it came through the doorway; and at every slow step there came a sigh from the hooded bearers, as if the burden were almost too much to carry. The Holy Mother stood at the top of the structure on a mound of blue and white flowers, her embroidered robe gleaming in the sunlight, her hands smeared with oil and honey. A priest with a censer walked before her; a dozen monks with candlesticks came behind, singing the *Avé* to the wailing of an *hautbois*.

I had little time to follow the music, however. As soon as the procession appeared, there was a moan from the people and we were jostled suddenly, violently, as the worshippers surged forward. *'Miséricorde!'* came the cry from a thousand throats, and the stench of oil and flesh and grime was overwhelming, mingling with the smoke from the silver censer, a scent of clove and holy dust. 'Pity! Pity for our sins!'

I stood upon the axle of my caravan and peered across the heads of the crowd. I was beginning to feel uneasy, for although I had seen religious frenzy before, this seemed unusually ferocious, the shrill note of zeal sharpened on something shriller, closer to the bone. Not for the first time, and with an almost unconscious cupping of the new roundness at my belly, I wondered whether it was not time to leave the life we were leading before it soured completely. I was in my twenty-third year. I was no longer young.

The black Doctor flapped his cloak, keeping a blister of space between himself and the crowd, a walking emptiness, and I noticed that the cries came louder at his passage and that some fell to their knees in his wake.

'Miséricorde! Pity for our sins!' We were too close to the procession to hope for a retreat and I steered my horse with care, keeping him dancing gingerly on the spot against the push of people that threatened to overturn us. The Holy Mother passed slowly, lurching like a laden barge through the crowd. I saw that many of the people carrying the platform went barefoot, like penitents, although this was not usual on the Virgin's Day. The monks were hooded like the bearers, but I

noticed that one had pushed back his hood a little, and his face was red and flushed with drunkenness or exhaustion.

We stood our ground. The platform swayed as it passed us, and for a moment, standing on my axle, I was eye to eye with the Virgin, close enough to see the dust of years gleaming in the intricacies of her golden crown, the flaking of paint across her pink cheek. There was a spider in the hollow of one blue eye, and as I watched, it began to move slowly down her face. No one else saw it. Then she passed by.

In her wake, the frenzy was mounting, with people falling to their knees even in the press of the multitude, dragging others with them. Others took their places, the ranks closing over their heads, their cries unheard. *'Miséricorde!* Pity for our sins!'

A woman to my left arched backwards into the crowd, eyes rolled up to the whites. For a moment she was held up like an effigy, floating effortlessly upon the outstretched hands, then she slid under and the people moved on.

'Hey!' I said. 'There's someone under there!'

Faces mooned at me without comprehension from the swell below. No one seemed to have heard me. I cracked my whip over their heads and my horse strained and pranced to stay level, eyes rolling. 'There's a woman under there! Stand back, for pity's sake! Stand *back*!'

But we had been carried too far. The injured woman was already behind us, and people were thronging forward to stare at the foolish patch of space I had cleared. There came a sudden lull in sound, reducing the cries to a drone above which the *Avé* was briefly audible, and I thought I read in the upturned faces a kind of hope, a new relief. Then came the catastrophe.

If it had been any other than a member of the procession no one would have noticed him fall. I learned afterwards that four people had been crushed underfoot during the celebrations, their heads smashed into the cobbles by the eager feet of pilgrims and revellers alike. But the procession was sacred, moving ponderously through a multitude held at bay by incense and adoration. I did not see him fall. But I heard the cry, a single note at first, then the chorus, rising in swift reaction far beyond that which we had previously witnessed. Leaping back onto the axle I saw what had happened, although even then I did not understand its significance.

The staggering monk at the tail of the procession had collapsed. The heat, I thought vaguely, or the fumes from the censer. A group of people had gathered around the fallen man; I saw the white blur of his exposed skin as they pulled open his habit. There was a gasp and a moan, then they were moving like ripples, as fast as they could back through the ranks.

In seconds, the ripples had become a powerful undertow, reversing the flow of people so that instead of pushing towards the procession they were pushing away with all their energies, the caravans rocking in the renewed counter-struggle, some even trying to climb up out of the crowd onto the caravans in their eagerness to be gone. The procession was no longer sacred; as I watched, the line trembled and broke in several places, the Holy Mother lurching to one side, uncrowned in the burst of panic as some of her bearers deserted.

Then I heard the cry: a high-pitched ululation of grief or terror, a single voice rising above them like a clarion, '*La peste! La peste!*'

I struggled to hear, to distinguish words in the unfamiliar dialect. Whatever it was, it ran through the crowd like summer fire. Fights broke out as people tried to escape; others climbed the walls of the buildings lining the street—some even jumped from the sides of the bridge in their eagerness to flee. I stood up to see what was happening, but I had become separated from the other caravans. Some distance ahead I could see LeMerle lashing at his mare's flanks, driving her onwards. But the crowd had him from both sides, rocking against the caravan's panels, lifting the wheels from the ground. Faces loomed at me out of the multitude. One caught my eye, and I was astonished at the hatred there. It was a young girl, her round red face distorted with terror and loathing. 'Witch!' she shrieked at me. 'Poisoner!'

Whatever it was, it was catching. I heard the cry bounce ahead of me like a stone across a lake, gathering momentum as it went, looking for somewhere to strike. The outpouring of hatred had become a tide; now it swelled against me, threatening to lift the caravan from the ground.

I was struggling with my horse; it was a quiet beast as a rule, but the girl struck it hard in the flank and it half reared, dancing out with its heavy-shod hooves. The girl screamed; I pulled back on the horse's harness to prevent it from trampling the people in front of me. It took all my attention and my strength—even so, the animal was panicked and I had to whisper a cantrip into his ear to calm him—and by the time I had done with that, the girl had vanished into the crowd, and the terrible wave of hatred had moved on.

Ahead of me, though, LeMerle was in trouble. I could see him shouting something, his voice lost in the roar of the multitude, but I was too far away to understand what it was. His horse, a nervy mare, was terror-stricken; I could hear the cries of *Witch!* and *Poisoner!* above her screaming. LeMerle tried to control her, but it was beyond his skill; he was alone, cut off from the rest of us, now lashing out over the heads of the crowd with his whip, trying to force them aside. The strain proved too much for the caravan's axle. It collapsed, toppling the vehicle, and now many hands tugged at the caravan's fastenings, ignoring the blows from LeMerle's whip. They had him now; there was nowhere for him to go. Someone threw a clod of earth; it hit him in the face and he lost his balance; hands reached to drag him from his perch. Someone else tried to intervene—an official, perhaps—I thought I could make out faint cries of *Order! Order!* as the two factions clashed.

Throughout all this I had been shouting at the top of my voice, trying to divert attention away from LeMerle; now I urged my horse forwards, heedless of the people in front of me. He saw me coming and grinned, but before I could reach him the crowd had closed in. Blows fell onto him as he was dragged away. LeMerle was lost from sight.

I would have followed on foot, although he was already too far away, except that Le Borgne, who had been hiding inside the caravan as I drove through the crowd, held onto my arm. 'Don't be stupid, Juliette,' he rasped in my ear. 'Don't you

65

know what's going on here? Haven't you been listening?'

I looked at him wildly. 'LeMerle—'

'LeMerle can take care of himself.' His hand tightened on my arm; in spite of his size, the dwarf's grip was painfully strong. 'Listen.'

I listened. I could still hear that cry, now grown rhythmic, swelled with the stamping of many feet, like a crowd calling for a favourite actress. *'La peste! La peste!'*

It was only then that I understood. The outburst of terror; the fallen monk; the accusations of witchcraft. Le Borgne saw my expression, and nodded. We looked at each other, and for a moment neither of us said anything. Outside, the cries redoubled.

'La peste!'

The plague.

CHAPTER TEN

♥

July 16th, 1610

The crowd was dispersing at last, leaving me still struggling to control the terrified horse. Bouffon reined in his own animal and brought it flank to flank with mine; Hermine, her caravan half overturned as she tried to cross the bridge, stood helplessly staring at the remains of a shattered wheel. Of the others, there was no sign. Perhaps they had been taken prisoner like LeMerle; perhaps they had fled.

66

I barely acknowledged Le Borgne's warning. Leaping down onto the road I ran towards the tail of the procession. Half the bearers had already gone; the rest were struggling to balance the Virgin's platform against the big marble fountain that dominated the square whilst ensuring the Holy Mother did not fall. I saw several bodies on the road, worshippers who had been crushed against buildings or trampled underfoot. LeMerle's caravan was lying there on its side. Of its occupant, living or dead, there was no sign.

'*Mon père.*' I addressed the priest as calmly as I could. 'Did you see what happened? My friend was in that caravan.'

The priest looked at me in silence. His face was yellow with road dust.

'Please tell me!' I heard my voice beginning to rise. 'He wasn't doing any harm. He was trying to protect himself!'

A woman in black—one of the bearers—glanced at me scornfully: 'He'll get what's coming to him, don't you worry.'

'What did you say?'

'Him and the rest of his brood.' The words were barely intelligible in their thick patois. 'We seen you poisoning the wells. We seen the signs.'

Behind her, the Plague Doctor stepped out of a side alley, his cloak slapping against the wall. The woman in black saw him and I caught the sign again, forked and secretive.

'Look. All I want is to find my friend. Where have they taken him?'

The woman gave a humourless laugh. 'Where d'you think? The courthouse. He won't fly away from there. None of you plague-bringers will.'

'What's that supposed to mean?' I must have looked threatening then, because the woman jerked away, poking the sign at me with trembling fingers.

'*Miséricorde!* God protect me!'

I took a quick step forward. 'Let's see if he does, shall we?'

But the Plague Doctor's hand was already on my shoulder, and I could hear his voice in my ear, muffled by the long-nosed mask. 'Be quiet, girl. Listen to me.'

I tried to pull away, but the grip on my shoulder was unexpectedly strong. 'It isn't safe here,' hissed the Doctor. 'Judge Rémy burnt four witches in this square last month. You can still see the grease marks on the cobbles.'

The dry voice seemed oddly familiar. 'Do I know you?'

'Quiet!' He turned away, his whitened mouth barely moving.

'I'm sure I know you.' There was something about that mouth; the thin, twisted look of it, like an old scar, which I recognized. And the smell, the dusty, alchemical smell from his robes . . . 'Don't I?'

There came an exasperated hissing sound from behind the Plague Doctor's mask. 'Oh for pity's sake, girl!' There it was again, that familiar voice, the clipped, precise intonation of a man who speaks many languages. He turned to me again and I could see his eyes, old and sad as a caged monkey's. 'They are looking for someone to blame,' he whispered harshly. 'Leave now. Don't even stay the night.'

He was right, of course. Players, travellers and

gypsies have always been useful scapegoats for any misfortune, be it crop failure, famine, bad weather or plague. I learned it in Flanders when I was fourteen; in Paris, three years later. Le Borgne knew it—Rico had learned it too late. The plague had pursued us sporadically across France, but by then, the worst of it was over. It had burnt itself out during the last epidemic, and few people died of it now except the old and the sick, but in Epinal this was only the last in a series of disasters. Dry cattle, spoiled harvest, rotten fruit, rabid dogs, unseasonal weather—and now this. Someone had to be held responsible. It didn't matter that it made no sense; plague takes over a week to spread its corruption, and we had barely been there an hour. Nor does it spread through water, even if we had tampered with the wells.

But I already knew that no one here would listen to reason. Witchcraft was what they believed in: witchcraft and poisoning. It's all there, in the Bible. Why look any further?

*   *   *

I came back to my caravan to find that Le Borgne had gone. Bouffon and Hermine, too, had disappeared, taking what they could of their possessions. I didn't blame them—the Doctor's advice was good—but I could not leave LeMerle to face the mob alone. Call it loyalty or foolish infatuation, I left the caravan where it was, led my horse to the fountain and followed in the wake of the crowd towards the courthouse.

It was already overflowing when I arrived. People were spilling out of the doors and down the steps, scrambling over each other in their eagerness to see, to hear. The town Sergeant was standing on a podium, trying to make himself heard above the noise. Armed soldiers flanked him on either side, and between them, looking pale but self-assured as ever, was LeMerle.

I was relieved to see him still standing. His face was bruised, and his hands were tied in front of him, but some official must have intervened before much harm was done. It was a good sign; a sign that someone was in control, someone who might listen to a reasonable argument. At least, I hoped so.

'Good people!' The Sergeant raised his staff and signalled for quiet. 'In God's name let me speak!' He was a short, plump man with a luxuriant moustache and a mournful look. He looked to me like every other vine-grower or corn merchant I had seen that summer, and even over the heads of the crowd, across the breadth of the courtroom and through the blur of their upheld arms, I could see that he was trembling.

There was a lull in the noise, but it did not subside completely. Instead, several people raised their voices, calling, 'Hang the poisoner!' and 'Hang the witch!'

The Sergeant rubbed his hands together in a nervous gesture. 'Good people of Epinal, peace!' he cried. 'I am no more empowered to try this man than the rest of you!'

'*Try* him!' came a harsh voice from the back of the room. 'Who said anything about that? All you need's a rope, Sergeant, and a branch to tie it to!'

There were murmurs of approval at this. The Sergeant waved his hands for silence. 'You can't

70

just go around hanging people. You don't even know if he's guilty. Only the Judge can—'

The harsh voice interrupted him. 'What about the portents, eh?'

'Ay, what about the portents?'

'What about the plague?'

Again the Sergeant appealed for calm. 'I can't make the decision!' His voice trembled like his hands. 'Only Judge Rémy can do that!'

The name of Judge Rémy seemed to have achieved what the Sergeant could not, and the noise sank to a dissatisfied murmur. Around me people crossed themselves. Others forked the sign. I lifted my eyes to meet LeMerle's—I stood half a head taller than most men in the room—and I saw that he was smiling. I knew that look; had seen it more times than I could remember. It was the look of a gambler as he plays his last coin, of a player about to begin the performance of his life.

'Judge Rémy.' His words carried effortlessly across the courtroom. 'I've heard that name before. A man of faith, I believe.'

'Two thousand witches across nine counties!' The harsh voice came from the rear of the hall, turning heads.

LeMerle lost none of his composure. 'Then it's a pity he isn't here now.'

'He'll be here soon enough!'

'The sooner the better.' The townsfolk were listening; intrigued in spite of themselves. Now that he had their attention, LeMerle had a presence they found difficult to ignore. 'These are dangerous times,' he said. 'You've a right to be suspicious. Where is Judge Rémy?'

'As if you didn't know!' brayed the voice—but

some of its heat had gone, and several people called out in protest.

'Be quiet! Let's hear the fellow speak!'

'What harm can it do to listen?'

The Sergeant explained that the Judge was away on business, but was due back any day. When the heckler called out yet again, heads turned angrily, but no one could make out quite where he was.

LeMerle smiled. 'Good folk of Epinal,' he said without raising his voice. 'I am only too pleased to answer your accusations. I can even forgive your rough treatment of me'—at this he touched his bruised face—'for did not Our Lord ask us to turn the other cheek?'

'The devil may speak fine if he pleases!' It was the heckler, standing closer to the podium now but still anonymous in the wash of faces. 'But let's see if the holy words don't blister your tongue!'

'With pleasure.' LeMerle's reply was prompt, and voices that had hitherto joined the chorus of accusations now lifted in encouragement. 'Unworthy though I may be, let me remind you before whom this court must bow. Not Judge Rémy, but a greater judge than he. Before we begin, let us join in prayer for His guidance and for His protection in these evil times.' And with these words, LeMerle took the silver cross from out of his shirt, and raised it in his bound hands.

I hid a smile. You had to admire the man. Heads bowed automatically as blanched lips mouthed the *Paternoster*. A tide had begun to turn for LeMerle, and when the now familiar voice called out again, it was met with a volley of angry rejoinders, so that once again the speaker's identity was lost. At the back of the room, blows were exchanged by several

72

parties, each of which held the other responsible for the outburst. The Sergeant blustered helplessly and LeMerle had to call for order.

'I demand respect for this court!' he snapped. 'Is this not the way the Evil One works, spreading discord so that honest men turn on each other and make a mockery of justice?' The culprits subsided into abashed silence. 'Is this not what happened only a few minutes ago, in the marketplace? Are you no better than animals?'

In the silence that followed, not even the heckler dared speak. 'The Evil One is in you all,' said LeMerle, dropping his voice to a stage whisper. 'I can see him. *You*'—he pointed to a big man with a red, angry face—'He touched you with Lust. I can see it, like a worm coiled behind your eye. And you'—to a sharp-featured woman near the front, one of the shrillest of his accusers before he turned the crowd around—'I see covetousness in you, and discontent. And you, and *you*'—his voice had risen now and he pointed to each one in turn—'I see avarice. Rage. Greed. Pride. *You* lied to your wife. *You* deceived your husband. *You* struck your neighbour. *You* doubted the certainty of salvation.'

He had them now; I saw it in their eyes. Even so, one false move and they would be on him without mercy. He knew it too; his eyes gleamed with enjoyment. 'And *you*!' Now he pointed to the centre of the room, clearing a swathe through the crowd with a sweep of his bound hands. 'Yes, you, in the shadows! You, Ananias, the false witness! I see you, clearest of all!'

For ten heartbeats there was silence as we looked at an empty space. Then we saw the heckler who had until then evaded us: a grotesque figure squatting in the shadows. Its head was large, its arms apelike, its single eye blazed. The people closest to it recoiled, and as they did so, the creature sprang towards the window and swung itself high onto the ledge, hissing with fury.

'Ye outwitted me this time, devil take ye!' it cried in its raucous voice. 'But I've not finished with ye yet, Frater Colombin!'

'God forgive us!' All around the courtroom, faces turned in wonder and disgust as people finally saw the creature that had voiced their suspicions.

'A monster!'

'The Devil's Imp!'

The one-eyed creature spat fire from its hideous mouth. 'This isn't over, Colombin!' it shrieked. 'You may have won the battle here, but in Another Place, the war goes on!'

Then the thing was gone, leaping out of the window into the courtyard below, leaving nothing but a reek of oil and smoke to prove that it had been there at all.

In the stunned silence that followed, the Sergeant turned open-mouthed towards his prisoner. 'Good God, I saw it! With my own eyes, so help me! The Devil's Imp!'

LeMerle shrugged.

'But he knew you,' said the Sergeant. 'He spoke as if you'd met before.'

'Many times,' said LeMerle.

The Sergeant stared at him. 'Suppose you tell me who you are, sir,' he said at last.

'I will,' said LeMerle, beginning to smile. 'But first, I'd be grateful if someone could find me a chair. A chair, and a glass of brandy. I'm tired and I've come a long way.'

He was a traveller, he told them, who had come to Epinal when he heard of the reputation of their evangelical Judge. News of his purges, said LeMerle, had reached from coast to coast. He himself had left the seclusion of a Cistercian cloister to seek the man out and to offer his services. He spoke of visions and portents, of marvels and blasphemies encountered upon his travels. Revealed the horrors of the sabbat, of the Jews and idolaters, the slaughtered children, poisoned wells, cursed crops, blighted harvests, churches struck by lightning, babies withered in the womb, stifled in the cradle. All this he had seen, he claimed. Would any man deny it?

No one did. They had seen the Devil's Imp with their own eyes. From its mouth they had heard his true name. In a few sentences LeMerle wove for them the tale of Brother Colombin, a man touched by God and driven to wipe out the Devil's children wherever he could find them. Travelling alone and in poverty from town to town he uncovered the Evil One's machinations wherever he passed, his only reward that of Satan's defeat. Not so strange, then, that he should have been taken for a gypsy, travelling as he was with a group of itinerant players, brief companions of the road. Seeing the people of Epinal in disarray the Imp had sought to trick them but had failed, praise the Lord, revealing its malice to its own undoing.

I had, of course, recognized Le Borgne. Throwing his voice was another of the dwarf's many skills, and he had used it to good effect on a

75

number of occasions. He must have crept into the courtroom before me—like many of his kind, he could be unobtrusive when he chose—providing LeMerle with a secret ally in the crowd. It is a trick often used by conjurers and carnival magicians; we had used it ourselves in our performances. Le Borgne was a fine actor; a pity that his short-ended legs made it impossible for him ever to perform anything but burlesques and tumbling acts. I promised myself to be kinder to him in future. He had a loyal heart, in spite of his gruff manner, and in this case, his courage and quick thinking had probably saved LeMerle's life.

Meanwhile, it seemed that once again LeMerle might be overwhelmed by the numbers of people wanting to touch him. Far from howling after his blood, however, it seemed that all were now desperate for his forgiveness. Hands reached out from every direction, plucking at his clothes, brushing his skin—I saw a man shake hands with him, and suddenly everyone in the room wanted to shake the hand of the one who had touched the holy man. Of course, LeMerle was enjoying every minute.

'Bless you, my brother. My sister.' Gradually, almost imperceptibly, I heard his register shift from pulpit to marketplace. The reckless light danced in his eyes. God help them, perhaps they took it for piety. And then, perhaps out of mischief, perhaps because the Blackbird could never resist a wager, he took it further.

'It's a good thing for you that I did come to Epinal,' he told them slyly. 'The air is thick with evil spirits here, the sky leaden with sin. If the plague has come upon you, ask yourselves the reason. You must know that the pure in heart are safe from the manifestations of the Evil One.'

There came uneasy murmurings from the audience.

'Ask yourselves how *I* manage to travel without fear,' he continued. 'Ask yourselves how a simple cleric could withstand hell's assault so surely for so many years.' His voice, though carrying, was persuasively soft. 'Years ago, a holy man, my tutor, devised a philtre against all forms of demonic aggression: evil visions, succubi and incubi, diseases and poisons of the mind. A distillate of twenty-four different herbs, salt and holy water, the whole to be blest by twelve bishops and used in infinitesimal quantities . . .' There was a pause as he studied the dramatic effect of his words. 'For the past ten years, this elixir has kept me from harm,' he went on. 'And I know of no place where it is more needed than in the town of Epinal today.'

I should have known LeMerle would not stop there. Why did he do these things? I asked myself. Was it revenge, contempt for their credulousness, the sheer glory of his adopted sainthood? Was it the chance to make a profit? Or was it just to win the game? I frowned at him from my place at the back of the courtroom, but he was in full voice now, and there was no stopping him. He saw my warning look, though, and grinned.

There was one problem, however, he told the crowd. Although he would willingly have given them the philtre at no cost, he had only one flask with him. He could make more, but the herbs were rare and difficult to come by, and besides, the twelve bishops made such a thing impossible to prepare at short notice. As a result, though it hurt him to ask, he would be obliged to take a modest sum from each person. Then, perhaps, if each of the good townspeople were to provide a small bottle of plain water or wine, then with an eyedropper he might create a more dilute mixture . . .

The takers were many. They lined the street until after sunset with their bottles and vials and LeMerle greeted everyone with solemn courtesy as he measured out the drops of clear fluid with a glass rod. They paid in coin and in goods. A fat duck, a bottle of wine, a handful of coins. Some drank the mixture straightaway, for fear of the plague. Many came back for more, having noticed an immediate, miraculous improvement in their health, although LeMerle generously made them wait until all the townsfolk had had their share before charging them a second time.

I could not bear to watch him preen any longer. Instead, I sought out the others, and helped them set up camp. I was angry to find that our caravans had been looted during the day and our torn and muddied belongings strewn across the marketplace, but told myself that it could have been much worse. I had few valuables in any case, the most serious loss to me being that of my casket of herbs and medicines; the only possessions I truly prized—the Tarot cards made for me by Giordano and the few books he left me when we separated in Flanders—I retrieved unscathed from an alleyway into which they had been thrown by looters with no idea of their use. Besides, I told myself, what were a few torn costumes against the wealth we had collected that afternoon? LeMerle must have made enough to buy back our finery ten times over. Perhaps this time, I thought wistfully, my share might be enough for me to buy a piece of land on which to build a cottage . . .

The small roundness at my belly felt very small to be leading my thoughts in this direction, but I knew that in six months' time l'Ailée would be earthbound for good, and something told me that perhaps I ought to make my bargain with LeMerle now, while I still could. I admired him—loved him still—but trusted him, never. He knew nothing of my secret, and he would not have hesitated to exploit the knowledge if he had.

And yet it was difficult to think of leaving him. I had considered it many times—I had even packed my bags once or twice—but until now there had always been something to give me pause. The adventure, perhaps. The perpetual adventure. I had loved my years with LeMerle; I loved being l'Ailée; I loved our plays and satires and flights of fancy. But now I sensed, more urgently than ever, that it was coming to an end. The child inside me already seemed to have a will of her own, and I knew that this was no life for her. LeMerle had never stopped chasing his tigers, and I knew that one day his audacity would drag us into some final game that would blow up in his face like one of Giordano's powders. It had almost happened at Epinal; only luck had saved us. How much longer would his luck hold out?

It was late when LeMerle finally packed up his baggage to leave. He declined the offer of a room at the inn, claiming to prefer simpler accommodation. A clearing just out of town served for our camp, and exhausted, we prepared for the night. I touched the small roundness at my belly for one last time as I curled onto my horsehair mattress. *Tomorrow*, I promised silently.

I'd leave him tomorrow.

*   *   *

No one heard him go. Perhaps he muffled his horses' hooves with rags, winding strips of cloth around his harness and wheels. Perhaps the dawn mist helped him, deadening the sound of his escape. Perhaps I was simply too tired, too absorbed in myself and my unborn child to care this time whether he stayed or left. Until that night there had always been a link between us, stronger than the infatuation I had once felt, or the nights we had been lovers. I thought I knew him. I knew his whims and his games and his random cruelties. There was nothing he could do that would surprise or shock me.

When I realized my mistake, it was already too late. The bird had flown, our trickery had been discovered, Le Borgne was lying under his caravan with a slit throat, and the soldiers of the new Inquisition were waiting for us in the false dawn with crossbows and swords, chains and rope. There was one thing we had all failed to take into account in our planning, one small thing, which made all of our winnings suddenly void.

During the night, Judge Rémy had come home.

CHAPTER ELEVEN

♥

July 17th, 1610

I have little recollection of that day. Any recollection would be too much, but it comes to me sometimes in still pictures, like a lantern show. The guards' hands as they dragged us from our beds. The discovery of Le Borgne, his face an open wound. Our clothes falling to the ground as they were cut from our bodies. More than anything else, I remember the sounds: the horses, the chink of metal harnesses, the cries of confusion, the shouted orders as we stumbled stupidly from sleep.

It took me too long to understand what had happened. If I had been more alert I might have escaped under cover of dark and the general chaos—Bouffon, especially, fought like a demon, and some of the guards had to leave us to attend to him—but I was still dazed, expecting LeMerle to appear at any moment with some plan for our release, and a moment later, the opportunity was lost.

He had abandoned us. He had saved himself, sensing perhaps the approach of danger and knowing that if we all fled together he would be more likely to be caught. Le Borgne, who might have revealed the trickery, was too dangerous to be left alive. They found the little man under his rig, his throat slit, his features deliberately mutilated. The rest of us—women, gypsies, dwarves, all easily replaceable—he flung to his pursuers like a handful of coins. What it came to, I told myself, was that LeMerle had sold us. Again.

But by the time I realized his betrayal it was too late. We were chained in a row with our wrists shackled, mounted guards watching over us on either side. Hermine was weeping noisily, her hair over her face. I walked behind her with my head held high. Bouffon limped along painfully at the back. The guard at my side—a fat swine of a man with mean eyes and a rosebud mouth—muttered a lewd comment, and put out his hand to brush my face. I looked at him in contempt. My eyes felt hot and dry as baking stones.

'Touch me once, even with the shadow of your little finger,' I told him softly, 'and I'll see to it your prick falls off. I know how to do it—a very *little* cantrip should be enough . . .'

The man bared his teeth. 'You'll get yours, bitch,' he mumbled. 'I can wait.'

'I'm sure you can, pig. But remember that cantrip.'

Foolish to threaten him, I know. But my rage was blistering me from within. I had to say something or I would explode.

The thought went round and round my mind, dogged and stupid as a mule around a well-wheel, slowly building as it went. How could he do that to me? To *me*? To Hermine, perhaps. To Bouffon and Bécquot. To the dwarves. But me? Why didn't he take me?

And it was this discovery about myself—the knowledge that if he had asked me to go with him I might have accepted—which fixed my hatred, then and for ever. I had assumed I was better than this, better than the others with their weaknesses and

82

their petty deceits. But LeMerle had held a mirror to my soul. Now I too was capable of betrayal. Of cowardice. Of murder. In my heart I saw it as I nursed my rage and dreamed of his blood. It rocked me as I slept. It clothed me as I walked.

The roundhouse cells were full, and they locked us in the cellars below the courthouse. It was cold, with a floor of trodden earth, the walls frosted with salty residue. I knew that mixed with a little sulphur and charcoal this white powder would make a satisfying explosion—but in this state, it was useless. There was no window, no way out but the locked door. I sat down on the damp floor and considered my position.

We were guilty. No one would dispute it. Judge Rémy could take his pick of the charges—God knows, LeMerle had given him enough to choose from. Theft, poisoning, impersonation, heresy, vagrancy, witchcraft, murder—any one of these deserved death according to the law. Someone else—a person of faith—might have found comfort in prayer, but I did not know how to pray. There is no God for the likes of us, Le Borgne used to say, for we were not made in His image. We are the holy fools, the half-made ones, the ones who came out broken from the kiln. How could we pray? And even if we could, what would we say to Him?

And so I set my back against the stone and my feet on the baked-earth floor, and I stayed there as the dawn approached, cradling the new life in my belly with both hands and listening to the sounds of sobbing from the other side of the wall.

Something woke me abruptly from my daze. The darkness was complete, but there was no mistaking the sound of a bolt being drawn, nor the stealthy approach of footsteps down the cellar steps. I struggled to my feet, keeping my back against the wall.

'Who's there?' I whispered.

Now I could hear the slow intake of a man's breath as he moved towards me, the sound of a robe brushing against the wall. I raised my fist in the darkness, my body trembling but my hand steady. I waited for him to come within range.

'Juliette?'

I froze. 'Who are you? How did you know my name?'

'Juliette, please. We don't have time.'

I lowered my fist gently to my side. I knew who it was; it was the Plague Doctor who had tried to warn me, whose voice had seemed so strikingly familiar. And I knew that smell, too, that dry alchemical smell. In the dark, my eyes widened.

'Giordano?'

There came an impatient hiss in the darkness. 'I said there isn't time, girl. Take this.' Something soft was flung across the cell towards me. A garment. It was a robe of some kind and smelt musty, but it was enough to cover my nakedness. Wondering, I pulled it over my head.

'Good. Now follow me, and quickly. You haven't got long.'

The trapdoor at the top of the steps was open. The Plague Doctor went through first, and helped me follow him. The light in the passageway seemed blinding to one so long accustomed to darkness, but came only from a single sconce. Still dazed, I turned towards my old friend and saw nothing but the long-nosed mask and black robe.

'Giordano?' I said again, putting out my hand to

touch the papier-mâché vizard.

The Plague Doctor shook his head. 'Must you always be asking questions? I put a purgative in the guard's soup. He's been rushing to the latrine every ten minutes. And this time he left his key.' He made as if to push me towards the courthouse door.

'What about my friends?' I protested.

'There's no time. If you escape alone, we both have a chance. Now will you go?'

I hesitated. In that moment I seemed to hear LeMerle's voice from behind the black mask, and my own whispering its ugly, foolish reply. *Take me. Leave the others. But take me.*

Not again, I told myself fiercely. If LeMerle had asked me, perhaps I might have gone. But *if* is a small, uncertain word on which to build a future. I felt my unborn child move inside me and I knew that if I followed my cowardice now LeMerle would always be there to taint my joy in her.

'Not without my friends,' I said.

The old man looked at me. 'Stubborn,' he hissed, as he fumbled with the locks. 'Stubborn hussy that you always were. Perhaps they're right, and you really are a witch. There must be some *dybbuk* inside that red head of yours. You'll be the undoing of us both.'

The dawn smelt of freedom. We drank it in furtively as we fled, each in a different direction. I would have stayed with the others but Giordano forbade it so furiously that I obeyed. Through the streets of Epinal we fled, hiding in the shadows, picking our way through back alleys knee-high in refuse. I was in a half-dream, every sense accentuated beyond comprehension so that our flight seemed touched with a feverish unreality. Slices of memory: faces at an inn, gaping in soundless song in the light of a red lantern; the moon riding over a bank of cloud, an edge of forest black beneath; boots, a packet of food, a coat hidden beneath a bush in readiness, a mule tethered close by.

'Take it. It's mine. No one will report it stolen.' He was still wearing his mask, but I knew him by his voice. A burst of affection for him almost overwhelmed me. 'Giordano. After all these years. I thought you were dead.'

He made a dry sound that might have been laughter. 'I don't die easily,' he said. 'Now will you be gone?'

'Not yet,' I said. I was trembling now, half in fear, half in excitement. 'I looked for you for so long, Giordano. What happened to the troupe? To Janette and Gabriel, to—'

'There isn't time. I could talk to you all night and still you'd be asking questions.'

'One question, then,' I said, gripping his arm. 'Just one, and I'll go.'

He nodded heavily. In his mask he looked like a big, sad carrion bird. 'I know,' he said at last. 'Isabelle.'

I knew at that moment that my mother was dead. All those years I'd kept her untouched, like a locket worn close to my heart: her proud figure, her smile, her songs and cantrips. But she'd died in Flanders, meaninglessly, of the plague; now all that I had of her was fragments and dreams.

'Were you there?' I said in a broken voice.

'What do you think?' said Giordano.

Love not often, but for ever—it might have been

86

my mother speaking, very quietly, behind the rasp of his breathing. I knew now why he had followed me, why he had risked his life for me and now could not bear to look at my face or reveal his own behind the Plague Doctor's mask.

'Take it off,' I told him. 'I want to see you before I go.'

He looked old in the moonlight, his eyes sunk so far into his face that it looked like a different mask, eyeless still and more tragic in its attempt to smile. Moisture leaked from the holes and into the deep channels at either side of his mouth. I tried to put my arms around him, but he pulled away abruptly. He had always disliked physical contact.

'Goodbye, Juliette. Get away as quickly as you can.' His voice was that of the old Giordano, crisp and sour and clever. 'For your safety and theirs, don't seek out the others. Sell the mule when you have to. Travel at night.'

I hugged him anyway, though he was stiff and unresponsive in my arms, and kissed his old brow. From his clothes I caught a familiar scent of spice and sulphur, the smell of his alchemical experiments, and I was engulfed in sorrow. In my arms I felt a tremor go through him, almost like a sob but deeper, from the bone, then he pulled away with a kind of anger.

'Every moment you lose is a wasted chance,' he said in a voice that shook a little. 'Be off with you, Juliette.' In his mouth my name sounded like a dry caress.

'What will you do?' I protested. 'What about you?'

He gave a tiny smile, and shook his head as he had always done when I said something

87

he considered particularly unintelligent. 'I've compromised my soul enough for you, girl,' he said. 'In case you'd forgotten, recall that I don't travel on the Sabbath.'

Then he lifted me onto the mule's back and slapped the creature's flanks so that it leaped forward onto the forest path, its hooves tapping smartly on the dry earth. I still remember his face in the moonlight, his whispered farewell as the mule trotted down the path, the scent of earth and ashes in my nostrils and his voice as it pursued me with his *Shalom*, with the voice of my thirteenth year like that of my essential conscience pursuing me sourly, like the voice of God on the mountain.

I never saw him again. From Epinal I travelled across Lorraine towards Paris, then back towards the coast as my belly increased. I foraged for food when Giordano's supplies gave out, and sold the mule on his advice. In the mule's saddlebags I found such things as my old mentor had salvaged from my caravan—a little money, some books, the jewellery discarded amongst my costumes, paste indistinguishable from real. I dyed my hair to avoid detection. I listened attentively to the reports form Lorraine. But still there was no news, no names, no rumours of burnings. And yet a part of me is waiting still, five years later, as if time has been suspended since then, a quiet interval between two acts, a conflict unresolved which must one day, inevitably, end in blood.

My dreams show me his face again and again. His woodland eyes. Our passion play continues there, the stage empty but not abandoned, waiting for the players to resume their roles, my mouth opening to speak lines I thought I had long since forgotten.

One more dance, he tells me as I twist and turn on my narrow bed. *You were always my favourite.*

*   *   *

I awake in sweat, certain this time that Fleur is dead. Even when I have checked a dozen times I dare not turn over but stay listening to the soft sound of her breathing. The dorter seems filled with unquiet murmurings. My jaw is a vice clenched around my fear. Release it and my scream will last for ever.

CHAPTER TWELVE
♥

July 18th, 1610

It was Alfonsine who saw them first. It was almost twelve o'clock, and they had to wait for the tide. Ours is not a true island; at low tide a broad pathway to the mainland is revealed, painstakingly cobbled to allow for safe passage across the flats. At least it appears safe, but there are currents across the bland surface strong enough to drag the cobbles free, sunk as they are in four feet of mortar. On both sides there is quicksand. And when the tide comes in, it sweeps the flats with terrible speed, spilling across the road and taking with it what it finds. And yet they moved with slow, relentless dignity across the sands, their progress mirrored in the shallows, the distant figures distorted in the rising column of hot air from the road.

She guessed who they were immediately. The carriage limped across the uneven causeway, the horses' hooves struggling for purchase against the green cobbles. Before it came a pair of liveried outriders. Behind it, a single man on foot.

I had spent the morning alone on the far side of the island. Waking early and unrefreshed, I left the abbey and took Fleur for a long walk, basket in hand, to pick the tiny dune pinks which, when infused and distilled, give peaceful sleep. I recalled a place where thousands of them grew undisturbed, but I was too restless for such work and I picked only a handful. In any case, the flowers were just another excuse to escape the cloister for a few hours.

As it was, we lost track of time. Beyond the dunes is a little beach of sand, where Fleur likes to play. There are broad white scars on the dune where she and I have worn away the grass, climbing and jumping, climbing and jumping, and the water is clear and shallow and filled with small jewelled pebbles.

'Can I swim today? Can I?'

'Why not?'

She swims like a dog, with shouting and splashing and great enjoyment. Mouche, her doll, watched us from the dunes' edge as I discarded my habit and joined Fleur in the water. Then I dried both of us with the skirt of my habit, and picked some small, hard apples from a tree by the side of the road, for I realized that the sun was high and we had missed lunch. Then, at Fleur's insistence, we dug a great hole, into which we flung pieces of seaweed to make a monster pit, and afterwards she slept for half an hour in the shade, Mouche under her arm, while I watched over her from the duneside path and listened to the whisperings of the turning tide.

It was going to be a dry summer, I thought. Without rain, harvests would be bad; forage meagre. The early blackberries were already burnt to a grey fluff on the stems. The vines, too, were stunted by drought, the grapes hard as dried peas. I pitied those who, like Lazarillo's players, travelled the road in the wake of such a summer.

The road. I saw it in my mind's eye, gilded with sunlight, strewn with the shards of my past. Was it really such a bad road? Had I suffered so much during those travelling years? I knew I had. We had endured cold and hunger, betrayal and persecution. I tried to recall those things, but still the road ahead of me gleamed like a path over quicksand, and I found myself remembering something LeMerle had once told me, in the days when we were friends.

'We have a natural affinity, you and I,' he had said. 'Like air and fire, combustion is our nature. You can't change the element you are born to. That's why we'll never leave the road, my l'Ailée; any more than fire can choose not to burn, or a bird leave the sky.'

But I had. I had left the sky, and for many years I had barely even raised my eyes to it. I had not forgotten, however. The road had always been there, patiently awaiting my return. And how I wanted it! What might I give to be free, to have a woman's name once more, a woman's life? To see the stars from a different place every night, to eat

91

meat cooked over my own campfire, to dance—maybe to fly? I did not need to answer the unspoken question. Joy leaped in me at the thought, and for a moment I might almost have been the old Juliette once more, the one who walked to Paris.

But it was ridiculous. Leave my life, my comfortable cloister, the friends who had given me refuge? The abbey was hardly the home I had longed for, but it provided the essentials. Food in winter, shelter, work for my idle hands. And leave it for what? For a few dreams? For a hand of cards?

The path, half-sand beneath my heavy boots, dragged at my feet. I kicked at it angrily. The explanation was simple, I told myself. Simple and rather stupidly obvious. The hot weather, the sleepless nights, the dreams of LeMerle . . . I needed a man. That was all. L'Ailée had had a different lover every night, choosing as she would—smooth or rough, dark or fair—and her dreams were scented and textured with their bodies. Juliette, too, was a sensual creature: Giordano scolded her for bathing naked in the rivers, for rolling in the morning grass and for the secret hours she spent with his Latin poets, struggling with the unfamiliar syntax for the sake of the occasional taut glimpse of Roman buttock . . . Either of them would have known how to dispel this malaise. But I—Soeur Auguste, a man's name and an old man, at that—what do I have? Since Fleur there have been no more men. I might have turned to women for comfort, like Germaine and Clémente, but those pleasures never appealed to me.

Germaine, whose husband cut her face with a kitchen knife fifteen times—once for every year of her life—when he found her with another girl, hates all men. I've seen her watching me. I know she finds me beautiful. Not like Clémente, of the Madonna face and filthy mind, but enough to please her. She sometimes watches me at work in the garden, but never says a word. Her light hair is cropped shorter than a boy's, and beneath the ungainly brown robes I can guess at a slim, graceful figure. Once, Germaine would have made a fine dancer. But something else is spoiled besides her face. Six years after the incident she looks older than I, her mouth pale and thin, her eyes almost colourless, like brine. She tells me she joined the convent so that she would never have to look at a man again. But she is like the sour apples and the dried-pea grapes, yearning to flourish but starved of rain.

Lovely, spiteful Clémente sees it and makes her suffer, flirting with me as I go about my duties. In chapel she sometimes whispers words of seduction, offering herself to me as behind her Germaine listens helplessly, stolid in her suffering, her scarred face impassive.

Germaine has no faith, no interest in religion of any kind. I spoke to her once about my female God—I thought it might appeal to her, hating men as she did—but she seemed as indifferent to that as she was to the rest. 'If such a thing ever was,' she told me dryly, 'then men have remade her. Why else should they want to lock us up and to make us ashamed? Why else should they be so afraid?'

I said that men had no reason to be afraid of us, and she gave another sharp laugh. 'Oh no?' She put her fingers to her face. 'Then why *this*?'

Perhaps she is right. And yet I don't hate men. Only one, and even he . . . I dreamed of him again last night. So close I could smell his sweat and his skin, smooth as my own. I hate him, and yet in my dream he was tender. Even with his face in shadow I would have known him anywhere, even without the moonlight that gilded the scorched flower on his arm.

The sound of birdsong awoke me. For an instant I was there again, before Epinal, before Vitré, with the blackbirds singing outside our caravan and my lover watching me with all of summer in his mocking eyes . . .

For a moment only. A sly incubus crept into my heart as I lay asleep. A ghost. There can be no part of me that still wants him, I tell myself.

No part at all.

* * *

It was long past noon when at last we returned to the abbey. I had taken off my wimple, but even so my hair was damp with sweat, my robe clammy against my skin. Fleur trotted beside me, Mouche dangling from one hand. There was no one in sight. Given the heat, this was not unusual, for many of the sisters, in the absence of authority, had taken to sleeping at that time, leaving what rudimentary duties they still performed until after Nones and the cooler evening. But when I saw the fresh horse dung by the abbey gate and the tracks of carriage wheels in the dust I was suddenly certain that what we had been expecting for thirteen days had finally happened.

94

'Is it the players coming back?' asked Fleur hopefully.

'No, sweetheart, I don't think so.'

'Oh.'

I smiled at her expression, and gave her a kiss. 'Play here for a while,' I said. 'I have to go inside.'

I watched her as she ran duck-footed along the path, then I turned towards the abbey, feeling as if a great weight had been taken from me. At last, then, this uneasy, unsettled time had come to an end. We had a new Abbess, a guiding hand for us in our aimlessness and fear. I could picture her already. She would be calm and strong, though no longer in the first blush of youth. Her smile would be grave and tranquil, but with the touch of humour necessary to lead so many disaffected women towards peace. She would be kind and honest, a good mainland woman, unafraid of hard work, her brown hands calloused but deft and gentle. She would enjoy music and gardening. She would be hard-headed; experienced enough in the world's ways to help us fend for ourselves and yet not too ambitious, not embittered by her knowledge but still able to face the world with simple joy, simple wisdom.

Looking back in amazement at my own simplicity I realize my fanciful picture owed a great deal to memories of my mother, Isabelle. Her remembered face has altered a little since I last saw her, I know. Only the eye of love could recall her as I do, so sweet and so strong, her beauty crystallizing in my mind so that she is far lovelier than Clémente or the Holy Mother herself, though I cannot quite remember the colour of her eyes, or the contours of her strong brown face. I put my mother's head onto the shoulders of our new Abbess before I even set eyes on her, and the relief I felt was like that of a child left too long in charge of a task too great for her, who, at last, sees her mother coming home. I began to run towards the strangely quiet building, my hair flying and my robes pulled up around my knees.

The cloister was dark and cool. I called out as I entered, but there was no reply. The gatehouse was unoccupied; the abbey seemed deserted. I ran down the broad, sunny slype between the dorters, but saw no one. I passed the refectory, the kitchens, the empty chapterhouse, making my way towards the church. Sext would be long past, I told myself. Perhaps the new Abbess had called a meeting.

As I approached the chapel I heard voices and chanting. Suddenly wary, I pushed open the door. All the sisters were present. I could see Perette; Alfonsine with her thin hands clasped at her chin; fat Antoine with her moony face and weak, excited eyes; stolid Germaine with Clémente at her side. There was silence as I came in and I blinked, disorientated by the dark and the reek of incense and the faces reflected in the light of many candles.

Alfonsine was the first to move. 'Soeur Auguste,' she exclaimed. 'Praise God, Soeur Auguste. We have a new—' Her voice broke in what might have been excitement. I was already looking beyond her, my eyes moving eagerly in search of the wise, bright lady of my expectation. But beside the altar I saw only a young girl of eleven or twelve, her small, pallid face impassive beneath a neat white wimple, her hand held out in a limp gesture of benediction. 'Soeur Auguste.' The voice was as small and cool as its owner, and I was suddenly very aware of my hoydenish appearance, of my flying curls, my glowing cheeks.

'Mère Isabelle.' Alfonsine's voice quavered with self-importance. 'Mère Isabelle, the Reverend Mother.'

For a second, my surprise was such that I almost laughed aloud. She could not be speaking of this child. The thought was absurd—this child with my mother's name must be some novice, some protégée of the new Abbess who must even now be smiling at my mistake . . . Then our eyes met. Hers were very light but without brilliance, as if all her vision were turned inwards. Looking into her wan young face I could see no gleam of humour, no pleasure, no joy.

'But she's so *young!*' It was the wrong thing to say. I knew it immediately and regretted it, but in my surprise I had spoken my thought aloud. I saw the girl stiffen, her lips half-open to reveal small, perfect teeth. *'Ma mère,* I am sorry.' Too late to unsay my words, I knelt to kiss the pale outstretched hand. 'I spoke without thinking.'

I knew even as I felt the cool fingers beneath my lips that my apology was not accepted. For a moment I saw myself through her eyes: a sweating, redfaced island woman, hot with the forbidden scents of summer.

'Your wimple.' Her coldness was catching, and I shivered.

'I—I lost it.' I faltered. 'I was in the fields. It was hot . . .'

But her attention was already elsewhere. Her pale eyes moved slowly, incuriously across the faces turned in expectation towards her. Alfonsine

97

watched her with an adoring expression. The silence was like ice.

'I was Angélique Saint-Hervé Désirée Arnault,' she said in a small, expressionless voice, which nevertheless penetrated me to the bone. 'You may think me young for the part God has chosen for me. But I am God's mouthpiece here, and He will give me the strength I need.'

For an instant I felt sorry for her, so young and defenceless, trying so hard to maintain her dignity. I tried to imagine what her life must have been, reared in the oppressive climate of the Court, surrounded by intrigue and corruption. She was a thin little thing: their banquets and sweetmeats, the guineafowl basted with lard, the pies, the *pièces montées*, the trays of peacocks' hearts and baked *foies gras* and larks' tongues in aspic only serving to sharpen her disgust of their excesses. A sickly child, not expected to survive beyond her teens, drawn to the Church through its ceremony, its dark fatalism, its intolerance. I tried to imagine what it must be like for her, cloistered at twelve, repeating as if by rote the pronouncements of her religious tutors, closing the door on the world before she even understood what it had to offer.

'There has been enough laxity here.' She was speaking again, her nasal intonation sharpening as she strained to be heard. 'I have seen the records. I have seen what manner of indolence my predecessor was pleased to tolerate.' She glanced briefly in my direction. 'I intend to change this from today.'

There was a low murmur amongst the sisters as her words reached them. I caught sight of Antoine, her face slack with puzzlement.

'First,' continued the girl, 'I wish to mention the matter of dress.' Another sharp flick of the eyes in my direction. 'I have already noticed a certain— carelessness—amongst some of you which I consider unbefitting to members of our sisterhood. I am aware that the previous Abbess tolerated the wearing of the *quichenotte*. This practice will cease.'

To my right, old Rosamonde turned a bewildered face towards me. Light from the window above her fell onto her white bonnet. 'Who is this child?' Her thin voice was querulous. 'What is she saying? Where is Mère Marie?'

I shook my head fiercely at her, miming silence. For a moment she seemed about to continue, then her wrinkled face crumpled, her eyes moist. I heard her mumbling to herself as the new Abbess continued: 'Even in so short a time I cannot help but notice certain irregularities in procedure.' The nasal voice might have been reading from an ecclesiastical textbook. 'Mass, for example. I find it difficult to believe that for a matter of years *no Mass at all* has been said in the abbey.'

There was an uneasy silence.

'We said prayers,' said Antoine.

'Prayers are not enough, *ma fille*,' said the child. 'Your prayers cannot be sanctified without the presence of a minister of God.'

I could feel laughter pressing against my belly at every word she spoke. The ridicule of the situation momentarily overturned my sensation of unease. That this sickly child should preach to us, frowning and pursing her lips like an old prude and calling us her daughters was surely a monstrous joke, like the valet dressing in his master's clothes on Fools' Day.

Christ in the temple was surely another such travesty, preaching contrition when he should have been running in the fields or swimming naked in the sea.

The child-mother spoke again. 'Henceforth Mass will be celebrated every day. Our eight daily services will be resumed. There will be fasting for all on Fridays and on holy days. I'll not have it said that my abbey was ever a place of indulgence or excess.'

She had found her voice at last. The reedy treble had taken on a demanding note and I realized that behind her wan self-importance there was hidden a kind of zeal, almost of passion. What I had taken for shyness I now recognized as high-bred contempt of the type I had not heard since I was at Court. *My abbey.* I felt a stab of annoyance. Was the abbey her plaything, then, and were we to be her dolls?

My voice was sharper than I intended as I spoke out. 'There's no priest but on the mainland,' I said. 'How can we have Mass every day? And who'll pay for it if we do?'

She looked at me again and I wished I had not spoken. If I had not already made an enemy of her, I thought, this scornful outburst must surely have tipped the balance. Her face was a bud of disapproval.

'I have my own confessor with me,' she said. 'My good mother's confessor, who begged to come with me to help in my work.' I could have sworn that as she spoke she flushed a little, her face slightly averted and a touch of animation colouring her flat voice. 'Let me introduce Père Colombin de Saint-Amand,' she said with a small gesture towards the

100

figure which only now detached itself from the shadow of a pillar. 'My friend, teacher and spiritual guide. I hope he will soon become as dear to you all as he is to me.'

As I stood there transfixed, I saw him with perfect clarity, the harlequin colours from the rose window illuminating his face and hands. His black hair was longer than I remembered, secured at the nape of his neck with a ribbon, but the rest was as my heart recalled him: the turn of his head into the light, the straight black brows, the woodland eyes. Black becomes him; consciously dramatic in his priest's robe, unadorned but for the gleam of his silver cross, he fixed his gaze directly at me and gave a small, audacious smile.

PART TWO
LEMERLE

CHAPTER ONE

♠

July 18th, 1610

What an entrance, eh? I was born for the stage, you know—or for the gallows, some might say, though there's little enough to choose between the two. Flowers and the trap, curtains at the end and the short, frenzied dance in the middle. There's a kind of poetry even there. But I'm not yet ready to tread those boards. When I am, be sure you'll be the first to know.

You don't seem pleased to see me. And after all these years. My Ailée, my one and only. How you flew in your day! Invincible to the last, you never fell, never faltered. I could almost have believed your wings were real, cleverly folded beneath your tunic to carry you shrieking to the edge of the sky. My adorable harpy. And to see you again here, wings clipped! I have to say you haven't changed. As soon as I saw that foxy hair of yours—that'll have to go, by the way—I knew you. And you knew me too, didn't you, sweetheart? Oh yes, I saw you blench and stare. It's good to have an appreciative audience—a *captive* audience, if you'll pardon the expression—before which I can really show the extent of my talent. This is going to be the performance of a lifetime.

You're very quiet. That can't be helped, I expect. Discretion is the better part of virtue—certainly of yours. But your eyes! Glorious! Velvet spangled with black sequins. Speak to me, my Harpy. Speak to me with your eyes.

I know what it is. It's that business, that little *fracas*—where was it now? Epinal? Shame on you. To hold that against me after so long. Don't deny it, you had me tried, found guilty, judged and hanged in an instant. Don't you want to hear my side? All right, all right. In any case, I was sure you'd escape. No fortress could hold my Ailée. She opens the sky with her wings. Shatters prison bars with a flick of her tongue.

I know, I know. Do you think it was easy for me? I was hunted, alone. Torture and death if they caught me. Don't you think I wanted to take you? I did it for your sake, Juliette. I knew that without me you'd have a better chance. I was going to come back. I swear. Eventually.

Is it Le Borgne? Is that what troubles you? He followed me as I prepared to leave. Pleaded with me to take him. Offered the rest of you as payment. Throats slit, he promised, nice and easy—if only I would take him with me. When I refused, he pulled his knife.

I was unarmed, exhausted from my day's exertions, bruised and sore from my treatment at the hands of the rabble. He aimed for my heart, but I saw him coming and he caught me in the shoulder, paralysing my knife arm. I struggled with him, he twisting at the blade until I almost passed out with the pain. In my attempt to break free I wrenched out the knife with my left hand, slashed him in the throat, and fled.

The blade must have been poisoned. Half an hour later I was too weak to ride, too dizzy to drive the rig. I did the only thing I could—I hid. Like a dying animal I crawled into a ditch and waited there for what might come.

Perhaps that was what saved me. They found the caravan four miles from Epinal, looted by scavengers; wasted time in finding and questioning the thieves. Weakened by the infected wound, I hid, feeding on the roadside plants and fruits you showed me when we were travelling together. Gaining strength, I made for the nearby forest. I lit a fire and made the infusions you taught me: wormwood for the fever, foxglove for the pain. Your teachings saved my life, dear witch. I hope you appreciate the irony.

You don't? What a pity. Your eyes are like blades. All right. Maybe I lied about Le Borgne, just a little. We both had a knife. I was clumsy and he got to me first. Did I ever pretend to you that I was a saint? A man cannot change the element into which he was born. There was a time when you would have understood that, my firebird. Let's hope, for both our sakes, that you still do.

Expose me? My dear. Do you really think you could? It might be amusing to see you try, but ask yourself this before you do. Who has the most to lose? And who is the most convincing? Admit it, I once convinced you myself. My papers are in order, you know. Their previous owner, a priest journeying by happy chance through the Lorraine, was suddenly taken sick (to the stomach, as I recall) as he entered a forest at dusk. A mercifully quick end. I closed his eyes myself.

Oh, Juliette. Still so suspicious? I'll have you know that I'm very fond of our little Angélique. You think she is too young for an Abbess. Believe me, the Church didn't think so, welcoming her—and her dowry—with an eagerness that was almost unseemly. And besides, the Church has, as always, the best of the bargain. Yet more wealth to swell her ever-glutted coffers, her ever-increasing lands, and all in exchange for a tiny concession, a remote abbey half-sunk in sand, its loose ways tolerated only because of its ex-Abbess's unrivalled skill with potatoes.

But I am forgetting my responsibilities. Ladies— or should I say sisters, daughters, even, to set the fatherly tone? Perhaps not. *My children*. That's better. Their eyes glitter in the smoky air like those of sixty-five black cats. My new flock. Funny, but they don't smell like women. I thought I knew that smell, its secret undertones, that complex of fish and flowers. Here there's nothing but the reek of incense. My God, don't they even sweat? I'll change that, wait and see.

'My children. I come to you in grief and in great joy. Grief for our departed sister'—what was her name again?—'Marie, but in a joy of anticipation of the great work we begin here today.'

Simple stuff, I know, but effective. Their eyes are enormous. Why did I think of cats? They are bats, their faces wizened, eyes enlarged beyond recognition but sightless, black wings drawn across hunched shoulders, hands folded across flat bosoms, perhaps in the fear that I should inadvertently catch a glimpse of forbidden curves.

'I speak of the great Reform of which my daughter Isabelle has already spoken, Reform on such a scale that very soon the whole of France will turn its eyes towards the Abbey of Sainte Marie-de-la-mer in awe and humility.'

Time for a quote, I think. Seneca, perhaps? *It is a rocky road that leads to the heights of greatness*?

No. I don't think this company is quite ready for Seneca. Deuteronomy, then. *Thou shalt become an astonishment, a proverb and a byword among all nations.* Of course, the wonderful thing about the Bible is that there's a quote to justify anything, even lechery, incest and the slaying of infants.

'You have strayed from the righteous path, my children. You have fallen into the ways of wickedness, and forgotten the sacred covenant you have made with the Lord your God.'

This voice was made to declaim tragedies; ten years ago, my play *Les Amours de l'Hermite* was already in advance of its time. Their eyes widen still further, and behind the fear I begin to see a different light, something like excitement. The words are themselves a kind of titillation.

'Like the people of Sodom, you have turned your faces from Him. You have pleasured yourselves whilst the holy flame grew cold in your keeping. You have harboured thoughts, which you believed secret, and revelled in your hidden vices. But the Lord saw you.'

Pause. A soft murmur thrills through the assembly as each enumerates her secret thoughts. '*I saw you.*'

In the semidarkness, faces blanch. My voice rises higher, growing in resonance until it might almost shatter glass. 'I see you still, though you may now hide your faces in shame. Your vanities are innumerable, lighting this place with the flames of your iniquity.'

A good line, that. I must remember it when I come to write my new tragedy. There is promise in some of these faces. I see it already. The fat woman with the moist eyes, mouth trembling wetly on the brink of tears. You jade, I saw you flinch when the child spoke of fasting.

And the sour one with the scarred face. What's *your* vice? You stand very close to your pretty neighbour, hands just touching in the shadows. Your eyes flick to her almost unwillingly as I speak, like a miser's to his hoard.

And you—yes, you—behind the pillar. Your eyes roll skywards like those of a shy mare. Tics and twitches distress your mouth. You plead silently with me, fingers clutching at your flattened breasts. Every word I speak makes you itch with fear and pleasure. I know your dreams: orgies of self-abasement, ecstasies of remorse.

And you? Flushed and panting, eyes shining with something more than religious zeal. My first disciple, face upturned to mine, hands outstretched. A single touch, she begs, a single look and I will be your slave. But I will not submit so quickly, my dear. A moment more of anticipation, a frown that darkens the room. Then the glimpse of salvation, the softening of the voice, the mellifluous hint of forgiveness in the grand soliloquy.

'But the Lord's mercy, like His wrath, is infinite. The erring lamb is inexpressibly more precious as it returns to the fold than its more virtuous brethren.' That's a laugh; in my experience the erring lamb is far more likely to become next Sunday's roast for its pains. 'Turn, o backsliding children,' says the Book of Jeremiah, 'for I am married unto you, and will lead ye to Zion.' For a second I allow my eyes to meet my disciple's. Her breathing quickens. She seems close to swooning.

My piece is said now. Scattering platitudes like

manna, I prepare to leave them to ferment. I have shown how strong I can be and how gentle; a missed step and a hand across the eyes, a quiet reference to my fatigue and to the discomforts of my long walk now illustrate my essential humanity. The eager sister—Alfonsine, was it?—is quick to offer her arm as support, gazing worshipfully into my face. Gently I draw away. No familiarities, please.

Not yet, anyway.

CHAPTER TWO
♥

July 18th, 1610

LeMerle! I had immediately recognized his style, a heady blend of the stage, the pulpit and the street crier's stall. The disguise, too, was very much his style, and from time to time his eyes met mine with the eloquent brightness I recognized, as if he were eager to share his triumph. For a while I wondered why he had chosen not to expose me.

Then I understood. I was to be his audience, his admiring critic. Pointless to give such a performance without someone with whom to share his secret, someone who could truly appreciate the daring of this imposture . . . This time, however, I refused to play his game. I could not avoid my duties in the salt fields that afternoon, but as soon as I could leave without giving cause for suspicion, I would collect Fleur and escape. I could take supplies from the kitchen, and although I disliked the thought of stealing from the nuns, the coffer containing the abbey's savings was easily accessible in a small storeroom at the back of the root cellar, the door's lock having long since been broken and never replaced. Our old Reverend Mother was a simple soul, believing that trust was the best defence against theft, and in all the time I was at the abbey I had never known anyone to take as much as a single coin. What did we need with money? We had everything we wanted.

He left us in a state of suppressed agitation, as no doubt he meant to, as we went to perform our various duties. As he went he shot me a comic look, as if to challenge me to come to him, but I ignored it and I was glad to see that he did not persist. The new Abbess hurried to investigate her little empire, Clémente ran to see to the horses, Alfonsine busied herself in making the new confessor at home in the gatehouse cottage, Antoine returned to the kitchens to begin preparing the evening meal, and I went in search of my daughter.

I found her in the barn, playing with one of the kitchen cats. In a few words I warned her: she was to stay out of sight for the rest of the day, wait for me in the dorter, speak to no one until I returned.

'But why?' She had fastened a pine cone onto a piece of string and was dangling it in the air for the cat to jump at.

'I'll tell you later. Don't forget.'

'I can talk to the kitty, though, can't I?'

'If you like.'

'What about Perette? Can I talk to her?'

I put my finger on my lips. 'Shh. It's a hiding game. Do you think you can keep very quiet, very still, until I come for you tonight?'

She frowned, eyes still on the cat. 'What about my dinner?'

'I'll bring it later.'

'And for the kitty?'

'We'll see.'

* * *

It had been decided that LeMerle should attend chapter with us but should not eat with the rest of us in the refectory. That didn't surprise me—our new policy of abstinence was unlikely to find favour with him. Nor did it escape my attention that LeMerle's cottage was just beside the abbey gates, giving him an ideal place to observe any traffic to or from the abbey. That made me anxious; it suggested advance planning and careful thought. Whatever his reasons, the confessor was intending to stay.

Still, I told myself, his plans were of no interest to me at present. His absence from the evening meal would offer me the ideal opportunity to prepare my escape. I would plead a stomach ache, collect my things, raid the kitchen and storeroom for supplies and hide my bundle of valuables somewhere within the abbey's outer walls. Fleur and I would go to bed as usual, then creep away when everyone was asleep, collect our belongings, and make for the causeway and the morning tide. When we were safely out of his reach, then I could deal with LeMerle. A note—a word to the right authorities—would be enough to expose him. The gallows would find him in the end, and maybe then my heart would find peace.

But when I came back to the dorter half an hour

before the evening meal, Fleur was not there to greet me. Nor was she in the garden, the cloister or the chickenhouse. I was annoyed, but not yet overanxious; Fleur was a lively spirit and often hid away at bedtime. I searched her secret hiding places, one by one, with no success.

Finally I went to the kitchens. It occurred to me that maybe Fleur had got hungry, and Soeur Antoine, the cook, was fond of the children, often giving them cakes and biscuits from the kitchen, or apples from the autumn windfalls. Today, however, she looked preoccupied, her eyes unusually reddened and with a slack look to her face as if her cheeks had been partially deflated. At Fleur's name she gave a wail of misery, as if remembering something she had been too busy to think about, and wrung her fat hands.

'The poor little one! I was going to tell you but—' She broke off, as if struggling to express several ideas at once. 'So many changes! She came into my kitchen, Soeur Auguste—I was making a confit for the winter stores, with goose fat and wild mushrooms—and she looked at me in that terrible, scornful way—'

'Who? Fleur?'

'No, no!' Antoine shook her head. 'Mère Isabelle. That terrible little girl.'

I made an impatient gesture. 'Tell me later. I want my daughter.'

'I was *trying* to tell you. She said it wasn't seemly for her to be here. She said it would be a distraction from your duties. She sent her away.'

I stared at her in disbelief. 'Sent her *where*?'

She eyed me humbly. 'It wasn't my fault.'

Something in her voice told me she thought it

114

was.

'You told them?' I grasped her sleeve. 'Antoine, did you tell them Fleur was mine?'

'I couldn't help it,' whined the fat sister. 'They would have found out sooner or later. Someone else would have let it slip.'

In rage I pinched her arm through her habit so that she almost screamed.

'Stop it! *Aii*! Stop it, Auguste, you're hurting! It's not my fault they sent her away! You should never have kept her here in the first place!'

'Antoine. Look at me.' She rubbed her arm, refusing to meet my eyes. 'Where did they send her? Was it to someone in the village?' She shook her head helplessly and I fought back the urge to strike at her. 'Please, Antoine. I'm just worried, that's all. I'm not going to tell anyone you told me.'

'You ought to call me *"ma soeur"*.' Antoine's face was puffy with resentment. 'Anger's a sin, you know. It's that hair of yours. You should cut it off.' She glanced at me with unusual daring. 'Now the Reform's coming, you'll have to anyway.'

'Please, Antoine. I'll give you the last bottle of my lavender syrup.'

Her eyes brightened. 'And the candied rose petals?'

'If you like. Where's Fleur?'

Antoine lowered her voice. 'I overheard Mère Isabelle talking to the new confessor. Something about a fisherman's wife, somewhere on the mainland. They're paying her,' she added, as if I were to be held responsible for the expense. 'But I was barely listening.

'The mainland! Where?'

Antoine shrugged. 'That's all I heard.'

115

I stood dazed, as the truth of it slowly sank in. It was too late. Before I had even dared raise my voice against him, the Blackbird had outmanoeuvred me. He must have known I would not run the risk of losing my daughter. Without her, I was forced to stay.

For a moment I considered making the attempt anyway. The trail was still warm, although by now I would have missed the tide and would have to await the next day's crossing. Everyone on the island knew Fleur; someone must have seen where she had been taken. But my heart knew it was useless. LeMerle would have anticipated that, too.

My stomach clenched. I imagined Fleur confused, unhappy, calling for me, thinking herself abandoned, taken away without even a cantrip or a star blessing to protect her. Who but I could keep her from harm? Who but I knew her ways, understood that she needed a candle near her cot on winter nights, knew to slice away the brown part of the apple before cutting it into quarters?

'I never even said goodbye.' I spoke for myself, but Antoine looked at me with returned sullenness.

'It isn't my fault,' she repeated. 'None of us ever kept our babies. Why should you be any different?'

I did not reply. I already knew whose fault it was. What did he want? What could I possibly have that he still wanted?

Returning to my cubicle I saw that the little cot had already been removed. My own things seemed untouched, my cache of books and papers behind the loose stone undisturbed. I found Fleur's doll,

Mouche, down the side of my bed, half hidden by the trailing blanket. Perette made it out of rags and scraps when Fleur was a baby, and it is her favourite toy. Mouche's arms and legs have been stitched back a hundred times, her hair is a bright tangle of multi-coloured wool, and her round face looks oddly like Perette's with its shoe-button eyes and rosy cheeks. Like her creator, too, Mouche is mute; where the mouth should be, there is only a blank.

For a while I stood with the doll in my hands, too numb to think. My first instinct was to find the new confessor, to force him to tell me—at knifepoint, if need be—where he had hidden my daughter. But I knew LeMerle. This was his challenge, his opening gambit in a game for which I did not yet know the stakes. If I went to him now, I played into his hands. If I waited, I might yet be able to call his bluff.

*   *   *

All night I turned and twisted on my hot bed. My cubicle is the furthest from the door, which means that although I have furthest to go if I wish to visit the reredorter in the night, at least I have the advantage of only one neighbour. I have the window, too, east-facing though it is, and the greater space which the end cubicles afford. The night was heavy, promising stormy weather, and as I watched sleeplessly into the small hours I saw the storm out at sea striding out on great silent stilts of lightning between the red-black clouds. But no rain came. I wondered whether Fleur saw it too or whether she slept, exhausted, her thumb in her

117

mouth, in a house of strangers.

'Shh, Fleurette.' In my daughter's absence, it was to Mouche that I spoke, stroking the woolly head as if it might have been Fleur's hair beneath my fingers. 'I'm here. It's all right.'

I traced the star sign on Mouche's forehead and spoke my mother's cantrip. *Stella bella, bonastella.* Pig Latin it may be, but there's comfort in an old rhyme, and although none of the ache in my heart subsided, I felt a slight diminishing of fear. After all, LeMerle must know that he would get nothing from me if any harm came to Fleur. I waited then, with Mouche under my arm, as all around me my sisters slept and lightning stalked the islands, one by one.

CHAPTER THREE
♥

July 19th, 1610

Today held little of Reform. The new Abbess spent much of the time in her private chapel with LeMerle, leaving us to our speculation. By now the holiday atmosphere had dissipated, leaving an uneasy vacuum. Voices were hushed, as if there were sickness in the place. Duties had been resumed, but mostly—with the exception of Marguerite and Alfonsine—in a slipshod manner. Even Antoine seemed ill at ease in her kitchen, her usual foolish good nature tempered by the previous day's accusations of excess. A number of lay workers came to inspect the chapel and scaffolding was erected on the west side, presumably to allow them to investigate the damaged roof.

Once again, my first impulse that morning had been to find LeMerle and to ask for news of my daughter. Several times I set out with this aim in mind, stopping myself just in time. No doubt that was precisely what he intended.

Instead I spent the morning at work on the flats, but my usually light touch was marred, and I found myself hoeing furiously at the salt stacks, pounding the careful white mounds into muddy sludge.

Fleur's absence is a pain that begins deep in the pit of my stomach, digging inwards like a canker. It touches everything, like a shadow behind bright scenery. It is stronger than I am, but I know that my silence is the only weapon I have. Let him be the first to reveal himself. Let him come to me.

I returned to find that LeMerle and the new Abbess had retired to their respective quarters early—she to the cell vacated by her predecessor, he to the gatehouse cottage just within the abbey walls—leaving the sisters in a state of unusual excitement. In their absence, there had been much whispered speculation on the nature of the intended Reforms, some murmured revolt and a great deal of ill-informed and ill-considered gossip.

Much of this surrounded LeMerle, and I was unsurprised to overhear a number of favourable opinions. Although some voices amongst us were raised in condemnation of the little chit who presumed to overturn our way of life, there were few who failed to be impressed by the new confessor. Alfonsine, of course, was completely overwhelmed, enumerating the qualities of the fake Père Colombin with the zeal of one newly converted.

'I knew it, Soeur Auguste. I knew it as soon as I saw his eyes. So dark, so *piercing*! As if he could see right through me. Right to the very soul.' She shuddered, eyes half closed, lips parted. 'I think he might really be a saint, Soeur Auguste. He has that holy presence. I can feel it.'

However, this was not the first time Alfonsine had been subject to a violent attack of hero-worship—she had suffered one, in fact, on the occasion of a local prior's visit which left her prostrate for a fortnight—and I hoped that given time this fervent admiration of LeMerle might subside. For the present she glowed at the sound of his name, murmuring *Colombin de Saint-Amand* to herself like a litany as she scrubbed the floors.

Marguerite, too, was deeply affected. Like Alfonsine, she developed a cleaning frenzy, repeatedly dusting and polishing every available surface; she twitched at sudden noises, and when LeMerle was close by she stammered and flushed like a girl of sixteen, though she was a dried-up thing of forty and had never known a man. Clémente saw her confusion and teased her mercilessly, but the rest of us held back. Somehow Marguerite's reaction to the new confessor went beyond humour and into a dark territory few of us cared to explore.

Marguerite and Alfonsine—who had always been bitter rivals—became temporary allies in the face of this joint infatuation. Together they had volunteered to clean out LeMerle's cottage, which was in a pitiful state, having been abandoned since the time of the black friars. In the morning they had gathered together what furniture they thought

120

might please the new confessor and brought it into the cottage, and before the day was over the place was spotless, with fresh matting on the earth floor and vases of flowers in its three rooms. Père Colombin expressed his gratitude with becoming humility, and from that moment the two sisters were his willing slaves.

The evening meal was a meagre affair of potato soup, which we ate in silence, even though the two newcomers were not present. But later, as I prepared for bed after Vespers, I was sure I saw Antoine crossing the courtyard towards the little cottage, carrying something on a large, covered dish. The new confessor, at least, would eat well tonight. As I watched, Antoine looked up at the window, her face a blur against the night, her mouth wide with dismay. Then she turned abruptly, pulling her wimple to cover her face, and fled into the darkness.

Tonight I read the cards again, drawing them silently and carefully from their hiding place in the wall. The Hermit. The Deuce of Cups. The Fool. The Star, her round painted face so like Fleur's with its wide eyes and crown of curly hair. And the Tower, falling against a red-black sky split with jagged bolts of lightning.

Tonight? I don't think so. But soon, I hope. Soon. And if I have to topple it myself, stone by stone, I will, be sure of it. I will.

CHAPTER FOUR

♠

July 19th, 1610

Terrible, isn't it? Divination; close enough to sorcery to scorch the flesh. The *Malleus Malleficarum* calls it 'a manifest abomination' whilst insisting it doesn't work. And yet her cards, with their painstaking detail, are strangely compelling. Take this Tower, for example. So like the abbey itself with its square turret and wooden spire. This woman, the Moon, her face half turned away but so strangely familiar. And the Hermit, this hooded man, only his eyes visible from beneath the black cloak, in one hand a staff, in the other a lantern.

You can't fool me, Juliette. I knew you'd have a hiding place. A child could have found it, tucked away behind a loosened stone at the back of the dorter. You were never much of a dissembler. No, I'll not accuse you—not yet, anyway. I may need you. A man needs an ally—even a man like me.

For the first day, I watched. Close enough in my cottage by the gates to see everything without offending ecclesiastical sensibilities. Even a saint may have desires, I tell Isabelle. Indeed, without them, where would be the sanctity, or the sacrifice? I will not live in the cloister. Besides, I value my privacy.

There's a door at the back of the cottage, which opens out onto a bare section of wall. The black friars were more concerned with grandiose architecture than with security, it seems, for the gatehouse is an impressive façade hiding little more than a hillock of tumbled stones between the abbey and the marshes. An easy escape route, if it ever comes to that. But it won't. I'll take my time over this business and leave when it suits me.

As I was saying, today I watched from afar. She tries to keep it from me, but I can see the pain in her, the tension in her lower back and shoulders as she strains to appear relaxed. When we were travelling together she never once cut short a performance, not even when she suffered an injury. The inevitable mishaps that occur in even the best troupes—sprains, damaged ligaments, even fractures of fingers and toes—never slowed her down. She always maintained the same professional smile, even when pain was blinding her. It was a kind of revolt, though against whom I never guessed. Myself, perhaps. I see it in her now, in her averted gaze, in the false humility of her movements. There is a pain which pride moves her to conceal. She loves the child. Would do anything to protect her.

Strange that I never imagined my Ailée bearing a child; I thought she was too much of a savage to accept that kind of tyranny. A pretty cub, with a look of her mother, and the promise of grace behind that little-girl slouch. She has her mother's ways, too: she bit me as I lifted her onto my horse, leaving the marks of her baby teeth in my hand. Her father? Some stranger of the road, perhaps, some chance-met peasant, peddler, player, priest.

Myself, even? I hope not, for her sake; there's vicious blood in my line, and blackbirds make bad parents. And yet I am glad that the child is in safe hands. She kicked me in the ribs as I handed her down, and would have bitten me again if Guizau hadn't stopped her.

'Stop that,' I said.

'I want my mamma!'

'You'll see her.'

'When?'

I sighed. 'I don't think you should ask so many questions. Now be a good girl and go with Monsieur Guizau, who will buy you a sugar pastry.'

The child glared up at me. There were tears running down her face, but they were of rage and not of fear. 'Crow's foot,' she shouted, making the forked sign with her stubby fingers. 'Crow's foot, crow's foot, curse you to death!'

That's all I need, I thought, as I rode away. To be witched by a five-year-old. It beats me why anyone should want a child anyway; dwarves are much easier to deal with, and far more amusing. She's a brave little cub, though, whatever her parentage; I think I can see why my Juliette cares for her.

Why then this sudden sting of chagrin? Her affection, weakness though it is, makes my position so much easier. She thinks to deceive me, my Wingless One, like a snipe luring the enemy from her nest. She feigns stupidity, evading me except when there is a crowd, or working alone on the salt flats, knowing that in that wide expanse of unpeopled space I cannot approach her with discretion. Twenty-four hours. I would have expected her to have come to me before now. Her stubbornness is a characteristic which both angers and pleases me. Perhaps I am perverse, but I do enjoy her resistance and I feel I might have been

124

disappointed if she had shown any less.

Besides, I already have my allies. Soeur Piété, who dares not meet my gaze; Soeur Alfonsine, the consumptive nun who follows me like a spaniel; Soeur Germaine, who detests me; Soeur Bénédicte, the gossip. Any of these might do to begin with. Or the fat nun, Soeur Antoine, nosing around the kitchen doorway like a timid sheep. I've been watching her, and I think I see potential there. Under the new order she now works in the garden. I've seen her digging, her cheeks marbled with the unaccustomed exertion. Another has been made cellarer in her place: the scrawny, twitching nun with the bright, wounded eyes. No more pies and pasties under *her* regime. No more unaccompanied trips to the market, or illicit samplings of old wine. Soeur Antoine's arms are plump and red, her feet in their narrow boots unusually dainty for her bulk. There is something maternal in her ample bosom, a generosity given free rein in her kitchens among the sausages and roasts. Where will it go now? In a single day her cheeks have already lost some of their roundness. Her skin has a sick and cheesy sheen. She has not yet spoken to me, but she wants to. I can see it in her eyes.

Last night, when she brought me my meal, I inquired innocently how they had dined. Potato soup, she said without looking at me. But for *mon père*, something more substantial. A fine pigeon pie, if monseigneur pleases, and a glass of red wine. Peaches from our own gardens, such a shame the drought has left us so few. Her eyes darted to mine in silent appeal. Ha, you jade! Don't think I didn't suspect you. Potato soup, indeed. Your lips grew moist as you spoke of peaches and wine. A creature of passions, this Antoine; and where will they go now their outlet is closed?

A day of fasting has dulled her bright and foolish good nature. She looks bewildered but sullen, a desperate sullenness veering towards spite. She is almost ready for me. Another day, I tell myself. Another day until she realizes what she has lost. I would have preferred a sharper tool with which to begin my work, but perhaps this one is fitting.

After all, I have to start somewhere.

CHAPTER FIVE
♥

July 20th, 1610

The daily services have been re-established. We were awoken at two o' clock today for Vigils with the ringing of the old bell, and for a moment I was sure some terrible calamity had happened: a shipwreck, a gale, a sudden death. Then I saw Mouche lying discarded on the pillow and the pain of remembrance was suddenly more than I could endure. I bit my pallet so that I should not be heard and sobbed into the packed straw, sparse, angry tears, which felt like runnels of powder on my face, ready at any moment to ignite.

It was at this moment that Perette found me, creeping to my bed so quietly that for a time I was not aware of her presence. If it had been anyone other than the wild girl, I would have lashed out like an animal in a trap. But Perette's little face was so simple and woebegone in the dim light of the cresset that I could not focus my anger.

In the last few days I know I have neglected my friend. More pressing things concerned me, things the wild girl could not understand. But I wonder whether I do not often underestimate Perette. Her birdlike voice speaks no tongue that I can understand, but there is intelligence in her bright gold-ringed eyes, and a deep, unquestioning devotion. She tried a smile, indicating her eyes with a speaking gesture.

I wiped my face with the back of my hand. 'It's all right, Perette. Go to Vigils.' But Perette was already taking her place on the mattress beside me, her bare feet curling beneath her, for shoes are clothing she continues to refuse. Her small hand crept into mine. For a second she reminded me of a sad puppy, offering comfort in humble, loving silence, and I was ashamed at the twist of contempt in the thought.

With an effort I returned the smile. 'Don't worry, Perette. I'm tired, that's all.'

It was true; it had taken me hours to get to sleep. Perette lifted her head and indicated the absence at the side of my bed where Fleur's cot used to be. When I did not reply she pinched my arm gently and pointed again.

'I know.' I did not want to talk about it. But she looked so woeful and concerned that I had not the heart to rebuff her. 'It won't be for long. I promise.'

The wild girl looked at me. Her head was cocked to one side and she looked more like a bird than ever. Then she put both hands to the side of her face, changing her expression as she did so to mimic the new Abbess with an accuracy that might in other circumstances have been comic.

I gave a wan smile. 'That's right. Mère Isabelle sent her away. But we'll get her back, you'll see. We'll get her back soon.'

I wondered whether I was speaking to myself, or whether Perette knew what I was saying. Even as I spoke, her attention had already passed onto other things, and she was playing with a pendant around her neck. There was an image of Saint Christina Mirabilis on the pendant, enamelled in orange and red and blue and white. She probably wore it because she liked the colours. The Saint was floating unharmed in her ring of holy fire, and Perette held the image in front of her eyes, crooning happily. She was still doing it when we finally arrived in the chapel and took our places in the crowd.

Vigils lasted longer than I had expected. The new Abbess kept the light to a minimum, passing occasionally with the cresset so that she could ensure no one was asleep. Twice she snapped a sharp rebuke at a lazy sister—Soeur Antoine was one, I think, and Soeur Piété the other—for the chanting was soft and almost soothing, and the night, warmed by eighteen hours of daylight, was not yet cold enough for discomfort. Almost two hours passed before the bell rang again for Matins, and I realized that the customary period of rest between the two services had been missed. I was shivering now in spite of my woollen stockings, though I could see the dawn piercing through the loose slates. The bell rang twice again for Lauds and a murmur went through the assembly as, once again, LeMerle made his entrance.

In a second, all drowsiness had dropped from

the air. Around me I could feel the small, barely perceptible movements of the sisters as they turned their sunflower faces towards him. I think I was the only one who did not look up. Eyes fixed firmly on my clasped hands, I heard him approach, heard the soft familiar sounds of his footsteps on the marble flags, sensed him standing at the lectern, motionless in his dark robe, one hand touching the silver crucifix he always wears.

'My children. *Iam lucis orto sidere*. The star of the morning has risen. Raise your voices now to greet it.'

I sang the hymn with my face still lowered, the words resonating strangely in my skull. *Iam lucis orto sidere . . . .* But Lucifer was the Morning Star before his fall, brightest of all angels, I thought, and at that I could not help but glance once at LeMerle as I sang.

Too late, I averted my gaze. *Iam lucis orto sidere . . . .* He was looking directly at me and smiling, as if I had revealed my thoughts. I wished I had not looked.

The hymn ended. The sermon began. I vaguely heard some reference to fasting, to penance, but I was alone in my circle of misery; nothing could reach me. Words droned past me like bees— *contrition—vanity—adornment—humility—penance.* But they meant nothing to me. All I could think of was Fleur, all alone without even Mouche to comfort her, and how I had not even had time to wipe her nose or tie a ribbon in her hair before they took her away.

Tsk-tsk, begone! I made the sign with my fingers. No more of that bad-luck thinking. Whatever his intentions, LeMerle wasn't planning to stay in the

129

abbey for ever. The moment he was gone, I would find my daughter. Meanwhile I'd play his game. I'd use every cantrip I knew to keep her from harm, and if by his fault anything happened to her, I would kill him. He knew I would; and he'd keep her safe. For now, anyway.

I was roused from my thoughts by a movement close by, and looked up. I had been standing near the back of the chapel; for a time I believed it was to receive a sacrament that we came forward one by one, heads bent in submission. A nun was kneeling at the altar, head bowed, her wimple in her hand. A line of sisters waited behind her, removing their wimples as they came, and I followed with the rest, as it seemed to be expected of me. As I came closer still, I passed the sisters as they returned from the pulpit. Shivering like lambs, they moved in a kind of dream, not meeting my eyes, their faces crumpled with indecision. Then I saw the shears in LeMerle's hand, and I understood everything. The Reform had begun.

In front of me I saw Alfonsine take her place before the pulpit, accepting the shears with a thrill of submission. Then it was Antoine's turn. I had never seen her without her wimple before, and the sudden beauty of her thick black hair was a startling revelation. Then came the shears and she was Antoine again, pale as a beached jellyfish, mouth working helplessly as LeMerle uttered the benediction. 'I hereby renounce all worldly vanities, in the name of the Father, the Son, the Holy Spirit.'

Poor Antoine. What vanities had she known in her sad, fearful time but those of the table and the cellarium? The moment of beauty, so fleetingly

130

glimpsed, was gone. She looked terrified, her hair standing out in uneven clumps, her eyes rolling and her fat hands kneading at each other as if in longing for the comforting routine of the bread pan.

Then it was Clémente, her flaxen hair catching at the light as she bowed her head. Oddly enough it was dour Germaine who cried out as the shears did their work. Clémente simply tilted her face at LeMerle, looking even younger than she had before the shearing; a wanton with the face of a little boy.

But hair was not the only vanity we were to relinquish. I saw old Rosamonde, her half-bald crown bared, reluctantly give up the gold cross that she wore about her neck. Her mouth moved, but her words did not reach me. She joined me a few moments later, her weak eyes roaming the chapel as if in search someone who was absent. Then it was Perette, whose hair was already cropped, sullenly emptying her pockets of treasures. Magpie treasures, that's all they were: a scrap of ribbon, a polished stone, a piece of rag—those small and harmless vanities that only a child could cherish. She was most reluctant to part with her enamelled pendant, and had almost succeeded in palming it when Soeur Marguerite pointed it out, and it was swept up with the rest. Perette bared her vicious little teeth at Marguerite, who piously looked the other way. From the corner of my eye I could see LeMerle, trying hard to keep himself from laughing.

Then it was my turn. I watched the ground dispassionately as my hair fell, curl by bright curl, amongst the mounting trophies. I expected to feel

131

something—anger, maybe, or shame—instead I felt nothing but the burn of his fingers at the nape of my neck as he stretched out and drew aside the tangle of hair, cutting with a deftness and precision which drew the eye from the more intimate gestures—a thumb pressed against the earlobe, a lingering touch in the throat's hollow—which he performed upon me in secret, without anyone noticing.

He spoke to me in two registers, the public one in which he intoned the *Benedictus*, and a thin, rapid whisper during which his mouth barely moved.

'Dominus vobiscum. *You've been avoiding me, Juliette.* Agnus Dei, *very unwise,* qui tollis peccata mundi, *we need to talk,* miserere nobis. *I can help you.*'

I shot him a glance of loathing.

'O felix culpa, *you look wonderful when you're angry.* Quae talem ac tanctum, *see me in the confessional,* meruit habere Redemptorem—*after Vespers tomorrow.*'

And then it was over, and I went back to my place feeling dizzy and strange, with my heart pounding and the ghosts of his fingers still fluttering like burning moths against my neck.

At the end of the session, all sixty-five of us were sitting in our places, newly cropped and demure. My face still felt flushed and my heart was beating wildly, but I hid it as best I could, and kept my eyes downcast. Rosamonde and some of the older nuns had been forced to exchange their old *quichenotte* for the crisp wimple favoured by the new Abbess, and they looked like a flock of seagulls in the semidarkness. Every cheap trinket, ring, necklace, every harmless scrap of braid or ribbon our old Reverend Mother had tolerated was gone. Vanity, LeMerle told us in his grave voice, was the jewel of gold in the pig's snout, and we had fallen to its lure. The Bernardine cross on our habits should be adornment enough, he said—whilst all the time the light played on his silver crucifix like a small malicious eye.

Then, after the communal blessing and act of contrition, which I mouthed with the rest, our new Abbess stood up and started to speak. 'This is the first of many changes I intend to make,' she began. 'Today will be a day of fasting and prayer in preparation for the task we will undertake tomorrow.' She paused, perhaps to feel the impact of so many pairs of eyes. 'The interment of my predecessor,' she continued, 'where it best befits her, in our own crypt.'

'But we—' The protest was out before I could stop it.

'Soeur Auguste?' Her gaze was scornful. 'Did you say something?'

'I'm sorry, *ma mère*. I should not have spoken. But the Reverend Mother was—a simple creature, who disliked the—the fanfare of church ceremony. We did what we thought best when we buried her. Surely it would be kinder now to leave her in peace?'

Mère Isabelle's small hands clenched. 'Are you telling me that it's *kinder* to leave that woman's body in some abandoned piece of ground?' she demanded. 'Why, I believe the place was actually a vegetable garden, or something! What can have possessed you?'

There was nothing to be gained in

133

confrontation. 'We did what we thought was right at the time,' I said humbly. 'I see now that it was a mistake.'

For a second Mère Isabelle continued to look at me with suspicion. Then she turned away. 'I must remember,' she said, 'that in such a remote area of the country old customs and beliefs still persist. There is not *necessarily* any sin attached to such a misunderstanding.'

Fine words. But the suspicion remained in her voice and I knew I was not forgiven. The safety of the abbey was eroding every minute I remained. Twice already I had attracted the critical attention of the new Abbess. My daughter had been taken from me. And now LeMerle held me between his careless, clever fingers; knowing perhaps that one more accusation—a hint of heresy, a casual reference to matters I had thought forgotten—would bring the weight of the Church's investigation to bear upon me. It had to be soon. I had to leave soon. But not without Fleur.

And so I waited. We repaired to the warming room for a time. Then Prime and Tierce, interminable chanting and prayers and hymns with LeMerle watching me all the time with that look of mocking benevolence in his eyes. Then to Chapter. In the hour that followed, duties were allocated, hours of prayer, days of fasting, rules governing decorum, dress, deportment laid down with military precision. The Great Reform was under way.

The chapel would be renovated, we were told. Lay builders would do much of the work on the roof, though the interior would be our own responsibility. The lay people who had until now done most of our menial duties were to be dismissed; it was unseemly for us to have servants to do our work whilst we spent our time in idleness. The rebuilding of the abbey must now be our main concern, and everyone was expected to take additional duties until the time of its completion.

I learned with dismay that our free time was to be curtailed to half an hour after Compline, to be spent in prayer and reflection, and that our excursions to the town and to the harbour were to cease at once. My Latin lessons to the novices, too, were to be discontinued. Mère Isabelle did not feel that it was appropriate for novices to learn Latin. To obey the Scripture was enough, she said; anything more was dangerous and unnecessary. A duty rota was established which reversed all our accustomed routines. Without surprise I noted that Antoine no longer governed the kitchens or the cellars and that henceforth my herb garden would be tended by strangers, but I accepted this, too, with indifference, knowing that my time at the abbey was coming to an end.

Then came the penances. Confession had never taken more than a few minutes in Mère Marie's day; this time it took over an hour, with Alfonsine setting the tone.

'I had impious thoughts about the new Reverend Mother,' she murmured, with a sidelong glance at LeMerle. 'I spoke out of turn in the church, when Soeur Auguste came in.' It was typical of her, I thought, to draw attention to my lateness.

'What kind of thoughts?' said LeMerle, with a gleam in his eye.

Alfonsine shifted beneath his gaze. 'It's what Soeur Auguste said. She's too young. She's only a child. She won't know what to do.'

'Soeur Auguste seems rather free with her opinions,' said LeMerle.

I stared into my lap and would not look up.

'I shouldn't have listened,' said Alfonsine.

LeMerle said nothing, but I knew he was smiling.

The rest soon followed Alfonsine's lead, initial hesitation giving way to a kind of eagerness. Yes, we were confessing our sins, and sin was shameful; but it was also the first time many of us had ever received such undivided attention. It was painfully compelling, like scratching at a nettle rash, and it was contagious.

'I went to sleep during Vigils,' said Soeur Piété, a colourless nun who rarely spoke to anyone. 'I said a bad word when I bit my tongue.'

Soeur Clémente: 'I looked at myself when I was washing. I looked at myself and I had a wicked thought.'

'I stole a p-pasty from the winter cellar.' That was Antoine, redfaced and stammering. 'It was p-pork and onion, with watercrust p-pastry. I ate it in secret behind the gatehouse wall, and it gave me a b-bellyache.'

Germaine was next, intoning her list—*Gluttony. Lust. Covetousness*—apparently at random. She, at least, had not been dazzled by LeMerle—her face wore a careful, colourless expression I recognized as scorn. Then came Soeur Bénédicte, with a tearful tale of shirked duties, and Soeur Pierre, with a stolen orange. At each new confession there came an increased murmur from the crowd, as if to urge the speaker onwards. Soeur Tomasine wept as she confessed lewd thoughts; several other nuns wept in sympathy, and Soeur Alfonsine eyed LeMerle while Mère Isabelle looked sullen and increasingly bored. Clearly she had expected more of us. Obediently, we gave it.

As the hour passed, the confessions grew more elaborate, more detailed. Every scrap of material was brought out for the occasion: tattered remnants of past transgressions, filched pie-crusts, erotic dreams. The ones who had been first to make their confessions now found their performance overshadowed; resentful looks were exchanged; the murmuring grew to a low roar.

Now it was Marguerite's turn to step forward. She exchanged glances with Alfonsine as she passed, and I knew then that there would be trouble. I forked the sign against evil into my palm; around me, the anticipation was so thick that I could barely breathe. Marguerite looked fearfully into LeMerle's face, twitching like a snared rabbit.

'Well?' said Isabelle impatiently.

Marguerite opened her mouth and closed it again without speaking. Alfonsine looked at her with barely concealed hostility. Then, haltingly, and without taking her eyes away from LeMerle's face, she began.

'I dream of demons,' she said in a low voice. 'They infest my dreams. They speak to me when I lie in bed. They touch me with their fiery fingers. Soeur Auguste gives me medicines to make me sleep, but still the demons come!'

'Medicines?' There was a pause, during which I felt Isabelle's eyes flick sharply at my averted face.

'A sleeping draught, that's all,' I said as the other sisters turned towards me. 'Lavender, and valerian, to calm her nerves. That's all it is.' Too late, I heard the edge in my voice.

Mère Isabelle put her hand on Marguerite's forehead and gave a small, chilly smile. 'Well, I don't think you'll be needing any of Soeur Auguste's potions any more. Père Colombin and I are here to take care of you now. In penance and humility we will expel all trace of the evil which plagues you.'

Then at last, turning to me, she said: 'So, Soeur Auguste. You seem to have something to say on almost every other subject. Have you no testimony to make here?'

I could see the danger, but was at a loss at how to avoid it. 'I—I don't think so, *ma mère.*'

'What? Not one? Not a transgression, not a weakness, an act of unkindness, a wicked thought? Not even a dream?'

I suppose I should have made something up, like the rest of them. But LeMerle's eyes were still on me, and I felt my face grow hot in revolt. 'I—forgive me, *ma mère.* I don't remember. I—I'm not used to public confession.'

Mère Isabelle gave a smile of singularly adult unpleasantness. 'I see,' she said. 'Soeur Auguste has a right to her privacy. Public testimony is beneath her. Her sins are between herself and the Almighty. Soeur Auguste speaks directly to God.'

Alfonsine sniggered. Clémente and Germaine grinned at each other. Marguerite piously raised her eyes to the ceiling. Even Antoine, who had blushed beet-red during her own confession, was smirking. At that moment I knew that every nun in the chapel felt the same guilty twist of pleasure at the humiliation of one of their own. And behind Mère Isabelle, LeMerle gave his angel's smile, as if none of this had anything to do with him.

CHAPTER SIX
♥

July 21st, 1610

My penance was silence. Two days' enforced silence, with instructions to the other sisters to report immediately any breach of this command. It was no punishment to me. In fact, I welcomed the respite. Besides, if my suspicions were correct, Fleur and I might soon be gone. *See me in the confessional after Vespers tomorrow*, LeMerle had said. *I can help you.*

He was going to give me Fleur. What else could he have meant? Why else would he risk a meeting? My heart leapt at the thought, all my caution swept aside. To hell with strategy. I wanted my daughter. No penance, however severe, could begin to compare with the pain of her absence. Whatever LeMerle wanted from me, he was welcome to it.

Alfonsine, the perpetual gossip, who had been given the same penance as I, was far more troubled, assuming a look of deep contrition which no one—to her chagrin—appeared to notice. Her cough had worsened in recent days, and yesterday she refused her food. I recognized the signs and hoped that this renewal of zeal would not provoke one of her attacks. Marguerite was put in charge of the clock for a month to cure her nightly visitations; henceforth she would be the one to ring the bell for Vigils, sleeping alone on a box-bed

139

suspended by ropes in the belfry and waking every hour to ring the time. I doubted that it would work, but Marguerite seemed exalted by her punishment—although her tic had worsened, and there was a new stiffness down her left side that made her limp when she walked.

Never had there been so many penances. It seemed as if half the sisters or more were under some kind of discipline, from Antoine's fasting—penance enough for her—and relocation to the overheated bakehouse, to Germaine's work digging the new latrines.

It created a strange climate of segregation between the virtuous and the penitent. I caught Soeur Tomasine looking at me with a kind of contempt as I passed her in the slype, and Clémente did her best to taunt me into speech, though without success.

*   *   *

Today passed with terrible slowness. Between services, I spent two hours in the refectory, whitewashing the faded walls and scrubbing a floor slick with built-up grease. Then I helped with the repairs to the chapel, silently passing buckets of mortar to the cheery, bare-chested workmen on the roof. Then came prayers over the potato-patch, with LeMerle intoning with incense and solemnity the Last Rites which the poor Reverend Mother had never received whilst I, Germaine, Tomasine and Berthe performed the unpleasant task of opening the new grave.

It was not yet noon, but already the sun was hot, the air sizzling with heat as we made our way with shovels and spades towards the burial mound. Soon we were sweating. The earth is dry and sandy here, whitish on the surface but becoming red at greater depth. Barely moist earth clung to the shroud and to our robes as we cleared away the sand from the body. It was a simple enough task, if one had the stomach for it; the earth had not had a great deal of time to settle and was still light enough to clear with a shovel. The body had been sewn into a sheet, now blackened where the corpse had rested against it so that the marks of head, ribs, elbows and feet were clearly visible against the creamy linen. Soeur Tomasine wavered as she saw this, but I have seen enough bodies to be unmoved and I reached for it myself, carefully and with as much reverence as I could muster. Mère Marie was heavier than she had been in life, weighted by the earth that clung to her, and I struggled to raise her with dignity, gripping her by the shoulders though her weight seemed strangely brittle, like that of a piece of driftwood washed onto the shore and half buried in sand. The shroud was badly stained on the reverse side, with the outline of the spine and ribs clearly defined, and as I heaved her from her unconsecrated resting place I uncovered a mass of brown beetles which boiled away into the sand like hot lead as soon as the sunlight reached them. At the sight of the creatures, Berthe gave a big, loose cry and almost dropped her end of the corpse. More of the beetles scattered along her sleeve and into the pit. I saw Alfonsine watching in appalled fascination. Only Germaine seemed unmoved, and she helped me hoist the body out of the hole, her scarred face impassive, her athlete's shoulders straining. There was a light, dry smell of earth and

141

ash, not too unpleasant at first, and then we turned Reverend Mother onto her front and the rankness struck us, a terrible midday blast of spoiled pork and excrement.

I held my breath and tried to stop myself from retching, but it was no use. My eyes streamed; I was all sweat. Germaine had brought up a fold of her wimple to cover her mouth, but it was not enough, and I could see distress in her face as she lifted the body to shoulder-height.

From a distance I was aware of Mère Isabelle watching us, a plain white handkerchief held to her nostrils. I cannot say for sure whether she was smiling, but her eyes seemed unusually bright, her face flushed with something more than the heat.

I think it was satisfaction.

*　　　*　　　*

We buried Reverend Mother in the ossuary at the back of the crypt, inside one of the many narrow grave-housings left behind by the black friars. They look something like stone bread ovens, each with a slab to cover the entrance, and some bear numbers, names, inscriptions in Latin. I noticed that some had been broken open, and I tried not to look too closely at these. There was dust and sand everywhere, and a cold, damp smell. I knew Mère Marie wouldn't have cared for it at all, but that was no longer my concern.

After the short ceremony the sisters went up to the chapel while I remained to seal the vault. A candle rested on the earth floor to light my work; there was a bucket of mortar and a trowel at my side. Above me I could hear the sisters singing a hymn. I was beginning to feel a little light-headed; my sleepless nights, the noon heat, the stench, the sudden cold of the crypt all combined with the day's fasting to create a kind of dark stupor. I reached for the trowel but it fell from my hand, and I realized I was close to fainting. I leaned my face against the wall for support, smelling saltpetre and porous stone, and for a second I was in Epinal again, and I grew cold with sudden fear.

At that moment, a draught from the vaults snuffed the candle, leaving me in darkness. Now panic bloomed horribly inside me. I had to get out. I could feel the dark pushing at my back, the dead nun grinning from her cell and the other dead ones, the black friars, sly in their dust, reaching out with withered fingers . . . I had to get out!

I took a shaky step in the darkness and knocked over the bucket of mortar. The ossuary seemed to yawn around me; I could no longer touch the walls. I felt a mad urge to laugh, to scream. I had to get out! I fell, with an immense clatter, striking my head against an angle of stone so that I lay half-dazed, dark roses blossoming behind my eyelids. The litany stopped dead.

Alfonsine was the first to reach me. By that time the unaccustomed panic had left me and I was sitting up, still dazed, my hand to my bruised temple. The light from her candle revealed how very small the crypt was after all, little bigger than a cupboard with its neat cells and low vaulting, killing the illusion of space. Her face was all eyes.

'Soeur Auguste?' Her voice was sharp. 'Soeur Auguste, are you all right?' In her eagerness she had forgotten our penance of silence.

I must have been less recovered than I thought.

For a moment the name by which she had addressed me meant nothing. Even her face meant nothing, the features behind the smear of candlelight those of a stranger.

'Who are you?' I asked.

'She doesn't know me!' The voice was unpleasantly shrill. 'Soeur Auguste, don't move. Help will be here in a moment.'

'It's all right, Alfonsine,' I said. The name had returned to me as rapidly as it had fled, and with it the wariness of years. 'I must have tripped on a broken slab. The candle went out. I was stunned for a moment.'

But my words came too late. The upheavals of the last few days, the darkness of the ossuary, the exhumation, the ceremony and now this new excitement—Alfonsine had always been more susceptible to these things than the rest of us. Besides which, Soeur Marguerite had stolen the scene the day before, with her visions of demons . . .

'*Did you feel that?*' hissed Alfonsine.

'Feel what?'

'*Shh!*' She lowered her voice to a stage whisper. 'Like a cold wind.'

'I felt nothing.' I got to my feet with difficulty. 'Here. Give me your arm.'

She flinched at my touch. 'You were down there a long time. What happened?'

'Nothing. I told you. I felt faint.'

'You didn't feel . . . a *presence*?'

'No.' I could see a number of sisters peering down into the crypt, their faces blurred in the uncertain light. Alfonsine's fingers were cold in mine. Her eyes seemed fixed upon a point just behind me. With a sinking heart, I recognized the

144

signs. 'Look, Alfonsine . . .' I began.

'I felt it.' She was beginning to tremble. 'It went right through me. And it was cold. Cold!'

'All right.' I agreed only to force her into motion. 'Maybe there was something. It doesn't matter. Now move!'

I had checked her excitement. She shot me a resentful look and I felt a sudden prick of mirth. Poor Alfonsine. It was cruel to rob her of her moment. Since the death of the Reverend Mother she has seemed more alive than at any time within the past five years. It's the *theatre* of it all that fires her: the tearing of hair, the penances, the public confessions. But for every performance there is a price to pay. She coughs more often than ever, her eyes are feverish and she has been sleeping almost as badly as I do myself. I hear her in the cubicle next to mine, whispering with the rhythms of prayer or cursing, sometimes whimpering and crying out but mostly the same soft repetition, like a litany repeated so often that the words have lost almost all their original meaning.

Mon père . . . Mon père . . .

I almost had to carry her back up the steps of the ossuary.

Suddenly she stiffened. 'Holy Mother! The silence! The *penance*!' I shushed her furiously. But it was too late. There were sisters all about us now, unsure whether or not to address us. LeMerle kept his distance. This performance was for his benefit, and he knew it. Mère Isabelle stood next to him, watching us with lips slightly parted. This was more like it, I thought fiercely. This was what she had hoped for.

'*Ma mère,*' brayed Alfonsine, falling to her knees

145

on the floor of the transept. '*Ma mère,* I am sorry. Give me another penance, a *hundred* penances if you must, but please forgive me!'

'What happened?' snapped Isabelle. 'What did Soeur Auguste say to make you defy your vow of silence?'

'Mother of God!' Alfonsine was stalling for time. I could hear it in her voice as she became aware of her audience. 'I felt it in the crypt, *ma mère*! We both felt it! We felt its icy breath!' Her own skin was icy as if in response. I could almost feel myself growing cold in sympathy.

'*What* did you feel?'

'It's nothing.' The last thing I wanted was to draw unwelcome attention to myself, but I could not allow this to pass. 'A draught from the undercroft, that was all. Her nerves are disordered. She's always—'

'Silence!' snapped Isabelle. She turned again to Alfonsine, whispered: '*What* did you feel?'

'The demon, *ma mère.* I felt its presence like a cold wind.' Alfonsine looked at me, and I thought I saw satisfaction in her face. 'A cold wind.'

Isabelle turned to me, and I shrugged.

'A draught from the undercroft,' I said again. 'It blew out my candle.'

'I know what I felt!' Alfonsine was shaking again. 'And you felt it too, Auguste! You told me so yourself!' Her face convulsed and she coughed twice. 'It blew into me, I tell you, the demon came right *into* me and—' She was choking now, clawing at her throat. 'It's still here!' I heard her cry. '*It's still here!*' Then she sank, convulsing, to the floor.

'Hold her!' cried Mère Isabelle, losing some of her composure.

But Alfonsine would not be held. She bit, spat, shrieked, kicked her legs immodestly, the attack redoubling whenever I came close. It took three of us—Germaine, Marguerite and a deaf nun called Soeur Clothilde—to hold her, to prise open her mouth to stop her from swallowing her tongue, and even then she continued to scream until finally Père Colombin himself came to bless her, and she lay rigid and still against him.

At that point Isabelle turned on me. 'What did she mean, "it's still here"?'

'I don't know,' I said.

'What happened in the crypt?'

'My candle blew out. I tripped and fell.'

'What about Soeur Alfonsine?'

'I don't know.'

'She says you do.'

'I can't help that,' I said. 'She makes things up. She likes the attention. Ask anyone.'

But Isabelle was far from satisfied. 'She was trying to tell me something,' she persisted. 'You stopped her. Now what was she—'

'For God's sake, can't this wait?' I had almost forgotten LeMerle, artfully positioned in a chance shaft of sunlight, with Soeur Alfonsine gasping like a beached fish in his arms. 'For the moment we must take this poor woman to the infirmary. I presume I have your authority to lift her penance?' Mère Isabelle hesitated, still looking at me. 'Or perhaps you would prefer to discuss the matter in your own good time?'

Isabelle flushed slightly. 'The matter must be investigated and dealt with,' she said.

'Of course. When Soeur Alfonsine is in a condition to speak.'

'And Soeur Auguste?'

'Maybe tomorrow.'

'But *mon père . . .*'

'By Chapter tomorrow we will know more. I'm sure you agree that it would be unseemly to act in haste.'

There was a long pause. 'So be it. Tomorrow, then. At Chapter.'

I looked at him then, to find his eyes on me again, bright and troubling. For a fleeting moment I even wondered whether he had known what was going to happen in the crypt, had arranged it in some way in order to bring me further into his power . . . I would have believed almost anything of him then. He was uncanny. And he knew me too well.

Well, whether he had planned it or not, this had been a demonstration. LeMerle had shown me that without him I was helpless, my safety as perilous as a frayed rope. Like it or not, I needed his help. And the Blackbird, I knew of old, never sold his favours cheap.

CHAPTER SEVEN
♠

July 21st, 1610

'Bless me, father, for I have sinned.'

At last. Confession. How good it feels to hold her captive like this, my wild one, my bird of prey. I can feel her eyes on me from behind the grille, and for a troubling moment I am the one who is caged.

It is a curious sensation. I can hear her quickened breathing, sense the enormous effort of will which keeps her voice level as she intones the ritual words. Light from the window above us filters dimly into the confessional, painting her face with a harlequin pattern of rose and black squares.

'Well, if it isn't my Ailée, giving up her wings for whiter ones in Heaven.'

I am unused to such intimacies as this, the casual exposure of the confessional. It makes me impatient—sends my mind wandering down overgrown paths best left forgotten. Perhaps she knows it; her silence is that of a confessor, and not a penitent. I can feel it, drawing out reckless words I did not intend to speak.

'I suppose you still hold that business against me.' Silence. 'That business at Epinal.'

She has withdrawn her face from the grille and the darkness speaks for her, blank and unremitting. I can feel her eyes on me, like irons. For thirty seconds I feel their heat. Then she folds, as I knew she would.

'I want my daughter.'

Good. It really is a weakness in her game; she's lucky we're not playing for money. 'I find myself obliged to stay here for a while,' I tell her. 'I can't risk you leaving.'

'Why not?' There is a savage note in her voice now, and I revel in it. I can deal with her anger. I can use it. Gently I feed the flame.

'You'll have to trust me. I haven't betrayed you, have I?'

Silence. I know she is thinking of Epinal.

Stubbornly: 'I want Fleur.'

'Is that her name? You could see her every day.

149

Would you like that?' Slyly: 'She must be missing her mother. Poor thing.'

She flinches then—and the game is mine. 'What do you want, LeMerle?'

'Your silence. Your loyalty.'

That sound was too harsh to be laughter. 'Are you mad? I have to get away from here. You've seen to that already.'

'Impossible. I can't have you spoiling things.'

'Spoiling what?' Too fast, LeMerle. Too fast. 'There's no wealth here for you. What's your game?'

Oh, Juliette. If only I could tell you. I'm sure you'd appreciate it. You're the only one who would. 'Later, little bird. Later. Come to my cottage tonight, after Compline. Can you get out of the dorter without being heard?'

'Yes.'

'Good. Till then, Juliette.'

'What about Fleur?'

'Till then.'

She came to me just after midnight. I was sitting at my desk with my copy of Aristotle's *Politics* when I heard the door open with a soft click. The glow from the single candle caught her shift and the copper-gilt of her cropped hair.

'Juliette.'

She had discarded her habit and wimple. Left them in the dorter, no doubt, to avoid arousing suspicion. With her hair cut short she looked like a beautiful boy. The next time we dance the classics I'll have her as Ganymede or Hyacinthus. She neither spoke nor smiled, and the cold draught from the open doorway swept between her ankles unnoticed.

'Come in.' I put down my book and drew up a chair, which she ignored.

'I would have thought it more appropriate for you to study some improving work,' she said. 'Machiavelli, perhaps, or Rabelais. Isn't *Do what thou wilt* your motto now?'

'It beats *Thy will be done*,' I said, grinning. 'Besides, since when were you in any position to preach morality? You're as much of an impostor as I am.'

'I don't deny it,' she said. 'But whatever else I may have done, I always stayed true to myself. And I've never betrayed a friend.'

With an effort, I bit back a retort. She had touched me on the raw. It was a knack she'd always had. 'Please, Juliette,' I said. 'Must we be enemies? Here.' I indicated a cut-crystal bottle on the bookcase beside the desk. 'A glass of Madeira.'

She shook her head.

'Food, then. Fruit and honey cake.'

Silence. I knew she had spent the day in fasting, but she seemed unmoved. Her face was mask-like, perfect. Only her eyes blazed. I put out my hand to touch her face. I never could resist playing with fire. Even as a child it was the dangerous games that appealed to me: walking the tightrope with a noose about my neck, firing wasps' nests, juggling knives, swimming the rapids. Le Borgne called it hunting tigers, and scorned me for it. But if there's no risk from the quarry, then where's the joy of the chase?

'You haven't changed.' I said, smiling. 'One false move and you'd take out my eyes. Admit it.'

'Get on with it, LeMerle.'

Her skin was smooth beneath my palm. From

her cropped hair I could smell the distant fragrance of lavender. I allowed my fingers to move down onto her bare shoulder. 'Is *that* it?' she said contemptuously. 'Is that what you wanted?'

Angrily I withdrew my hand. 'Still so suspicious, Juliette? Don't you realize what I have at stake here? This is no ordinary game. It's a scheme of such daring and ambition that even I—' She gave a sigh, stifling a yawn beneath her fingers. I paused, stung. 'I see you find my explanation tedious.'

'Not at all.' Her inflection was a precise parody of my own. 'But it's late. And I want my daughter.'

'The old Juliette would have understood.'

'The old Juliette died in Epinal.'

That hurt, although I had expected it. 'You know nothing about what happened in Epinal. For all you know I might be completely innocent.'

'As you say.'

'What, did you think I was a saint?' There was an edge to my voice that I could not subdue. 'I knew you'd manage to get out of it; if you hadn't, I'd have thought of something. Some kind of scheme.' She waited politely, eyes averted, one foot turned out in a dancer's gesture. 'They were too close, damn you. I'd tricked them once already, and now they were onto me. I could feel it: my luck was running out. I was afraid. And the dwarf knew it. It was Le Borgne who set the dogs on me, Juliette. It could only have been him. In any case he was ready enough to trade your necks for his own, the bastard, and to deal me a foul blow with a poisoned knife. What, did you think I'd deserted you? I would have come back for you if I'd been able. As it was I was lying sick and wounded in a ditch for days after your escape. You felt a little pique,

152

perhaps. A little anger. But don't say you needed me. You never did.'

I must have sounded convincing—in fact, I almost convinced myself. But her voice betrayed nothing as she repeated: 'I want Fleur.'

Once more I bit down upon my anger. It tasted metallic, like a bad coin. 'Please, Juliette. I've already told you. I can let you see Fleur tomorrow. Not to bring her back, not yet in any case, but I can arrange it. All I ask in return is a truce. And a favour. A little favour.'

She stepped towards me then, and put her hands on my shoulders. Again I caught the scent of lavender from the folds of her shift.

'No, not that.'

'What then?'

'A joke. A practical joke. You'll enjoy it.'

She hesitated. 'Why?' she said at last. 'What are you doing here? What could we possibly have that would interest you?'

I laughed. 'A moment ago you didn't care.'

'I don't. I want my daughter.'

'Well, then. Why ask?'

She shrugged. 'I don't know.'

You can't fool me, Juliette. You care about these poor toadstools, cowering in their darkness. They are your family now, as once we were in the *Théâtre des Cieux*. I have to say it's a poor substitute, but each to his own. 'Call it a game, if you like,' I said. 'I've always wanted to play the priest. Now take these.' I handed her the tablets of dye. 'Don't get any of the colour on your hands.'

She looked at me with suspicion. 'What do you want me to do with it?'

I told her.

'And then I can see Fleur?'

'First thing in the morning.' Suddenly I wanted her to leave. I was tired and my head had begun to ache.

'You're sure this is harmless? It won't hurt anyone?'

'Of course not.' Well, not exactly.

She looked again at the tablets in her hand. 'And it's just this—little thing.'

I nodded.

'I want to hear you say it, LeMerle.'

I knew that she wanted to believe me. It's in her nature to do so, as it is in mine to deceive. Blame God for making me this way. I made my voice gentle as I put my arm around her shoulders, and this time she did not flinch.

'Trust me, Juliette,' I murmured.

Till tomorrow.

CHAPTER EIGHT
♥

July 22nd, 1610

I made my way back to the abbey in haste. It was not truly dark; a sliver of moon lit the clear sky and the stars were bright enough to cast shadows on the road beyond the gatehouse. In the distance, just above the dim line of the sea, I could see a bank of cloud darker than the sky. Rain, perhaps. As I entered the dorter, I strained my ears for sounds of wakeful breathing, but heard nothing.

In five years I have become familiar with the

sounds of my neighbours' breathing. I know the casual sprawl of their limbs beneath the rough blankets, their nocturnal habits, the sighs and whimperings of their dreams. I passed Soeur Tomasine, first by the door, snoring in her high, whistling manner. Then Soeur Bénédicte, always on her face with her arms outstretched. Then Piété, prim in sleep as she is in waking; then Germaine, Clémente and Marguerite. I needed all my dancer's agility to pass without alerting *her*; even so she stirred as I passed, one hand outflung in grasping, blind entreaty. Then came Alfonsine's empty cubicle, and opposite that, Antoine, hands folded demurely on her breast. Her breathing was light, effortless. Was she awake? She gave no sign of it. And yet she seemed too still, too quiet, her limbs arranged with more dignity and grace than sleep usually affords.

It could not be helped. If she was awake, I could only hope that she suspected nothing. I slid into my own bed, the hiss of my skin against the blanket very loud amongst the sounds of breathing. As I turned to the wall to sleep I heard Antoine give a sharp snore and felt some of my fear slip away, but even as it did so, it occurred to me that the sound rang false, too studied, too perfect in its timing. Resolutely I closed my eyes. It didn't matter. Nothing mattered but Fleur. Not Antoine, not Alfonsine—not even LeMerle, alone now in his tiny study surrounded by books. And yet it was LeMerle, and not my daughter, who followed me into my dreams. I cared nothing for his games, I told myself as sleep closed over me. All the same I dreamed of him, standing on the far bank of a flood-gorged river with his arms outstretched,

155

calling out to me above the roar of the water in words I could never quite hear.

I awoke with tears on my face. The bell for Vigils was ringing and Soeur Marguerite was standing at the foot of my bed with a cresset in one uplifted hand. I muttered the customary *Praise be!* and rose in haste, feeling between my mattress and the bed for the tablets of dye LeMerle had given me, wrapped in a scrap of cloth so that my fingers should show no tell-tale stains. It would be easy, I knew, to dispose of the tablets as instructed. That done, I would see my daughter.

All the same I hesitated. I lifted the tiny package and smelt it. It had a resinous, sweetish scent and I could detect the smell of gum arabic and the scarlet pigment Giordano called Dragon's Blood through the weave. There was something else, too: something spicy like ginger or aniseed. Harmless, he had promised.

LeMerle was not at Vigils, nor at Matins, nor Prime. Eventually he made his appearance at Chapter, but said that he needed to attend to some business in Barbâtre, and selected two sisters—at random, or so it seemed—to assist him. I was one. Antoine was the other.

As Père Colombin addressed the Chapter and Antoine saw to the hens and ducks in the barnyard, I fetched LeMerle's horse for the journey into Barbâtre. Antoine and I would walk, of course, but the new confessor would ride as befitted his noble status. I brushed the animal's dappled flanks and strapped on the saddle whilst Antoine fed the other beasts—a mule, two ponies and half a dozen cows—from the bins of hay at the back of the barn. It was over an hour before LeMerle joined us, and

156

when he returned I saw he had put aside his clerical robe in favour of the breeches and boots more suited to riding. He wore a wide-brimmed hat to protect his eyes from the sun, and thus clad he looked so like the Blackbird of the old days that my heart twisted.

It was market day, and he explained as we set off that he wanted us to arrange some food purchases and other errands on his behalf. Antoine's eyes lit up as he mentioned the market and I kept mine cautiously lowered. I wondered what favour Antoine had performed—or might be called upon to perform—in return for this outing, or whether she had indeed been a random choice. Perhaps it simply amused him to see the fat nun sweat and struggle in the dust at his horse's flanks. It didn't matter in either case. Soon I would see Fleur.

We walked more slowly than my racing heart would have wished, and even so Antoine suffered from the heat. I was more used to walking, and although I was carrying a large basket of potatoes on my back for sale at the market, I felt no fatigue. The sun was hot and high as we reached Barbâtre, and the harbour and the square beyond were already thronged with market-goers. The traders come from everywhere on the island, sometimes even from the mainland if the causeway is open, and today it was; in the harbour the tide was at its lowest, and the place was riotous with people.

As soon as we entered the main street we tethered the horse next to a drinking trough, Antoine went off, basket in hand, on her errand, and I followed LeMerle into the crowd.

The market had been in progress for some time. I could smell roasting meats and pastries, hay, fish, leatherwork and the sharp scent of fresh dung. A cart half-blocked the passage while two men unloaded cases of chickens onto the road. Fishermen unloaded lobster pots and cases of fish from their craft. A group of women were at work with the fishing nets, picking them clean of weed and retying broken mesh. Children straddled the wall of the churchyard and gawped at passers-by. The air was hot with stench and crackling with flies. The noise was overwhelming. After five years of virtual seclusion I had grown unused to this press of people, these cries, these smells. There were too many people; too many criers and peddlers and gossips and pamphleteers. A one-legged man behind a table stacked with tomatoes and onions and glossy aubergines winked and made a bawdy comment as I passed. Customers held their noses as they queued at a butcher's stall, purple with flies and black with old blood. A beggar with no legs and only one arm sat on a ragged blanket; opposite him a piper played, while a little girl in a shabby overall sold packets of herb salt from the back of a small brown goat. Old women seated in a close circle made lace with incredible deftness, their grey heads almost touching over the needlework as their withered fingers danced and twisted. What pick-pockets they would have made! I lost my bearings in the throng; paused at a vendor of printed sheets, selling illustrated accounts of the execution of François Ravaillac, Henri's murderer, and a fat surly woman with a tray of pies attempted to push past me. One of the pies fell to the ground, splitting open in a startling burst of red fruit. The fat woman turned upon me, squealing her displeasure, and I hurried on, my face burning.

It was then that I saw Fleur. Amazing that I had not noticed her before. Not ten feet away from me, head slightly averted, a grubby cap covering her curls and an apron, much too large for her, tied around her waist. Her face was set in an expression of childish disgust, and her hands and arms were stained with the leavings from the fish cart behind which she stood. My first instinct was to call her name, to run to her and take her in my arms, but caution halted me. Instead I looked at LeMerle, who had reappeared at my side and was watching me closely. 'What's this?' I said.

He shrugged. 'You asked to see her, didn't you?'

There was a drab-looking woman standing beside Fleur. She too wore an apron, and false sleeves over her own to protect them from the stinking merchandise on display. As I watched, a woman pointed out the fish she wanted and the drab woman handed it to Fleur to gut. Her face twisted as she slid the short blade into the creature's belly, but I was surprised at my daughter's deftness with the unaccustomed task. There was a bandage, now slick with a fishy residue, on her hand. Perhaps she had not always been so deft.

'For God's sake, she's five years old! What business have they to make her do that kind of work?'

LeMerle shook his head. 'Be reasonable. The child has to earn her keep. They have a large family. An extra mouth to feed is no little thing for a fisherman.'

A fisherman! So Antoine had been right about that. I looked at the woman, trying to determine whether or not I had seen her before. She could have been from Noirs Moustiers, I supposed; she had that look. On the other hand, she could easily be from Pornic or Fromentine; even maybe from Le Devin or one of the smaller islands.

LeMerle saw me watching. 'Don't concern yourself,' he said drily. 'She's being well looked after.'

'Where?'

'Trust me.'

I did not reply. My eyes were already taking in every detail of my daughter's transformation, each one bringing with it a new kind of pain. Her pinched cheeks, their roses gone. Her lank hair under the ugly cap. Her dress, not the one she wore at the abbey but some other child's cast-off of prickly brown wool. And her face: the face of a child with no mother.

I turned back to LeMerle. 'What do you want?'

'I told you. Your silence. Your loyalty.'

'You have it. I promise.' My voice was rising and I was powerless to stop it. 'I promised last night.'

'You didn't mean it last night,' he said. 'You do now.'

'I want to talk to her. I want to take her back!'

'I can't allow that, I'm afraid. Not yet, anyway. Not until I'm certain you won't just take the child and disappear.' He must have seen murder in my eyes then, because he smiled. 'And in case you were wondering, there are precise instructions to be carried out in case of any misfortune happening to me,' he said. 'Very *precise* instructions.'

I sheathed my gaze with an effort. 'Let me talk to her, then. Just for a moment. Please, Guy.'

It was harder than I had expected. LeMerle had told me that if I caused any mischief or suspicion,

160

then there might be no further opportunities to see Fleur. But I had to take the risk. I moved slowly, curbing my impatience, through the crowd to the fish cart. There was a woman on either side of me, one demanding fifty red mullet, the other exchanging recipes with the fishwife. At my back, more customers jostled. Fleur lifted her eyes to mine and for a moment I thought she had not recognized me. Then her face lit up.

'Shh,' I whispered. 'Don't say anything.'

Fleur looked puzzled, but to my relief, nodded.

'Listen to me,' I said in the same low voice. 'I don't have much time.'

As if to confirm this, the fishwife shot a suspicious gaze in my direction before returning to the order of mullet. I gave a silent prayer of thanks for the woman who wished to buy such an unusually large quantity of fish.

'Have you brought Mouche?' Fleur's voice was tiny. 'Have you come to take me home?'

'Not yet.' Her small face was grey with woe, and again I fought the urge to take her in my arms. 'Listen, Fleur. Where are they keeping you? A cottage? A caravan? A farm?'

Fleur glanced at the fisherman's wife. 'A cottage. With children and dogs.'

'Did you cross the causeway?'

'*Excuse* me.' A big woman pushed between us, stretching out her arms for a packet of fish. I stepped sideways into a line of customers; someone called out in annoyance.

'Hurry up, sister! Some of us have families to feed!'

'Fleur. Listen. Is it on the mainland? Is it over the causeway?'

161

From behind the large woman, Fleur nodded. Then, infuriatingly, she shook her head. Someone stepped into the space between us, and once again my daughter was lost to sight.

'Fleur!' I was almost weeping with frustration. The large woman was wedged beside me, the crowd was pushing at my back, and the customer who had called out had begun a noisy diatribe on people who stood around gossiping in queues. 'Sweetheart. Did you go over the causeway?'

For a second, then, I thought she would tell me. Puzzled, she seemed to be trying to articulate or remember something, to give me some clue which would reveal to me where she was being kept. Was it the word 'causeway' that she had not understood? Had she been taken to the mainland in a boat?

Then the woman with the mullet turned to face me, and I knew my chance to discover the truth was over. She looked at me and smiled, holding out her basket of fish to me in her meaty red arms. 'What do you think?' she said. 'Will it do for tonight's dinner?'

It was Antoine.

*　　　*　　　*

The journey home was difficult. I carried the fish on my back as I had the potatoes, the stench of it growing in the sun in spite of the quantities of seaweed intended to keep it cool. The load was heavy, too, fishy water dripping through the weave of the basket onto my shoulders and into my hair, soaking my habit with brine. Antoine was in cheery mood and talked incessantly of what she had done

162

at the market, of the gossip she had heard, the sights she had seen, the news she had exchanged. A peddler from the mainland had brought news of a group immolation in honour of Christina Mirabilis, a woman had been hanged in Angers for masquerading as a man, and there were rumours that a man from Le Devin had caught a fish with a head at both ends—a sure sign of disaster to come. She did not mention Fleur, and for that, if nothing else, I was grateful. However, I knew that she had seen her. I could only hope that she would hold her tongue.

We followed the coastal path back to the abbey. It was a longer route, but LeMerle insisted upon it—after all, he was riding, and the extra mile or so meant nothing to him. It had been one of my favourite walks in happier times, passing by the causeway and along the dunes, but laden as I was, lurching through the soft sand with the fish basket, I found little enjoyment in it. LeMerle, on the other hand, seemed to derive great pleasure from watching the sea, and asked a number of questions about the tides and the crossing times from the mainland, which I ignored but which Antoine seemed more than happy to answer.

It was mid-afternoon when we reached the abbey, by which time I was exhausted, half-blind from squinting at the sun and heartily sick of the smell of fish. With relief I delivered the stinking basket to the kitchens, then, my head still ringing from the heat and my throat parched, I made my way across the outer courtyard towards the well. I was about to throw down the pan for the water when I heard a cry from behind me; turning, I saw Alfonsine.

She seemed fully recovered from the previous day's attack; her eyes were bright and her cheeks were flushed with excitement as she ran towards me. 'For God's sake, don't touch that water!' she panted. 'Don't you know what's happened?'

I blinked at her. I had completely forgotten LeMerle's tablets of dye, and the instructions he had given me for their use. My daughter's face seemed stamped across everything I saw, like the after-image one gets from looking too long at the sun.

'The well, God save us, the well!' cried Alfonsine impatiently. 'Soeur Tomasine went down to fetch water for the cookpots and the *water had turned to blood*! Mère Isabelle has forbidden anyone to use it.'

'Blood?' I repeated.

'It's a sign,' said Alfonsine. 'It's a judgement on us for burying poor Mère Marie in the potato patch.'

In spite of my weariness, I tried not to smile. 'Perhaps it's a vein of iron oxide in the sand,' I suggested. 'Or a layer of red clay.'

Alfonsine shook her head contemptuously. 'I should have known you'd say something like that,' she said. 'Anyone would think you didn't *believe* in the devil, the way you always try to find reasons for everything.'

No, it was demonic influence, she was sure of it. Mère Isabelle was sure of it, and to such an extent that the new Abbess was to order Père Colombin to bless the well and the entire abbey grounds if necessary. Alfonsine felt unclean too, she said, and would not rest easy until Père Colombin had examined her minutely to ensure that no taint remained in her. Following this pronouncement, Soeur Marguerite had developed a tic in her left leg, which the new confessor also promised to investigate. If this continued, I told myself, the place would soon be closer to an asylum than an abbey.

'What about the water?' I asked. 'What are we going to do?'

Her face lit. 'A miracle! A carter arrived near midday with a delivery of twenty-five barrels of ale. A present, he said, for the new Abbess. While the new well is being dug, no one will go thirsty.'

That evening we dined on bread, ale and mullet. The food was good, but I had little appetite. Something was wrong—in the layout of the tables, the silence of the assembly, the look of the food on our plates—which made me uneasy. When we danced for King Henri at the Palais-Royal and were led through his Hall of Mirrors I had the same sense of things reversed, slyly reflecting an altered truth, though perhaps the difference was in my mind only.

Mère Isabelle said Grace, and after that there was no conversation—no sound at all, in fact, but for Rosamonde's toothless gums sucking noisily at her food, the nervous tapping of Marguerite's left foot and the occasional tick of cutlery. I motioned to Soeur Antoine that she should take from my plate what I did not eat, and she did so with gleeful deftness, her small weak eyes bright with greed. She glanced at me several times as she ate, and I wondered whether she took the extra food as payment for keeping silent about Fleur. I left her most of the ale too, eating nothing but the bread. The smell of fish, even cooked, made my stomach turn.

Perhaps it was that, or worry over Fleur, that made me slow this evening, for I had been at table for ten minutes or longer before I realized the source of my disquiet. Perette was not at her usual place amongst the novices. LeMerle too was absent, though I had not expected to see him. But I wondered where Perette could be. The last time I remembered seeing her was at the funeral yesterday, I realized; since then, nowhere—be it amongst the cloisters or in the performance of my duties in the bakehouse, or later at Sext in the chapel, or at Chapter, or now at dinner—nowhere had I glimpsed my friend.

Guilt at my disloyalty burned my cheeks. Since Fleur's disappearance I had paid little attention to Perette—in fact, I had barely noticed her. She might be ill—in a way I hoped she was. That, at least, would explain her absence. But my heart told me she was not. What plans he might have for her, I could not guess; she was too young for his taste, and too much of a child to be of any use to him, but all the same, I knew. Perette was with LeMerle.

CHAPTER NINE

♠

July 23rd, 1610

Well, it's a beginning. Act one, if you like, of a five-act tragi-comedy. The main roles are already established—noble hero, beautiful heroine, comic relief and a chorus of virgins in the style of the

166

ancients, all in their proper places—except for the villain, who doubtless will make his appearance in due course.

The blood in the well was a poetic touch. Now everyone's out looking for omens and prodigies—birds flying north, double-yolked eggs, strange smells, unexpected draughts—all are grist to the mill. The irony is that I barely have to do anything to help it along; the sisters, cloistered for so long with nothing to relieve the boredom, will see—with a little encouragement—precisely what I want them to see.

Soeur Antoine is proving invaluable to me. Easily bought—for an apple, a pasty or even a kind word—from her I hear the abbey's gossip, its little secrets. It was Antoine, acting on my instructions, who caught the six black cats and let them loose around the abbey, where they wrought havoc in the dairy and brought bad luck to no fewer than forty-two nuns who inadvertently crossed their path. She, too, it was who found the monstrous potato shaped like the Devil's horns, and served it to Mère Isabelle at dinner; and who frightened Soeur Marguerite into a spasm by hiding frogs in the meal bin. Her own little secret—that of her child and its untimely death—I know from Soeur Clémente, who scorns the fat nun and seeks to be my favourite. Of course she is not, but she too is easily flattered, and to tell the truth I prefer her to Alfonsine, breastless as the wooden panels in the chapel, or Marguerite, dry as kindling and riddled with tics and twitches.

Soeur Anne is less cooperative. A pity, that, for there are distinct advantages in having an accomplice who will not speak, and if I read the signs correctly, then the wild girl is brighter than she looks. As easy to train as a good dog, in any case, or even a monkey. And Juliette cares for her, of course—an added bonus in case my hold on the child should somehow slip.

Ah, Juliette. My Winged One remains unamused at my little jokes, though she is secretly exasperated at the commotion they have caused. That's like her; a lifetime of spells and cantrips has done little to alter her essential practicality. I knew she would not be fooled by tricks and vapours, but now she is as responsible for the confusion as I am myself, and will not betray me. I am tempted, sorely tempted to take her into my confidence. But I have taken enough risks already. Besides, she has a regrettable tendency towards loyalty, and if she knew what I was planning, she would probably try to stop me. No, my dear; the last thing I need with me on this trip is a conscience.

Today I rode out to Barbâtre and spent most of the afternoon at the causeway watching the tides. It is a pastime that never fails to calm my thoughts, as well as providing a welcome respite from the abbey and the increasing demands of the good sisters. How can they bear it? To be caged like chickens, pecking over and over the same little backyard? For myself, I have never been able to bear enclosed spaces. I need air, sky, roads rushing away in every direction. Besides, I have letters to send which are best delivered without my Isabelle's knowledge; a week's ride should do it, payment on reply. The tide takes eleven hours to turn around—a fact that few islanders have bothered to note, even though it is useful knowledge—leaving the causeway clear for just under three hours every time. Some have written that the moon draws the tide, as some heretics whisper the sun draws the earth; certainly, the tide comes higher at full moon, and shows less movement with the new. As a boy I was repeatedly punished for my interest in such matters—*idle curiosity*, they called it, presumably to distinguish it from the industrious apathy of my devout tutors— but they never quite cured me of my inquiring tendency. Call me perverse, but *God made it thus* never seemed a satisfactory enough explanation to me.

CHAPTER TEN
♥

July 24th, 1610

Today and yesterday we spent in a fury of activity. Services in chapel have been officially suspended as LeMerle deals with the special services, though we had Vigils and Lauds as usual. I have been set to digging the new well with Soeur Germaine, and as a result we are excused from all but the most necessary of duties. Perette is still absent, but no one talks of her disappearance and something prevents me from asking too many questions; of course, I dare not speak of it to LeMerle. As for the others, they talk of nothing now but devils and curses. Every book in the scriptorium has been consulted, every old wives' tale brought out. Piété remembers a man in her village, years ago, who was bewitched to death by bleeding. Marguerite speaks of the sea of blood in Revelation, and swears the

Apocalypse is at hand. Alfonsine recalls a beggar who may have muttered an incantation against her when she refused to give him money, and fears she may have been cursed. Tomasine suggests a charm of rowan berries and scarlet thread. It would have been funny if it had not also been a little frightening; although there had been no official acknowledgement of our island Saint by the new Abbess and her confessor, by noon there must have been fifty tapers burning under the statue of Marie-de-la-mer, plus a little pile of offerings at her feet—mostly flowers, herbs and pieces of fruit—and the air was blue with incense.

Mère Isabelle was furious. 'You have no business trying to take matters into your own hands!' she snapped when Bénédicte protested that we were only trying to help. 'It is completely irregular to ask for the intervention of the Saint—if indeed she *is* a saint—in a situation such as this. As for these'—she gestured at the offerings—'they are tantamount to paganism, and I shall have them removed.'

Meanwhile, LeMerle was everywhere. Throughout the morning I heard his voice ringing across the courtyard, calling, hectoring, encouraging . . . instructions to workmen here—he has three of them on the chapel roof to inspect the damage and to estimate the cost of repairs—there to a carter with a delivery of food, sacks of flour and grain, green and white cabbages from the market, a case of pullets for breeding. Soeur Marguerite is now in charge of supplies as well as the cooking, and gloats visibly over Antoine's envious expression. I noticed that she gloats over LeMerle, too, pausing frequently to ask his opinion on the best way to store grain, the drying of herbs, and whether the consumption of fish counts as fasting.

Then came the exorcism at the well, with prayers and incantations before the cover was fastened shut with wattle and mortar. Then to the chapel again, and talk of roofing and stacks and arch supports. Then back to the gatehouse and Isabelle, who follows him everywhere like a small, sullen wraith.

In the terrible heat, work on the well was slow and laborious, and by mid-morning my habit was caked with the yellow clay that forms a thick stratum below the surface sand. This clay prevents the water that filters from beneath from evaporating. Penetrate it and the water will ooze out, brackish at first but becoming clearer and sweeter as the well fills. It is sea water, I know, its salt content sifted out by the banks of fine sand upon which the island sits. We are halfway there now, and we save the clay carefully for Soeur Bénédicte, the abbey's potter, who will use it to make the bowls and cups we use in the refectory.

Midday came and went. As manual workers, Germaine and I lunched on meat and ale— although under Mère Isabelle's new order our main meal is now after Sext, with the midday meal reduced to a frugal handful of black bread and salt—but even so I was exhausted, my hands puckered from the brackish water, my eyes raw. My feet were peeling painfully, and stones dug into the arch of my instep as I trod blindly around the darkening hole. The water was deeper now, the yellow clay giving place to a black ooze in which fragments of mica sparkle. Soeur Germaine pulled the buckets of ooze into the sunlight where they would be used on the vegetable beds, for this evil-smelling stuff is barely salty at all and rich as alluvial soil.

As cool evening fell and the light began to fail, I climbed out of the well, helped by Soeur Germaine. She too was mud-spattered, but I was many times caked with filth, my hair stiff with it in spite of a rag tied around my head, my face smeared like a savage's.

'The water is good here,' I told her. 'I tasted it.'

Germaine nodded. Never a woman of many words, she has been almost entirely silent since the new abbess's arrival. It was strange, too, I noticed, to see her without Clémente at her side. Perhaps they had quarrelled, I told myself, for in the old days they had been inseparable. It is a bitter thought that barely three weeks after the death of Reverend Mother, I can already think of my previous life here as *the old days.*

'We'll have to shore up the sides,' I told Germaine. 'The clay seeps and taints the water. Wood, then stone and mortar, are the only things that can keep it out.'

She gave me a sour look that reminded me of Le Borgne. 'Quite the engineer, aren't you?' she said. 'Well, if you think you can gain favour this way, you're likely to be disappointed. You'd do better having a fit in church, or tattling on someone in Confession, or better still, reporting a monstrous potato, or thirteen magpies in a field.'

I looked at her in surprise.

'Well, that's what everyone wants, isn't it?' said Germaine. 'All this talk—this nonsense about devils and curses. That's what she wants to hear, and that's what they give her.'

'Give who?'

'The girl.' Germaine's words were eerily similar to those Antoine had spoken the day they took Fleur. 'That dreadful little girl.' She was silent for a moment, a strange smile on her thin lips. 'Happiness is such a frail thing, isn't it, Soeur Auguste? One day you have it, the next it's gone, and you don't even realize how.'

It was a long, strange speech for Germaine, and I did not know how to reply to it, or even whether I wanted to. She must have read my expression, because she laughed then, a sharp barking sound, turned on her heel and left me standing by the well in the gentle dusk, suddenly wishing I could call her back, but unable to think of anything to say.

Dinner was a solemn, silent business. Marguerite, who had taken Antoine's place in the kitchens, had none of her cooking skills, and the result was a meagre, oversalted soup, with watery ale and more of the hard black bread. Although I scarcely noticed the unappetizing fare, others were inclined to balk at the absence of meat on a weekday, though nothing was said openly. In the old days there would have been animated discussion of this at Chapter, but now, although the silence was laden with discontent, it remained unbroken. Soeur Antoine, sitting at my right, ate with thick, fierce bites, her black brows drawn together. She looked different now, her flabby moon-face pinched and sullen. Her work in the bakehouse was long and difficult; her hands were covered in burns from the stone ovens.

A row away, Soeur Rosamonde ate her soup in happy ignorance of the Abbess's disapproval. The old nun's distress at the changes in the abbey had been short-lived; she existed now in a state of placid bewilderment, going about her duties in a willing but haphazard fashion, called to services by a novice specially assigned the task of ensuring she did not stray too far. Rosamonde lived in a half-world between past and present, cheerfully confusing names, faces, times. Often she spoke of people long dead as if they were still alive, addressed sisters by names that were not their own, helped herself to others' clothes, went to collect supplies from a barn demolished in winter storms twenty years before. But she seemed well enough, and I have seen this kind of thing many times before in the very old.

Yet her behaviour irked the Abbess. She ate noisily at table, smacking her gums. Sometimes she forgot to observe silence or mistook the words of prayers. She dressed carelessly, often going to church without some necessary item of clothing until the novice was charged with her supervision.

The wimple was an especial burden to an old woman who had worn the *quichenotte* for sixty years and could not understand why it was suddenly to be forbidden. Even more irksome to the new Abbess was her refusal to acknowledge her authority, and her querulous calls for Mère Marie. True, Angélique Saint-Hervé Désirée Arnault had not had much exposure to senility. Her life—what there had been of it—was a nursery where mechanical toys replaced playmates and servants replaced family. For her there had been no clear window onto the world, her only view a procession of priests and doctors. The poor were kept safely out of sight. The old, the sick, the infirm were not a part of Mère Isabelle's Creation.

Soeur Tomasine said Grace. We ate in a silence

174

punctuated occasionally by slurping sounds from Rosamonde. Mère Isabelle looked up once, then her wrathful gaze returned to her plate. I could see her mouth tightened almost to invisibility as she ate in small, delicate jabs of her spoon.

An unusually loud smacking noise caused a ripple to move down the novices' bench, perilously close to laughter. The Abbess seemed about to say something, but her lips tightened once more and she was silent.

It was to be the last time Rosamonde took a meal with the rest of us.

*　　　*　　　*

I went to LeMerle's cottage again that night. I am not certain why I went except that I could not sleep and that my need drew me, like a barb through the heart. Need for what, I cannot say. I knocked, but there was no reply. Looking in through the window I saw a soft glow from a dying fire, and on the rug a shape—no, two shapes—illuminated in the firelight.

The man was LeMerle. I saw on his arm the black scarf that hid the old brand. The girl was young, slender as a boy, face averted, cropped hair the colour of raw silk beneath his hands, beneath his mouth.

Clémente.

I crept back to the dorter then, and silently I returned to my bed. Everyone sounded asleep. Even so a phantom mutter of laughter pursued me as I fled, burning with shame, to my place by the wall, past Clémente's cubicle . . . I froze in mid-step. Germaine was sitting bolt upright and

175

motionless in Clémente's bed. A stray strand of moonlight bisected her scarred face and I could see her eyes shining. She did not seem to see me, and I passed by without a word.

CHAPTER ELEVEN
♥

July 25th, 1610

Perette returned this morning as if nothing had happened. It was a disturbing fact of the new regimen that no one had mentioned her absence, not even in Chapter. If it had been any other than she, then perhaps someone would have spoken. But the wild girl was no true sister—or even novice—of Sainte Marie-de-la-mer. A strangeness clung to her, an aloofness which no one had yet managed to penetrate. Even I had been too absorbed in my own affairs to pay any real attention to the absence of my friend. It was as if Perette had never been there at all, her disappearance from collective memory as complete as her removal from every aspect of our daily life. This morning, however, she was back: demure as a marble saint, she took her place as usual without a glance at anyone.

But there was something about her manner that disturbed me. She was too quiet, her face expressionless as only Perette can be, her gold-ringed eyes as flat and bright as the gilding on our altarpiece. I wanted to speak to her, to find out where she had been for the past three days—but

176

Soeur Marguerite had already rung the bell for Vigils, and there was no time for questions, even if Perette had been inclined to reply.

LeMerle made no appearance until Prime. He never was an early riser, not even in the old days, preferring to roll out of bed at eight or nine, having read until midnight, squandering candles—wax ones, not tallow—while the rest of us had barely enough food to keep body and soul together. It was always his way, accepted by all as if it were his due, as if he were the master and we his servants. The worst thing was we *liked* it; served him willingly and for the most part without resentment; lied for him, stole for him, made excuses for his most outrageous behaviour. 'It's the way he is,' Le Borgne once told me, one day when my exasperation had been too much to contain. 'Some people have it, and some don't, that's all.'

'Have what?'

The dwarf gave his crooked smile. 'Grace, my dear, or what passes for it these days. That gilding that some of us receive at birth. That special gilding which sets his kind apart from mine.'

I didn't understand, and I said so.

'Oh yes you do,' said Le Borgne with unusual patience. 'You know he's worthless, you know he doesn't give a damn, and that he'll betray you some day or another. But you want to believe in him all the same. He's like those statues you see in churches, all gold and glitter on the outside, plaster on the inside. We know what they're made of really, but we pretend we don't, because it's better to believe in a false god than in no god at all.'

'And yet you follow him,' I said. 'Don't you?'

He looked at me with his one eye. 'I do,' he said,

'but then I'm a fool. Every circus has one.'

Well, LeMerle, I thought as all eyes turned hungrily to watch him make his entrance, you can certainly take your pick of fools this morning. Late nights and privations had taken no toll on him, I noticed; he looked rested and well in his ceremonial robes, his hair tied back neatly with a piece of ribbon. The embroidered scapular of his office had been flung over his black soutane and as always he wore the silver crucifix, his pale hands resting upon it. As if by chance, he had chosen to stand just beneath the single stained-glass window, through which reached the first rose-gold fingers of dawn. I guessed immediately that something was afoot.

With him was Alfonsine. Since her attack there had been a number of rumours, though most of us knew Alfonsine well enough to discount the wildest of these. Even so, her presence at LeMerle's side attracted no little attention, and she played it for all she was worth, affecting a haunted look and a faltering step, and coughing repeatedly into her fist. She behaved as if her fit of hysterics in the crypt had elevated rather than disgraced her, and her adoring eyes never left LeMerle.

Others were watching him too with varying expressions of hope, fear and admiration; I caught Antoine staring, and Clémente, and Marguerite, and Piété. Not all looks were adoring, however. Germaine's face was set in a look of dogged indifference, but I read a clearer message from her eyes. I knew that look, and LeMerle was a fool if he failed to recognize the threat. If Germaine had the chance, she would do him harm.

Then silence fell, and LeMerle began to speak.

'My children,' he said. 'It has been a testing time for us, these past few days. The contamination of our well by means unknown; the disruption to our services; the uncertainty of change.' A murmur of acquiescence passed through the crowd. Soeur Alfonsine seemed close to swooning. 'But the testing times are over,' said LeMerle, beginning to move from the pulpitum to the altar. 'We have survived them, and must be strengthened thereby. And as a token of our strength, our hope, our faith'—he paused, and I could sense the expectation in the air—'we shall now take Communion, a sacrament which has been neglected here for all too long. *Quam oblationem, tu Deus, in omnibus quaesumus, benedictam . . .*'

At this Soeur Piété, who was in charge of the sacristy, moved slowly to the tiny cabinet where our few treasures were kept and brought out the chalice and holy vessels for Communion. We seldom used these. I myself had taken the sacrament only once since my arrival, and our old Reverend Mother had been overawed by the finery of the treasures left by the black monks, ordering them to be kept safe and rarely allowing them to be seen at all. LeMerle broke that rule, as all others. There is an oven at the back of the sacristy for the baking of the holy wafers, but to my knowledge it had been twenty years since it was last used. Where he had got the wafers I can only guess; maybe he baked them himself, or maybe Mère Isabelle had one of the sisters make them. Bowing her head, Soeur Alfonsine carried the Host to LeMerle, as he poured the wine into a dull-silver chalice knuckled with polished gems.

Mère Isabelle was first at the altar, kneeling to

179

receive the sacrament. LeMerle put a hand on her forehead and took a wafer from the silver plate.

'*Hoc est enim corpus meum.*'

At those words I felt my hackles rise, and I forked the sign against malchance. Something was about to happen. I could feel it. It was in the air, like a promise of lightning.

'*Hic est enim calyx sanguinis mei . . .*'

Now for the chalice, huge in her small hands. Its rim was blackened, the uncut gems no brighter than pebbles. Suddenly I wanted to leap up and warn the child, to tell her not to drink, not to trust him, to refuse the false sacrament. But it was madness; I was already in disgrace, already under penance; I forked the sign again and could not watch as she parted her lips, drew the cup towards them and . . .

'*Amen.*'

The cup passed and moved on. Now Marguerite took Isabelle's place in front of the altar, her leg quivering uncontrollably beneath her habit. Then Clémente. Then Piété, Rosamonde and Antoine. Had I been wrong? Had my instincts deceived me?

'Soeur Anne.' Beside me, Perette flinched at the unfamiliar name, the unfriendly voice. The Abbess's tone was crisp, commanding. Any sweetness the Communion might have opened in her was sealed up like honey in a bee's cell. Perette took a step backwards, heedless of the nuns behind her. I heard someone grunt as her bare heel stamped down on an unsuspecting foot.

'Soeur Anne, you will come forward and take the sacrament, if you please,' said LeMerle.

Perette looked at me in appeal and shook her head.

'Perette, it's all right. Just go to the altar.' My whisper was hidden in the crowd. Still the wild girl held back, her gold-ringed eyes pleading. *'Go on!'* I hissed, pushing her forwards. 'Trust me.'

Perette knelt before him, conspicuous in her novice's habit, her nostrils flaring like a dog's. She whimpered a little as LeMerle placed the wafer on her tongue. Then he passed her the chalice. Her fingers closed around it and I saw her glance backwards at me as if for comfort. Then she drank.

For an instant I thought I had been mistaken. His *Amen* rang clear in the bright air. He reached out to help Perette to her feet. Then she coughed.

Suddenly I was reminded of the monk in the procession at Epinal. The crowd drew away with just the same low sigh of distress, the fallen monk rolling to the ground, the chalice falling from his grasp.

Perette coughed again, leaned forward, then suddenly, shockingly, vomited between her feet. There was a silence. The wild girl looked up, as if for reassurance, then a new paroxysm of vomiting struck her, and she tried too late to cover her mouth. An appalling blurt of red sprayed from between her lips, spattering her white skirt.

'Blood!' moaned Alfonsine.

Perette clapped her hands to her mouth. She looked terrified, ready to bolt. I tried to reach her, but Alfonsine got in my way, crying: 'She defiled the sacrament! The sacrament!' Then she too doubled up, coughing, and I was back in Epinal, watching as the crowd drew away from the stricken brother, hearing the human tide turn, crushing everything in its path. For a minute I could hardly breathe as the nuns in front of me backed me against the wall of the transept.

Then LeMerle stepped forwards, and the sisters wavered back into uneasy half-silence. Alfonsine was still coughing, hectic patches of red standing out on her thin cheeks. Then she too bent over and retched, and a terrible wad of blood spattered the marble between her feet.

That ended all hope of rational discourse. In vain I tried to remind the nuns that Soeur Alfonsine had coughed up blood before, that this was the nature of her illness—the crowd heaved back just as it had in Epinal, and the panic began.

'It's the blood plague!' cried Marguerite.

'It's a curse!' said Piété.

I struggled against it, but their excitement had reached me too and I was drowning in it. My mother's cantrip—*evil spirit, get thee hence*—calmed me a little, although I knew that it was a man, and not a spirit, who had set this in motion. All around me faces mooned, eyes rolled. Marguerite had bitten her tongue and there was blood on her lips. One of Clémente's flailing arms had caught Antoine in the face, and she was cursing, a hand clapped to her bloody nose. I'd seen a painting once, by a man named Bosch, in which the souls of the damned clawed and clutched at each other in just such an ecstasy of savagery and fear. It was called *Pandaemonium*.

But now LeMerle had raised his voice, and it rolled across the hall like the wrath of God. 'For God's sake, let us have respect for this place!' Silence returned, filled with eddies and small whimperings. 'If this is a sign, and the Unholy One has dared to come upon us'—the murmur came again, but he stilled it with a gesture—'I say if the

Evil One has dared assail us now in the very sanctity of our church, to desecrate God's very sacrament—then I am glad of it.' He paused. 'As you should *all* be glad of it! Because if a wolf threatens the farmer's herd, it's the farmer's duty to *flush that wolf out*! And if a cornered wolf tries to bite, then what does that farmer do?'

We watched him, eyes wide.

'Does that farmer turn and run?'

'*No.*' It was a thin cheer, like a splash of spray above the rolling wave.

'Does that farmer weep and tear his hair?'

'*No!*' It was stronger now, more than half the sisters joining in the cry.

'No! That farmer takes what weapons he can—staff, spear, pitchfork—and he takes his friends and neighbours and his brothers and his good strong sons, and he hunts down that wolf, he hunts it down and kills it, and if the Devil has made himself a home here, then I say it's time we hunted him down and sent him back to hell with his tail between his legs!'

They were with him now, whimpering their relief and admiration. The Blackbird basked for an instant in that applause—so long since he stood like this before a crowded house—then his eyes met mine, and he grinned. 'But look to yourselves,' he went on softly. 'If the Devil has breached your defences, ask yourselves how you let those defences drop. With what unshriven sins, what secret vices have you fed him, in what shameful practices has he taken his solace during the unclean years?'

Once more the crowd lifted its voice, touched now with a new note. *Tell us*, it murmured. *Guide us.*

'The Unholy One may be anywhere.' His voice dropped to a whisper. 'In the very sacraments of our church. In the air. In the stones. Look to yourselves!' Sixty-five pairs of eyes flicked furtively sideways. 'Look to each other.'

On that note LeMerle turned away from the pulpit, and I knew the performance was over. It was his style—opening, development, soliloquy, grand finale, and then, at last, to business. I'd heard that piece—or variations thereon—many times before.

His voice, so haunting and evocative before, changed register, became the brisk, impersonal tone of an officer giving orders. 'Leave here now, all of you. There can be no more services until this place has been cleansed. Soeur Anne'—he turned to Perette—'will remain with me. Soeur Alfonsine will return to the infirmary. The rest of you may return to your duties and your prayers. Praise be!'

I had to admire it a little. From the beginning he had held them in the palm of his hand, cleverly guiding them from one extreme of feeling to another—but for what? He had hinted at some grander motive than his usual robberies and deceits, although I could not begin to guess at what profit he might find in a little abbey hidden away off the coast. I shrugged to myself. What could I do? He had my daughter. Let me deal with that first and foremost. The rest was the Church's business.

CHAPTER TWELVE

♥

July 26th, 1610

We devoted that morning to duties, prayer and
speculation. We held public confession at Chapter,
during which it was revealed that five other nuns
had tasted the tainted blood in their mouths after
taking Communion. Mère Isabelle blames this
inflammation of the senses on strong meats and
excessive drink, and has decreed that nothing red—
no red meat, no tomatoes, red wine, apples or
berry fruits—should be used in the kitchen or
served at mealtimes, and that our food should
henceforth be only of the plainest kind. Now that
the new well is almost complete, the ale too has
been restricted, to the dismay of Soeur Marguerite,
who in spite of her ailments had become almost
exuberant under its nourishing influence. Soeur
Alfonsine is in the infirmary with Perette. Soeur
Virginie watches over them both, with orders to
report back anything unusual to Mère Isabelle. I
find it impossible to believe that any of my sisters
can truly suspect either of them of being possessed.
Rumours abound, however. More dragon's teeth of
LeMerle's sowing.

After dinner today we had half an hour to
ourselves before prayer, confession and evening
duties. I went to my herb garden—mine no
longer—and ran my fingers over the neat bushes of
rosemary and silver sage, releasing their dim
sweetness into the darkening air. Bees droned from

the purple spikes of the lavender and the small fragrant blooms of the thyme. A white butterfly paused for a moment on a patch of cornflowers. Fleur's absence was suddenly very immediate, very final, the memory of her orphan's face clear as the turn of an evil card. I felt the grief which I had kept at bay come flooding back. A few seconds stolen in a crowd, a glimpse. It wasn't enough. And I had paid for it dearly. Four days had passed. And still there was no sign from LeMerle, no hint of a second visit. A cold feeling entered me as I considered the thought that perhaps now that he had Clémente, there would be no more visits to Fleur. I was too old, too familiar for his tastes. LeMerle's palate was for something younger. I had been too cold, too sure, too wilful. I had lost my chance.

I knelt down on the path. The scents of lavender and rosemary were heady and nostalgic. Not for the first time, and with increasing urgency, I wondered what the Blackbird had planned. If only I knew his mind, then maybe I could gain some hold over him. Was there gold in the abbey, upon which he planned to lay his greedy hands? Had he somehow discovered the existence of a secret treasure, which he hoped I would uncover during my excavation of the well? We'd all heard stories, of course, of monks' treasures, buried under crypts, immured in ancient walls. But that's my romantic imagination again. Giordano deplored it, preferring the poetry of mathematics to that of high adventure. *You'll come to a bad end, girl,* he would say in his dry voice. *You've the soul of a buccaneer.* And then, with a twinkle in his eye as I seemed to approve of the comparison: *The soul of a pirate, and the mind of a jackass. Come now, back to this formula . . .*

I know what Giordano would have told me. There was no gold in the abbey walls, and anything buried in that shifting soil would long since have been lost for ever. Such things happened only in stories. And yet LeMerle was more like myself than my old tutor; more buccaneer than logician. I know what motivates him. Desire. Mischief. Applause. Sheer pleasure taken in wrongness, in biting his thumb at those who thwart him, in the tumbling of altars, defiling of graves. I know this because we are still alike, he and I, each a small window into the soul of the other. Many passions run hot and cold in his strange blood, and wealth is only one of the lesser of these. No, this is not a question of money.

Power, then? The idea of having so many women under his thumb, for his use and manipulation? That was more like the Blackbird I knew, and would tally with his secret trysts with Clémente. But LeMerle could have had his pick of beauties; had never lacked for success in that direction, either in the provinces, or in the Paris salons. He had never valued these things before, had never gone out of his way to pursue them. What then? I asked myself. What drives a man like that?

There came a sudden cry from behind the wall of the herb garden close by, and I leapt to my feet. *'Miséricorde!'* The voice was so shrill that for a second I did not recognize it. I ran to the garden wall and hoisted myself to look over.

The orchard and herb garden give directly onto the west side of the chapel so that the plants and

187

trees may be protected from the cold in winter. As I peered over the wall I could see the west entrance barely fifty feet away and poor old Rosamonde, her hands clasped to her face, wailing fit to split.

'*Aiii!*' she screeched. '*Men!*'

With an effort I pulled myself to the top of the wall and straddled it. There were six men at the west entrance. A contraption of ropes and pulleys had been left at the open door, and next to it a pile of logs as if in preparation to roll something heavy.

'It's all right, *ma soeur*,' I called encouragingly. 'They're only workmen. They've come to mend the roof.'

'What roof?' Confused, Rosamonde turned to look at me.

'It's all right,' I repeated, swinging my legs over onto her side. 'They're workmen. The roof's been leaking, and they're here to mend it.' I gave her a friendly nod and allowed myself to drop lightly into the long grass.

Rosamonde shook her head in bewilderment. Then: 'Who are you, young woman?'

'It's Soeur Auguste,' I told her. 'Remember me?'

'I don't have a sister,' said Rosamonde. 'Never did. Are you my daughter?' She peered short-sightedly at me. 'I know I should know you, my dear,' she told me. 'But I can't quite remember . . .'

I put my arm gently around her shoulders. I could see a small group of sisters watching from the chapel door. 'Never mind,' I said. 'Look, why don't we just go into the chapterhouse and—'

But as I turned her to face the chapel Rosamonde gave another shriek. 'Look!' she cried. 'Sainte Marie!'

Either old Rosamonde's eyes were not as feeble

188

as I had thought, or she had actually been in the chapel when the work commenced, for I had seen nothing amiss in the group of workmen at the west entrance. But as I watched now I saw that none of the equipment that had been left at the door was for roofing. Indeed, no scaffolding had been erected up the walls, not even a ladder. One man was positioning rollers. Two others levered the statue into position. Two more at the rear kept her steady whilst the foreman directed the operation. And thus, tethered like a great beast, inch by inch on her wooden rollers came Marie-de-la-mer.

A few nuns were already watching in silence. Aldegonde was amongst them, and Marguerite. Rosamonde looked at me in baffled distress. 'Why are they taking the Saint outside?' she demanded. '*Where* are they taking her?'

I shook my head. 'Perhaps they're going to transport her to somewhere more appropriate,' I said without conviction. What could be more appropriate than our own chapel, our own entrance, where she could be seen from every part of the building, touched by anyone entering?

Rosamonde was making her way as quickly as she could towards the group of workmen. 'You can't take her!' she shouted hoarsely. 'You can't steal her from us!'

I hurried after her. 'Be careful, *ma soeur,* you'll do yourself an injury.'

But Rosamonde was not listening. She hobbled to the doorway where the men were taking pains to avoid chipping the marble steps.

'What are you doing?' demanded Rosamonde.

'Careful, sister,' said one of the men. 'Don't get in the way!' He grinned, and I saw the crooked line

189

of his blackened teeth.

'But it's the Saint! The *Saint!*' Rosamonde's eyes were round with outrage.

In a way I understood her. The big saint—if saint she was—had been a part of the abbey for years. Her stony face had watched us live and die. Countless prayers had been uttered beneath her mute, impassive gaze. Her round belly, her massive shoulders, the black bulk of her tender, indifferent presence had been a comfort, a touchstone to us across changes and seasons. To remove her now, in this time of crisis, was to make orphans of us at a time when we needed her most.

'Who ordered this?' I said.

'The new confessor, sister.' The fellow barely glanced at me. 'Mind yourself, she's coming down!'

I thrust Rosamonde away from the steps just as the statue, supported on either side by the workmen and from beneath by the rollers, came crashing down the steps onto the path. Dust puffed up from the cracked earth. The man with bad teeth steadied the Saint, while his assistant, a young man with red hair and a cheery smile, manoeuvred a cart into position on which to load her.

'Why?' I insisted. 'Why remove it at all?'

The red-haired man shrugged. 'It's just orders,' he said. 'Maybe you're getting a new one. This one looks old as God.'

'And where will you put it?'

'Dump it in the sea,' said the red-haired man. 'Orders.'

Rosamonde clutched at me. 'They can't do that!' she said. 'Reverend Mother will never let them do it! Where is she? Reverend Mother!'

'*Ma fille,* I'm here.' The voice was small and flat,

190

almost colourless like its owner, and yet Rosamonde stopped struggling and stared, her poor baffled face tugging between hope and dread.

Mère Isabelle was standing at the church door, hands folded. 'It's time we were rid of this blasphemy,' she said. 'It has been here too long already, and the islanders are a superstitious folk. They call it the Mermaid. They pray to it. It has a *tail*, for God's sake!'

In spite of myself I spoke out. 'But *ma mère . . .*'

'This object is not the Holy Mother,' said Isabelle. 'And there is no such saint as Marie-de-la-mer. There never was.' Her nasal voice rose a little. 'How can you bear it here? This thing at our chapel! Pilgrims coming to touch it! Women— *pregnant* women—scraping dust from it to brew their charms!'

I began to understand. Not the Saint herself, but the use to which she had been put; the touch of fertility in the barren house of God.

Isabelle took breath. Now she had begun to speak it seemed she could not stop herself. 'I knew it the moment I set foot here. The unconsecrated burials. The secret excesses. The curse of blood.' It was almost hysteria, but she was cold for all that. Angélique Saint-Hervé Désirée Arnault had her own formula and would stick to it no matter what.

'And now,' she said. 'It dares to attack me. Me! Taunts me with blood! My confessor locates the source and purifies it. But the evil remains. The evil remains.'

She stayed for a minute in silence, contemplating the evil. Then, with a crisp *Praise be!*, she turned and was gone.

191

The bell for Vespers went soon afterwards, and there was little time for discussion. Not that I would have dared voice my doubts in any case, for the fear of losing contact with Fleur kept me from speaking my mind. Throughout Nones I found my mind straying to Mère Isabelle's words on the chapel steps, words of which she herself seemed barely conscious.

The curse of blood. The evil remains.

The new well is close to complete now, its water as sweet and clear as she could have wished. LeMerle has exorcized the chapel itself, the font, the sacristy and all the holy vessels, declaring them free from taint. He has intimated the same of Perette and Alfonsine, too, to my relief, although there are still rumours. Alfonsine seems quite disappointed that she is to be given this clean bill of spiritual health, and her visible chagrin causes Marguerite to speak slightingly of actresses and attention-seekers.

And yet *the evil remains.*

I tried to keep my eyes from wandering, but time and again found myself staring at the giant emptiness that had once held Marie-de-la-mer. A small sacrifice, I told myself, compared with the return of my daughter, for what was a statue to a living child, a frightened child?

LeMerle was behind it, of course. What he wanted with the statue I could not guess, but its removal—that of the one symbol of our unity and our faith—had brought us one step closer to surrender. He must become our symbol now, I realized; he was to be our only salvation. During the service he spoke of female martyrs, of Saint Perpetua and Saint Catherine and Christina Mirabilis, of the mystery of death and the purity of fire, and he held us in his palm.

CHAPTER THIRTEEN

♠

Abbaye de Sainte-Marie la Mère,
Ile des Noirs Moustiers,
July 26th, 1610

Monseigneur,
It is with the Greatest Pleasure that I am able to inform Monseigneur that Everything He has so wisely foreseen is proceeding according to Plan. My Charge shows the most Commendable Zeal in all the Reforms she has instigated, and the Abbey is almost Restored to Former Glory. The Church Roof still requires some Labour, and I regret to say that much of the South Transept has been grievously Damaged by Weathering. However, we entertain Great Hopes of seeing the Whole Complete by the Beginning of Winter.

The Original Name of our Abbey, as Monseigneur will have Noticed, has also been Restored and all Signs and Intimations of the Vernacular Name erased in favour of the Above. I add my most earnest Entreaties to those of Your Niece, Monseigneur, that if Your busy Schedule enables You to Grace us with a Visit in the Coming Months, we should be most Honoured and Gratified to receive Your August Presence.

I remain your most obedient servant,

Blah, blah, blah.

I have to admit I've a neat turn of phrase. *Your August Presence*. I like that. I'll have it sent in the morning by special envoy. Or maybe I could ride out to Pornic myself and send it from there— anything to get out of the stink of this place for a few hours. How Juliette can bear it, I can't imagine. I only bear it because I have to; and because I know I won't be here for long. These cloistered ones, these toadstools, have a very special rankness, and the scent of their hypocrisy turns my stomach. Imprisoned here I can hardly breathe, hardly sleep; I must ask Juliette to make me a soothing draught.

Sweet Juliette. The fair girl—what's her name? Clémente?—is well enough for my needs, and touchingly eager to please too, but she's no worthy quarry. For a start, her eyes are too large. Their colour, that of a flawless summer sky, lacks that discordant note of slate and embers. Her hair, too, fair as foam, is hopelessly wrong. Her skin too white, her legs too smooth, her face unmarred by sun and grime. Call me ungrateful if you like. A honey-fall like that, and I must hanker after that stiff-necked maypole with her flinty eyes. Perhaps it's her hatred of me that gives it spice.

There's no heat in Clémente. Her pallor freezes my bones. She whispers constantly in my ears tales of romance, dreams of Belle Yolande, Tristan and Iseult, Abelard and Héloïse . . . In any case, there's no danger of her talking. The little fool's in love. I subject her to more and more prolonged miseries, but she seems to revel in each indignity. For myself,

194

I enhance my pleasure how I can with dreams of red-haired harpies.

There's no escaping her. The other night she came to me—in a vision, or so I thought. I saw her for an instant only, her face pressed to the pane of my window, her eyes reflecting the soft glow of the firelight so that for a moment she looked almost tender.

Clémente moved beneath me with the little bleating cries that masquerade as passion with her. Her eyes were closed and I saw her hair and flanks illuminated in fire. I felt a hot sudden surge of joy in my loins, as if the woman at the window and the one in my arms were unexpectedly become one and the same, then the face at the window vanished and I was left with nothing more than Clémente gasping like a landed fish in my hands. My pleasure—no great delight in any case—was marred by the growing certainty that Juliette's face at the window had been no phantasm. She had seen us together. The look on her face—shock, disgust and something that might have been chagrin or even rage—haunted me. For a second I could almost have run after her, ruinous though that would have been to all my careful plans. Wild thoughts fired me. I stood up and went naked to the window in spite of Clémente's protests. Was that a pale figure half hidden in the shadows of the gatehouse? I could not be sure.

'Colombin, please.' I looked over my shoulder to see Clémente crouching by the hearth, her hair still deceptively brazen in the light of the dying embers. A sudden wave of fury washed over me and in two strides I was upon her.

'I gave you no leave to use my name.' I yanked

her to her feet by a fistful of hair and she gave a stifled scream. I slapped her then, twice, not as hard as I should have liked, but enough to bring brief roses to her cheeks. 'Who do you think you are, some Paris courtesan in her salon? Who do you think *I* am?'

She was weeping now, in braying sobs. For some reason this enraged me still more and I dragged her to the couch, still squealing.

I didn't really hurt her. A red handprint or two on a white shoulder, a white thigh. Juliette would have killed me for far less. But Clémente watched me from her couch, her eyes reproachful but nevertheless bright with a strange satisfaction, as if this were how she expected things to be.

'Forgive me, *mon père*,' she breathed. One childish hand cupped a breast scarce bigger than a green apricot, making the nipple pout with imagined seductiveness. My stomach revolted at the thought of touching her again. But I had perhaps given too much away. I took a step towards her and brushed her forehead with languid fingers.

'Very well,' I said. 'I'll overlook it this time.'

CHAPTER FOURTEEN

♥

July 27th, 1610

Sainte Marie-de-la-mer was taken in the stonebreakers' wagon to the easternmost point of the island, where the coast is ragged from the eroding tides. There her remains were given to the

196

sea. I was not present to see it—only LeMerle and the Abbess were there—but we were told later that a great wind blew up from the sea where the effigy fell, that the water boiled and that black clouds obscured the sun so that day became night. Since LeMerle told us this, no one disputed it aloud, although I met Germaine's cynical gaze during his performance.

Of course, she has lost someone to him too. Her face seems narrower these days, the scars very prominent on her pale skin. She sleeps as little as I do; in the dorter I hear her pretending sleep, but her breathing is too shallow, her lack of movement too disciplined to be that of rest.

Last night before Vigils I heard her quarrelling with Clémente in a low, harsh voice, though I could not make out the words she spoke. There was silence from Clémente—in the darkness I guessed she had turned her back—and during the long hours between Matins and Lauds I heard Germaine weeping with long, harsh sobs, but dared not approach her.

As for LeMerle . . . He had not sought me out since my visit to the market, and I had become increasingly convinced that Clémente—who, after all, shared his bed—had also stolen his heart. Not that *that* troubled me, you understand. I'm long past caring where he lays his head at night. But Clémente is spiteful; and she has no love for Fleur or for me. I hated to think of the power she might wield over all of us, if LeMerle had succumbed to her charms.

I was working in the laundry house when at last he came looking for me. I knew he was there; knew the sound of his feet against the flagstones, and knew from the clink of his spur against the step that he was dressed for riding. I did not turn round at once, but plunged an armful of linens into one of the vats of boiling water, face averted, not daring to speak. My cheeks were burning, but that might have been the steam, for the laundry house was hot and the air was filled with clouds. He stood watching me for some minutes without a word, but I would not return his gaze, nor speak until he spoke first. At last, he did, in the tone and style he knew had always infuriated me.

'Exquisite harpy,' he said. 'I trust I am not interrupting your ablutions. Cleanliness, if not godliness, dearest, must be the prerequisite of your calling.'

I used the baton to pound the laundry. 'I'm afraid I've no time for games today. I have work to do.'

'Really? What a pity. And on market day, too.'

I stopped.

'Well, after all, perhaps I have no reason to go to market,' said LeMerle. 'Last time the stench of fish and the common folk was almost unendurable.'

I looked at him then, not caring that he saw the pain in my eyes. 'What do you want with me, Guy?'

'Nothing, my Ailée, but your own sweet company. What else should I desire?'

'I don't know. I daresay Clémente could tell me.' It was out before I could stop it. I saw him flinch, and then he smiled.

'Clémente? Let me see now . . .'

'You know her, LeMerle. She's the girl who comes to your cottage at night, in secret. I should have known you wouldn't be here long without finding yourself a comfortable bedfellow.'

198

He shrugged, unabashed. 'Light entertainment, that's all. You wouldn't believe how tedious I find the clerical life—and do you know, Juliette, she's begun to bore me already?'

Yes, that was like him. I hid an unwilling smile. But it's hard to keep a secret in a place like this, and even Mère Isabelle was not so besotted that she would overlook a charge of lechery. 'They'll find out, you know. You can't trust Clémente to keep a secret. Someone will talk.'

'Not you,' he said.

His eyes had remained on me, and I felt uncomfortable beneath their scrutiny. I poured more water into the vat, my eyes stinging at the rise of steam over the lye soap. I would have poured more—it was needed for the starch rinse—but LeMerle took the water jug from me and set it down very softly on the floor.

'Leave me alone.' I made my voice sharp to stop it from trembling. 'The laundry won't wash itself, you know.'

'Then let someone else finish it. I want to talk to you.'

I turned and faced him. 'What about?' I said. 'What can you possibly want from me that you haven't already taken?'

LeMerle looked hurt. 'Must it always be a question of what *I* want?'

I laughed. 'It always was.'

He was displeased at that, as I knew he would be. His mouth thinned, and a gleam came into his eyes; then he sighed and shook his head. 'Oh, Juliette,' he said. 'Why so unfriendly? If only you knew how hard it's been these past few months. All alone, no one to confide in—'

199

'Tell that to Clémente,' I said tartly.

'I'd rather tell you.'

'You want to tell me something?' I reached for the baton to pound the clothes. 'Then tell me where you're hiding Fleur.'

He gave a soft laugh. 'Not that, sweetheart. I'm sorry.'

'You will be,' I told him.

'I mean it, Juliette.' I had removed my wimple to do the laundry, and he brushed the nape of my neck with his fingertips. 'I wish I could trust you. There's nothing I'd like better than to see you and Fleur reunited. As soon as I've finished my business here . . .'

'Finished? When?'

'Soon, I hope. Enclosed spaces do nothing for my constitution.'

I poured another jug of hot water into the vat, sending up a great billow of stinging steam. Then I pounded the laundry some more, and wondered what his game was. 'It must be important to you,' I said at last. 'This business.'

'Must it?' There was a smile in his voice.

'Well, I don't imagine you're here just to play practical jokes on a few nuns.'

'You may be right,' said LeMerle.

I took the wooden tongs, fished the linens out of the vat and dumped them into the starch bath. 'Well?' I turned towards him again, tongs in hand. 'Why are you here? Why are you doing this?'

He took a step towards me, and to my surprise, on my hot forehead he placed the lightest of kisses. 'Your daughter's at the market,' he said gently. 'Don't you want to see her?'

'No games.' My hand was shaking as I put down

the tongs.

'No games, my Ailée. I promise.'

*   *   *

Fleur was waiting for us by the side of the jetty. Although it was market day, there was no sign today of the fish cart or the drab-faced woman. This time there was a man with her, a white-haired man who looked like a farmer in his flat hat and rough-woven jacket, and a couple of children, both boys, who sat close by. I wondered what had happened to the fishwife; whether Fleur had been staying with her at all, or whether this had been a ruse to put me off the scent. Was this white-haired man my daughter's keeper? He said nothing to me as I walked up to them and took Fleur in my arms. His milky-blue eyes were flat and incurious; from time to time he chewed on a piece of liquorice and his few remaining teeth were stained brown with its juice. Other than that, he gave no sign of movement; for all I knew he might have been a deaf-mute.

As I had feared, LeMerle did not leave me alone with my daughter, but sat, face averted, on the edge of the sea wall a few yards away. Fleur seemed a little uneasy at his presence, but I saw that she looked less pale, a clean red pinafore over a grey dress and wooden sabots on her feet. It was a bittersweet satisfaction; she has been gone for little more than a week and already she is beginning to adapt, the orphan look fading into something infinitely more frightening. Even in this short time she seems altered, grown; at this rate in a month she will look like someone else's child altogether, a stranger's child with only a passing resemblance to my daughter.

I did not dare ask outright where she was being kept. Instead, I held her in my arms and put my face into her hair. She smelt vaguely of hay, which made me wonder whether she had been kept on a farm, but then she smelt of bread, too, so it might have been a bakery. I ventured a glance at LeMerle, who was watching the tide, apparently lost in thought. 'Aren't you going to introduce me to Monsieur?' I said at last with a nod to the white-haired man.

The old man seemed not to hear. Neither did LeMerle.

'I'd like to thank him, anyway,' I went on. 'If he's the one taking care of you.'

From his observation point, LeMerle shook his head without bothering to look round.

'Mmm-mm. Suppose. Am I coming home today?'

'Not today, sweetheart. But soon. I promise.' I forked the sign against malchance.

'Good.' Fleur did it too, with plump baby fingers. 'Janick taught me how to spit. D'you want to see how I do it?'

'Not today, thank you. Who's Janick?'

'A boy I know. He's nice. He's got rabbits. Did you bring Mouche?'

I shook my head. 'Look at the pretty boat, Fleur. Can you see boats from where you're staying?'

A nod from Fleur—and a glance from LeMerle from his place on the wall.

'Would you *like* to go on a boat, Fleur?'

She shook her head furiously, bouncing her flossy curls.

202

Urgently now, seeing my chance: 'Did you come here on a boat today? Fleur? Did you take the causeway?'

'Stop that, Juliette,' said LeMerle warningly. 'Or I'll see to it that she doesn't come back.'

Fleur glared. 'I *want* to come back,' she said. 'I want to come back to the abbey and the kitty and the hens.'

'You will.' I hugged her, and for a second I was close to tears. 'I promise, Fleurette, you will.'

*   *   *

LeMerle was unexpectedly gentle with me on the return journey. I sat behind him on the horse and for a time he spoke in reminiscent tone of the old days, of L'Ailée and the *Ballet des Gueux*, of Paris, the Palais-Royal, the *Grand Carnaval*, the *Théâtre des Cieux*, of triumphs and trials past. I said little, but he seemed not to care. The merry ghosts of past times drifted by us, brought to life by his voice. Once or twice I found myself close to laughter, the unfamiliar smile sitting strangely on my lips. If it had not been for Fleur I would have laughed aloud. And yet this is my enemy. He is like the piper in the German tale who rid the town of rats, and when the townsfolk did not pay him his fee, led their children dancing to hell's mouth and piped them in, the earth covering their screams as they fell. Such a dance he must have led them, though, and with such a merry tune . . .

CHAPTER FIFTEEN

♥

July 27th, 1610

We returned to find the abbey in turmoil. Mère Isabelle was waiting at the gatehouse, looking ill and impatient. There had been an incident, she said.

LeMerle looked concerned. 'What kind of incident?'

'A visitation.' She swallowed painfully. 'A damnable visitation! Soeur Marguerite was in the chapel, praying. For the soul of my p-predecessor. For the soul of M-Mère Marie!'

LeMerle watched her in silence as she stammered out her tale. She spoke in short, bitten-off sentences with much repetition, as if trying to make the business clear in her mind.

Marguerite, still greatly troubled by the events of the morning, had gone to the chapel alone to pray. She went to the closed gate of the crypt and knelt on the little *prie-dieu* which had been placed there. Then she shut her eyes. A few moments later she was roused by a metallic sound. Opening her eyes she saw at the mouth of the crypt a figure in a Bernardine nun's brown habit with its linen tucker, the face hidden inside a starched white *quichenotte*.

Standing up in alarm, Marguerite called out, demanding that the strange nun name herself. But her legs were weak with terror and she sank to the ground.

'Why this dread?' asked LeMerle. 'It might have

been any of our older sisters. Soeur Rosamonde, perhaps, or Soeur Marie-Madeleine. All have occasionally worn the *quichenotte*, especially in this hot weather.'

Mère Isabelle turned on him. 'No one wears it now! No one!'

Besides, there was more. The lappets of the strange nun's white bonnet, the tucker, even the hands of the apparition were stained with red. Worse still—here Mère Isabelle's voice dropped to a whisper—the cross stitched onto the breast of every Bernardine nun had been torn off, the stitches still faintly visible against the bloody cambric.

'It was Mère Marie,' said Isabelle flatly. 'Mère Marie, back from the dead.'

I had to intervene. 'That isn't possible,' I said crisply. 'You know what Marguerite is like. She's always seeing things. Last year she thought she saw demons coming out of the bakehouse chimney, but it was only a nest of jackdaws under the eaves. People don't come back from the dead.'

Isabelle cut me short. 'Oh, but they do.' The little voice was hard. 'My uncle, the Bishop, dealt with a similar case in Aquitaine years ago.'

'What case?' Impossible for me to keep the scorn from my voice. She looked at me, no doubt concocting some penance to inflict upon me at a later time.

'A case of witchcraft,' she said.

I stared at her. 'I don't understand,' I said at last. 'Mère Marie was the kindest, most gentle woman alive. How could you possibly believe—'

'The Devil may take a pleasing countenance if he chooses.' Her tone was cold and final. 'The signs—the curse of blood, my dreams, and now this damnable visitation . . . How can anyone doubt it? What other explanation can there be?'

I had to stop this. 'A person given to fanciful imaginings may see things which are not,' I told her. 'If anyone else had seen this—apparition . . .'

'But they did.' The small voice was triumphant. 'We all did. All of us.'

Her pronouncement was not strictly true. When Marguerite screamed, maybe half a dozen nuns were within earshot, Mère Isabelle among them. Running from the dazzling sunshine into the dark chapel, their vision unused to the gloom, what they saw was little enough. A shape, a white bonnet . . . The vision turned at their approach and seemed to flee into the crypt. By then more nuns had arrived. Later each claimed to have seen the same apparition—even the latecomers who could only have witnessed the ensuing disturbance. I even found so-called witnesses to the incident who had been working in the fields all afternoon. But Mère Isabelle, armed with crucifix and lantern, flanked by Marguerite and Tomasine, entered the crypt to search for evidence of human interference, having first unlocked the gate through which no mortal could have passed. Their search was in vain. No sign of the ghostly nun was found. But by Mère Marie's tomb, its seal unbroken and the mortar still fresh, they found traces of the same sweet-smelling red ichor that had tainted the abbey water, a dribble of the stuff having seemingly leaked from the stone cell containing Mère Marie's coffin . . .

LeMerle looked concerned and insisted upon going to inspect the scene of the incident at once. I returned to my duties. It was clear Mère Isabelle was annoyed that I had accompanied LeMerle to Barbâtre—though she grudgingly accepted his assurance that I was needed to carry food and medicines to a poor family there—and I was put to work in the kitchens, peeling vegetables for the evening meal. There I had plenty of time to think over what had happened.

It seems too much of a coincidence. Last week I went to Barbâtre and Perette vanished for three days. This week, Marguerite saw visions, once more in my absence. Both times I was with LeMerle. Had he engineered this purposely to have me out of the way? Certainly I should have tried to intervene in both cases if I had been there. But what reason can he have for such action? A practical joke, he told me when he gave me the tablets of dye for the well. And a fake vision of a hooded nun might as easily be another. I can envisage Clémente accepting to take part. But what reason can he have for such a cruel succession of practical jokes? Surely the last thing he wants is to attract notice to the abbey or to himself. And yet LeMerle is subtle, cunning. If he planned it so, it must have been for a reason. What that reason may be eludes me. If only I could somehow find out who played the ghost and how she managed to escape seemingly into thin air . . . But the frenzy of interest this prank has already ignited must be enough to still the most voluble of tongues. Did he plan that too? And how many other trifling favours has he granted, payment to be deferred? And who are his acolytes here? Alfonsine? Clémente? Antoine? Myself?

CHAPTER SIXTEEN

♥

July 29th, 1610

A dissolution is taking place amongst us, the sisterhood broken into pieces as far flung as the figure of our patron. Clémente seems distant, banished to dig latrine trenches for a week as penance for idleness. I find myself wondering whether it is the stench of her work that has given LeMerle a distaste for her, or whether this cruel caprice is merely his nature. A blackbird may decimate the fruit on a tree, pecking hither and thither at random, spoiling but never finishing. Does she love him? Her dreamy abstraction, the look in her eyes when he does not notice her, suggests she does. The more fool she. Germaine's company she will no longer tolerate, though the other woman has volunteered to help her with the latrines in a desperate measure to be close to her.

First thing this morning I eventually spoke to Perette, but she was restless and abstracted, and I could make no sense of her. Perhaps she is angry; with Perette it is always so difficult to tell. I would like to tell her about LeMerle and Fleur and the contaminated well, but my silence keeps Fleur safe. I must believe that, or lose my mind. And so I deceive my friend, and try not to mind if she holds me in contempt. I miss her, but I miss Fleur so much more. Perhaps there can be room only for one in my hard heart.

Rosamonde is no longer with us. Two days ago

she was moved to the infirmary, where the sick and dying are kept. Soeur Virginie, the young novice entrusted with her care, has taken vows at last and has taken over the duty of hospitaller. A plain girl, as I recall from our Latin classes, with little spirit and less imagination, her angular features even now beginning to take on the coarse and ungrateful look of so many of the island women. Mère Isabelle has, I think, warned her against me. I can tell from her sharp looks and evasive replies. She is barely seventeen. Rosamonde is a foreign country to her. Her youth calls to the new Abbess, whom she copies slavishly.

I saw Rosamonde yesterday over the wall of the infirmary garden. Seated on a small bench, huddled into herself as if by doing so she could somehow present the world with a smaller target for its cruelties, she looked more bewildered than ever. She looked up at me, but without recognition. Robbed of her routine, the thin thread that bound her to reality, she drifts in aimless anxiety, her only contact with the rest of us the sister who brings her meals and the bland-faced, unsmiling child appointed her keeper.

I was enraged enough at the pitiful sight to bring up Rosamonde's case at Chapter this morning. LeMerle is not normally present at Chapter, and I hoped to be able to sway the Abbess out of his presence.

'Soeur Rosamonde is not ill, *ma mère*,' I explained in a humble voice. 'It is not kind to keep her from what small pleasures she can still enjoy. Her duties, her friends . . .'

The Abbess looked at me from the distant continent of her twelve years. 'Soeur Rosamonde is seventy-two,' she said. Sure enough, that must have seemed an eternity to her. 'She barely recalls what day it is. She recognizes no one.' Ay, I thought. That was more like it. The old woman had not recognized *her*. 'And she is feeble,' continued Isabelle. 'Even the simplest duties are too much for her now. Surely it's kinder to let her rest than to set her to work in her condition? Surely, Soeur Auguste,' she said, her eyes glinting slyly, '*you* do not begrudge her this well-earned respite?'

'I grudge her nothing,' I said, stung. 'But to be shut up in the infirmary, just because she's old and sometimes slops at her food—'

I had said too much. The Abbess put up her chin. '*Shut up?*' she echoed. 'Are you implying that our poor Soeur Rosamonde is a prisoner?'

'Of course not.'

'Well then . . .' She let her voice trail for a moment. 'Anyone who wishes to visit our ailing sister may do so, of course, provided Soeur Virginie feels she is strong enough to receive visitors. Her absence from the dinner table merely means that she can be allowed a more nutritious diet and more regular meals than the rest of us, at times more agreeable to her age and condition.' She gave me a sly look. 'Soeur Auguste, you would not deny our old friend her few privileges? If you live to be her age, I'm sure you'll be glad of them too.'

Clever, the little minx. LeMerle was teaching her well. Anything I said now would seem like envy. I smiled, conceding a point, even though my heart seethed. 'I'm sure we all will, *ma mère*,' I said, and was pleased to see her lips tighten.

Well, that was the end of my attempt at rescue.

As it was, I had almost overstepped the mark; Mère Isabelle looked at me askance throughout the rest of Chapter and I narrowly escaped another penance. Instead I accepted a turn of duty in the bakehouse—a hot, filthy, disagreeable task in this sultry weather—and she seemed satisfied. For the present, anyway.

*　　*　　*

The bakehouse is a round, squat building on the far side of the cloister. Its windows are glassless slits, most of the light coming from the huge ovens in the centre of the single room. We bake in clay ovens as the black monks did, on flat stones heated red by the heaped faggots beneath. The smoke from the ovens escapes through a chimney so wide that the sky is visible through its mouth, and when it rains the droplets of water fall onto the domed ovens and turn to hissing steam. Two young novices were making dough as I arrived, one picking out the weevils from a stone jar of flour, the other mixing yeast in a basin, preparing to make the mixture. The ovens were stoked and ready, and the heat was like a shimmering wall. Behind the wall was Soeur Antoine, sleeves rolled up over her thick red forearms, hair tied into a rag that she had rolled about her head.

'*Ma soeur.*' Antoine looked different somehow, her usually kind, vacuous look replaced by something harder and more purposeful. She looked almost dangerous in the red light, the muscles of her wide shoulders rolling beneath her fat as she kneaded the dough.

I set to work, kneading the bread in the huge

211

pans and placing the loaves on the oven shelves to bake. It is a tricky business; the stones need to be heated perfectly even, for too high a heat will scorch the dough whilst leaving the inside raw, and too low a heat will bake flat, sad loaves as dense as stones. We worked in silence for a time. The wood in the oven crackled and snickered; someone had stoked it with green wood and the smoke was acrid and foul. Twice I burned my hands on the heated bakestones and cursed under my breath. Antoine pretended not to notice, but I'm sure she was smiling.

We finished the first batch of loaves and began the second. An abbey needs at least three batches of baking a day, each batch making twenty-five white or thirty black loaves. Plus the hard biscuit for winter when fuel is less abundant, and cakes for storing and special occasions. The smell from the loaves was good and rich in spite of the smoke that made my eyes sting, and I felt my stomach growl. I realized that since Fleur's disappearance I had hardly eaten. Sweat trickled through my hair, soaking the rags that bound it. My face was bearded with sweat. My vision doubled momentarily; I put out my hand to steady myself and touched the hot bread-pan instead. The metal was cooling but still hot enough to sear the tender webbing between my finger and thumb, and I gave a sharp cry of pain. Antoine looked at me again. This time there could be no doubt about it; she was smiling.

'It's hard at first.' She spoke softly enough for me to hear her, no more. The young novices were sitting near the open door, too far to catch her words. 'But you get used to it eventually.' Her mouth was very red, too ripe for a nun's, and her eyes reflected the fire. 'You get used to anything eventually.'

I shook my burned hand to cool it and said nothing.

'It would be a pity if someone found out about you,' Antoine went on. 'You'd probably be here for good then. Like me.'

'Found out about what?'

Antoine's lips curled wolfishly and I wondered how I could ever have thought her stupid. There was mean intelligence behind the small, bright eyes, and in that moment I almost feared her. 'Your secret visits to Fleur, of course. Or did you think I hadn't noticed?' Now there was bitterness in her voice too. 'No one expects fat Soeur Antoine to notice anything. Fat Soeur Antoine thinks of nothing but her belly. I had a child once, but I wasn't allowed to keep it,' she said. 'Why should you keep yours? What makes you any different to the rest of us?' She lowered her voice, the little red light still dancing in her eyes from the oven. 'If Mère Isabelle finds out, that will be the end of it, whatever Père Saint-Amand says. You'll never see Fleur again.'

I looked at her. She seemed a thousand leagues away from the fat soft woman of last month who wept when I pinched her arm. It was as if some of the Saint's black stone had entered her. 'Don't tell, Antoine,' I whispered. 'I'll give you—'

'Syrups? Sweetmeats?' Her voice was harsh and the young novices looked up curiously to see what was happening. Antoine snapped a sharp command at them and they dropped their heads at once. 'You owe me, Auguste,' she said in a low voice. 'Just remember that. You owe me a favour.'

213

Then, turning, she went back to check her loaves as if nothing had passed between us, and I saw nothing but the stolid curve of her back for the rest of that long morning.

Perhaps I should have felt reassured. It was clear Antoine did not intend to disclose my secret. And yet her unwillingness to be bought was unnerving; more so was the phrase she had used—*you owe me a favour*—the Blackbird's habitual coin.

*   *   *

This evening I went to the well after Compline to collect a jug of washing water. The sun had set and the sky was a dark and brooding violet, striated with red. The courtyard was deserted, as most of the nuns had already retired to the warming room or the dorter in preparation for sleep, and I could see the warm yellow lights shining from the unprotected windows of the cloister. The well is still incomplete, awaiting a stone finish to its rough earthen walls and a protective wall around. Today it is almost invisible in the shadows, a primitive wooden fence erected in haste around the hole to prevent anyone from falling in by accident. A crossbar, furnished with a bucket, rope and pulley, looks like a thin figure standing against the purple ground. Twelve paces. Six. Four. The thin figure detached itself from the wellside with a sudden start. I saw a small, pale face made violet in the reflected sky, eyes wide with surprise and—I could have sworn—guilt.

'What are you doing here?' Her voice was suspicious. 'You should be with the others. Why are you following me?'

214

There was something in her hands, a bundle like wet rags. My eyes fell to it and she tried to hide the bundle in the folds of her skirt. In the shadows I thought I saw staining on the linen, dark blotches which in that poor light looked black. I held out my jug.

'I needed some water, *ma mère.*' I made my voice toneless. 'I didn't see you.' Now I could see the bucket of water at her feet, its contents slopping over to form a puddle on the trodden earth of the courtyard. The bucket also seemed to contain rags or clothing. Isabelle saw the direction of my gaze and seized the rags. They slapped against her skirt, but she made no attempt even to wring them dry.

'Get your water, then,' she said curtly, pushing the bucket with a clumsy foot. It overturned, spreading a dark stain on the darker ground.

I would have done as she asked, but I could feel the tension coming from her. Her eyes were huge and strangely brilliant, and in a stray sliver of light I noticed her face was sheened with moisture. There was a smell, too, a bland and sweetish scent I recognized.

Blood.

'Is anything wrong?'

For a second she stared me out, her face rigid with the effort of maintaining her dignity. Her chest hitched once. The front of her skirt was dark with water from the dripping rags.

Then she began to sob, the raking, pitiful tears of a confused child, a child who has wept so bitterly and for so long that she no longer cares who hears her. For an instant I forgot with whom I was dealing. This was no longer Mère Isabelle, formerly of the house of Arnault and latterly Abbess of Sainte-Marie la Mère. As I stepped forwards she clung to me and for a second it might have been Fleur in my arms, or Perette, in despair over some real or imagined sorrow such as only children endure. I stroked her hair. 'There, little one. It's all right. Don't be afraid.'

Against the breast of my habit she spoke, but her words were muffled. I could feel water from the stained rags—which she still held tightly in her hand—trickling down my back. 'What happened? What's wrong?' The swampy scent of fever was sharp on her, like that of the marshes after rain. Her brow was so hot that I wondered whether she were truly ill. I asked her the question.

'Cramps,' said Isabelle with an effort. 'Belly cramps. And blood. *Blood!*'

There had been so much talk of blood in the past few days that for an instant I did not understand. Then it came to me. Her words—*the curse of blood*—the stained rags which she had tried to hide. The cramps. Of course. I held her closer.

'Am I going to die?' The flat voice quavered. 'Am I going to go to hell?'

No one had ever told her. I was lucky; my own mother had no false delicacy. The blood was neither wicked nor unclean, she told me. It was a gift from God. Janette told me more as she taught me how to fold the pad and tie it into place; it was *wise* blood, she whispered mysteriously. Magical blood. Her quick hands fingered the cards, the new game of Tarot, which Giordano had brought with him from Italy. Her eyes were pale with cataracts, yet she had the most piercing eyes I knew. See this

216

card? The Moon. Giordano says the tides follow the moon's cycle, in, out, high, low. So are a woman's tides, dry at the wane, and full at the waxing of the moon. The pain will pass. To receive the gift, it may be necessary to suffer a little, a very little. But this is the magical gem of which *Le Philosophe* speaks. The fountain of life.

Of course, I could say nothing of this to Isabelle. But I explained as well as I could until her sobs lessened and her limp body grew rigid next to mine, and she finally pulled away. 'Your own mother should have told you,' I said patiently. 'It's certain to be a shock to you otherwise. But it happens to all girls when they become women. It's no shame.'

She looked at me, already hardening. Her face was contorted with disgust and rage.

'There's nothing bad about it.' For the child's sake, I had to make her understand. 'It isn't the Devil, you see.' I tried to smile at her but her gaze was accusing, hateful. 'It only happens once a month, for a few days. You fold the pad like this . . .' I demonstrated with a panel of my habit, but Isabelle seemed barely to be listening.

'Oh, you liar!' She pulled away from me, kicking my water jug aside with such violence that it flew through the fence pickets and into the well. 'You *liar*!'

I tried to protest, but Isabelle struck out at me wildly with her fists. 'It isn't true! It isn't! It isn't!'

I knew then that I had committed the unforgivable sin. I had seen her without defences. I had offered compassion. Worse, I knew a secret now, a secret she considered shameful enough for her to wash her soiled rags at night to ensure privacy . . .

I read all this in her last look at me as she turned momentarily to face me. 'You liar! You filthy witch! You're the one! You're the Devil's whore and I can prove it!'

I tried to call her back.

'I won't listen!' Even then I could feel pity for her: her youth, her frailty, her terrible loneliness . . . 'I *won't* listen! You've always hated me! I see you watching me with your insolence! Comparing me!' She gave an angry sob. 'Well, I won't be deceived! I know what you're trying to do and I won't—I *won't!*'

Then she was gone.

PART THREE
ISABELLE

CHAPTER ONE
♥

August 1st, 1610

Three days have passed with the slick certainty of nightmare. Since the incident at the well, Mère Isabelle speaks to me rarely and without reference to what has passed between us, but I sense her mistrust and dislike. Her words on that occasion, the accusations and threats, have not been repeated, in private or otherwise. Indeed, she treats me with something like tolerance, which was not her manner from the first. But she looks unwell: her face mottled with angry-looking blemishes, her eyes purplish and heavy.

LeMerle has twice more invited me to his cottage. He hints at favours to be won, but I am afraid of what he may ask me to abet this time. Already, Marguerite's apparition has been seen in various parts of the abbey, each sighting growing more detailed in the telling so that now the ghostly nun sports hideous features, red eyes and all the trappings of popular romance.

Unsurprisingly, Alfonsine has seen her too, in far greater detail, and I wonder to what extent the ghostly nun is not an invention of their mutual rivalry. Alfonsine, who looks paler and more ecstatic as the days pass, even swears that she recognized Mère Marie's kindly face beneath that sinister coiffe, now distorted with hate and demonic glee. It will not be long before Marguerite finds something even more distressing to report, and thereby steals Alfonsine's thunder once again; meanwhile, she spends her free time in cleaning and prayer, while her rival fasts and prays—and coughs with increasing frequency.

What is becoming of us? We talk of little else but of blood and Visitations. Normal relations between us have been suspended. Penances have reached a level hitherto undreamed of, with Soeur Marie-Madeleine keeping vigil in the chapel for two nights without sleep for having dared to query some novice's tale. Our diet now consists of nothing but black bread and soup, Mère Isabelle having decreed that anything richer inflames the baser appetites. She says this with such ferocity that the bawdy jokes to which such a pronouncement might once have given rise in the days of Mère Marie stick in the throat.

We thrive on gossip and whispered scandal. Clémente has revealed herself to be a zealous informant at Chapter. Few escape her innocent, wide-eyed spite. If Soeur Antoine gobbles her bread before Grace, Clémente sees it. If Tomasine closes her eyes during Vigils, if Piété shows ill-temper when disturbed at prayer, if Germaine speaks slightingly of the Visitations . . . This last is especially cruel. Words spoken in confidence are revealed in public with bland complacency. Mère Isabelle commends Clémente on her sense of duty. LeMerle seems not to notice.

Germaine accepted her penance with cold indifference. She looks stony now, her damaged face as rough and hard-looking as the effigy of Marie-de-la-mer, the saint who never was. And yet it is easier for us to believe, in our abbey buffeted by the bitter west winds, in a Goddess of the Sea, a watchful, dangerous Goddess with stony, gouged-out eyes. Easier in any case than in the Mother of God, that Virgin claiming still to be the mother of us all.

Three days ago a fine marble statue of the Holy Mother arrived by cart from the mainland, in replacement for our loss. A gift, said Mère Isabelle, from her favourite uncle, for whom we will say forty Masses in thanks for his generosity. She is all white, this new Marie, smooth and bland as a peeled potato. She sits in the doorway of the chapel where the old Marie used to be, her lips curved in a tiny, meaningless smile, one hand outstretched in a limp gesture of benediction.

The morning after her arrival, however, the new Marie was found defaced, obscene words scrawled across her features in black grease-pencil. Germaine—who had been doing penance in the chapel on the night of the outrage—claimed to have seen nothing during her vigil, though her mouth curled as she said it. Perhaps a mysterious robed nun did it, she suggested insolently, or a monkey from the Far East, or a manifestation of the Holy Ghost. She began to laugh then, softly at first. We watched her, embarrassed and anxious. Patches of scarlet marbled her cheeks. For an instant she turned to Clémente with an expression of entreaty on her scarred face. Then she fell backwards, stiffly onto the flagstones, hands clutching at air.

Germaine went to the infirmary after that. Soeur Virginie declared that she was suffering from the *cameras de sangre* and spoke of a possible recovery with noisy confidence whilst in private she shook her head and whispered that the patient was unlikely to live out the month. Soeur Rosamonde, too, is causing concern. During the past week her decline has been dramatic; now she remains in the infirmary all day, barely moving and refusing to eat. Of course she is very old—almost as old as poor Mère Marie—but until the removal of the Saint she had been a cheery soul, sound in body if not in mind, and enjoying what small pleasures she could with enviable simplicity.

I feel oddly responsible, and would try to intercede on her behalf, but I know that to do so would accomplish nothing. In fact, at this point, Mère Isabelle is far more likely to show sympathy to Rosamonde if I seem unaware of her condition.

It is a part of his trap, of course. Every day I spend here deepens the pit into which I have dug myself. LeMerle knows it; doubtless he meant it so. He despises my loyalty to the sisters, but understands that I will not leave them while Fleur is safe and they are not. I have become my own jailer, and although every instinct tells me with increasing urgency that I must escape, I am afraid of what may happen if my vigilance is withdrawn. Every night I tell the cards, but they show me nothing but what I already know: the Tower in flames with the woman falling, arms outstretched, from the top; the hooded Hermit; the cruel Six of Swords. Disaster, poised like a crushing rock above our heads, with nothing I can do to prevent its fall.

CHAPTER TWO

♠

August 1st, 1610

At last, a reply to my letters. Monseigneur takes his time, it seems, and sees no reason to thank me for all my hard work. I am privileged to be given the chance to devote my life to the noble house of Arnault. However, the generous gift, the marble statue which accompanied his letter, shows his unspoken approval. Monseigneur is most gratified to hear of his niece's reforms. As well he might—a pretty picture I drew of the young Abbess, radiant in her innocence and unearthly beauty; of adoring nuns; of birds flocking to hear her speak. I hinted at marvels; showers of rose leaves; spontaneous healings. Soeur Alfonsine will be pleased to hear that she has been restored to health from a fatal illness. Soeur Rosamonde, too, has regained the use of her withered arm. One must not speak too hastily of miraculous cures, but one must always hope, and if God wills it . . .

The lure is cast. I have little doubt but that he will take it. I have suggested the fifteenth of August as a favourable date. It seems appropriate, it being the day of the Virgin, to celebrate thus our reclamation of the abbey.

Meanwhile, I must work day and night to have things ready in time. Fortunately I have my helpers: Antoine, strong, slow and undemanding; Alfonsine, my visionary and spreader of rumours; Marguerite, my catalyst. Not to mention Piété, who runs errands, my little Soeur Anne, and Clémente . . .

Well, maybe that *was* a miscalculation. Despite her meek appearance she is by far the most demanding of my disciples, and I find it hard to keep up with her changes of mood. Purring like a housecat one day, the next perversely cold, she seems to take pleasure in goading me into violence, only to indulge in extravagant protestations of love and repentance afterwards. I believe I am expected to find this appealing. Many would, I am sure. But I'm no seventeen-year-old any more, to be ensnared by a pretty face and some girlish simpering. Besides, I have so little time to give her. My hours have become at least as long and as wearisome as those of the nuns. My nights are divided between various clandestine pursuits; my days are filled with blessings, exorcisms, public confessions and other everyday blasphemies.

Following the first sighting of the Unholy Nun there have been a number of further incidents which may or may not be of a demonic nature: crosses removed from nuns' habits during the night; obscene writings on statues in the chapel; red dye in the font and on the stones in front of the altar. Père Colombin, however, remains defiant in the face of these new outrages, and spends hours each day in prayer; an occasional catnap saves me from complete exhaustion, and Soeur Antoine ensures that I do not starve.

And what of you, my Juliette? How far will you follow me, and for how long? The market at Barbâtre has served its purpose. There cannot be another visit there without arousing suspicion. Isabelle watches me with something akin to jealousy, and her vigilance, assiduously honed, is a compass needle ever pointing in my direction. Père Saint-Amand is an innocent for all his worldly wisdom, easily swayed by feminine wiles. Far harder on her own sex than any man could be, she knows this my essential weakness and values this proof of my humanity. If she learned of my involvement with Clémente now, she would take my side, assuming that the girl led me into temptation. But her eye is on Juliette. Instinct shows her where the enemy lies. My Winged One works in the bakehouse—hard enough work, I'm told, but an easier task than digging the well. She does not approach me, though she must long for news of her daughter, but preserves that look of stolid, almost stupid docility that goes so ill with what I know of her. Only once she slipped and drew attention to herself when the old nun was taken to the infirmary. Yes, I heard about that. A foolish lapse, and for what? What loyalty can such as she have to these people? She always had too soft a heart. Except, of course, with me.

This morning I spent two hours I could ill afford with Isabelle in confession and prayer. She has a study of her own next to her bedchamber with a shrine, candles, a portrait of herself by Toussaint Dubreuil and a silver figurine of the Virgin taken from the sacristy treasures. Time was when I would have coveted that figurine, and the treasures too, but the time for pilfering is long past. Instead I listened to a spoilt girl's rantings with a grave, compassionate air, whilst deep in my stomach, I grinned.

Mère Isabelle is troubled. She tells me so with the unconscious arrogance of her breeding, an adult's pride masking the child's fears. For she does fear, she tells me. For her soul; for her salvation. There have been dreams, you see. She sleeps only three or four hours a night—is the sea never quiet?—and what sleep she finds is stitched through with uneasy dreams of a kind she has never before known.

'Of what?' I narrowed my eyes to hide the smile within. She may only be a child, but her senses are alert, her instincts uncanny. In another life I might have made a fine card-player of her.

'Blood.' Her voice was low. 'I dreamed blood flowed from the stones of the crypt and into the chapel. Then I dreamed of the black statue in the doorway, and blood came welling from beneath it. Then I dreamed of Soeur Auguste'—I told you her instincts were sound—'and of the well. I dreamed blood came from the well Soeur Auguste was digging, and *it was all over me!*'

Very good. I never credited my little pupil with such an imagination. I notice that her face is marked with a number of small blemishes about the mouth and chin, indicating ill-health. 'You must not push yourself so hard, *ma fille,*' I told her gently. 'To encourage physical collapse through self-denial is no way to ensure the completion of our work here.'

'There's truth in dreams,' she muttered, sullen. 'Was not the well water tainted? And the sacrament?'

Gravely I nodded. Difficult to remember that she is twelve years old; with her pinched small face and reddened eyes she looks ancient, used up.

'Soeur Alfonsine saw something in the crypt.' Again that mutter, half sullen, half imperious.

'Shadows,' I told her crisply, feeding the flame.

'No!' Her shoulders hunched instinctively; she put her hand to the pit of her stomach with a grimace.

'What is it?' My hand lingered at the nape of her neck and she pulled away.

'Nothing. *Nothing!*' she repeated, as if I had contradicted her. A cramp, she tells me. An ache, which has afflicted her for the past few days. It will pass. She seemed about to tell me more, the wizened mask falling for an instant to reveal the child she might have been. Then she recovered, and for a moment I could clearly see her uncle in her. It's a welcome resemblance; it reminds me that this is not a normal child that I am dealing with, but one of a vicious and degenerate brood. 'Leave me now,' she told me haughtily. 'I wish to pray alone.'

I nodded, hiding a smile. Say your prayers, little sister. The house of Arnault may need them sooner than you think.

CHAPTER THREE
♥

August 3rd, 1610

Last night, Germaine killed herself. We found her this morning, hanging from the crossbar halfway down the well. Her weight had dragged down the wooden strut from which she was suspended without dislodging it from the earth walls. A few more feet and the corpse might have tainted the well water more certainly than LeMerle's red dye.

As it was, Germaine's suicide was as cryptic as she was in life. Close by, we found obscene, barely decipherable messages on the chapel walls as well as on several statues, scrawled in the same black grease-pencil which had been used to deface the new Marie, and she had removed the Bernardine cross from the front of her habit, carefully unpicking the tiny stitches, as if to spare us the shame of seeing it on the breast of a suicide.

I saw only a glimpse of her face as they pulled her from her vertical grave, but it seemed to me virtually unchanged. Even in death her mouth had just the same pinched and cynical look, that look of always expecting and receiving the worst life had to offer, which hid a heart more vulnerable and more easily bruised than anyone knew.

She was buried without ceremony before Prime, at the crossroads beyond the abbey grounds. I dug the grave myself, remembering our work on the well together, and I spoke a few silent, sorry words to Sainte Marie-de-la-mer. Tomasine wanted to put a stake through the corpse's heart, to prevent her from walking, but I would not allow it. Let Germaine rest as she could, I said; we were nuns, not savages.

Tomasine muttered something sullen and indistinct.

'What did you say?'

'Nothing.'

I could sense the unrest, however. Throughout the day it walked with me, in the abbey, in the garden and the chapel; it worked alongside me in the bakehouse and in the fields. It did not help that the heat had soured. Overnight the air had become flat and humid, and the sun was a tarnished coin behind a sheet of cloud. Beneath it we sweated; sweating, we stank. No one spoke aloud of Germaine's suicide, or even of the Unholy Nun, but it was there nevertheless: a murmur of revolt, a fear that grew with every silent hour. This was, after all, the second death in as many months—and both had occurred in unusual circumstances. A third outrage seemed only a matter of time.

Then, this evening, it finally came. Soeur Virginie arrived from the infirmary with the unwelcome news that during Chapter Soeur Rosamonde had died. Oh, it was to be expected at her age, but it was a blow nevertheless. Certainly it was enough to set rumours flying: Rosamonde had died of shock following a new Visitation by the Unholy Nun; she had been bewitched to death by the same evil spirit that had killed Mère Marie; she had committed suicide; she had died of the cholera, and everyone was trying to cover it up; she had perished of an overzealous bleeding, authorized by Mère Isabelle.

I was more inclined to believe this. Virginie's handling of the old woman had been misguided from the start, and, separated from her friends and cut off from the rest of the abbey, Rosamonde had soon fallen into a fatal decline. Her death was ill-timed, however. No amount of reasoning could persuade the other sisters that they were in no danger. Death is not contagious, I protested; only disease. At her own insistence I agreed to make a medicine bag for Soeur Piété to protect her from evil humours, and I promised strengthening draughts for Alfonsine and Marguerite, who had grown even thinner under Virginie's care. After the evening meal several of the novices came to me for advice and protection; I told them to avoid excessive fasting, to drink only the water from the well, and to wash with soap morning and night.

'What good will *that* do?' asked Soeur Tomasine when she heard of it.

I explained that regular washing sometimes prevented disease.

She looked sceptical. 'I don't see how it can,' she said. 'You need holy water, not soap and water, to drive out evil.'

I sighed. It is sometimes very difficult to explain these things without sounding heretical. 'Some evils are waterborne,' I explained carefully. 'Some travel by air. If the water or the air is tainted, then disease may spread.' I showed her the scented pomander I had made to dispel foul air and flying insects, and she turned it over suspiciously in her hand.

'You seem to know a lot about these things,' she said.

'Only what I've heard.'

* * *

At Vespers tonight LeMerle spoke to us, looking tired after a day of fasting and prayer. Exhausted and afraid, the sisters brightened a little at the sound of his voice, but Père Saint-Amand seemed reluctant to mention the long day's troubling business, and spoke of the trials of Saint Felicity with a forced cheer which convinced no one.

Then Mère Isabelle addressed us. I had noticed that the more LeMerle spoke to us of caution and restraint, the more agitated she became, as if she were purposely defying the new confessor. Today her address was longer and more confused than

232

ever, and though she spoke to us of the Light of God in the darkness, her speech held little illumination.

'We must try to find the light,' she told us in a voice that quavered a little with fatigue. 'But today it seems that try as we might we are infested, even to the heart. Even to the soul. Oh, we mean well. But even the best of intentions may lead the soul into hell. And sin is everywhere. No one is safe. Even a hermit alone for fifty years in a lightless cave may not be free of sin. Sin is a plague, and it is contagious.'

'There have been dreams,' she whispered, and a murmur rose from the assembly like poison smoke, 'dreams and blood,' and the murmur echoed again like the voice of our longings—*blood, yes*—'and now the ichors of hell flow free among us, touching us with monstrous thoughts, monstrous cravings . . .' *Yes*, whispered the voice of the multitude, *Oh yes, yes, yesss!*

At her side LeMerle seemed to smile—or was it the candlelight?—his face ringed in the glow from the sacristy lantern so that a soft nimbus surrounded him.

'There have been lecheries!' cried Mère Isabelle. 'Blasphemies! Secret abominations! Can anyone deny it?'

Before her Soeur Alfonsine began to wail, arms held out. Clémente too held out her hands in seeming entreaty. Behind them, a dozen more joined the chorus. 'All of us, guilty!'

Guilty, yessss! An ecstasy of release.

'All of us tainted!'

Tainted, yes!

The candles, the incense, the stench of fear and

233

excitement. The dark, teeming with shadows. A gust of wind slammed the door against the wall and set the candles guttering. A hundred shadows against the walls doubled, trebled, becoming three hundred, three thousand, an army from hell. Someone screamed. Such was the nervous power of Mère Isabelle's soliloquy that the cry was echoed by a dozen more.

'See! It comes! It comes! It is here!'

Everyone turned to see who had cried out. Set slightly apart from the rest of the crowd stood Soeur Marguerite, arms uplifted. She had cast aside her wimple and her head was thrown back, revealing a face distorted with tics and tremors. Her left leg was shaking perceptibly through the thick folds of her habit, a vibration that seemed to pass through every muscle and nerve in her body.

'Soeur Marguerite?' LeMerle spoke in a clear, calm voice. 'Soeur Marguerite, is anything wrong?'

With a visible effort, the thin nun turned her eyes towards him. Her mouth opened, but nothing came. The tic in her leg intensified.

'Don't touch me!' said Marguerite, as Soeur Virginie moved to help her.

LeMerle looked concerned. 'Soeur Marguerite. Come here please. If you can.'

It was clear she wanted to obey. But her limbs refused to do so. I had seen a similar case in Montauban, in Gascony, where several people had been afflicted by St Vitus' Dance. But this was not the same malady. Marguerite's leg jerked and danced as if some evil puppeteer were pulling her strings. Her face worked frantically.

'She's faking,' said Alfonsine.

Marguerite's head twisted to face her.

234

Grotesquely, her body kept the same unnatural posture. 'Help me,' she said.

Isabelle had been watching in silence. Now she spoke. 'Can you doubt it now?' she said in a low voice. 'Possessed!'

LeMerle said nothing, but looked well satisfied with himself.

All around them, the sisters had begun to murmur. The word—unspoken until this moment—filled the air like a plague of moths.

Only Alfonsine looked sceptical. 'That's ridiculous,' she said. 'It's a tic, or the palsy. You know what she's like.'

Privately, I agreed with her. There had been more than enough excitement in the abbey during the past weeks to provoke a frenzy in one as susceptible as Soeur Marguerite. Besides, Alfonsine had been coughing up more blood than ever in recent days, and it was getting hard to compete.

Isabelle, however, was not pleased. 'There have been cases!' she snapped. 'Who are you to question this one? What do you know about it?'

Alfonsine, abashed at the rebuke, began to cough. I could hear her forcing it, raking at her throat. If she'd had any sense she would have accepted the linctus I had prepared for her, and bandaged her throat with linen. Even so I knew that such remedies would not cure her, but would merely slow the progress of her illness. The consumption is not an ill that can be cured with syrups.

Meanwhile, Marguerite's affliction had not abated. The tremor had passed to her right leg, and now both legs were infected with the dancing sickness. Her eyes rolled in dismay as her feet seemed to move independently of the rest of her body, rocking her from side to side. The word—*possessssed*—rolled around the vaults, picking up momentum as it went.

Isabelle turned to LeMerle. 'Well?'

He shook his head. 'It's too early to say.'

'How can you doubt it?'

The Blackbird looked at her. 'I can doubt it, child,' he said with an edge of irritation, 'because, unlike you, I have seen many things, and I know how easily judgement may be clouded by impatience and lack of thought.'

For a moment Isabelle held his gaze defiantly, then her eyes dropped. 'Forgive me, *mon père*,' she said through her teeth. 'What shall I do?'

He thought about it for a while. 'She should be examined,' he decided, with a seeming reluctance. 'Immediately.'

CHAPTER FOUR
♥

August 4th, 1610

Only I could appreciate how deftly the Blackbird had handled last night's scene. By seeming to hold back, by adopting a reasoned posture at variance with the atmosphere of fear and mistrust he had already created, he had made it seem as if they, and not he, were making the decisions. Soeur Marguerite was taken to the infirmary, where she remained with LeMerle and Soeur Virginie throughout the night and the following day. According to the rumours, Marguerite's tic had continued for more than an hour after the aborted service. She was bled twice, on Soeur Virginie's recommendation, after which she was too exhausted to be examined, and had to be put to bed.

I listened to the reports with barely restrained impatience. Of course I know that Soeur Virginie is a silly girl who should never have been put in charge of the infirmary. Already weakened by fasting and nervous exhaustion, the last thing Marguerite needs at the moment is bleeding. She needs rest, quiet and good, wholesome food: meat, bread and a little red wine—all the things, in fact, that Mère Isabelle has forbidden. Demons respond to sanguineous humours, declares Soeur Virginie, and to prevent infestation it is essential to thin the blood. In fact, the colour red would have been outlawed altogether except for the crosses stitched onto our habits, and Mère Isabelle looks with suspicion on any sister who does not share her own sickly pallor. Red is the Devil's colour: dangerous, immodest, blatant. For the first time I am glad that I wear the wimple, and hope that she does not remember the colour of my hair.

In this sullen heat, ill-humour and suspicion breed like the plague. There are cantrips to bring rain, but I dare not use them; already I sense the disapproval of Soeur Tomasine and others, and I want no more unwelcome attention. Instead, this evening, alone by the chapel, I sat at the feet of the new Marie, lit a candle for Germaine and Rosamonde, and tried to compose my thoughts.

Tsk-tsk, begone! But the Six of Swords is not so

easily banished. It hangs above my head like a curse, and will not be satisfied. I looked inside at the pew where, only the night before, Marguerite had suffered her attack of the tremors, and foreboding warred with curiosity in my heart. Was this what LeMerle had intended? Was this another stage of his mysterious plan?

I tried a little prayer—a heresy, you might call it, but the old Saint would have understood. The new one, however, just stood in her chilly silence and gave no sign of having heard. She knows only good Latin, this new Marie, and the prayers of such as I are of no interest to her. Once more I thought of Le Borgne—and, too, of Germaine and Rosamonde, and I began to understand the desire to attack this clean new Saint; to bring her down, deface her, make her more like ourselves.

Observing her more closely I could see that she was not all white, as first I had thought. There was a slim ribbon of gilt running around the edge of the Virgin's mantle, and her halo, too, was picked out in gold. Carved from the finest marble, veined in the tenderest rose, she stood on a pedestal of the same material, engraved with her name and that of our abbey in gilded letters. There was a crest carved underneath, which on close scrutiny I recognized as that of the house of Arnault, and this time I also noticed another, rather smaller crest, modestly placed beneath, the design of which—a white dove and the Holy Mother's fleur-de-lys picked out against a gilt background—suddenly looked strangely familiar . . .

A gift from her uncle, Isabelle had said; her favourite uncle, for whom we must say forty Masses in thanks. Why then should I know his emblem?

238

Why then should I feel myself on the brink of some revelation that would cast light on all that had happened during the past weeks? Even more puzzling was the half-memory which accompanied the feeling: a scent of sweat and wax, a great light and heat, a sensation of dizziness, the clamour which was the Théâtre-Royal, that good year in Paris . . .

Paris! The memory locked into place with a click. I could see him now: a tall man, gaunt with genteel self-deprivation, his eyes so light they seemed gilded, as if from looking at too many altars. He only spoke once in my hearing, but I remembered his words, uttered in rage on the night of our *Ballet des Gueux*, as he left the hall in a surge of applause.

A Blackbird's voice may haply be silenced, he had said. *Even though such quarry is the vassal's preserve, if its song offendeth . . .*

A man of strange pride, my Blackbird, in spite of his lack of morals; a strange marriage of arrogance and knavery. So many things are a game to him; so few things matter in his life. But he understands revenge. I know that path myself, after all, and if now I choose to give it up it is only because Fleur takes up a greater part of my heart than I can afford to waste on such foolish things. LeMerle has no Fleur, and for all I know, no heart. Pride is all he has.

I returned to the dorter in silence, my head finally clear. I knew now why LeMerle had come to the abbey. I knew why he had adopted the role of Père Saint-Amand, why he had given orders to taint the well, why he had encouraged the frenzies in the chapel, and why he had taken such pains to keep me from escaping. But knowing why is not enough. Now I must discover *what* it is that he intends to do. And what is to be my role in this play of travesties? And how will it end—in tragedy or farce?

CHAPTER FIVE
♠

August 5th, 1610

Well done, my Ailée. I knew it would be only a matter of time before you put the facts together. You remember the Bishop, then? Monseigneur had the bad taste to disapprove of my *Ballet Travesti*. To order my removal from Paris. My ignominious removal.

My *Ballet des Gueux* outraged him, with its sequined ladies; my *Ballet Travesti* more so, with the ape dressed as a bishop and the Court beaux in petticoats and corsets. To tell the truth, I meant it so. What right had he to censure? No harm was done. A few left outraged, prudes and hypocrites for the most part. But the applause! It seemed never-ending. We stood for five minutes with our smiles melting beneath the lamps and the greasepaint running down our faces. The boards glittered with flung coins. And you, my Ailée, too young yet to have earned your wings but lovely in your scandalous breeches, hat in hand, eyes like stars. It was our great triumph. Do you remember?

And then, more abruptly than we could understand, came the end. Evreux's public letter to

De Béthune. The furtive glances, the mumbled excuses from those I had counted as friends. The polite messages—*Madame has left town. Monsieur is not at home tonight*—whilst more favoured visitors came and went with barely concealed disdain.

I was expected to leave quietly, discreetly, accepting my disgrace. But the Blackbird's song is not so easily silenced. As they burned me in effigy at the steps of the Arsenal I bought a new wardrobe. I paraded with vulgar exhibitionism about the town. I wore my women like costume jewellery, two on each arm. Madame de Scudéry's salon was closed to me now, but there were many others not so choosy. The Bishop watched me, enraged, but what more could he do?

I learned soon enough. A beating at the hands of lackeys, no less, as I returned drunk from a night of revelry. Without De Béthune as my benefactor I was defenceless, unprotected even by the law, for who would think to take my side against Monseigneur the Bishop? I was unarmed, without even a dress sword at my side. There were six of them. But I was less drunk—or more desperate—than they imagined. I was forced to run, hiding in alleys infested with rats, crouching in open drains, skulking through shadows, heart pounding, head aching, mouth dry.

It could have been an Italian farce: Guy LeMerle, running from a Bishop's flunkeys, his silver-buckled shoes slipping in the street slops, his silk coat spattered with mud. Better, I suppose, than LeMerle lying in the gutter with his ribs broken. But it was enough; I lost the game. And there would be another time for Monseigneur. And another. My credit had finally run out, and we both knew it.

But memory is long on the road, with only whores and dwarves for company. And the road is a long one, crossing and recrossing with incestuous intimacy. We met there before, if you recall, in a village near Montauban, and after that in a cloister just outside Agen. All roads lead to Paris, and we met there too, several times. On one occasion there I relieved you of a silver cross—I wear it still, you'll be glad to know—but once again you held the aces, and retaliation was swift. Shame on you, *mon père.* I lost a player, and one of my caravans. But the Blackbird's feathers were barely singed. And after that, our stakes were higher.

Every man has a weakness, Monseigneur Bishop. It took me some time to find yours. But my dark star led me at last to the cradle of your ambition. Congratulations, by the way. Such a devout family. Two brothers highly placed in the clergy, a sister Prioress of an abbey in the south. Innumerable cousins in monasteries and cathedrals throughout France. You'd have to be blind to miss the streak of nepotism that runs through the house of Arnault. But a line so rich in virgins must soon be doomed to sterility. Your one regret, *mon père,* must be that you never fathered a son to carry your line. Instead you lavished what affection you could on your dead brother's daughter: Angélique Saint-Hervé Désirée Arnault, henceforth to be known as Mère Isabelle, Abbess of Sainte-Marie la Mère.

She looks like you. She has the same suspicious face and silver-gilt eyes. She has your contempt for the common man, and she has your pride, too—beneath your pious attitudes you Arnaults conceal a level of hubris worthy of Classical tragedy. In all but name she is your daughter. You schooled her well. She reads your letters with the devotion of Héloïse to Abelard; even from the nursery her piety exceeded expectations. She eats no meat, drinks no wine but at Communion, fasts on Fridays. She does you credit, and such credit may be turned to good advantage—why not? After all, one cannot remain a bishop forever. A cardinal's hat might sit well on Monseigneur, or at the very least an archbishop's mitre. Cunningly, you paved her way to Mother Church's door: spread rumours of visions, angelic voices and unofficial but well publicized acts of healing. Your secret wish is of a canonization in the family—without sons, this is the only continuation your line can hope for—and with Mère Isabelle, this may not be entirely out of the question. Although her late mother judged her too young to take the veil, *you* took her in hand; encouraged the girl to dream of an abbey in the same way that a normal child might wish for a doll's house.

If you'd only seen her when I gave her the news! God, I almost loved her for that, her eyes narrowed into crescents of ill-temper, her mouth turning spitefully downwards.

'Abbess of *where*?' she wailed. 'But that's *nowhere*! Nowhere at all!'

You spoiled her, Monseigneur. Made her believe, young as she was, that she might look higher. Perhaps she coveted Paris, the minx, with its towers and conceits and worldly whores on their knees in front of her. It would have been her style.

Or maybe it was for the penance I made her do for her anger, for my rebuke and the tenderness of my absolution when she had finished, for there is a hunger in her which I'm sure you never saw, a part of her in which sin rubs against sanctity to form a single, bright blade. One day she'll be sharp enough to cut with, Monseigneur d'Evreux. Till then, beware.

*   *   *

Juliette came to me tonight, as I knew she would. It was a risk; she must have suspected Clémente might be with me, but having discovered my secret she could not stay away.

It was like her, too, to confront me at once. In her place I would have kept my counsel and played a close game; my Winged One, as always, rushes forth in the heat of the moment, showing all her aces in her eagerness to confront me. It's a flaw in her play—a beginner's flaw, at that—and although it serves my purpose in this case, I cannot help feeling a little disappointed. I thought I'd taught her better.

'So *that*'s why you're here,' she said, when I opened the door. 'The Bishop of Evreux.'

'Bishop of where?' I feigned innocence, but poorly; just to see the look of triumph in her eyes.

'And you used to be *such* a good liar,' she said, pushing past me into the cottage.

I shrugged modestly. 'Maybe I'm out of practice.'

'I don't think so.'

She sat down on the arm of my chair, one leg swinging. There was dust on the soles of her brown feet; her face was alight with her imagined victory. 'So,' she said. 'When are we expecting him? And what will you do when he's here?'

'*Are* we expecting him?' I said, smiling.

'If not, you've lost your touch.'

I shrugged, conceding the point. 'You can't imagine I would have told you,' I said. 'After all, you haven't shown much trust in *me* so far, have you?'

'Why should I?' she said. 'After Epinal—'

'Juliette, you're being tiresome. I explained about that already.'

'Explained, but not excused.' Her tone was harsh, but there was something in her manner, a kind of obscure softening—as if her discovery, instead of increasing her suspicion of me, had somehow brought her reassurance. 'Tell me about the Bishop,' she said in a softer voice. 'You know I won't betray you.'

I smiled. 'Loyalty? I'm touched. I—'

'Hardly,' she said. 'You have my daughter.'

Ouch. Another hit. However, in the course of a long game, a calculated surrender may serve as well as a victory. 'Very well,' I said, drawing her gently towards me. She did not pull away.

I confessed enough to allay her fears and to flatter her—just a little—though she thought her face expressionless as she listened to me in silence. Women hear so often what they want to hear, even my Harpy—who has every reason to believe the worst. And a partial truth is often so much more effective than a total lie.

She has guessed the obvious, of course. I'd accounted for that. Perhaps she can even understand me a little—she's a resentful piece, in spite of her assumed holiness, and she has no more reason to love the Bishop than I have myself. All I

245

want from her now is a little time; after all, good scandal, like good wine, takes time to ferment and mellow. Château d'Evreux, not a subtle vintage but with a certain brazen charm which you, my Juliette, may find appealing. Let the brew froth just a little longer. When he arrives I want him drowned in a wave of suds.

Oh, I was convincing. Juliette listened first with scepticism, then with satisfaction, then with a reluctant kind of sympathy. When I had finished, she nodded slowly, looking into my eyes. 'I thought it might be that. A special performance, to make him pay for that time in Paris? A return match?'

I managed to look rueful. 'I don't like to lose.'

'And you think *this* is winning?' she said. 'Have you any idea of the harm you've done? The harm you're still doing?'

'Me?' I shrugged. 'All I did was set the stage. You did the rest yourselves.'

Her mouth thinned; she knew I was right. 'And after the show?' she demanded. 'What then? Will you ride away again, both of you, in your different directions, and leave us in peace?'

'Why not?' I said. 'Unless you'd like to come with me.' She ignored that, as I expected her to. 'Come on, Juliette,' I said, seeing her expression. 'Give me credit for some intelligence. How far do you think I would get if I actually *harmed* the Bishop? Did you hear what they did to Ravillac? And in any case, if I'd wanted to kill Evreux, don't you think I would have found some way to do it by now?' I let her think that over for a while. 'I want him humbled,' I told her quietly. 'Monseigneur has high ambitions; pretensions to greatness for his line. I want them quashed. I want the Arnaults in

246

the dust, along with the rest of us, and I want him to know that I was the one who put them there. A dead Bishop is only a step removed from canonization; I want this one to live a long, long time.'

I stopped, and for several minutes she was silent. Then, finally, she nodded. 'You're taking a terrible risk,' she said. 'I doubt whether the Bishop would extend the same privilege to you.'

'I'm touched by your concern,' I said, 'but a game without stakes is no game at all.'

'Must there always be a game?' she asked, so earnestly that I could have kissed her.

'Why, Juliette,' I said gently. 'What else is there?'

CHAPTER SIX
♥

August 6th, 1610

Last night, at long last, the rain came, but it fell to the west onto Le Devin, and did not refresh us. Instead we sweltered uncomfortably in the dorter and watched the heat lightning as it chased its tail across the bay. The sultry weather had brought a plague of midges from the flats, and that night they swarmed through the windows, settling on every inch of our unprotected flesh, drawing out our blood. We slept poorly—or not at all—throughout that night, some slapping at the midges in a frenzy, others lying exhausted and resigned. I used citronella leaf and lavender to banish the creatures

from my cubicle, and in spite of the heat I slept a
little. I was one of the lucky ones; in the morning I
awoke to find myself virtually free of insect bites,
though Tomasine was in a pitiful state, and
Antoine, with her warm blood, was a quivering
mass of red blotches. To make matters worse, the
chapel too was infested with the flying creatures,
which seemed unaffected by either incense or
candle smoke.

Matins passed, and Lauds. Day broke, and the
midges withdrew to their stronghold in the
marshes. By Prime, however, the air had thickened
still further and the sky was hot and white,
promising worse to come. No one was still. We
were a mass of tics and itches; even I, who had
escaped the scourge, could feel my skin prickling in
sympathy. It was to this that LeMerle made his
morning appearance, looking cool and grave. Soeur
Marguerite was at his left side, Mère Isabelle at his
right.

A murmur ran through the chapel. This was the
first time that Marguerite had attended a service
since her attack, and we were still awaiting an
official pronouncement on the nature of her
affliction. Opinions were divided. Some said St
Vitus' Dance, others the palsy, yet more were
convinced she was bewitched or bedevilled.
Certainly she *looked* quiet enough—her tic was
gone and her eyes were unusually dark and wide.
That would be the poppy I had slipped into her
strengthening draught, I told myself. I hoped it
would be enough.

But I could hardly dose all sixty-five of us.
Alfonsine was flushed and restive; Tomasine was so
covered in bites that she could barely keep still;

248

Antoine scratched at her legs continuously; even Clémente, usually so meek, looked agitated. Perhaps Germaine's death had distressed her more than we had thought, for her eyes were heavy and her features drawn. I noticed that she watched LeMerle constantly, but he took care not to pay her any attention, or even to meet her eye. Perhaps he really *had* tired of her, then; I was annoyed at myself for the satisfaction the thought gave me.

'My children,' he said. 'For three days you have waited patiently for news of our sister Marguerite.'

We nodded, shifted, shuffled. Three days was long enough. Three days of rumour and uncertainty; three days of potions and possets. Superstition had never been very far, not even in the days of Mère Marie; now, robbed of our Saint's comforting presence, we turned to it more than ever. Order was what we needed, order and authority in the face of this crisis. Instinctively, we turned to LeMerle to provide it.

But Père Colombin was looking troubled. 'I have examined Soeur Marguerite closely,' he said. 'And I have found nothing amiss with her—body or soul.'

A whisper of revolt went through the crowd. There had to be *something*, it said. He had led us to this; had fed us such scraps as had given us an appetite for his words. There was evil in the abbey; who could question it?

'I know,' said LeMerle. 'I understand your doubts. I have prayed; I have fasted. I have consulted many books. But if there are spirits in Soeur Marguerite, I cannot make them speak. All that I can conclude is that the forces which have infested our abbey are too powerful for me to deal with alone. I have failed.'

No! The murmur went through the crowd like the wind through wheat. The Blackbird, hanging his head in fake humility, could not resist a smile. 'I thought I could hunt the Devil with nothing more than my faith and your trust in me,' he said. 'But I could not. I have no alternative but to inform the proper authorities and place the situation—and myself—in their hands. Praise be.' And with that he stepped down from the pulpit and motioned to Isabelle to take his place.

The rest of us looked at each other, remembering the last time Isabelle had addressed us, and a ripple of dissatisfaction and revolt ran through the crowd. We could not rely upon Isabelle to keep order, we knew. Only LeMerle could control us.

Isabelle herself had been taken completely by surprise. 'Where are you going?' she asked, in a quavering voice.

'I'm no use to you here,' said LeMerle. 'If I catch the morning tide, I should be able to bring help within a week.'

Now Isabelle was close to panic. 'You can't leave,' she said.

'But I must. What else can I do?'

'*Mon père!*' Clémente, too, was looking alarmed. At her side Antoine turned her mottled face towards him in silent entreaty. A rumour, louder than before, swept over the crowd. We had lost everything else; we could not lose Père Colombin. Without him, chaos would descend upon us like a flock of birds.

He tried to explain above the mounting noise. If the evil could not be located—if the culprit was not found . . . But the thought that he might leave them

250

at the mercy of that evil had taken possession of the sisters and they began to wail, an eerie, catlike sound, which began at one side of the chapel and swelled until it had engulfed the entire assembly.

Mère Isabelle was almost beside herself. 'Evil spirits, show yourselves!' she commanded shrilly. 'Show yourselves and speak!'

The wave of sound passed over us again, and Perette, who was standing near me, put her hands to her ears. I made the sign against malchance behind my back. That cry had sounded too close to a cantrip for my liking. I whispered my mother's good-luck charm under my breath, but doubted that it would have very much effect in such surroundings.

LeMerle, however, was watching with an air of cool satisfaction. They were his now, I knew; they would perform at his command. The only question was: who would be first? I glanced around me. I saw the imploring face of Clémente, the moony features of Antoine, Marguerite, already twitching at the mouth as the draught began to wear off, and Alfonsine . . .

Alfonsine. At first she seemed utterly still. Then the slightest of tremors went through her, a fluttering like that of a moth's wing. She seemed unaware of what was happening around her; her entire body quivered. Then, very slowly, she began to dance.

It began in her feet. With tiny steps, hands splayed as if for balance, she might have been a rope-dancer feeling for the measure with her bare toes. Then came the hips: a scarcely perceptible, undulating motion. Then the fingers: the sinuous arms, the rolling shoulders.

251

I was not the only one to have noticed. Ahead of me, Tomasine took a sharp breath. Someone cried out shrilly, 'Look!'

Silence fell; but it was a dangerous silence, like a rock about to fall.

'Bewitched!' moaned Bénédicte.

'Just like Soeur Marguerite!'

'Possessed!'

I had to put a halt to this. 'Alfonsine, stop it, this is ridiculous!'

But Alfonsine could not be stopped. Her body turned and twisted to an unheard rhythm, first to the left, to the right, then revolving round like a top, snaking and circling with grave deliberation, her skirts flying out about her ankles. And there was a sound coming from her mouth, a sound that was almost a word. '*Mmmmm . . .*'

'They're here!' wailed Antoine.

'Speaking to us . . .'

'*Mmmmm . . .*'

Someone behind me was praying. I thought I heard the words of the *Ave Maria*, oddly distorted and elongated into a mess of vowels. '*Marie! Marie!*'

The front row before the pulpitum had begun to take up the chant. I saw Clémente, Piété and Virginie throw their heads back almost at the same time and begin to rock in cadence.

'*Marie! Marie!*'

It was a slow rocking, heavy as the rolling of a huge ship. But it was contagious. The second row joined the first, then the third. It became a wave, inexorable as a wave, bringing each row—choir, pews, stalls—into surging motion. I felt it myself, my dancer's reflexes returning to life, fears, sounds, thoughts submerging in this dizzy vortex of movement. I threw back my head; for a moment I saw stars in the vaulting of the chapel roof and the world tilted enticingly. I could feel warm bodies all around me. My own voice was lost in a thick murmur. There was complete and unspoken cooperation in this slow frenzy of dance; the tide dragged us to the right, then to the left, all of us treading a measure all seemed to know by instinct. I could feel the dance calling, urging me to join it, to plunge my being into the black surf of movement and sound.

I could still hear Mère Isabelle shouting above the crowd, but had no understanding of what she was saying; she was a single instrument in an orchestra of chaos, voices blending and rising, hers a shrill counterpoint to the dark-mawed roar of the multitude, a few cries of protest—mine amongst them—in the howling tide of affirmation but lost as the rhythms, the raw-throated harmonies of pandaemonium engulfed us all . . .

And yet a part of my mind remained clear, floating coolly above the rest like a bird. I could hear LeMerle's voice without quite making out his words; in this shared madness it sounded like a refrain, a reminder of steps, of cadences in this *Ballet des Bernardines*.

Was this, then, to be his special performance? In front of me, Tomasine stumbled and fell to her knees. The dance shifted gracelessly to accommodate her, and another figure stumbled over her hunched from. They fell heavily together, and I recognized Perette, sprawling on the marble, the other nuns now snaking and spinning, oblivious, around her.

'Perette!' I pushed my way to my friend's side.

She had struck her head in the fall and a bruise already marked her temple. I picked her up, and together we pushed our way towards the open door. Our intrusion—or their exhaustion—seemed to quell some of the dancers, and the wave faltered and broke. I noticed Isabelle watching me, but had no time to wonder what her look of suspicion might portend. Perette was clammy and pale, and I forced her to breathe deeply, to put her head between her knees and to smell the little sachet of aromatics I carry in my pocket.

'What's that?' asked Mère Isabelle in the sudden lull.

The noise had begun to abate. I realized that several of the assembled nuns had broken their trance and were looking in my direction. 'This? Just lavender, and anise, and sweet balm, and . . .'

'What were you doing with it?'

I lifted the sachet of herbs. 'Can't you see? It's a scent sachet, you must have seen one before.'

There was a silence. Sixty pairs of eyes now turned towards me. Someone—I think it was Clémente—said softly, but very clearly: '*Witchcraft!*'

And I seemed to hear the murmur of acquiescence, the voice that came from no throat but from the small movements of many pairs of fluttering hands as they made the sign of the cross, the *hishh* of skin against cambric, of tongues moistening dry lips, of breath quickening. *Yes*, it whispered, and my heart flipped over like a dead leaf.

Yes.

CHAPTER SEVEN

♠

August 6th, 1610

I could have stopped it with a word. But the scene was so compelling, so classic in its perspectives that I had not the heart to do so. The evil omens, the visions, the portentous death and now the dramatic revelation amidst the carnage . . . It was magnificent, almost Biblical; I could not have scripted it better myself.

I wonder if she was conscious of the tableau she presented: head high, coiffe pulled back to reveal the dark fire of her curls, the wild girl clasped to her breast. Of course it is regrettable that tableaux should now be so out of fashion; more so that there should be so few here present able to appreciate it. But I have hopes for little Isabelle. An apt pupil in spite of her stolid upbringing, I could not have planned a more rousing performance myself.

Naturally, it was I who taught her all she knows, nurtured her, coaxed her from her meek obedience into this. I have, as you see, a vocation. A sense of pride moves me as I recall the tractable little girl she once was. But the good children, we are told, are always the ones to be careful of. A moment comes when even the most acquiescent of them may reach a point beyond which the cartographers of the mind can map nothing more. A declaration of independence, perhaps. An affirmation of self.

She thinks in absolutes, like her uncle. Dreams of sanctity, of battles with demons. A fanciful child,

255

in spite of everything, tormented by the visionary yearnings and uncertainties of her youth, the rigid conventions of her line. I suspected she'd declare herself today. You might say I staged it: a little *divertissement* between two acts of a great drama. Even so she surprised me. Not least by her perversity in choosing as her scapegoat the one woman I should have preferred her not to accuse.

Impossible to think that the girl suspects anything. It is instinctive with her, a child's love of defiance. She feels the need to prove to me the rightness of her suspicions—I, who have always remained maddeningly calm, almost sceptical in the face of her growing conviction—to earn my praise, even my discomfiture. For there is more to her now than submissive adoration. The declaration of self has elevated her, bred seeds of dissent in her that I must nurture whilst struggling to control. Her awe of me remains, coloured now with a sullenness, a renewed suspicion . . . I must take care. Given her head she might fall upon me as easily as upon you, my Ailée, and in this the two of you are more alike than you know. She is a knife, which I must handle with cunning. Perverse enough to welcome the subtle humiliations of my erstwhile designing, the core of breeding in her is strong, her pride obdurate.

You see, Juliette, that this changes things between us. I must not be seen to favour you. Both our heads might roll. I must be discreet now, or my plans will come to naught. I do admit to feeling a pang for you, however. Maybe when all this is done . . . But for now the risk is too great. Your weapon against me is gone now, even if you choose to use it. The word that stutters and hushes about the chapel must silence all accusations you may try to voice. You know it; I can see it in your eyes. And yet in spite of this it rankles to submit to the Arnault girl, even if it furthers my plans. My authority has been challenged. And as you know, a challenge is something I can seldom resist . . .

'There is no cause as yet to cry witchcraft upon our sister.' My voice was even and a little stern. 'You are ignorant, led only by your fear. In its face a lavender sachet becomes an instrument of the dark arts. A gesture of mercy takes sinister meaning. This is foolish beyond permission.'

For an uneasy moment I sensed their revolt. Clémente called out: 'There was a presence! *Someone* must have sent it out!'

Voices joined hers in agreement.

'Ay, I felt it!'

'And I!'

'There was a cold wind . . .'

'And the dancing . . .'

'The dancing!'

'Ay, there *was* a presence! Many presences!' I was improvising now, using my voice as a bridle to rein in this wild and spirited mare. 'The very presences that were unleashed when we opened the crypt!' Sweat ran into my eyes and I shook it away, afraid to show the beginnings of a tremor in my clenched hands. '*Vade retro, Satanas!*'

Latin has an authority that common tongues sadly lack. A pity that necessity should force me to perform in the vernacular, but these sisters are sadly ignorant. Nuances evade them. And for the moment they were too distraught for subtleties. 'I tell you this!' My voice rose above the murmur. 'We sit upon a well of corruption! A century-old bastion

257

of hell has been threatened by our Reform, and Satan fears its loss! But be of good cheer, sisters! The Evil One cannot harm the pure in heart. He works through the soul's corruption, but cannot touch one of true faith!'

'Père Colombin has spoken well.' Mère Isabelle looked at me from her small colourless eyes. There was something in her expression I did not quite like: a calculating look, a look almost of defiance. 'His wisdom puts our feminine fears to shame. His strength keeps us from falling.'

Strange words, and not of my choosing. I wondered where she was leading. 'But piety may hold its own dangers. The innocence of our holy father precludes true vision, true understanding. *He* has not felt what we have felt today!'

Her eyes moved to the doorway of the chapel where the new Marie, newly scrubbed, stood in gracious lethargy. 'There is a rot here,' she continued. 'A rot so deep that I have not dared voice my suspicions openly. But now . . .' She lowered her voice like a child exchanging secrets. I have taught her better than I knew, for her voice was clearly audible, a stage whisper that carried to the eaves. 'Now I can reveal it.'

Breathless, they awaited her revelation.

'Everything begins with Mère Marie. Did not the first Visitation appear from the crypt in which we interred her? Did not the apparitions you have seen wear her features? And did not the spirits speak to us in her name?'

There came from the crowd a low murmur of acquiescence.

'Well?' said Isabelle.

I didn't like it. 'Well what?' I said. 'Are you

258

saying that Mère Marie was in league with Satan? That's absurd. Why—'

She interrupted me—*me!*—and stamped her little foot. 'Who was it gave the order to bury Mère Marie in unhallowed ground?' she demanded. 'Who has repeatedly defied my authority? Who deals in potions and charms like a village witch?'

So that was it. Around her the sisters exchanged glances; several forked the sign against evil. 'Can it be a coincidence,' Isabelle went on, 'that Soeur Marguerite took one of her potions just before she got the dancing sickness? Or that Soeur Alfonsine went to her for help before she began to cough up blood!' She blanched at my expression, but went on nevertheless. 'She has a secret compartment next to her bed. She keeps her charms in there. See for yourself, if you don't believe me!'

I bowed my head. She had declared herself, then, and there was nothing I could do to prevent it. 'So be it,' I said between clenched teeth. 'We'll make a search.'

CHAPTER EIGHT
♥

August 6th, 1610

LeMerle followed her to the dorter, the sisters flocking at his back like a clutch of hens. He had always been good at hiding his anger, but I could see it in the way he moved. He did not look at me. Instead, his eyes flicked repeatedly to Clémente, trotting alongside Isabelle with her face modestly averted. Let him draw what conclusions he would, I thought; for myself, I had little doubt as to the identity of the informant. Perhaps she had seen me coming from his cottage last night; perhaps it was simply her instinctive malice. In any case, she followed with deceptive meekness as Mère Isabelle, looking nervous but defiant, led us straight to the loose stone at the back of my cubicle.

'It's there,' she announced.

'Show me.'

She reached for the stone and worked at it with her small, uncertain fingers. The stone held fast. Mentally, I enumerated the contents of my cache. The Tarot game, my tinctures and medicines, my journal. That in itself was enough to condemn me—to condemn us both. I wondered if LeMerle knew of it; he seemed calm, but all of his body was tensed and ready. I wondered whether he would try to make a run for it—he had more than a fighting chance—or whether he would risk a bluff. A bluff, I thought, was more his style. Well, two could play at that.

'Are we all to be searched?' I said in a clear voice. 'If so, may I suggest that Clémente's mattress might bear investigation?'

Clémente gave me a dirty look, and a number of the sisters looked uneasy. I knew for a fact that at least half of them were hiding something.

But Isabelle was undeterred. 'I will decide who is to be searched,' she said. 'For the moment . . .' She frowned impatiently as she struggled with the loose stone.

'Let me do it,' said LeMerle. 'You seem to be having some difficulty.'

The stone came away easily beneath his card-player's fingers, and he pulled it out and laid it aside on the bed. Then he reached into the space. 'It's empty,' he said.

Isabelle and Clémente turned towards him with identical looks of disbelief. 'Let me see!' said Isabelle.

The Blackbird stepped aside with an ironic flourish. Isabelle pushed past him, and her little face contorted as she saw the empty cache. Behind her, Clémente was shaking her head. 'But it was right there . . .' she began.

LeMerle looked at her. 'So you're the one who has been spreading rumours.'

Clémente's eyes widened.

'Malicious, unfounded rumours to breed suspicion and to bring down our fellowship.'

'No,' whispered Clémente.

But LeMerle had already moved away, searching along the rows of cubicles. 'What might *you* be hiding, Soeur Clémente, I wonder? What will I find beneath your mattress?'

'Please,' said Clémente, white to the lips.

But the sisters around her had already begun to take up the bedroll. Clémente began to wail. Mère Isabelle watched, teeth clenched.

Suddenly, there came a cry of triumph. 'Look!' It was Antoine. She was holding a pencil in her fist. A black grease-pencil, of the type that had been used to deface the statues. And there was more: a clutch of red rags, some with the black stitching still visible—the crosses that had been maliciously removed from our clothes as we slept.

There was a heavy silence, as every nun who had been obliged to do penance for the damage turned her eyes on Clémente. Then, they all started shouting at once. Antoine, who had always been quicker with her hands than with her voice, dealt Clémente a sharp slap which tumbled her against the side of the cubicle.

'You milksop bitch!' yelled Piété, grabbing a handful of Clémente's wimple. 'Thought it was funny, did you?'

Clémente struggled and squealed, turning instinctively to LeMerle for help. But Antoine was already upon her, knocking her to the ground. There had been tension between them earlier, I recalled; some foolishness in Chapter.

Now Isabelle turned to LeMerle in distress. 'Stop them,' she wailed above the noise. 'Oh, *mon père*, please stop them!'

The Blackbird looked at her coldly. 'You began this,' he said. 'You drove them to this. Didn't you see I was trying to calm them?'

'But you said there were no demons—'

He hissed at her. 'Of *course* there are demons! But now was not the time to reveal all! If you had only *listened*.'

'I'm sorry! Please stop them, *please*!'

But the scuffle was already at an end. Clémente crouched on the ground, her hands over her eyes, whilst Antoine stood above her, redfaced and nose bleeding. Both were out of breath; around them, sisters who had not raised a finger to aid either party were panting in sympathy. I ventured a quick glance at LeMerle, but he was at his most cryptic, and his expression betrayed nothing of his thoughts. I knew I had not imagined it, however; that moment of surprise when he saw the empty cache. Someone had cleared it without his knowledge; I was sure of it.

*   *   *

Clémente and Antoine were both taken to the infirmary, on LeMerle's orders, and I was put to work in the bakehouse for the rest of the day, where, for three hours, my toils afforded me little enough time for thought. During that time, I made the dough in batches, shaped the long loaves on the trays, shoved them into the deep, narrow bays, so like the dark cells in the crypt where the coffins are laid to rest.

I tried not to recall the morning's events, but my mind returned to them again and again. Alfonsine's dance, the swaying bodies, the frenzied beginnings of possession. And the moment when LeMerle's eyes met mine, even then so close to laughter but behind the laughter a kind of fear, like a man on a wild horse who knows he will be thrown but who can still laugh with sheer delight at the chase.

For a time I had been certain he would not speak for me. He had lost control somehow, though I was sure that the madness was part of his plan. It would have been so easy for him to allow the blame to fall upon me, to use it to bring his followers to heel. But he had not. Absurd to feel gratitude. I should hate him for what he has done to me, to all of us. And yet . . .

I had almost completed the morning's work. I was alone, I had my back to the door and was cleaning out ash from the last of the ovens with a long wooden slat. I turned at the sound of her footsteps. Somehow I already knew who it was.

She had taken a risk coming to me, but not such

a great one; the infirmary lay just alongside the bakehouse, and I guessed she must have climbed the wall. The midday heat was still blinding; most of the sisters would be indoors. 'No one saw me,' said Soeur Antoine, as if to confirm my thoughts. 'And we need to talk.'

The change I had begun to see in her a week ago was more pronounced now. Her face looked leaner, her cheekbones defined, her mouth hard and determined. She would never be a slender woman, but now her fleshiness seemed powerful rather than soft; thick slabs of red muscle sheathed in the fat.

'You shouldn't be here,' I told her. 'If Soeur Virginie finds out you're here—'

'Clémente will talk,' said Antoine. 'I've been listening to her in the infirmary all morning. She knows about Fleur. She knows about you.'

'Antoine, I don't know what you're talking about. Go back to—'

'Will you listen?' she hissed. 'I'm on your side. Who do you think took those things from behind the loose stone?' I stared at her. 'What?' said Antoine. 'You think I'm too stupid to know about your hiding place? Poor, fat, stupid Soeur Antoine who wouldn't know an intrigue if she fell over it during the night? I see more than you think, Soeur Auguste.'

'Where did you hide my things? My cards, and—'

Antoine shook a plump finger. 'Quite safe, *ma soeur*, quite hidden. But I'm not ready to give them back just yet. After all, you owe me a favour.'

I nodded. I had not expected her to forget it.

'Clémente will talk, Auguste,' she said. 'Not now,

264

perhaps. She may be in disgrace today, but Mère Isabelle believes in her. Sooner or later, she will accuse us. And when she realizes that Père Colombin will not defend her, then she will bring him down.'

She paused for a moment to make sure I understood. My head was spinning. 'Antoine,' I said. 'How did you—'

'That isn't important,' said Antoine in a harsh voice. 'The little girl will believe her. I know little girls. I was one myself, after all. And I know'—at this her red face twisted in a painful smile—'I know that even the sweetest and most docile little girl will one day rise up to defy her father.'

There was a long silence. 'What do you want?' I said at last.

'You know about herbs.' Now Antoine's voice was soft, persuasive. 'You know what to do with them. I could—I could slip her a dose while she's safe in the infirmary. No one would know.'

I stared at her, incredulous. '*Poison* her?'

'No one would know. You could tell me what to do.' She sensed my disgust and gripped my arm tighter. 'It's for all of us, Auguste! If she speaks against you, you'll lose Fleur. If she speaks against me . . .'

'What?'

There was a long silence. 'Germaine,' she said at last. 'She knew about Clémente and Père Colombin. She was going to tell.'

I tried to understand. But it was hot; I was tired; Antoine's words sounded like meaningless noise. 'I couldn't let her,' she went on. 'I couldn't let her accuse him. I'm strong—stronger than she was, anyway. It was very quick.' And Antoine gave a tiny smile.

It was almost too much for me to take in. And yet it made a kind of sense. I told you: the Blackbird's skill was in making people see what they most wanted in him. Poor Antoine. Robbed of her child at fourteen, her only remaining passions those of the table, at last she had found another outlet for her maternal nature.

A sudden thought struck me, and I turned to her in dismay. 'Antoine. Did *he* tell you to do it?'

I don't know why the thought appalled me. He's killed before, and for less reason. But Antoine shook her head. 'He knows nothing about it. He's a good man. Oh, he's no saint,' she added, dismissing the seduction of Clémente with a gesture. 'He's a man, with a man's nature. But if that little girl turns against him . . .' She gave me a sharp look. 'You see why it has to be done, don't you, Auguste? A painless dose—'

I had to stop this. 'Antoine. Listen.' She looked at me like a good dog, with her head to one side. 'It would be a mortal sin. Doesn't that mean anything to you?' Admittedly it meant little enough to me, but I had always thought her a true believer.

'I don't care!' Her face was flushed, her voice rising dangerously. It occurred to me that her very presence here could be a danger to me.

I motioned her to be silent. 'Listen to me, Antoine. Even if I knew the plants to use, whom would they suspect? All poisons take time, you know, and any fool can recognize the symptoms.'

'But we *can't* let her tell!' said Antoine stubbornly. 'If you won't help me, I'll have to take action.'

'What do you mean?'

266

'I hid your treasures, Auguste,' she said. 'I can always find them again. You'll be watched all the time, now you've been accused. Do you think he'd speak for you again? And if you were examined, what do you think would happen to Fleur?'

In Aquitaine all the witch's household follows her onto the pyre. Pigs, sheep, housecats, chickens . . . I saw an engraving once of a burning in Lorraine: the witch above the pyre, and below her, cages in which smaller crudely drawn stiff figures crouched, hands outstretched. I wondered what the custom was in the islands.

Antoine watched me with a look of terrible patience. 'You have no choice,' she said. Nodding, I had to agree.

CHAPTER NINE
♠

August 7th, 1610

So the Abbess is mine again, if only for the moment. As she mouthed her Act of Contrition, on her knees, head bowed beneath my accusations, she wept; but they were thin tears, tears of resentment rather than of true repentance. She has defied me once already; never forget she may do so again.

'This fiasco is of your doing!' My voice was harsh against the stones of the cell. The silver crucifix gleamed in the candlelight. A tiny silver *encensoir* diffused frankincense into the dim air. 'Your refusal to ask for assistance has jeopardized God knows how many innocent souls!'

Her mutter was almost defiant behind the Latin. '*Mea culpa, mea culpa, mea maxima—*'

'It cost Soeur Germaine her life!' I continued mercilessly. 'It may well cost Soeur Clémente her soul!'

I lowered my voice a little. Cruelty is a precision instrument, better used to flay than to bludgeon. 'And as for your own'—she gave me a sharp look of fear then, and I knew I was close to reaching her—'only you know the depth of your sin and of your soul's defilement. The greatest demon of all has violated you. Lucifer, the demon of Pride.'

Isabelle flinched and seemed ready to speak, but instead put down her head and would not meet my eyes. 'Is it not true?' I insisted in a cold, soft voice. 'Did you not think you could solve all our troubles yourself, alone and unaided? Did you not imagine the triumph of victory, the homage the Catholic world would pay to the twelve-year-old girl who, single-handed, defeated the armies of hell?' I drew close to her ear and whispered in it. The hot scent of her tears was exhilarating. 'What did the Foul One put into your mind, Angélique?' I murmured. 'With what lures did he blind your eyes? Did you hope for fame? Power? Canonization, perhaps?'

'I thought . . .' her whimper was small, childish. 'I thought . . .'

'*What* did you think?' Coaxingly now, not unlike the seductive voice of Satan as imagined by these foolish virgins. 'What did you think, Angélique?' She did not seem to notice that I had reverted to her childhood name. 'Did you want to be a saint? To make of this place a shrine for the worldly? To have them bruise their knees before you in awe and adoration?'

She cringed. I knew her too well, you see. I saw these ambitions in her before she did herself, and I nurtured them for just such a moment. 'I didn't . . .' She was sobbing now, the hot, heartbroken tears of the child she is. 'I didn't think—I didn't know . . .'

I held her then, letting her weep against my shoulder. I felt no compassion for such as her, believe me, but it was expedient. Necessary. This might be the last time I was able to wield such power over her. Tomorrow might bring a new wave of self-declaration, a new revolt. Already I fancied I could see in her small colourless eyes a measuring look, a look almost of awareness . . . But for the present I was still the good Father, the warm, the forgiving, the rebuking Father . . .

'What must I do?' Her eyes were watery and, for the moment, trusting.

I struck at once.

CHAPTER TEN
♥

August 8th, 1610

I ground the morning glory seeds with some oil taken from the kitchen supplies, to which Antoine still has a key. The result was a paste which, when mixed with food, is difficult to detect. I flavoured it with a little sweet almond to mask the bitter taste, and gave it to Antoine camouflaged in a loaf of bread. She would administer the dose to Clémente, she told me, at supper.

She seemed to have no doubt as to my mixture's efficacy, nor any suspicion concerning my change of heart; I could only pray that her trust would last long enough for me to set my own defences in place. The morning glory seed, though dangerous in use, is far from lethal. I hoped that, having realized that, Antoine would hold her tongue. For a while, at least.

My deceit was simple enough. The dose of ground seeds, even administered twelve hours in advance, would ensure Clémente was unfit to be examined next day at Chapter. The symptoms are severe, ranging from vomiting to visions to complete unconsciousness over a period of twenty-four hours. That, then, was the time I had left.

That night the dorter was slow to settle. Perette lingered close to my cubicle, watching me—waiting, I thought, her bright birdlike eyes glittering—until at last I motioned her to go to bed. She seemed inclined to persist, her small face pinched with anxiety or impatience, and I sensed she wanted to signal something to me. But now was not the time. I repeated the gesture of dismissal and turned away, pretending to sleep. But for a long time after the lights were extinguished I could still hear the small sounds of wakefulness—sighs, turnings, the *click-click* of Marguerite's bead rosary—in the darkness so that I wondered whether I dared risk leaving at all. The small oblong of sky above my bed glowed purplish-blue—in August here the sky is never quite dark—and I could see a dim scatter of stars in the distance and hear the soft sigh of the surf across the marshes. Close by, Alfonsine moaned, and I wondered whether she was observing me. Her moanings might be genuine sleep sounds or a fakery of sleep to lull me into unwary action; the thought kept me in my bed for almost an hour longer until desperation drove me out. After all, I could not wait for ever, I told myself, and by morning I might have lost my only chance of escape.

Forcing myself to breathe silently, I rose and crossed the dorter barefoot. No one moved. I ran softly down the steps and across the courtyard, expecting at any moment to hear cries at my back, but the courtyard remained cool and dark, but for a shard of moon cutting across an angle of brickwork, the windows unlit.

LeMerle's cottage too was unlit, but I could see a dim glow from his fire reflected onto the ceiling, and I knew he was awake. I tapped at the door; a few seconds later he opened it cautiously, and his eyes widened. He was in his shirt, with breeches replacing his priest's robes. From his coat, carelessly discarded on a nearby chair, and his muddied boots, I guessed that he too had been on the prowl about the abbey, but he gave no indication of his business there.

'What the hell are you playing at?' he hissed, as he pulled me in and latched the door behind me. 'Isn't it enough that I risked my neck for you?'

'Things have changed, Guy. If I stay I may be accused.'

I explained my meeting with Antoine and her murderous request. I told him of my compromise, of the morning glories, the twenty-four hours. 'Do you see now?' I asked him. 'Do you see why I have to collect Fleur and leave?'

LeMerle frowned and shook his head.

271

'But you have to help me!' I sounded shrill to myself, afraid. 'Don't think I'll stay silent if I'm accused! I owe you nothing, LeMerle. Nothing at all.'

He sat down, one booted foot flung casually over the chair arm. His anger was gone and now he looked tired and—genuinely, I thought—rather hurt. 'What's this?' he said. 'Don't you trust me yet? Do you think I would stand and let you be accused?'

'You did it before, remember?'

'All in the past, Juliette. I suffered for it, believe me.'

Not half enough, I thought, and said as much.

'I'm sorry. I can't let you go.' His voice was final.

'I wouldn't betray you.'

Silence.

'I *wouldn't*, Guy.'

He stood up, putting his hands on my shoulders. I was suddenly aware of his scent, a dark aroma of sweat and damp leather, of the fact that in spite of my height he dwarfed me.

'Please,' I said in a low voice. 'You don't need me.'

The touch of his hand was like a breath from the ovens, crisping the hairs at the nape of my neck. 'Trust me,' he said. 'I do.'

Ten years ago I would have given anything to hear those words. It alarmed me a little that a part of me might still want them, and I closed my eyes to evade his. It was a trap. Didn't I know him by now? His skin was smooth, smooth as my dreams.

'As what? A pawn in your game of Bishops?' I pushed him away with my hands, but somehow my body drew him closer so that we stood entwined,

272

his fingers clasped at the nape of my neck, tracing letters of fire on my raised hackles.

'No.' His voice was very gentle.

'Then why?'

He shrugged and said nothing.

'*Why*, LeMerle?' I cried in angry desperation. 'Why this charade? Will you risk both our lives for your revenge? Because a man once had you exiled from Paris? Because of a *ballet*?'

'No, Juliette. Not for those things.'

'Then *why*?'

'You wouldn't understand.'

'Try me.'

It must have been witchcraft. Or madness, perhaps. I fought against it, scarring his wrists with my fingernails even as I clung to him, sealing his mouth with mine as if by so doing I might consume him whole. We shed our clothes in ferocious silence, he and I, and I saw that his body was still hard and strong, as I remembered it, and I was startled to realize just how tenderly I recalled every mark, every scar, as if they were my own. The ancient brand on his arm shone silver-snakeskin-pale in the moonlight, and though some part of me protested that I was making an irrevocable mistake, I could hardly make it out above the roaring in my mind. For a time I was more than flesh. I was sulphur, I was a pillar of fire which raged and fed and thirsted. It was what Giordano had always warned me about; the hidden savagery in my nature that he had always taken such care to subdue—and with so little success. It occurred to me then that although Giordano may have been learned in the properties of elemental substances, there were far more powerful alchemies in the world than his: alchemies that melded flesh and burned away the past and changed hatred back into love with a simple cantrip.

After a time the fire slipped from us and we lay gently, like lovers. My anger had left me, and a new languor possessed my limbs, as if the past five years had been a dream, nothing more, grim shadowplay on a wall which reveals itself to be nothing more than the movement of a boy's hand in the sunlight.

'Tell me, LeMerle,' I said at last. 'I want to understand.'

In a sickle of moonlight I saw him smile. 'It's a long tale,' he warned me. 'If I tell you, will you stay?'

'Tell me,' I repeated.

Still smiling, he did.

CHAPTER ELEVEN

♠

August 8th, 1610

Well, I had to tell her *something*, and she would have worked it out in the end. A pity she's a woman; if she'd been born a man I might almost have thought her my equal. As it was, I still had a weapon to wield, and the battle was sweet for a time. Her hair smelt of burnt sugar, the scents of baking and lavender warm on her skin. I swear this time I meant to keep my promise. My mouth on hers, I could almost believe it was true. We could take to the road again, I promised; together we could take to the air. L'Ailée might fly again—in

274

fact, I never doubted she would. Sweet fantasy, my Winged One. Sweet lies.

She wanted the tale, so I told it in words that would please her. More than I intended, perhaps, lulled by her sly caresses. More, perhaps, than was entirely safe. But my Ailée is a romantic at heart, wanting to believe the best in everything. Even this. Even me.

*   *   *

'I was seventeen.' Imagine that. 'The son of a local girl and some passing seigneur: unwanted, unacknowledged. It was understood that as such I belonged to the Church. No one asked me if I understood it. I was born a few miles away, near Montauban, and I was sent away to the abbey at five years old—that was where I learned my Latin and Greek. The Abbot was a weak but kindly man who had left society twenty years before to join the Cistercians. His connections remained good, however; and although he had renounced his name, it was reputed to have once been a powerful one. Certainly, the abbey was wealthy enough under his direction, and it was large. I grew up in a mixed environment, with monks on one side and nuns on the other.'

The tale is almost true—the name of the other protagonist eludes me but I recall her face beneath the novice's veil, the fine spray of freckles across the bridge of her nose, her eyes the colour of burnt umber ringed with gold.

'She was fourteen. I worked in the gardens, too young even to have earned my tonsure. She was a minx; she would glance over the wall at me as I

275

worked, laughing with her eyes.'

As I said, almost true. There was more, my Ailée, darker, uglier currents and cross-currents you would not so easily understand. In the reading room I would linger over the Song of Songs and try not to think of her whilst my masters watched me closely for signs of rapture.

I am the rose of Sharon, and the lily of the valleys.

I never could bear the sight or the smell of those flowers, afterwards. A summer garden is filled with bitter memories.

'For a time it was an idyll.'

This is what she wants to hear, a tale of innocence corrupted, of vanquished love. She is more troubadour than buccaneer, my Winged One, in spite of her sharp claws. You'd understand that, Juliette, with your sweet and sheltered childhood amongst the painted tigers.

For myself the idyll was a darker thing, the scents of that summer's flowers coloured with those of my solitude, my jealousy, my imprisonment. I neglected my lessons; I did penance for what sins they could discover, and on the rest I brooded in growing resentment and longing. I could hear the sound of running water beyond the abbey walls, and wondered where the river led.

'It was summer.' I'll let you believe it was love. Why not? I almost convinced myself. I was drunk on moonlight, on sensations: a curl of her hair, cut in secret and passed to me in a missal, the imprint of her feet on the grass, the imagined scent of her as I lay on my pallet, looking up at that tiny square of stars . . .

A garden enclosed is my sister, my spouse; a spring shut up; a fountain sealed.

We met in secret in the walled gardens, exchanged shy kisses and tokens like lovers long versed in the arts of intrigue. We were innocents ... Even I, in my way.

'It could not last.' This, my Ailée, is where our tales diverge. 'They found us together, grown careless perhaps, giddy with delight at our forbidden pleasures ...'

She screamed, the little fool. They called it rape.

'I tried to explain.' I had pulled down her uncut hair; it hung in ringlets to her waist. Beneath her robe I could feel her small breasts. Solomon said it most sweetly: *Thy breasts are like unto two young roes that are twins, which feed among the lilies.*

How could I have known she'd be such a little prude? She screamed and I silenced her, pinning her arms to her sides and my hand over her mouth.

'Too late.' They dragged me off, protesting. It was no fault of mine, I swore; if any was to blame, let it be Solomon, with his twin roes. My convent passionflower pleaded innocence; the fault was all mine, she hardly knew me, had not encouraged my advances. I was locked in my cell. My scribbled note to her was returned unopened. Too late I realized we had misunderstood each other. My reluctant sweetheart dreamed of Abelard, not Pan.

'I was imprisoned for three days, awaiting judgement. For all that time, no one spoke a word to me. The brother who brought me my meals did so with his face turned away. But to my surprise, I was not starved or beaten. My disgrace was too profound for any ordinary penance.'

I have always hated being enclosed, however, and my imprisonment was all the more painful for the scent of the garden outside my window and the sounds of summer beyond the walls. They might have let me out if I had repented, but my stubborn lack of shame cut me from them. I would not recant my story. I would not submit to their judgement. Who were they to judge me, anyway?

On the fourth day a friend managed to pass me a note, informing me that the Abbot had sought the advice of a visiting clergyman—a well-regarded man of noble house—concerning the matter of my punishment. I was not greatly troubled by the prospect. I could take a whipping if I needed to, although the kind Abbot had always been lenient towards me, and rarely used such measures.

It was late that afternoon when I was finally brought from my cell. Restless, sullen and desperately bored, I blinked in the sudden sunlight as the Abbot led me from the dark passageway into his study, where a tall, distinguished man of about thirty-five was awaiting me.

He was dressed in the black town habit and cloak of an ordinary priest, with a silver cross around his neck. His hair was black to the Abbot's grey, but they had the same high cheekbones and light, almost silvery eyes. Seeing them there, side by side, there could be no doubt that the two men were brothers.

The newcomer studied me expressionlessly for a moment. 'So this is the boy. What's your name, boy?'

'Guy, if it pleases you, *mon père*.'

His mouth thinned as if it did not please him at all. 'You've indulged him, Michel,' he said to the Abbot. 'I should have known you would.'

The Abbot said nothing, though it cost him an effort.

'A man's nature cannot be altered,' continued the stranger. 'But it can—it *must*—be subdued. By your negligence, an innocent girl has been corrupted, and the reputation of our house—'

'I didn't corrupt her,' I protested. It was true; if anything, she had corrupted me.

The newcomer looked at me as if I were carrion. I gave him back his look, and his cold eyes grew colder. 'He persists, then,' he said.

'He's young,' said the Abbot.

'That's no excuse.'

Refusing once more to acknowledge my crime, I was taken back to my cell. I rebelled at being locked up again; fought the brothers who had been sent to fetch me, blasphemed, flung abuse. The Abbot came to reason with me, and I might have listened to him if he had been alone, but his guest was with him, and something in me revolted at the thought of giving in to this man who had apparently judged and detested me on sight. Exhausted and angry, I slept; was awoken at dawn—for Matins, I thought—and led outside by two brothers who refused to meet my eye.

In the courtyard, the Abbot was waiting for me, with the brothers and the nuns standing around him in a circle. At his side, the priest, his silver cross gleaming in the pale light, his hands folded. Among the nuns I caught sight of my little novice, but her face was averted, and remained so. Others bore expressions of pity, dismay or vague excitement; there was an atmosphere of breathless expectancy.

Then the Abbot stood aside and I saw what he had been concealing. A brazier, heated to buttercup-yellow under the banked embers, and a

279

brother, with heavy gloves to protect his hands and arms from the heat, now hauling the iron from beneath the coals.

A sigh rose from the ranks, almost of pleasure. *Ahhhh*.

Then the newcomer spoke. I don't remember much of what he said; I was too preoccupied with the scene before me. My eyes returned again to the brazier in disbelief; to the small square iron heated to the colour of your hair. Dimly I began to understand. I struggled, but was held; a brother pulled up my sleeve to expose bare flesh.

It was at this point that I recanted. There's pride, and there's stupidity, after all. But it was too late. The Abbot looked away, grimacing; his brother took a step closer to me and whispered something in my ear, just as the iron made its dreadful contact.

I have occasionally prided myself on a certain turn of phrase. Some things, however, can never be adequately described. Suffice it to say that I feel it still, and the words he spoke to me in that moment lit a spark that still endures.

*   *   *

Perhaps, Monseigneur, I owe you *something*; after all, you spared my life. But a cloistered life is no life at all, as Juliette could no doubt tell you, and to be expelled from mine was probably the best thing that could have happened to me. Not that you acted out of any concern for me. In fact, you doubted I'd survive. What skills did I have? Latin, reading, a certain natural perverseness. *That* served me well, if nothing else; you wanted me dead, so I decided to live. Even then, you see, I was shameless. So was born the Blackbird, strident and indomitable, flinging his idiot song in the faces of those who despised him, raiding their orchards beneath their very noses.

Years later, as Guy LeMerle I came to Court. My enemy was a bishop now, the Bishop of Evreux. I should have known a simple parish would not have contained him long. Monseigneur wanted more. He wanted the Court; more than that, he wanted the ear of the King. There were too many Huguenots around Henri for his liking; it offended your exquisite sensibilities. And what glory to the house of Arnault—in heaven and on earth—if he were to bring a royal lamb back to the fold!

Once burned, twice shy. Not in my case. I escaped the second time, but narrowly. I could almost smell the reek of burning feathers. Well, this time it's my turn. They say Nero fiddled whilst Rome burned. Paltry fellow that he must have been with his one fiddle. When my time comes I'll greet Monseigneur d'Evreux with a whole damned orchestra.

*   *   *

I was sweating. My hand was unsteady on her breast. My pain was scented with flowers. It coloured my tale with truth, Juliette. I saw her eyes widen with pity and understanding. The rest was easy. Revenge, after all, is something we can both understand.

'Revenge?' she said.

'I want to humiliate him.' Answer with care, LeMerle. Answer so that she believes you. 'I want him to be implicated in a scandal which even his influence cannot suppress. I want him ruined.'

She gave me a sharp look. 'But why now? Why now, after all this time?'

'I saw an opportunity.' This, like the rest of my tale, is close to the truth. But a wise man makes his own opportunities, just as a good card-player makes his own luck. And I am a very good player, Juliette.

'There's still time to change your mind,' she said. 'Only harm can come of such a plan. Harm to yourself, to Isabelle, to the abbey. Can you not leave things as they are and free yourself from the past?' She lowered her eyes. 'I might come with you,' she said. 'If you decided to go.'

A tempting offer. But I had invested too much in this to turn back. I shook my head in genuine regret. 'A week,' I said softly. 'Give me a week.'

'What about Clémente? I can't drug her for ever.'

'You need not fear Clémente.'

Juliette looked at me suspiciously. 'I won't let you harm her. Or anyone else.'

'I won't. Trust me.'

'I mean it, Guy. If anyone else is harmed—by you, or on your orders—'

'Trust me.'

Almost inconceivable, that I should be forgiven. Yet her smile tells me that haply all might be as it was. Guy LeMerle—if I were only he—might have taken that offer. Next week will be too late; by then there will be more blood on my hands than even she could absolve.

CHAPTER TWELVE

♥

August 9th, 1610

The air was cool, and there were livid smears of false dawn on the night's palette. Soon the bell would chime for Vigils. But my head was too full for sleep, still ringing as it was with LeMerle's words.

What was this? Some witchcraft, some drug slipped to me as I slept? Could it be that I believed him now, that in some way he could have regained my trust? Silently I berated myself. What I had said—what I had done—was said and done for Fleur. Whatever I had promised was for both of us. As for the rest—I shook aside visions of myself and LeMerle on the road again, friends again, maybe lovers . . . That would never happen. Never.

I wished I had my cards with me, but Antoine had hidden them well; my search of her bedroll and of her place in the bakehouse had discovered nothing. Instead I thought of Giordano, and tried to hear his voice over the pounding of my heart. *More than ever I need your logic now, old friend.* Nothing discomposed your ordered, geometric world. Loss, death, famine, love . . . The wheels that turn the universe left you unmoved. In your numbers and calibrations you glimpsed the secret names of God.

Tsk-tsk, begone! But my cantrips are useless in the face of this greater magic. Tomorrow night at moonrise I will pick rosemary and lavender for protection and clear thinking. I will make a charm of rose leaves and sea salt and tie it with a red ribbon and carry it in my pocket. I will think of Fleur. And I will not meet his eyes.

*　　　*　　　*

Clémente was not at Matins this morning, nor at Lauds. Her absence was not mentioned, but I noticed that Soeur Virginie was also excused from prayers, and drew my own conclusions. The drug was working, then. The question was, for how long?

Such was the speculation about Soeur Clémente that it was some hours before I noticed that Alfonsine, too, was absent. At the time I did not give it much thought; Alfonsine had recently become very friendly with Soeur Virginie, and had offered to help her on a number of occasions. Besides, LeMerle was so often in the infirmary block that Alfonsine needed no other reason to haunt it.

But at Prime, Virginie came alone, and with news. Clémente was very sick, she said. She had fallen into a deep lethargy from which nothing was able to rouse her, and she had been running a high fever since dawn. Piété shook her head and swore she had suspected the cholera all along; Antoine smiled serenely. Marguerite declared that we were all bewitched, and suggested a harsher system of penances.

But there was more unwelcome news. Alfonsine, too, was ill once more. In her case there was no fever, but she was unusually pale, and had been coughing fitfully for most of the night. Bleeding had seemed to quiet her a little, but she was still very listless and would not eat. Mère Isabelle had been to visit her and had declared her unfit for duties, although Alfonsine had tried to persuade her she was quite well. But any fool could see it was the *cameras de sangre*, declared Soeur Virginie; and unless the bad blood were drained away, the patient would surely die within the week.

That troubled me far more than the news about Clémente. Alfonsine was already weak from overexcitement and self-inflicted penances. Bleeding and fasting would kill her with far greater efficiency than disease. I said as much to Soeur Virginie.

'I'll thank you not to interfere,' she said. 'My method worked perfectly well for Soeur Marguerite.'

'Soeur Marguerite had a narrow escape; besides, she's stronger than Alfonsine. Her lungs are not compromised.'

Virginie looked at me in open disdain. 'If we're to speak of being compromised, *ma soeur*, you should look to yourself.'

'What do you mean?'

'I mean that although you may have got away with it last time, there are some of us who think that your—*enthusiasm*—for potions and powders might not be as innocent as Père Colombin thinks.'

I dared not make any comment after that, either to help Alfonsine or to advise on the treatment of Clémente. It was too close to the truth, and although LeMerle might speak lightly of the possible danger, I was only too aware of the precarious line I was now treading. Virginie had the Abbess's ear; they are alike in some ways, as

285

well being closer to each other in age than the rest of us; and she has never liked me. It would take only a little thing—words spoken by Clémente, perhaps, in delirium or otherwise—to ensure that I was once more accused.

I would have spoken of it to LeMerle, but he made no appearance today, remaining in the infirmary or in his study, surrounded by books. Very soon, if I knew my plant lore correctly, Clémente's fever would break and she would regain consciousness. What happened then was up to LeMerle. He could control Clémente, he had said; I did not share his optimism. He had chosen me publicly over her; that was something no woman would forgive.

I slept badly, and dreamed too well. My own voice awoke me, and after that I was afraid to close my eyes in case I spoke again and betrayed myself as I slept. In LeMerle's cottage, a little light burned. I had almost made up my mind to go to him when Antoine got up to use the latrines in the reredorter, and I had to lie back, eyes closed, feigning sleep. She got up twice more during the night—our diet of black bread and soup evidently disagreed with her—and so we were both alert to the sound of the alarum as it sounded across the courtyard from the infirmary.

Finally, Clémente was awake.

CHAPTER THIRTEEN

♥

August 9th, 1610

Antoine and I were the first to reach the infirmary. We did not look at each other as we raced along the slype towards the walled garden, but we could already hear Clémente's feverish cries as we approached. There was a light at one of the windows and we followed the light, with Tomasine, Piété, Bénédicte and Marie-Madeleine arriving soon after.

The infirmary consists of a single, large and rather stuffy room. There are beds lined up against the wall—six of them, although there is provision for more. No cubicle wall separates the beds, so that sleep is almost impossible here among the sighs and coughs and whimperings of the sufferers. Soeur Virginie had made some effort to isolate Clémente; her bed was at the far end of the room, and she had placed a curtain screen to one side of it, cutting off some of the lamplight and giving the afflicted girl some privacy. Alfonsine was positioned by the door, as far from Clémente as possible, and I caught sight of her open eyes as I passed: two points of brightness in the dark.

The Abbess was already there. Virginie and Marguerite, who must have given the alarum at her command, were beside her, looking fearful and excited. LeMerle stood at a distance, grave in his black robe with his silver crucifix held in one hand. On the bed, her ankles fastened into place by two straps fixed to the wooden frame, sprawled Clémente. A pitcher of water had been spilt across a small bedside table; a stinking basin pushed beneath the bed itself. Her face was white; her pupils were dilated so much that the blue of her irises was almost invisible.

'Help Soeur Virginie to tie her down,' ordered the Abbess to Marguerite. 'You—yes you, Soeur Auguste! Bring a calming infusion.'

I hesitated for an instant. 'I—perhaps it might be better if—'

'At once, you fool!' The nasal voice was sharp. 'A calming drink, and a change of bedclothes! Go quickly!'

I shrugged. The morning glory seed requires an empty stomach to avoid ill effects. But I obeyed; ten minutes later I returned, carrying a light infusion of skullcap leaves sweetened with honey, and a fresh blanket.

Clémente was delirious. 'Leave me alone, leave me alone!' she screamed, flailing at the proffered cup with her unsecured left hand.

'Hold her down!' cried Mère Isabelle.

Soeur Virginie poured most of the infusion down Clémente's throat as she opened her mouth again to scream. 'There, *ma soeur*. That will make you better,' she shouted above the noise. 'Just try to rest—'

Her words were barely uttered when Clémente vomited with such force that reeking liquid splattered against the wall of the infirmary. I shrugged inwardly. Virginie, who had been liberally showered, shrieked, and Mère Isabelle, beside herself, slapped her smartly, as a spoiled child might slap her nurse in a fit of temper.

288

Clémente vomited again, leaving a trail of slime over the new blanket. 'Fetch Père Colombin.' Her voice was hoarse with shrieking. 'Fetch him now!'

LeMerle had been standing in silence. Now he moved closer, delicately avoiding the patches of vomit on the floor. 'Let me pass.' In fact there was no one obstructing him, but we responded to the voice of authority. Clémente too responded; she turned her face towards him and whimpered softly.

LeMerle held out his crucifix.

'*Mon père!*' For an instant the afflicted woman seemed quite lucid. She whispered in her hoarse voice: 'You said you'd help me. You said you'd help . . .'

LeMerle began to speak in Latin to her, still holding the crucifix between them as if a weapon. I recognized the words as a fragment of the exorcism service, which he would no doubt perform in full at some later date.

'*Praecipio tibi, quicumque es, spiritus immunde, et omnibus sociis tuis hunc Dei famulum obsidentibus . . .*'

I saw Clémente's eyes widen. 'No!'

'*Ut per mysteria incarnationis, passionis, resurrectionis, et ascensionis Domini nostri . . .*'

In spite of everything I felt a sudden surge of guilt at her suffering.

'*Per missionem Spiritus Sancti, et per adventum ejusdem Domini.*'

'Please, I didn't mean it, I'll never tell anyone—'

'*Dicas mihi nomen tuum, diem, et horam exitus tui, cum aliquo signo—*'

'It was Germaine—she was jealous, she wanted me for herself . . .'

When Janette used the drug in ceremonies and

divination, it was in tiny doses after a long period of meditation. Clémente had been unprepared. I tried to imagine the depth of her terror. Now, at last, the drug was reaching its final stage. Soon the attack would be over, and she would sleep again. LeMerle made the sign of the cross over Clémente's face. '*Lectio sancti Evangelii secundum Joannem.*'

But his refusal to acknowledge her seemed to contribute to her agitation. She grasped at the sleeve of his robe with her teeth, almost knocking the crucifix from his hand. 'I'll tell them everything,' she snarled. 'I'll see you burn.'

'See how she recoils from the Cross!' said Marguerite.

'She's ill,' I said. 'Delirious. She doesn't know what she's doing.'

Marguerite shook her head stubbornly. 'She's possessed,' she said, her eyes shining. 'Possessed by the spirit of Germaine. Didn't she say so herself?'

Now was no time to argue. I could see Mère Isabelle watching us from the corner of my eye, and knew she had heard every word. But LeMerle was unmoved. 'Demons who have infested this woman, name yourselves!'

Clémente whimpered. 'There are no demons. You yourself said—'

'Name yourselves!' repeated LeMerle. 'I command you! In the name of the Father!'

'I only wanted—I didn't mean to—'

'Of the Son!'

'No—please—'

'Of the Holy Spirit!'

At this, Clémente finally broke. 'Germaine!' she screamed. 'Mère Marie! Behemoth! Beelzebub!

290

Ashtaroth! Belial! Sabaoth! Tetragrammaton!' She was weeping now in fast, gasping sobs, the names—many known to me from Giordano's various texts, but doubtless gleaned by Clémente from Alfonsine's raptures—coming from her lips in a desperate rush. 'Hades! Belphegor! Mammon! Asmodeus!'

LeMerle laid a hand on her shoulder, and such was her agitation that she shrieked again and drew away.

'Possessed!' whispered Marguerite again. 'See how she burns at the touch of the Cross! Hear the names of the demons!'

LeMerle half turned to face the rest of us. 'Evil news indeed,' he said. 'I was blind enough yesterday to believe there might be another explanation for her illness. But now we have it from her own mouth. Soeur Clémente has been infested by unclean spirits.'

'Let me help her, please.' Unwise, I knew, to draw attention to myself, but I could bear it no longer. All the same I was very aware of Virginie's eyes on me, and behind her, those of our little Abbess.

LeMerle shook his head. 'I must be alone.' He looked exhausted, the outstretched hand which held the crucifix visibly shaking with the effort. 'Anyone who stays here puts their soul in peril.'

Clémente, between sobs, began to recite the Lord's Prayer.

LeMerle took a step backwards. 'See how the demons taunt us!' he said. 'You have named yourself, demon, now let us see your face!'

As he spoke, a cold draught blew from the open door, flickering the flames in the candles and cressets that illuminated the room. Instinctively I turned; others followed my lead. Beyond the door, in the darkened hallway, a white figure hesitated just out of the range of our light. I could barely make out its shape. It appeared to float vaguely down the passageway, skirting the light with delicate precision so that all we saw of it was the habit it wore—so similar to our own—and the pale *quichenotte* that hid its face completely.

'The Unholy Nun!'

I grabbed a cresset from Virginie and sprang forwards with its small flame in my hand. Marguerite shrieked and clawed at my sleeve. I paid no attention but took three paces into the passageway, carrying my light before me.

'Who's that?' I cried. 'Show yourself!'

The Unholy Nun turned, and I had time to see dark-stockinged legs beneath the robe. So much, then, for its ghostly floating. The hands, too, were gloved in black. Then the figure began to run down the passage, moving lightly and quickly away from the light.

Someone at my back called out impatiently: 'What did you see?'

Someone else tugged at my wimple, my arm. I dislodged the grip with some difficulty, fighting to keep hold of the cresset. When I looked back the apparition had gone.

'Soeur Auguste! What did you see?' It was Isabelle, clutching me as if she never meant to let go. At close quarters her complexion looked worse than ever, small angry red sores blooming around her mouth and nose. Janette would have prescribed fresh air and exercise. *Fresh air and sunshine,* she would have said with her familiar cackle. *That's the thing for a growing child. That's what made me the beauty you see before you.* If only Janette were here now.

'Yes indeed, Soeur Auguste, what *did* you see?' The polite tone was LeMerle's, touched now with a note of mockery only I could hear.

'I . . .' I heard my voice waver. 'I'm not sure.'

'Soeur Auguste is a sceptic,' said LeMerle. 'Perhaps even now she doubts the presence of demons in Soeur Clémente.'

I kept my eyes fixed to the cresset's light, not daring to face his smile.

'Soeur Auguste,' said Isabelle shrilly. 'Tell us at once. What did you see? Was it the Unholy Nun?'

Slowly, reluctantly, I nodded.

A wave of questions followed. Why had I pursued her? Why had I stopped? What exactly had I seen? Was there blood on the bonnet? And on the surplice? Had I seen the face?

I tried to answer them all. Where lies were needed, I lied. Every word I uttered drove me further into LeMerle's power, but I had no choice, no strength to resist it; I lied by necessity. For in the second when the spectre turned to me, face to face and almost close enough to touch in the dim passageway, I had recognized the Unholy Nun. My dearest friend, her gold-ringed eyes wide with something almost like amusement. As if this were a game with nothing more at stake than a handful of glass marbles.

It made perfect sense. Her innocence protected her. Her silence was assured. And only I had heard the faint bird-laughter which followed the spectre's disappearance into the gloom, that hooting, inhuman note which no other throat could quite duplicate.

There could be no mistaking that sound, those eyes.

It was Perette.

PART FOUR
PERETTE

CHAPTER ONE

♠

August 10th, 1610

So far, so good. But the task which remains is a delicate one. I have only five days until his arrival, and the threads of my delicate weaving become ever more twisted and tortuous. Clémente remains in her bed in the infirmary, quiet now, but not, I suspect, for long. I have spent many hours at her side with Virginie in attendance, incense and holy water in hand. A sharp needle concealed in one sleeve ensured her cooperation throughout the final stage of her drug's effects; with it I pricked her with scientific precision when a scream or a curse was required, and in her dazed condition she was unable to distinguish the pains of her visions from those of the hidden instrument.

With becoming gravity I pronounced Clémente possessed by two hundred and fifty demons. I spent much of the remainder of the morning in my library, engrossed in several texts on the subject, then emerged some little time before midday with a list of their names. This I proceeded to read to Clémente in slow, measured tones whilst Virginie watched in slack-mouthed awe and the doomed girl on the bed writhed and pleaded.

I knew that Juliette would refuse to administer another dose of her morning glories, but I had enough for my immediate needs, and as the day wore on and I saw Clémente begin to regain her senses I began to foresee the need for a repetition

297

of the procedure. I knew already that my Ailée would disapprove. But what could she do?

Mass was, of course, cancelled. I 'studied' in my rooms, with a book of Aristotle's maxims hidden within the covers of the *Malleus Malleficarum*. Services without me were a dull affair, I gather, but I made a show of fearing another repetition of the frenzies and the Dancing Mass.

Meanwhile, Marguerite watched over Clémente and—in spite of strict instructions from me not to breathe a word of the day's events—diffused the terrible news of her possession throughout the abbey. Of course this had been my intention all along, and the rumours, all the more appealing for being forbidden, were soon repeated, expanded, embellished and otherwise disseminated as widely as dandelion seed.

My principal source of unease lies in Juliette. Her discovery of the identity of my Unholy Nun was perhaps inevitable, but nevertheless troubles me a little. The wild girl is her friend, so I'm told, and she feels loyalty to her. Not so the wild girl, who can be bought for a trinket and whose silence is beyond rubies, but if Juliette were to learn the full extent of my plans . . .

Foolishness, of course. Perette is a primitive creature, an unformed mind with no more intelligence than a trained monkey. It took me a little time to break her—indeed, I spent two sleepless nights in the crypt curing her of her unreasonable fear of the dark—but now she fawns on me as trusting as a spaniel, her small hands cupped, begging for the next treat. I'm sorely tempted, when I leave this place, to take Perette with me. There are so many uses to which I could put her. And Juliette— But I must not think of Juliette. By the Sunday she will have learned the full extent of my treachery, and I cannot hope to be forgiven this time. But Perette is another matter. Even untrained, she is nimble beyond expectation. Sleight-of-hand is child's play to her. She can move unseen and unheard in a room of sleepers without disturbing a single one. She can run like the wind, climb like a squirrel, curl up and hide in the tiniest of spaces. I could even teach her to dance on a rope. No one could hope to equal my Ailée, but perhaps with practice . . . I could paint her face with walnut juice and pass her off as a savage from Canada. They'd pay to see that.

Yes, amongst all the rest I might yet save Perette.

CHAPTER TWO

♥

August 10th, 1610

Of course, after what I had seen in the infirmary I went to Perette as soon as I could. That was in the morning, after Prime. We all went to our duties a little late, for the Abbess was with her confessor and we guessed that discipline might be a little relaxed. I found Perette, as I expected, in the stables where we kept our beasts. She had taken some stale bread with her, and the place was awash with the hens and ducks and speckled pullets which had followed her in. She looked at me inquiringly.

'Perette.' She smiled then, a wide-open smile of

299

delight, and indicated the birds. She looked so happy—and so innocent—that I felt oddly reluctant to speak of that morning's incident. I steeled myself nevertheless. 'Never mind the hens. Perette. I saw you in the infirmary this morning.' She looked at me pertly, head to one side. 'I saw you pretending to be the Unholy Nun.'

Perette gave the hooting cry which in her passes for laughter.

'It isn't funny.' I took her arms and turned her to face me. 'It could have been very dangerous.'

Perette shrugged. She is clever enough at some things, but when we broach the subject of might-have, or could-have-been, or would-be, she tends to lose interest.

I spoke slowly, patiently, using simple words she knew. 'Perette. Listen to me. Tell me the truth.' She smiled at me, giving no sign of whether or not she understood. 'Tell me, Perette. How many times have you—' No, that was wrong. 'Perette. Have you played this game before?'

Perette nodded and hooted happily.

'And did—did Père Colombin ask you to play this game?'

Again, the nod.

'Did—did Père Colombin say *why* he wanted you to play this game?'

That was more difficult. Perette thought for a moment, shrugged, then held out a grimy palm. In it rested a small brown object. A piece of sugar. She looked at it, licked it, then replaced it carefully in her pocket.

'Sugar? He gives you sugar when you play the game?'

Perette shrugged again. Then, fumbling around

300

her neck, she drew out the small medallion I had seen LeMerle take from her only a few weeks ago, now secured by a piece of twine. Christina Mirabilis smiled out from the bright enamelled disc.

Again I made my voice slow and coaxing. 'So, Perette. You played the game for Père Colombin.' Perette smiled and ticked her head from one side to the other. The medallion winked in the sunlight. 'But why did he want you to play the game?'

The wild girl shrugged and turned the medallion over in her fingers, catching the light. I tried to curb my impatience. 'Yes, Perette, but *why* did he ask you? Did he tell you why?'

Again she shrugged. What did it matter why he wanted it, said the shrug, as long as there was sugar and trinkets?

I gave her a gentle shake. 'Perette. What you did was a bad thing.'

She looked puzzled at that, beginning to shake her head in denial. 'A bad thing!' I insisted, raising my voice a little. 'It wasn't your fault, but it was bad all the same. Père Colombin was bad to make you do it.'

Perette turned her mouth down sulkily and made as if to pull away. I held her back. 'Do you remember Fleur?' I said suddenly. 'Do you remember when they took Fleur away?'

Perhaps she did not, I told myself. It had been almost a month since Fleur's disappearance, and Perette might already have forgotten her young playmate. For a moment she looked puzzled, then raised her hand in the gesture she had always used to indicate the child.

'It was Père Colombin who took Fleur away,' I

301

told her. 'He may seem very nice, he may give you presents, but Perette, he's a bad man, and I need to know what he's planning!' My voice had risen again, and I was gripping her arm painfully. Her blank expression told me that I had gone too fast, that I had lost her. 'Perette, look at me!'

But it was too late. The moment of contact was gone, and Perette had returned her attention to the birds. As I turned away, furious at my own impatience, I saw her sitting in a clucking mound of them, arms outstretched, her lap a mass of white, brown, speckled, golden, green and red feathers.

And yet I cannot give up. If there is a key to this enigma, it is she. My sweet Perette, my innocent. Whatever he is planning, she knows it. It may be beyond her understanding, but his secret is there, hidden within her as securely as in a Chinese puzzle-box. If only I knew what it was. If only I could break your locks, my dear.

CHAPTER THREE
♥

August 11th, 1610

I tried to talk to LeMerle all yesterday, but he avoids me and I cannot afford to draw attention to myself. Last night his door was locked, the light extinguished. I wondered whether he was in the infirmary, but dared not go to see. Clémente is still incapable of rational speech, so Antoine tells me, alternating long periods of lethargy with intervals of wild, wakeful delirium. During those times she has to be secured to the mattress for fear she injures herself. Often she tears at her clothing, exposing herself, thrusting violently at the air as if ridden by a demon lover. At these times she may scream or moan in terrible pleasure, or claw at her face in an agony of self-loathing. Better to tie her down, though she pleads to be released, thrashing her head from side to side and spitting with uncanny accuracy at anyone who dares approach her.

I am not allowed to visit. Antoine, too, has been removed from the infirmary, though Virginie remains to care for the possessed woman. Antoine tells me this with sly satisfaction: Clémente seems crazed, and may never regain her sanity. So Virginie tells her. Antoine's eyes are small and mean as she speaks of it. She has volunteered to help in the infirmary, washing blankets and preparing broths for the afflicted woman, into which, no doubt, she slips a regular dose of morning glories.

Lovely Clémente is no longer quite so lovely, she reports in that new, sly voice; her face will be scarred by the repeated assault of her fingernails; her hair is coming out in patches. I would have liked to go to her, to comfort her perhaps or to explain to her ravaged face that it wasn't my fault . . .

What good would it do? Antoine's hand may have given her the dose, but it was I gave her the means. I would do it again in the same circumstances. LeMerle, wisely keeping his distance, knows it. Again he has opened a gulf inside me, has opened the dark budget of possibility within my entrails.

Thou shalt not suffer a witch to live.

Giordano used to say that in the original Hebrew the word *witch* meant *poisoner*.

I wonder if Giordano would recognize his pupil now.

CHAPTER FOUR

♠

August 12th, 1610

As expected, my affairs proceed according to plan. Mère Isabelle remains docile—for the present. She spends much of her time in prayer, heedless of her increasingly unruly flock. Access to Clémente is limited, for even I can hardly dose the girl continuously, and her ravings have become increasingly violent.

Instead, I build upon my pupil's fears with lore and nonsense culled from a hundred books both sacred and profane. Whilst seeming to lull her terrors I artfully nourish them with anecdotes and fancies. The world is filled with horrors: burnings, poisonings, bewitchings and evil enchantments—you name it, Père Colombin knows it, and he knows exactly how to bring the horrors to life. A chequered career may provide useful fuel for such deceits; after all, I even met the famous jurisconsult Jean Bodin at one of Mme de Sévigné's soirées—and was thoroughly bored by the lengthiness of his discourse. The rest I borrowed from the great fictions of history. Aeschylus, Plutarch, the Bible . . . Clémente herself is quite unaware that the demoniac names she utters in her frenzies are for the most part merely the secret, forgotten names of God, reborn as blasphemies in her tortured brain.

My pupil has hardly slept for days. Her eyes are sunken and red. Her mouth is pale as a scar. Sometimes I see her watching me, she thinks in secret. I wonder if she suspects. In any case, it is too late for her. A dose of Clémente's morning glories would be enough to kill her revolt, though I would only administer it in dire emergency. I want it to come to Arnault from a blue sky. The end of his hopes. Irrevocable.

Ironically, my pupil now takes what comfort she can at the prospect of Sunday's treat, the long-awaited Festival of the Virgin. Now that our abbey has been reclaimed from the apostate saint, Marie-de-la-mer, we should be able to count on a personal intervention from the Holy Mother in our regrettable affairs. So she thinks, anyway; and redoubles her prayers. Meanwhile, I work on our spiritual defences with many Latin incantations and a great quantity of incense. No demonic force must be allowed to penetrate on our abbey's holiest day.

*   *   *

Juliette came to find me in my rooms early this morning. I knew she might, and I was ready for her, raising my head from a stack of books to face her. She was fiercely prim in her clean, starched linen, not a stray curl softening the line of her pale, set face. This was about Perette, I told myself warily, and I must tread lightly.

'Juliette. Is the sun up already? The room seems brighter than it was a moment ago.'

Her expression told me that now was not the time for flattery. 'Please.' Her voice was sharp, but with anxiety, I noticed, rather than anger. 'You have to keep Perette out of this. She doesn't understand the danger. Think of the risk, if she were to be found out!' Then, as I said nothing: 'Really, LeMerle, you must see that she's only a child!'

Ay, that was it. That was the mother in her. I tried misdirection. 'Isabelle is feeling unwell,' I said gently. 'While she rests in her rooms, I might arrange for you—and Antoine—to slip out for a time. To take a basket of food to—for example—a poor fisherman and his family?'

She looked at me for a second, and I could see the hunger in her eyes. Then she shook her head. 'That's very like you, LeMerle,' she said without heat. 'And what would happen with me out of the way? Another Apparition? Another Dancing Mass?' She shook her head again. 'I know you,' she said softly. 'Nothing is free. You'd want something in return, then something more, then—'

I interrupted her. 'My dear, you mistake my intentions. I made the suggestion out of concern for you, nothing more. You're no danger to me, Juliette; you're already as guilty as I am.'

She lifted her chin at that. 'I?' But there was fear in her eyes.

'Your silence alone is proof of guilt. You recognized the Unholy Nun. And have you forgotten the business with the well? Or the poisoning of Soeur Clémente? And as for your vow of chastity . . .' I let the phrase hang maliciously.

She was silent, her cheeks flaring.

'Believe me,' I said, 'a charge of witchcraft might

306

be levelled upon you for any one of these things. And we have long since passed the point where you could have damaged me. No one alive could turn them against me now.'

She knew it was true.

'I am the rock,' I told her. 'The anchor in the storm. To suspect me is unthinkable.'

There was a long pause. 'I should have spoken when I had the chance,' said Juliette. I was not mistaken by her tone; her eyes were almost admiring.

'You wouldn't have done it, my dear.'

Her eyes told me she knew that, too.

'Perette has been very useful to me during the past weeks,' I said. 'She's quick—almost as quick as you were, Juliette—and she's clever. She hid in the crypt, you know, the first time you saw the Unholy Nun. All the time you were searching she was there, curled up behind one of the coffins.'

Juliette shivered.

'But if you're so concerned about her, then maybe . . .' I pretended to hesitate. 'No. I need her still, Juliette. I cannot give her up. Not even to please you.'

She took the bait. 'You said there was a way.'

'Impossible.'

'Guy!'

'No, really. I should never have spoken.'

'*Please!*'

I never could resist her pleading. An exhilarating delicacy, seldom tasted. I pretended reluctance in order to savour the moment. 'Well I suppose there might be . . .'

'What?'

'If you agreed to take her place.'

307

There. The trap swings shut with an almost audible click. She ponders it for a moment. No fool she. She knows how she has been manoeuvred. But there is the child . . .

'Fleur was never on the mainland,' I told her gently. 'I placed her with a family not three miles from here. You could see her within the hour if only—'

'I won't poison anyone,' said Juliette.

'That won't be necessary.'

She was beginning to weaken. 'If I agree,' she said, 'you swear Perette's involvement will cease?'

'Of course.' I pride myself on my look of honesty. This is the true, open look of a man who never cocked a card or loaded a die in all his life. Amazing that after all these years it still works.

'Three days,' I said, sensing her resistance. 'Three days till Sunday. Then it ends. I promise.'

'Three days,' she echoed.

'After that, Fleur can come home for good,' I said. 'You can have everything back as it was. Or—if you like—you can come with me.'

Her eyes shone—with scorn or passion, I could not tell—but she said nothing.

'Would it really be so bad?' I said gently. 'To take the road again? To be l'Ailée—to be back where you belong'—I lowered my voice to a whisper—'back where I need you?'

There was silence, but I felt her relax, just a little, just enough. I touched her cheek fleetingly. 'Three days,' I repeated. 'What can happen in three days?'

Rather a lot, I hope.

CHAPTER FIVE
♥

August 12th, 1610

Fleur was waiting for me, as LeMerle had promised, not three miles from the abbey. A salter's croft, built low to the ground, with a turf roof and walls of whitened daub, screened from view by a row of tamarisk bushes. I could have passed by it a hundred times and not seen it. Behind the croft, a shaggy pony cropped grass; beside it, a wooden hutch housed half a dozen brown rabbits. All around, the ditches of the salt marsh formed a kind of shallow moat, in which a couple of flat-bottomed *platts* were moored for access to the fields. Herons stood in the reeds at the water's edge; in the long yellow grass I heard the *scree* of cicadas.

LeMerle, knowing that I would not abandon Perette, had seen no need to accompany me this time. Instead he sent Antoine as my guard, eyes narrowed in sly complicity beneath the sweat-stained wimple. I wondered if I was hers. The poisoner and the murderer, arm in arm, like inseparable friends.

I clasped Fleur to my heart as if by so doing I could merge our flesh into one and so never be parted from her. Her skin is soft and brown, startlingly dark against the flaxen hair. Her beauty almost alarms me. She was wearing her red dress, now grown a little short for her, and she had a fresh scrape on one knee.

'Sunday,' I whispered in her ear. 'If all goes well, I'll be here on Sunday. At noon, wait for me here by the tamarisk bushes. Don't tell anyone. Don't let anyone know I'm coming.'

*　　　*　　　*

Of course, LeMerle had tricked me. As soon as I returned from my visit to Fleur I knew from the reek of incense and burning that he had been at work on them once again. There had been another Dancing Mass, said Soeur Piété excitedly, more frenzied even than the first; pressed for explanations she spoke of their raptures, of her own possession by a lustful imp, of howlings and animal noises uttered by the unfortunates driven to their knees by the army of demons unleashed in rage against the holy sacrament.

With tears in her eyes she spoke too of Soeur Marguerite, of how in spite of her prayers she was forced to dance until her feet bled, and of Père Colombin, of his purification by fire of the infested air, of his struggle with the forces of evil until he too was brought to his knees in his attempt to wrestle them to the ground.

Mère Isabelle was with him now, revealed Piété. As the evil spell had begun to fall from the congregation, as the nuns, released from their frenzies by the sound of his voice, began to turn towards each other in wonder and bewilderment, Père Colombin had fallen to his knees, swooning, the pages of the *Ritus exorcizandi* slipping from his fingers. A minute of chaos as the bereft and panic-stricken nuns thronged to his aid, certain he had himself succumbed to the forces of darkness . . .

310

But it was merely exhaustion, explained Piété. To the relief of the nuns Père Colombin managed to raise himself to his feet, held on either side by a member of his faithful flock. Raising a trembling hand he declared himself in need of rest, and allowed himself to be borne off to his cottage, where even now he rests, surrounded by books and holy artefacts, working on a further solution to the ills that plague us.

It must have been a fine show. A rehearsal, I supposed, for Sunday's opening performance, but why had LeMerle arranged for me to be absent? Could it be, in spite of his bold words, that somehow he fears what I may discover? Is there some part of this performance that LeMerle does not want me to see?

CHAPTER SIX
♥

August 13th, 1610

Alfonsine has been officially pronounced possessed. So far the demons of her infestation number fifty-five, though Père Colombin swears there are more. The ritual of exorcism may not be completed until every one of these has been named, and the walls of his cottage are papered with lists to which he is constantly adding more names. Virginie too has acquired a pale and haggard look and has been seen on several occasions walking in tiny circles around the walled garden and muttering to herself. When asked to stop and rest she merely looks up with an air of terrible calm and says, 'No, no,' before reverting to her interminable circling. Rumour has it that it is only a matter of time before she too is declared a victim of the infestation.

Mère Isabelle has not left her rooms today. LeMerle denies that she is possessed, but with so little optimism that few of us are convinced. A brazier of coals has been lit outside the chapel, on which have been scattered sanctuary incense and various powerful herbs. So far, this has served to protect us from renewed attack. Another burner was placed outside the infirmary, and yet another at the abbey gates. The smoke is sweet when fresh, but turns sour very quickly, and the air, already stifling, hangs like dusty curtains across the white-hot sky.

As for the Apparitions, the Unholy Nun has been seen twice today and three times yesterday, once in the dorter, twice in the slype and twice more in the gardens. No one has yet commented that the Nun seems oddly grown in stature, or has noticed the large footprints she left in a vegetable patch. Perhaps by now such things are no longer meaningful to us.

We spent the rest of today in idleness not unlike that which followed the death of the old Reverend Mother. Mère Isabelle was unwell, LeMerle was studying, and robbed of our direction we once more fell into the roles to which we were accustomed, our thoughts returning to the events of the last week with increasing fear and anxiety. Our ship drifted rudderless towards the rocks and we were powerless to stop it, turning instead to gossip and unhealthy self-examination.

Soeur Marguerite scrubbed the already spotless floors of the dorter until her knees bled. Then she scrubbed the blood with increasing frenzy until she was returned to the infirmary for examination. Soeur Marie-Madeleine lay upon her bed, whimpering and complaining of itching between her legs that no amount of scratching could assuage. Antoine left the confines of the infirmary—there were now four sufferers there, strapped to their beds, and the noise, she said, was driving her mad—and regaled me with gruesome details, embellished no doubt to considerable effect. In spite of myself I listened.

Soeur Alfonsine, she says, is very ill. The smoke from the brazier, far from cleansing her lungs, seems to have exacerbated her condition. Soeur Virginie takes this as a sign of possession, for the afflicted woman has been coughing up more blood than ever before, in spite of her cures and LeMerle's frequent visits.

As for Soeur Clémente, reports Antoine, for three days she has taken no food and hardly any water. So weak that she can barely move, she looks at the ceiling with glazed, unseeing eyes. Her lips move, but senselessly. It will be a merciful release.

'What did she do to you, Antoine?' The question was out of me before I knew it. 'What harm did she do to you, that you hate her so much?'

Antoine looked at me. I suddenly recalled the one moment in which I thought her beautiful: the thick sheaf of blue-black hair released from the wimple, the roundness of her rosy shoulders, her soft nape as LeMerle reached for the shears. She has changed beyond recognition since then. Her face was like basalt, remote and pitiless.

313

'You never did understand, Auguste,' she said with mild contempt. 'You tried to be kind to me in your way, but you never understood.' She surveyed me for a moment, hands on hips. 'How could you? You always had it easy. Men looked at you and saw something they wanted. Something beautiful.' She smiled, but the smile darkened her face rather than illuminating it. 'I was always the dray-horse, the fat slut, too stupid to hear their laughter, too good-natured even to hate them in my secret heart. To the men, just meat, just enough warmth for a quick fumble, just a pair of legs, a pair of tits, a mouth and a belly. To the women I was stupid, too stupid to keep a man, too stupid even to—' She broke off abruptly. 'I never cared about the father. Never asked myself who he was. My child was all my own. No one even suspected the fat slut was with child at all. My belly was always round. My tits were always heavy. I'd planned to have it in secret, to hide it perhaps, to keep it mine.' Her eyes were suddenly hard. 'It was going to be the one thing I really owned. All mine. Needing me, not caring that I was fat or stupid.' She looked at me. 'You might have known how to carry it off. Don't think I ever believed in your tale, Auguste. I may be stupid, but even I know you were no more a rich widow then I was.' She smiled, not unkindly, but without warmth. 'You kept your child, fatherless or no. There was no one to tell you what to do, or if there was, you ignored them. Isn't that so?'

'It is, Antoine.'

'I was fourteen. I had a father. Brothers. Aunts and uncles. They all assumed I wouldn't know what to do. They had it all arranged before I could say a word. They said I wouldn't know how to care for a

314

baby. They said I'd never live with the shame.'

'What happened?'

'They were going to give it to my cousin Sophie,' said Antoine. 'I was never even consulted. Sophie had three children already, and she was only eighteen. She would raise mine with hers. The scandal would soon be forgotten. Laughed over. Fancy that! The stupid fat girl had a child! But my dears, who was the father? A blind man?'

'What happened?' I said.

'I took a pillow.' Her voice was low and reflective. 'I put it over my child's head. My little son's soft dark head. I waited.' She gave a smile of terrible tenderness. 'No one wanted him, Auguste. He was the one thing I'd ever had of my own. It was the only way I could keep him.'

'And Clémente?' My voice was a whisper.

'I told her everything,' said Antoine. 'I thought she was different. I thought she understood. But she laughed at me. Just like the others . . .' Again the smile, and just for a second I glimpsed once again the dark beauty of the woman. 'But it doesn't matter,' she said with a hint of malice. 'Père Colombin promised . . .'

'Promised what?'

She shook her head. 'This is mine, my secret. The secret I share with Père Colombin. I don't want to share it with you. You'll know soon enough, anyway. You'll know on Sunday.'

'Sunday?' I was dancing with impatience. 'Antoine, what did he say?'

She put her head to one side, an absurdly coquettish gesture. 'He promised. All the women who laughed at me. All the ones who made fun of me and made me do penances for greed. No more

315

poor Soeur Antoine, stupid Soeur Antoine to blame or to bully. On Sunday we light a flame.'

And from then on she was silent and would say no more, but folded her fat arms onto her bosom and turned away with that maddening, angelic smile.

CHAPTER SEVEN

♠

August 14th, 1610

She found me in the chapel at daybreak. For once I was alone. The air was rancid-sweet with last night's incense, the thin sunlight filtering through layers of floating airborne dust. For the luxury of a moment I closed my eyes and smelled the hot reek of smoke, the scorch of flesh . . . But not mine, this time, Monseigneur. Not mine.

How they would dance! The habits, the virgins, the hypocrites. What an act it would be! What a rapturous, unholy finale!

Her voice jolted me from a reverie which had sunk me almost into slumber. True, I had not slept in three days. 'LeMerle.'

Even half-conscious I knew that note. I opened my eyes. 'My harpy. You've worked well for me. You must be looking forward to seeing your daughter tomorrow.'

Three days ago that ploy might still have worked. As it was she barely acknowledged my words, shaking them aside as a dog may shake water from its pelt.

'I've spoken to Antoine.'

Ah. A pity. I always knew my plump disciple to be a little unstable. It was like her to let something drop without considering the implications. A loyal slave, Antoine, but no thinker. 'Yes? I trust she was a stimulating conversationalist.'

'Stimulating enough.' The sequin eyes glittered. 'LeMerle, what's happening?'

'Nothing that need concern you, my Winged One.'

'If you're planning to harm anyone, I'll stop you.'

'Would I lie to you?'

'I know you would.'

I shrugged and held up my hands. 'Forgive her, Lord, her hurtful remark. What more can I do to make you trust me? I've kept Fleur safe. I've asked nothing more of Perette. I was thinking that tomorrow you could skip Mass and collect your daughter—take the road while I'm tying up my few loose ends—meet me, perhaps, on the mainland, and—'

'No.' Her tone was final.

I was beginning to lose patience. 'What then? What more do you want of me?'

'I want you to announce the Bishop's visit.'

I wasn't expecting that; trust you, my Winged One, to find my weakness. 'What, and spoil my surprise?'

'We don't need any more surprises.'

I touched her face with my fingertips. 'Juliette, it's of no importance. Tomorrow we'll be in Pornic, or in Saint Jean-de-Monts, drinking wine from silver cups. I have money put aside; we can start again, start a theatre troupe or anything you'd like . . .'

317

But she was not to be cajoled. 'Announce it at Chapter,' she said. 'Do it tonight, Guy, or I'll do it myself.'

*   *   *

Well, that was my cue. I should have liked your co-operation, my dear, but I had never really expected it at this final stage. I found Antoine by the well—the spot seems to hold a special place in her heart since Germaine's hanging—and she reacted quickly to the signal she has been anticipating for the past week. Perhaps she is not as slow-witted as I take her for, for I saw her face light up in real pleasure at the task. In that moment she looked neither dull-witted nor ugly, and I felt a moment's unease. Still, she follows me without question, which is what counts; she does not have your scruples, and she at least understands revenge.

Oh really, Juliette. You always were a simpleton despite your learning. What do we owe to anyone but ourselves? What do we owe to the Creator, sitting there on his golden throne dispensing judgement? Did we *ask* to be created? Did we ask to be thrown into this world like dice? Look around you, little sister. What has he dealt you that you should take his side? Besides, you should know better by now than to play against me; in the end, I always win.

I knew she would wait until Chapter. Knowing that, I struck first, or rather, Antoine struck, with the help of Soeur Virginie. It was a rousing performance, so I hear—a vision led them to your cache and to the evidence concealed therein: the

318

Tarot cards, the poisons and the bloodied *quichenotte* of the Unholy Nun. You would have fought, but were no match for Antoine's brute strength; on the orders of the Abbess, you were taken to the cellarium and imprisoned there, awaiting a decision. The rumours took wing at once.

*   *   *

'Is she . . .'
  '*Possessed?*'
  'Accused?'
  'No, not Auguste . . .'
  'I always knew she was a . . .'
It is a sigh almost of satisfaction, the whisper taken up—*wishwishwish*—with a coyness, a fluttering of eyelash and lowering of lids more at home in a Paris salon. These nuns have more feminine tricks than a battery of society prudes, exercising their false modesty to captivate. Their desire smells of sour lilies.

I made my voice grave. 'An accusation has been made,' I announced. 'If this is true, then we have— we have nurtured—hell's catamite in our mist from the very first.'

The phrase enticed them. *Hell's catamite.* A good name for a burlesque or a *tragédie-ballet.* I saw them squirm in scarce disguised excitement.

'A spy, mocking our rituals, secretly in league with the forces that seek to destroy us!'

'I trusted you,' you said as I led you to the cellar door. And then you spat in my face, and would have gone for me with your nails if Soeur Antoine had not pushed you into the room and shut the

319

door.

I wiped my brow with a Cholet handkerchief. Through the slit in the door I could see your eyes. Impossible to tell you at this time why I have betrayed you. Impossible to explain that this is the one measure which may save your life.

CHAPTER EIGHT
♥

August 14th, 1610
Nones

At first I was disorientated. The room—a storeroom annex to the cellarium, hastily reconverted into a cell for the first time since the black friars—was so like the cellar in Epinal that for a time I wondered whether the past five years had not been a dream, my mind's attempt to play its fleeting sanity like a fish on a line, reeling it inwards and inwards until understanding breaks the surface.

Giordano's cards were enough to confirm their suspicions. I wish now that I had paid more attention to their warning: to the Hermit, with his subtle smile and cloaked lantern; to the Deuce of Cups, love and forgetfulness; to the Tower aflame. It is past noon now, and the storeroom is dark except for half a dozen slices of sunlight against the back wall from the ventilation slats; too high to reach, in any case too small to present any hope of escape.

I have not wept. Perhaps some part of me

expected his betrayal. I cannot even say that I feel sorrow—or even fear. Five years have sown a kind of serenity. A coldness. I think of Fleur at noon tomorrow, waiting by the tamarisks.

Today this room reverts to its original function. The black friars once did penance in such cells, hidden from the daylight, their food pushed through a narrow slot in the door, the air rank with the stink of prayers and guilt.

I will not pray. Besides I do not know to whom I should do so. My Goddess is a blasphemy, my Marie-de-la-mer lost to the sea. I can hear the surf from here, carried across the marshes by the west wind. Will she remember me, my child? Will she grow with my face in her heart, as I kept my own mother's image close to my own? Or will she be the child of strangers, unwanted, or worse—to grow to love them as her own, to be grateful, glad to be rid of me?

The thought is useless. I try to regain my serenity, but her image troubles me too much. My heart aches for her touch. Once more, I ask Marie-de-la-mer. Whatever it costs me, once more. My Fleur. My daughter. It is not any prayer Giordano would understand, but it is a prayer nevertheless.

Time's black rosary counts the interminable seconds.

CHAPTER NINE

♥

August 14th, 1610
Vespers

I think I slept. The darkness and the hush of the
surf lulled me, and for a time I dreamed. Bright
images pranced by me: Germaine, Clémente,
Alfonsine, Antoine . . . The snakeskin-silvery scar
on LeMerle's arm, the smile in his eyes.

Trust me, Juliette.

My daughter's red dress, the scrape on her knee,
the way she laughed and clapped at the players in
the dusty sunlight a thousand years ago. I awoke to
find the slices of sunlight high up on the wall,
reddened as the sun began its descent. I judged it
to be early evening. Feeling refreshed in spite of
everything, I rose to look about me. The room still
smelt of the vinegar and preserves that had been
kept there. In clearing space a pickle jar had been
broken and a damp patch remained on the earthen
floor, redolent of clove and garlic. I searched the
floor, thinking perhaps to find a sliver of glass
overlooked in their haste, but there was nothing. In
any case I do not know what I would have done
with it if there had been one; the thought of my
blood on the earth, mingling perhaps with the aloes
and vinegar of the spilled pickles, revolted me.
Tentatively I touched the walls of my cell. These
were stone, the good grey granite of the region
which sparkles with mica in sunlight but in shadow
looks almost black. There were indentations

scratched into the stone, I realized, short, even marks chiselled at intervals in the granite which my fingertips discovered in the semi-darkness; five marks, then a neat cross-stroke, five marks, then another. Some brother had perhaps tried to mark his time in this way, covering half the wall with the orderly down- and cross-strokes of his days, his months.

I went to the door. It was locked, of course, the heavy wooden panels banded with iron. A metal hatchway—secured from the outside—might serve as a means to deliver my meals. I listened at the door, but could hear nothing to indicate whether or not anyone kept watch over the prisoner. Why should they? I was safe enough.

Daylight waned until it was nothing but a purplish blur. My eyes, accustomed to the dim light, could still make out the shapes of the door, the twilit pallor of the ventilation slats, a heap of flour sacks that had been left in a corner to serve as bedding, a wooden bucket in the opposite corner. Without my wimple—it was removed when I was led here, as was the cross at the breast of my habit—I felt oddly estranged from myself, a creature from a different time. Yet this Ailée was cold, and her quick calculation of time was like that of a mariner measuring the approach of a coming storm, not that of a prisoner awaiting the hours to execution. In spite of everything there was still power to be had, to be used, if only I knew how.

Interesting, that no one had come to speak to me. Strangest of all that LeMerle should not have come—to justify himself, or to gloat. Seven rang, then eight. The sisters would be making their way to Vespers.

Was this, then, what he had planned? Was I to be removed from the scene until his game—whatever it was—had been played out? Was I still a danger to him? And if so, how?

I was roused from my meditations by a rattling at the door. A clang as the spyhole was flung open, then a clattering as something was thrust through, bouncing noisily off the hard floor as it fell. I saw no light at the spyhole, heard no voice as the metal hatch was locked again from the outside. I felt on the ground for the object that had been pushed through, and had little difficulty in finding a wooden plate, from which a piece of bread had rolled.

'Wait!' I stood up, the plate in my hand. 'Who's there?'

No response. Not even the sound of footsteps receding. I concluded that whoever it was must be waiting behind the door, listening.

'Antoine? Is that you?'

I could hear her breathing behind the metal trap. Five years' worth of nights in the dorter had taught me to recognize and identify the sounds of breathing. These short, asthmatic breaths were not Antoine's. I guessed it was Tomasine.

'Soeur Tomasine.' My guess was correct. I heard an indrawn shriek, stifled against a forearm. 'Talk to me. Tell me what's going on.'

'I won't—' The voice was almost inaudible, a high whimper in the dark. 'I won't let you out!'

'That's all right,' I whispered. 'I'm not asking you to.'

Tomasine paused for a second. 'What then?' The high note was still in her voice. 'I'm—I'm not supposed to talk to you. I'm not supposed to—look

324

at you.'

'In case of what?' I said scornfully. 'In case I fly through the hole? Or send an imp to leap down your throat?'

She whimpered again.

'Believe me,' I said, 'if I could do any of those things, would I still be here?'

A silence as she digested that. 'Père Colombin lit a brazier. Demons can't pass through the smoke.' She swallowed convulsively. 'I can't stay. I—'

'Wait!'

But it was too late. I heard her footsteps recede into darkness.

'Damn.'

And yet it was enough to begin with. LeMerle wanted me hidden, had frightened poor Tomasine so badly that she did not even dare to speak to me. What was it he wanted to conceal? And from whom—the Bishop, or myself?

I paced the cell after that, forcing myself to eat the bread Tomasine left me, though it was dry and I had never been less hungry. I heard the bell chime for Compline, then Matins. I had maybe six hours. To do what? Pacing, I asked myself the question. There was no means of escape, even though there was no one posted at my cell door. No one would help me. No one dared disobey Père Colombin. Unless—no. If Perette were going to come, she would have done so already. I had lost her the day in the barn, lost her to LeMerle and his trinkets. I was a fool to believe that she, of all people, might help me. The clear gold-ringed eyes were witless as a sparrow's, pitiless as a hawk's. She would not come.

Suddenly there came a scratching at the door.

325

Shh-shh. Then a low hooting sound, like that of a baby owl.

'Perette!'

The moon was up; the light from the ventilation slats was silver. In its reflected glow I saw the hatch open a crack, saw Perette's luminous eyes from its mouth.

'Perette!' Relief suffused me so that I felt almost weak, stumbling in my haste to reach her. 'Did you bring the keys?'

The wild girl shook her head. I moved closer to the hatch, close enough to be able to touch her fingers through the opening. Her skin was ghostly in the moonlight.

'No?' I forced myself to be calm, even through my disappointment. 'Perette, where are they?' I spoke as slowly as I could. 'Where are the keys, Perette?'

She shrugged. A speaking gesture of the shoulders, a movement of the right hand to indicate width, a round face: Antoine.

'Antoine?' I said eagerly. 'You say Antoine has them?'

She nodded.

'Listen, Perette.' I spoke slowly and clearly. 'I need to get out of here. I need you—to bring me—the keys. Can you do that?'

She gave me her blank look. Desperate now, my voice rising in spite of myself, I pleaded. 'Perette! You have to help me! Remember what I said—remember Fleur.' I was gabbling now in my desperation to reach her. 'We have to warn the Bishop!'

At my reference to the Bishop she cocked her head abruptly to one side and hooted. I stared at

326

her. 'The Bishop?' I questioned. 'Did you know he was coming? Did Père Colombin mention his visit?'

Again, the hooting sound. Perette grinned.

'Did he tell you what—' It was the wrong question. I rephrased it as simply as I could. 'Are you playing another game tomorrow? A trick?' My excitement was clenching my fists, fingernails scoring my palms, knuckles cracking. 'A trick to play on the Bishop?'

The wild girl gave her eerie laughter.

'What, Perette? What trick? What trick?'

But she was already half turning in sudden lack of interest, her attention caught by some other thought, some shadow, some sound, her head ticking to one side then to the other as if to some unheard rhythm. One hand came up slowly to close the hatch.

Click.

'Perette, *please*! Come back!'

But she was gone, without a sound, not even a cry, not even a farewell. I laid my head on my knees and I wept.

CHAPTER TEN
♥

August 15th, 1610
Vigils

I must have slept again, for when I awoke the moonlight had faded to a greenish blur. My head was pounding and my limbs were stiff with cold, and a draught at the level of my ankles made me shiver. I stretched out first my arms, then my legs, chafing my frozen fingers to restore the circulation, and I was so preoccupied with this that for a moment I did not realize the significance of that draught, which had not been there before.

Then I saw. The door was open a crack, allowing dim light to penetrate into the cell. Perette was standing in the doorway, a hand to her mouth. I sprang to my feet.

She gestured urgently at her mouth, to indicate silence. She showed me the key in her hand, slapped her thigh, then mimed Antoine's lumbering gait. I applauded her soundlessly. 'Good girl,' I whispered, moving towards the door, but instead of allowing me to pass, Perette motioned me frantically to let her though. Slipping past me, she pushed the door shut behind her and squatted on the floor.

'No, Perette.' I tried to explain. 'We have to go—now—before they find the keys are gone.'

The wild girl shook her head. Holding the keys in one hand, she performed a series of rapid movements with the other. Then, seeing that I did not understand, she repeated them more slowly and with barely concealed impatience.

A stern countenance, a sign of the cross. Père Colombin.

A bigger sign of the cross. A quick, amusing mime of horseriding, one hand holding a mitre which threatened to be blown off by the wind. The Bishop.

'Yes. The Bishop. Père Colombin. What then?'

She clenched her fists and hooted in frustration.

A fat woman, rolling as she walked. Antoine.

Père Colombin again. Then a mime of Soeur Marguerite, twitching and dancing. Then a complicated mime, as if repeatedly touching something hot. Then a gesture I did not understand, arms outstretched as if in readiness to fly.

Perette repeated it with greater insistence. Still I did not understand.

'What, Perette?'

The flying gesture again. Then a silent grimace, miming the torments of hell beneath the fluttering movements. Then, once again, the 'hot' gesture as Perette sniffed the air and wrinkled her nose, as if at a stench.

Almost I began to understand. 'Fire, Perette?' I asked her hesitantly but with growing comprehension. Perette beamed at me, showing me her clenched fists. 'He's going to light another fire?'

Perette shook her head and pointed at herself. Then she motioned at the roof, a circular gesture which encompassed the abbey, herself, everyone in it. Then the flying gesture again. Then she took out the pendant of Christina Mirabilis from her garment and showed me, insistently, the miraculous virgin, ringed with fire.

I stared at her, beginning at last to understand. She smiled.

CHAPTER ELEVEN
♥

Matins

You see now why I cannot leave.

LeMerle's plan was more vicious, more implacable than anything I could have imagined—even of him. With the help of gestures, hootings, mimes and scratchings in the dirt, Perette explained it, occasionally laughing, occasionally losing interest like the innocent she was, distracted by a piece of mica shining against the granite, or the cry of a night bird beyond the walls. She was wholly innocent, my sweet Perette, my wise fool; quite unaware of the sinister implications of the favour LeMerle had asked of her.

That had been his only mistake. He had underestimated my Perette, believing her to be under his control. But the wild girl is no one's creature, not even mine. She is like some bird that can be trained but not tamed; let the glove slip, for even an instant, and she will bite.

For now, at least, I have her attention. I may lose it at any time, but she is my only weapon as I try to devise a plan of my own. I do not know whether my wit is a match for the Blackbird. What I do know is that I must try. For myself, for Fleur. For Clémente and Marguerite. For all those he has damaged and deceived and crippled and mocked. For all those to whom he has fed the pieces of his bitter heart and poisoned thereby.

This may mean my death. I have faced that. If I

330

succeed it may certainly mean his, and I have faced that too.

CHAPTER TWELVE
♥

Lauds

Perette has locked me back in the cell. Anything else is simply too dangerous. I hope Fleur will understand if my plan goes awry—and I hope Perette remembers her part. I hope—I hope. Everything seems to be built upon those two words, those two fragile syllables like the cry of some forlorn seabird: I—hope.

Birds are singing outside. In the far distance, though not as loud as last night, I hear the sounds of the surf on the island's western shore. Somewhere in the breakers, the statue of Marie-de-la-mer rolls endlessly against the fine sand, polishing, dwindling, to be scoured by the shoreline into slow oblivion. Never have I been so conscious of time—of that which remains to us, of its passing, its tides.

Some minutes ago someone tried the door and, finding it locked, went away. I shiver to think what might have happened if Perette had left it unlocked. My breakfast, a piece of bread and a cup of water, was pushed through the hatchway, the trap slamming shut as soon as I collected them as if I were infected with the plague. The water smelt sharp, as if someone had fouled it, and though I am thirsty, I did not drink. The next hour will tell whether or not my hopes are founded.

If she remembers. If LeMerle suspects nothing. If my skill holds. If my one shaft hits true.

If.

Perette, do not fail me.

CHAPTER THIRTEEN

♠

Lauds

Since last night, the sisters have been busy preparing for this morning's festival. Flowers cover every surface; hundreds of tall, white candles have been lit in the chapel, and the altar is decked with an embroidered banner, which I am told dates back to before the black monks, and which is used only for this ceremony. The chapel's holy relic—a fingerbone of the Virgin, in a gold reliquary—is on display, along with a selection of the Virgin's ceremonial robes and dresses. The new Sainte-Marie has been draped in blue and white, with lilies—what else?—at her feet. I can smell the flowers from twenty yards away, even over that of the extra braziers which have been installed at every entrance in spite of the heat, burning frankincense and sandalwood to dispel evil thoughts. There are torches, too, hanging against the walls, and votives on every surface. The air is more than half smoke; against it, the light from the stained-glass window looks almost solid, as if it might be possible to pluck gems from the air.

I watched in secret from the opposite side of the

causeway as the Bishop's retinue approached. I could tell his colours even at that distance—pitiful, that he should still need so much pomp and ceremony. It speaks of a pride that has even now not been mastered, doubly inappropriate in a man of the cloth. Liveried soldiers, gilded harness glinting in the sun . . . I'll make a fine blaze of all his trumpery soon enough, but first we'll dance our little measure, he and I. I have looked forward to it for so long.

Of course, he missed the tide. I meant him to; not for nothing have I observed the comings and goings at the causeway. He expected to reach us last night, before Vespers, but on this coast, the tide takes eleven hours to turn. There is an inn on the other side, however; conveniently placed for such occasions, and he must have stayed the night there—no doubt angrily berating the fool who misinformed him. Low tide was at seven. I'll give him two hours more to reach the abbey, and all is set. With luck—and a little judicious planning—he should arrive just in time for my little comedy to begin.

A Blackbird's song may haply be silenced, indeed. But not by such a gilded scarecrow as yourself, Monseigneur. You'll not walk out of this performance, I promise. A pity that my Ailée cannot be among us at the finale, but that I suppose was inevitable. A pity, nevertheless; she would surely have appreciated it.

CHAPTER FOURTEEN

♠

Prime

It was time; all were gathered in the chapel as I made my entrance. Even my poor afflicted ones had been brought to the service—though they had been given seats throughout the long service, and were not obliged to stand or kneel. Perette was missing, of course, but no one paid much attention; her comings and goings had always been erratic and she would not be missed. Good. I hoped she would remember her part. A small role, but a pretty one; I would be very disappointed if she failed to carry it off.

'My children.' I had coached them well; glassy-eyed with the burning incense, they watched me as if I were their only salvation. Mère Isabelle was standing at my right side, close to the brazier; through the smoke, her face was ash. 'Today we celebrate the most sacred and most dear to us of our holy days. The festival of the Holy Mother.'

A rumour ran through the congregation, an *ahhh* of satisfaction and release. Above it, I could just hear the sound of drops beginning to fall on the roof slates; at last, it had begun to rain. I couldn't have planned it better. Come to think of it, a little strategic thunder would not come amiss. Perhaps the Lord would provide some when the time came, thereby proving that he does have a sense of irony. But I digress. Back to the Virgin, then, before she loses her freshness. Where was I?

'The Mother, who watches down upon us in the presence of evil. The Virgin who comforts us in our times of need, whose purity is that of the dove and the white lily'—nice touch, LeMerle—'whose forgiveness and compassion know no bounds.'

Ahhh. Not for nothing do we use the language of love to seduce these foolish virgins; pulpit rhetoric is indecently close to that of the bedroom, just as some of the more interesting sections of the Bible echo the pornographies of the ancients. I played now on this kinship in words they knew well, promising raptures beyond the realms of human endurance, ecstasies without limit in the arms of the Lord. Earthly suffering is less than nothing, I told them, in the face of the pleasures to come: the fruits of Paradise—I could see Antoine beginning to drool—the joys of unending service in the House of God.

It was a promising start. Already I could see Soeur Tomasine grinning alarmingly; beside her, Marguerite's face was a mass of twitches. Good. 'But today is not simply a time of rejoicing. It is also our day of battle. Today we throw down the final challenge to the evil that has plagued us, and plagues us still.'

Ahhh. Wrested from their pleasant thoughts, the sisters flinched and pranced like nervous mares.

'I do not doubt that today we shall defeat the forces of darkness—but if the worst happens, and we are once more tested to the limits of our faith, be of stout heart. There is always an escape for those of true faith with the courage to embrace it.'

Isabelle's face was set in a grimace of determination. Saint or martyr, that look told me; this time, she was not to be thwarted. Angélique

Saint-Hervé Désirée Arnault always gets her way.

Now, outside, I could hear a distant sound of horses' hooves on the road, and I knew that my enemy was near; and just in time, too. Timing, the greatest tool of an artist in my trade: good timing is a precision instrument, coaxing comedy or tragedy to one climax after another; bad timing is a bludgeon which kills all suspense and ruins both drama and punchline. By my reckoning I had maybe eight or ten minutes until Arnault's grand entrance; time enough, anyway, to whip up the welcome he deserved.

'Courage, my children, courage. Satan knows we await him. We have faced him together, and we stand now united in our faith and our conviction, ready to go to war. The Devil comes in a thousand guises: fair-faced or foul, he may be a man or a woman, a child or a beast, he may take the features of a loved one, of a man of power, even, on occasion, of a bishop or a king. The next countenance you see will be his, my children; already the Dark One approaches. I can hear the sound of his infernal carriage as it thunders towards us. Satan, we are here. Show us your face!'

Seldom has any audience—at Court or in the provinces—ever been so entranced by a single performer. Already, they were watching me as if their souls depended upon it. The braziers lit my face like the fires of Purgatory. Above us, the rain was cathartic; after so many days of heat and drought it exalted them, turned their faces towards the heavens, sent them staring towards the rafters as their feet began to move independently of their minds and my *dea ex machina* prepared to take the stage . . .

♥

The Bishop's retinue was arriving. I could see them, half a mile or less along the road; I could hear the outriders' horses and the sound of the carriage wheels in the rain. It was a large group, even for a bishop; as they approached I could see two banners, and I understood that the Bishop had brought along a colleague, perhaps a superior, to share in his family's triumph. I looked down into the chapel and I saw that Perette, with the swiftness that served her so well in her role as the Unholy Nun, had slipped once again into the shadows. I could only trust that she remembered all the instructions I had given her. Her eyes were bright with birdy intelligence, but I knew that the smallest distraction—a flight of gulls at a window, the lowing of cows on the marshes, the colours of the stained glass reflected upon the flagstones—might mean our undoing.

My hiding place was high in the bell-tower, not far from the bell itself, which hangs from an iron crosspiece in the narrowest part of the spire. My eyrie was perilous, accessible only from the rough scaffolding erected by the workmen repairing the roof, but it was the only place from which I could work. Even so I could be certain of nothing; this performance could have no rehearsal, no second showing. The light was poor. From a cloudy sky only a little murky daylight filtered through the broken slates, and from below the candlelight looked hazy beneath the pall of incense, a necklace of fireflies in the greater dark. In my habit I was the colour of smoke; over my head I wore a hood so that the pale blur of my face did not attract attention. The rope—I hoped it was long enough—was looped three times around my waist, the end weighted with a piece of lead. My breathing seemed to fill the whole abbey as silence fell, and LeMerle began his performance.

Oh, he was very good. He knew it, too; and although I could not see his face from my position, I could tell from his voice that he was enjoying himself. The acoustics of the chapel were ideal for his purpose; they picked up every word to fling them unerringly to the back of the hall. The scenery was all in place: braziers, candles, flowers, a promise of heaven or hell. Much may be achieved, as LeMerle taught me in our Paris days, by the artful positioning of a few simple props: a lily in the hair or a pearl rosary in the hand suggest purity—even of the most debauched of whores; a flashy sword-hilt carried ostentatiously at the belt will discourage attackers—even when there is no sword attached. People see what they expect to see. That's why he wins at cards, and it's why the sisters failed to identify the Unholy Nun. That's his style: art and misdirection, and though I could see the bales placed all around the hall, although I could smell the oil with which he had saturated the straw and guess at the oil-soaked rags which ran beneath every bench and pew, the sisters were blind to them for the moment, smelling only smoke and incense, seeing nothing but the stage and the performance into which they had been so carefully drawn.

But I—I could see it all from my privileged position. Giordano had taught me something about engines and fuses; the rest needed only a little guesswork. A spark, correctly placed—from the pulpitum, for example—might be enough to set it

338

off. And then, as Antoine had said, *we light a candle*.

I must be careful, I told myself. Timing was essential. I thought I knew his mind; now I prayed that I was right. He would not act until he had revealed himself; the temptation to gloat a little was too much for him to pass by. Vanity is his weakness. Above everything else, he is a performer, and he needs his audience. That, I was hoping, would be his downfall. I waited, then, biting my lip, as a murmur went through the congregation and the Bishop made his long-awaited entrance.

*   *   *

♠

Here he was; right on cue. Time for some music, I thought. Music is a great enhancer of moods, lending extra pathos and drama to a dull performance. Not that this one was likely to be dull, but I find a little Latin always does the trick; besides, it would buy us more time, allowing Arnault to enter freely. Psalm 30, then; I gave the sign and the congregation shuffled to its feet.

'*In te, Domine, speravi, non confundar in aeternum: in justitia tua libera me.*' I could see Marguerite flinch at the Latin words. Clémente's head lolled and she grinned widely.

'*Inclina ad me aurem tuam, accelera ut eruas me.*' Of course, Clémente was never an apt scholar in that tongue; perhaps she had begun to associate it in her mind with our nightly sessions, stimulated in turn with Juliette's decoctions and with the sly workings of my hidden needle. In either case she began to rock nervously, her movement

339

accelerating in tempo as the psalm continued. Behind her, Tomasine echoed her movements, shifting uneasily from one foot to the other.

'Esto mihi in Deum protectorem, et in domun refugii: ut salvum me facias.'

The unease had already spread to Virginie, who, face upturned, was staring into the air with idiot intensity. At the name of God she gave a tiny shriek and clutched at her breasts. Piété giggled. I awaited the inevitable with a smile of satisfaction as Arnault and his little retinue made their way to the main doors.

The scent of incense was thick and muskily sexual—I hope it offended his priggish nostrils!—mingling as it did with the scent of female flesh. If I have taught them nothing more, I thought, at least I have wrought that change in them, that now they sweat—ooze—*reek*—their fear, their appetites. I have opened something in them, a secret garden, if you like (see how Solomon continues to inspire me!), rank with avidness and life. I hoped he could smell it too, most rank of all on his niece, his precious niece, the family's pride. I hoped it would choke him.

Ah. Just in time. The stink caused him to frown a little, his delicate nostrils flaring. He raised a scented handkerchief to his face as if to reassert his expression of benevolence. At my gesture—which was also a sign to Perette—the choir began a sweet but ragged rendition of Psalm 10, *In Domino confido,* and his smile returned, a professional smile, like mine, but not nearly as trustworthy. Behind the words of the psalm I could still hear their voices, their one voice, the voice of their affirmation, the voice of the demons I had awoken in them.

I had taken a step backwards. Thanks to the shadows and the smoke from the braziers, my face was partially obscured. In any case, Arnault did not recognize me, but moved forward into the chapel, the Archbishop at his side. He was visibly displeased with the situation, but could not interrupt the psalm. His gilded eyes flicked self-consciously towards the Archbishop, whose face was now a mask of disapproval.

Below me I could feel the sisters becoming restless, tiny, almost imperceptible movements rippling across them like dead leaves in a breeze. I had made sure to seat Tomasine, Virginie, Marguerite and the other more susceptible ones in the front rows; their faces were slack, observing the visitors with glazed, frightened eyes as they moved slowly through the crowd towards the altar.

I needed only to speak one word, and the trap was sprung.

'Welcome.'

♥

I saw it begin. One upturned face, then another—for a second I was certain this meant discovery, but the eyes were blanks. Another face turned upwards, the arms outflung in sudden rapture, then the ripple ran through the entire congregation as, like fire, it leapt from one sister to the other. The psalm faltered, stopped as the cries began, pleas, incantations, obscenities. The Dancing Mass had refined itself since I last attended. Pandaemonium unfurled new petals in the face of this newcomer, strutting, prancing, falling to its knees or lifting its skirts in daring lewdness . . . In a few seconds it would be impossible to stop it. Arms flailed the smoky air. Faces surfaced only to submerge once more amongst hopeless cries. Clothes were rent and cast off. Virginie, always eager to take the lead, began to revolve madly, skirts wheeling out around her.

The Bishop was taken completely by surprise. This was so far from what he was expecting that he was dazed, still looking among the cries and the scenes of chaos for the triumphant tableau he had been expecting to see. Isabelle was watching him from her place by the brazier, her face scarlet in the flames, but she made no move to greet him. Instead her small fists clenched against the side of the pulpit and her mouth dropped open as the noise redoubled and LeMerle stepped out into the light.

'Welcome.'

♠

Such a moment was meant to be savoured. Imagine this if you can: the greatest scion of the house of Arnault, a half-naked nun on one side, a grinning ecstatic on the other, and all the wild beasts of this hellish circus grunting and squealing and bellowing about him like the lowest and most debauched of sideshows!

For a second I was afraid that he had not recognized me, but it was rage that silenced him, not incomprehension. His eyes widened as if they might devour me; his mouth opened, but no sound emerged. Outrage swelled him from within like the frog in the fable, so that his voice, when it finally came, was a ridiculous croak: 'You here? *You here?*'

Even now he did not completely understand.

342

Père Colombin Saint-Amand, the man with whom he had corresponded, could not be this man. This interloper had somehow taken the place of the holy man, and the nuns, the nuns . . . But the nuns seemed to recognize him. Hands outstretched, pleading, praying. Even Isabelle—poor child, grown so wan in the past months, her face ravaged by sickness and disquiet—even she looked to him as to a saviour, tears silvering her small pinched face as her hand reached out towards some object hidden behind the pulpitum . . .

Stupid disbelief slowed all his faculties. I couldn't have that. I signalled to Isabelle to hold back, and to Perette, who must still be lurking out of sight, to take her place.

Meanwhile Arnault stared at me as if one or the other of us must be mad. 'You here! How dare you? How *dare* you?'

'Oh, I'll dare anything. You said so yourself, on one or another of our meetings.' I addressed the sisters, who had forsaken their raptures in curiosity and now stared at us open-mouthed. 'Did I not warn you of how a fair face may conceal a foul one? The man before you is not what he appears.' I controlled my audience with a gesture as the crowd surged forward. Already the liveried guards of the retinue had been separated from their masters. The Archbishop was cut off—though I was glad to see he was well positioned to witness everything— and only the Bishop stood between me and the congregation.

Don't let anyone tell you it isn't worth it. The longer you have to wait, the more exquisite it is. I could see fear in him now—only a little, for he still believed this to be some kind of dream, but it

343

would grow. Behind him, someone wailed and collapsed. They were beginning to move again, restlessly; a ripple that would soon once more become a wave. I took off my cross by the leather thong that bound it, and raised it in front of me. Then I laid it—negligently, or so it seemed—by the side of the pulpitum, and waited for the finale to begin.

*   *   *

♥

This must be the moment, I thought, when Perette was due to appear. I sensed a drop in the voices below me, a slight hesitation in his delivery that no one perceived but myself. I could appreciate his timing: the lull during which the Unholy Nun was to make her last and most dramatic appearance. Unlike myself, however, he had not placed all his trust in Perette. She was not fundamental to his plans, but an artistic touch without which he could manage quite well if he needed to. He would be disappointed, certainly; but I hoped her absence would arouse no suspicion in him. He knew Perette was too volatile to trust; I was about to gamble my life on the hope that she was not.

The Bishop advanced, too angry for caution or curiosity. He was a tall man, taller even than LeMerle, and from my perch he looked more like a bird, a black crane, perhaps, or a heron, as he marched up the steps towards the pulpitum with his robes flapping behind him. The smoke from the brazier stung my eyes and there was rain dripping on my neck, but I had to see this confrontation. I had to be sure—I had to know that there was no

344

other way than the one I had chosen—before I made my move.

Their voices were clear below me, only slightly distorted by the shape of the bell-tower. LeMerle's clear tones, and those of the Bishop, hoarse with disbelief and righteous anger, calling out instructions to his guards which they could not obey without cutting a swathe through a crowd of ecstatic nuns.

I could not yet make my move. LeMerle was still too close to the brazier, and if cornered might light the fuse and set the terrible sequence into motion. Had I left it too late? Was I to watch helpless as LeMerle carried out his revenge?

Then, as if in answer to my prayer, the Bishop mounted the pulpitum and in the same moment, miraculously, LeMerle stepped away from the brazier. Now was the time, I thought, now—and, with a quick cantrip to ensure my safe footing and a whispered prayer to Saint Francis of the Birds, I took the rope in both hands and flung it out into the smoky air.

♠

'*Mon père.* I'm touched.' I used my other vocal register so that the sound would not carry. 'After last time, I'd hardly anticipated such a warm welcome.'

Behind me, Isabelle was watching, white to the lips. Perette had failed me—a pity, though hardly of the essence—but now came the real test. Would Isabelle play her part to the end? Had I broken her, or would she declare herself against me? I have to admit the uncertainty excited me somewhat. Besides, I thought, my escape route was

345

safe with Antoine to keep it clear. At this stage I could risk a little self-indulgence.

'I'll see you burn for this!' Hardly original, but it fitted the script. 'I'll finish you once and for all!' You see how unwittingly he played my game; his emotions betrayed his every move, as any card-player could tell you. With murder in his silvery eyes he came striding up towards me like a great gilded crow. For a second I was sure he would try to strike me, but I was younger and quicker than he was, and he dared not risk his dignity for a missed blow. Even now I could see that he believed it to be nothing but a trick of breathtaking impudence; he was too concerned about Isabelle and the now-unwelcome presence of the Archbishop to consider my deeper motives.

'This man is no priest!' he said, turning to address the sisters in a voice that shook with rage. 'He is an impostor! A trickster, a common stage actor!'

Less of that, Father. I'll have you know I was years ahead of my time. 'Is that likely?' I said with a smile. 'Is it not more believable that this—this mitred abomination—is the real impostor?' Their voices told me they believed it, though there were a few cries of dissent among the many. 'Certainly, there is one Deceiver in this hall,' I said. 'And who is to say where? False priest, false bishop. Or are we *all* false? Can any of you say in all honesty that you have stayed true to yourself? Tell me, Father'—here I addressed the Bishop in an undertone—'how true were you? How much more worthy to wear that robe than an actor—or a lecher—or an ape?'

He lunged at me then, as I knew he would;

346

laughing, I evaded the blow. But it was a feint; instead of going for me, he made a grab for the silver cross I had forgotten on the side of the pulpitum, and brandished it with a cry of triumph.

His triumph was brief, however. At once and with a cry of pain, he dropped the cross and looked at his hand, where even now white blisters were beginning to rise like fresh dough. It was a simple trick: placed so close to the brazier, the metal had become too hot to handle, but logic had long since abandoned my susceptible sisters, and the cry went up from the first row, spreading to the back in a matter of seconds.

'The Cross! He cannot touch the Cross!'

'That's ridiculous!' shouted the Bishop over the noise. 'This man is an impostor!' But the crowd was pushing forward, straining in the pews; the guards were still too far away to be of use, and Monseigneur looked about to use his fists when he thought better of it and lowered his hands, teeth clenched.

'Very wise,' I told him, beginning to smile. 'Lay a hand on me—lay even a finger—and all of hell breaks loose.'

♥

The rope caught at the first try. I felt the lead connect with the scaffolding opposite with a dull smacking sound. I tugged gently at the rope, but it held firm. Good. There was no time for further checks or precautions, and I secured the rope as well as I could to the rotten structure at my back. It was slacker than I usually like it, but I could not risk losing more time. I dropped my cloak from my shoulders, stepped out of the brown habit that had concealed me and stood on the narrow platform in my white shift. A swathe of blue cloth covered my all too recognizable hair. A moment of terror—it was too late, too much time had gone by, I would fall, I would fall—then the glacial cloak of the Winged One dropped over me, untouched by the passing years, and with it a kind of joy.

Head raised high, bare feet gripping the cord, arms slightly outstretched, l'Ailée stepped out proudly into the dark air.

♠

I knew her at once. You don't believe that? My first and best pupil—my only perfect achievement—of course I knew her. Even without her sequinned wings, veiled and with a cloth tied over her hair I knew her grace, her assurance, her style. I was the first; seconds later others had seen her too. I knew a moment of pride—ay, that was my Ailée, all eyes drawn to her in envy and longing—even in my astonishment and growing understanding.

I should have known. That was her audacity. I wondered what had alerted her to my plan—pure instinct, perhaps, that malicious instinct of hers to thwart me at every turn and to lay low my pride— even doomed to failure as it was, it was still a brave attempt.

From this low angle I could see no rope supporting her. The muted candle glow made of her a figure of mist, a warm, hazy apparition that seemed to shine with an inner light. A distant rumble of thunder from across the sea served as her introductory drum roll.

From the frenzy came a voice: 'Look! Above you! Look, I say!'

More faces turned to watch. More voices, clamorous at first, then falling to an awed hush as the white figure glided across the shadowy air, seemingly to hover right above their heads. 'Mère Marie!' wailed one voice from the depths of the congregation.

'The ghost of Germaine!'

'The Unholy Nun!'

The veiled figure paused for a moment in its passage over thin air and made the sign of the cross. Silence, awed silence, fell once more, as she prepared to speak.

♥

'My children.' My voice sounded terribly distant, the words resonating so far into the throat of the tower that they seemed barely recognizable. I could hear the beating of the rain against the wooden slats not five feet from my head and, somewhere across the water, a growl of thunder. 'My children, do you not recognize me? I am Sainte-Marie-de-la-mer.' The voice I had chosen was deep and resonant, like those of the tragedians of my Paris days. A flutter went through the sisters like a breath of wind on the sea. 'My poor, deluded children. You have been the victims of a cruel deception.'

LeMerle was watching me. I wondered at what point he would realize that all was lost for him; what he would do.

'Père Colombin is not what you think, my children. The man you see before you is a cruel impostor. No priest at all. A deceiver, whose true name is known to me.'

The collective gaze moved from the man to the

woman, the floating woman to the man . . . The silence was terrible. Then LeMerle lifted his eyes towards me and I could see the challenge in his face far below.

Will it be war, then, Harpy?

No malice in the unspoken question, simply a bright look of anticipation, the gambler's fever heightened to furnace intensity.

I nodded, almost imperceptibly, but I knew he understood.

Cue thunder. That was luck, Juliette; it could just as easily have been mine.

Did she expect me to run, I asked myself? Did she expect me to hide in the shadows? She should know better. And yet it pleased me in some absurd way that my pupil should seek to outplay the master at his own game of deceit. She looked down at me, my lovely bird of prey, and we understood each other completely. In spite of myself, in spite of the danger, I played your game, eager to know how well I taught you.

♥

The crowd was all faces, mouths open as if to receive honey from the sky. Above me, the storm was approaching fast; the rain had turned to a hail that rattled against the slates like dice. Although I was partly shielded by the roof above me, it was in poor condition, and I was uncomfortably aware that a single one of those hailstones might be enough to break my concentration and topple me from my perch. Was this what he hoped for? I'd expected him at least to deny my accusation, but he

350

seemed to be waiting, almost as if he had something else planned . . .

The realization, when it struck me, almost cost me my footing. Of course! Even from my vantage point, with everything laid out below me, I had been misdirected, like the rest of them. I had been so busy watching LeMerle that I had hardly noticed Isabelle eclipsed in his shadow. Only now, as I scanned the little scene, did I understand his full intent. Isabelle herself was to be the fuse. What he wanted was not to light the flame himself, but to watch the Bishop's face as his niece sacrificed her own life, and who knows how many others', in a desperate attempt to beat the Devil. She was poised to do it; a word might trigger her reaction. Now I understood the repeated sermons, the constant references to such martyred saints as Saints Agatha, Perpetua, Margaret of Alexandria, or holy miracle-workers like Christina Mirabilis who passed unhurt through flame to heavenly bliss.

I could see it in my mind: heavily robed and anointed with oil, she would leap into flame as quickly as summer stubble. I'd heard of it happening on stage, in the ballet, as a tulle skirt brushes the overheated glass of one of the footlights and fire jumps like an acrobat from one dancer to another, making lanterns of them all, torching their hair, vaulting ceiling-high in a trembling tower of fire and smoke. Whole troupes devoured in seconds, said LeMerle, who had once seen it happen, but—my God!—what a performance!

I could feel her eyes on me, now that I was awake to her gaze. I had to tread more carefully than ever; it was not enough to have interrupted

351

LeMerle's oratory or to have liberated the others from the dancing frenzy, it was not even enough to have thrown Père Colombin into doubt by endorsing the Bishop's claim against him. It was Isabelle I had to convince—only Isabelle. The question was, how much of the original Isabelle was left?

'There is no such saint as Marie-de-la-mer.' It was as if she had sensed my thoughts. Around her, the sisters awaited their cue and LeMerle observed his pupil with the smile of a man with a hand of aces.

'As I told you before,' he said in a calm voice, 'there is at least one Deceiver here. Which is it to be? Whom do you trust? Who has never lied to you?'

Isabelle looked up at me, then back at LeMerle. 'I trust you,' she said quietly, and put out her hand towards the brazier.

♠

Her rope is too slack. I saw that at once. A moment ago I saw her change position and she swayed, gripping the invisible rope with her toes to stop it from swinging out of control. Where to now, my harpy? Ten seconds and the place will be ablaze. A brave try, Juliette, but late, much too late. The pang I feel for you is real enough, but you chose this. I have to say I never imagined you'd really betray me, but a wise man anticipates every eventuality. You'll fly from your perch in flames, my bird. A better end, perhaps, than to live, wings clipped, among barnyard geese.

'*Vade retro, Satanas!*'

Isabelle's hand faltered an inch from the coals.

352

Even then it might have been enough, but for a sudden draught from the open side door. Damn it, Antoine. I told you not to leave your post, whatever happened. In any case, the girl faltered, looked up in spite of herself, recognizing the language of ancient authority. That was a foul blow, Juliette; using my own weapons against me. But is it good enough? And, seeing your advantage, will you play or will you fold?

'The Devil knows his Latin, too,' I reminded Isabelle softly. I began to move, very slowly, towards the side door and the second brazier. A wise man always covers his bets, and if one fuse fails to light, it's safer to have a second in reserve. But Antoine was standing at the side door, barring my exit with her huge body, and I saw that she too was watching the fake Virgin with a strange expression on her face.

'Listen to me, all of you.' The Winged One speaks again, and I can hear a hoarse note in her voice. 'Père Colombin has lied to you. He has deceived and tricked you since the moment he arrived. Remember the curse of blood? That was only dye, red dye, that he slipped into the well to frighten you. And the Unholy Nun? That was—' She stopped then, realizing her mistake, and I grinned and began to recite the rite of exorcism.

'*Praecipio tibi, quicumque es, spiritus immunde . . .*'

'Look at his arm!' cried the fake Marie, in the voice of Juliette. 'Make him show you the mark of the Virgin on his left arm!'

Timing, my dear, timing. If you'd thought of that at the start, you might have hurt me badly. But we've passed the time for signs and symbols. At this stage we need something more visceral, something

353

closer to the nerve.

'Name yourself,' I told her, smiling. 'Name yourself, because I don't think anyone here believes you're the Mother of God.'

'He is Guy LeMerle, he's a theatre actor and a—'

'I said name yourself!' Once more, Isabelle's hand began to creep towards the brazier. 'In the name of the Father!'

'He's doing this for revenge—'

'In the name of the Son!'

'Against the Bishop of Evreux!'

'In the name of the—' She was going to do it; her hand was an inch from the coals; her long sleeve had begun to smoke—

'The Bishop, *his father*!'

That was such an unexpected blow that I actually staggered. All around me the sisters had frozen. Isabelle was staring at me; the Bishop's face was cheesy with shock. The liveried guards were beginning once more to push through the crowd, swords loosened at their belts. And still my Ailée went on. 'Admit it, LeMerle,' she cried. 'Isn't he? *Isn't he?*'

My God, I thought, she's good. Wasted on these tame things, she should be setting stages alight in Paris theatres. I gave her a little bow to acknowledge it, then I turned to the Bishop, who was watching me with a look of sick horror. 'Well, Father,' I said, smiling. 'Aren't you?'

♥

The storm was almost over our heads now. Through the gaps in the roof I could watch its approach, hell's black circus striding across the

354

flats. Below me the candles grew suddenly dim as a cold gust rushed in from beneath the doors. A sound arose from the crowd below, a throbbing like that of a rotten tooth. Eyes flicked from Bishop to Priest, from Virgin to Bishop. My ankle began to wobble with the strain of standing still for so long, and I shifted slightly to ease it.

'Well?' said LeMerle, almost caressingly. 'Aren't you?'

There was a pause. Now I could see how cleverly LeMerle had used my intervention. If the Bishop denied the Virgin's accusation, then he validated LeMerle's imposture and Isabelle would light the fuse. If he admitted it, he was publicly disgraced in front of the Archbishop, his retinue, and the entire abbey full of nuns. But there was one detail LeMerle had forgotten, though I was not yet sure how—or if—I could turn it to my advantage. At the side door, almost invisible in the smoke from the brazier, stood Soeur Antoine, head lowered like a bull about to charge.

♠

I suppose I should be grateful, my Juliette. How you knew, I cannot guess—witchcraft, perhaps. But what a way to force him into a confession! My own plan was more dramatic, perhaps—I always enjoy a fire, you know—but I should have guessed you'd try to protect these poor sheep you call your sisters. Well, my dear, have it your own way. Let them keep their lives—if you can call it life. In either case, justice is done.

'Well, Father?'

Arnault gives a single nod.

Ahhh. The sound is like a tower of cards falling.

♥

'It's a lie,' said Isabelle.

'No, my dear. It's the truth.' LeMerle, watching the Bishop, with a sudden movement opened his priest's robe and let it drop to the ground. A cry went up from the sisters. Underneath the discarded robe he was dressed for travel: booted and spurred, with a leather vest leaving bare his branded left arm. It was the Blackbird of the old days who stood now smiling before the assembly, and as if to complete the tableau, lightning chose that moment to crack its bright whip across the sky, framing him in a sudden blaze of white.

The moan from the crowd had reached a pitch I could barely tolerate, dragging at my heels like undertow. For a second I looked directly below me, and the world gave a sudden lurch. I felt the beginning of a tremor in my left leg, a tiny ticking of the calf muscle which, if left unchecked, would jerk the rope from under me into the kicking air.

I understood that this was precisely what LeMerle was waiting for, that the apparent recklessness of this unveiling had been as coolly calculated as the rest of his plan. One against sixty were odds even he might have hesitated to play, but if I were to fall . . .

Once more I shifted, uncomfortably aware of the slackness of the rope and of their white coiffes below me, waiting like gulls on a sea of eyes.

♠

Ten more seconds and she will fall. Ten seconds more, eyes fixed on the white figure in the air. The diversion should be enough—the moment of flight,

356

the broken shape on the marble—moment enough for me to find my exit. If not that, then to grab a weapon. Any of these sisters might buy my escape, but I would prefer Isabelle as hostage. A sword, a horse, and hotfoot across to the mainland. I'll maybe leave the chit's body in a ditch for him to find, or better still keep her with me. I could find uses enough for her where I'm going, and every day I'd fix in her flesh the barbs of my revenge. Not for myself—no, not this time. But for her, for Juliette, my sweet deceiver.

That I should live to see the day when I wished my Ailée to fall! He'll pay for that too, you'll see, in full coin. The congregation has become a chorus. The note—the long drawn-out vowel of their despair—rises, swoops, soars again. Some weep in confusion, some tear their faces. But all eyes are on us both now, I watching her, she watching me. A turn of the friendly card—Jack below, Queen above—and our roles can be reversed once more. Even the guards remain frozen, swords half drawn, awaiting an order which never comes.

*　　　*　　　*

♥

I know what you're doing, LeMerle. You're waiting for me to fall. Buying time. I can feel you willing me, *wishing* me to slip, to stumble, the rope arcing into empty air without me, the long slice of darkness to the ground. I can feel your thoughts pressing against me. I am drenched with the rain now as water spurts from the gutter into the tower. The bell, barely three feet above me, spatters its note in a thousand droplets of sound. I will not—

will not fall. But the gulf beneath draws me, and my cramping muscles scream for respite. I feel as if I have been here motionless for hours.

The rope jerks again in response to some involuntary spasm. The keening of my sisters makes me dizzy. And yet I will not—

—must—

—not—

—fall—

♠

I see it happen with a dreamlike clarity. A series of tableaux, each fixed by the lightning as it strikes nearby—several times, in rapid succession. She slips, kicks out against the swing of the rope and loses it—for an instant I see her arms flung wide, embracing the dark. *Strike.* Thunder, louder than ever before, so close overhead that for a moment I almost believe the strike has hit the tower itself . . . And in the brief interval of darkness that follows, I hear the rope give way.

I know I should run now, while their attention is elsewhere. But I cannot; I have to see for myself. Soeur Antoine is guarding the door. There is a dangerous expression on her face, but she is surely too slow to hinder me. As I glance at her, she begins to move towards me. Her face is set in stone, and now I remember the strength in her big red arms, the size of her meaty fists. Nevertheless, she is only a woman. Even if she has turned against me now, what can she do?

The sisters crowd round, no doubt to see the body on the floor. At any moment there will come the cries, the confusion, and in that confusion I will make my escape. Soeur Virginie is looking at me, her small fists clenched; beside her, Soeur Tomasine, her eyes narrowed into crescents. I step forward once again and the nuns cluck like frightened hens, too stupid even to move aside. My sudden fear is absurd, I know. Ridiculous, to think that they might try to stop me; you might as well expect barnyard geese to attack the fox.

But something has gone wrong. The eyes that should have been gazing at the body on the floor are turning instead towards me. Even geese, I recall from my childhood days, can be savage when driven. And now they dare to block my way, to peck at me, to surround me with their stink and their reproaches . . . As I push forwards into the space, Soeur Antoine raises a fist which I could deflect with my arms behind my back, but already I am felled with astonishment, stumbling even before her blow lands. What witchcraft is this? I drop to my knees, my head ringing from a vicious punch to the back of the neck, but all I feel is a remote and silent amazement.

There is no body on the floor.

Strike.

And the tower is empty.

CHAPTER FIFTEEN

♥

September 7th, 1611
Théâtre Ambulant du GrosJean,
Carêmes

Some memories never fade. Even in the warmth of this good autumn, this good town, some part of me remains *there*, at the abbey, in the rain. Perhaps some part of me died there—died, or was reborn, I am not sure which. In any case, I, who did not believe in miracles, witnessed *something* that changed me—only a little, but for ever. Maybe, in that moment, Sainte Marie-de-la-mer was with us. Sitting here now, a twelve-month later, I can almost believe even that.

I felt the rope go. A muscular spasm, perhaps, or the slackness of the cord, or the rotten wood of the scaffolding as it gave way. I knew a moment of utter calm, frozen in the lightning flash like a fly in amber. Then reaching for nothing in a last gesture of desperation, my mind a blank but for the thought *If only I were a bird*, my fingers splayed but finding nothing, nothing.

And then there was something in front of my face: a cobweb, a figment, a rope. I did not question its miraculous presence; as I fell, it was almost out of my hands before I had the wit to catch it. I missed it altogether with the right hand, but my reflexes were still good and I caught fast with the left, dangling for a second in midair with nothing in my mind but stupid disbelief—then I saw a pale face, twisted now in an urgent grimace as she mouthed at me from the hole in the roof, and I understood.

Perette had not failed me. She must have climbed up the scaffolding left by the workmen and watched everything through the gaps in the slates. I hoisted myself up—the ability to climb a rope, like that of balancing upon a line, is not easily lost—and dragged myself like a wet fish onto the slippery roof.

I lay there for a while, exhausted, whilst Perette embraced me, hooting with joy. Below us I could hear a surge of sound, incomprehensible as the tides. I think I lost consciousness; for a moment I drifted, washed by the rain, the smell of the sea in my nostrils. I would never fly again. I knew it; this had been l'Ailée's final appearance.

But now Perette put out her small hand and shook me urgently. I opened my eyes; saw her sketch one of her quick hand-mimes. A horse; the sign for 'haste'; the gesture she had always used to indicate Fleur. And again: Fleur, riding, haste. I sat up, my head swimming. The wild girl was right. Whatever the outcome of LeMerle's drama, it would not be wise to remain. Soeur Auguste, too, had given her final performance, and I found that, after all, I did not regret it.

Perette took my hand, guiding me deftly towards the ladder, still in place some fifteen feet down the steep slope below us. She seemed quite unafraid of the danger but climbed with catlike ease, balancing delicately upon a ridge of broken guttering as she moved to let me pass. Rain stung our faces and hammered on our heads, thunder rolled over us like rocks, a hundred yards away a lightning-struck tree was ablaze, touching everything with a dim, apocalyptic light. And in the middle of it all we laughed, Perette and I, like mad things; laughed with the sheer joy of the rain and the storm, at the relief of my escape, and most of all, at the look on his face, the look on LeMerle's face as he prepared to receive the pounding of his life from a gaggle of angry nuns . . .

I heard later that he went without a fight and with only a token protestation of innocence, still gazing in puzzlement at the place where I had been. It was as if the ground had been cut from under him, I heard, his words losing their witchcraft in the face of this new, greater sorcery. Certainly it must have seemed to them as if I disappeared into thin air. A miracle, came the cry, a miracle, and surely this floating lady was indeed Sainte Marie-de-la-mer, come to rescue her own, as in the old legends.

The discovery of a lightning-struck tree not a hundred yards from the chapel also sparked rumours of miraculous delivery. I hear that today there is a small shrine to the Holy Mother of the Sea, that the new Marie has returned to the mainland and that a new Mermaid, so like the old one as to be almost identical, has reappeared in the abbey chapel. Already she is said to have healing powers, and pilgrims come from as far as Paris to see the place where she appeared in front of over sixty witnesses.

The Bishop of Evreux was quick to corroborate the Apparition's tale, revealing LeMerle as an impostor in a catalogue of deceit and corruption. The miraculous appearance of the fleur-de-lys, emblem of the Holy Virgin, on the arm of the accused man was interpreted as definitive proof of the Apparition's authenticity and of his own alliance with dark powers and he was taken, dazed and unprotesting, into the custody of the secular court.

I cannot help but grieve a little. I have hated him in the past, but since then I think I came to know him better, and if not to forgive, at least to understand. He was taken to the mainland, I heard, to be examined by the judge in Rennes. I was in Rennes myself for a time, and saw the roundhouse in which he was being kept, and read the notices upon its doors telling of his arrest. These announced his forthcoming execution—I thought I detected the vindictive hand of the Bishop in some of the details, which rivalled the execution of Ravillac, the King's murderer, in their ingeniousness and brutality.

The Bishop and his niece returned to Montauban, the ancestral home of the Arnaults. Apparently Isabelle had expressed the wish for a simpler life, far from the coast, and had joined a reflective order—this time as an ordinary sister, where, I hope, she learned to live in peace and forgetfulness.

The Bishop himself fared less well. Though he protested that his false confession in our chapel had been extracted by fear, he never quite recovered from its effects. Rumours of his cowardice spread insidiously; open doors were softly closed, friendships withdrawn, ambitions quashed. I have heard reports that he too is planning to retire—ostensibly on the grounds of ill-health—to the same monastery of which his late brother was Abbot.

As for myself, I left the abbey that day. I could not stay and risk arrest—besides, too much had passed in that place for it to be a home for me again. So I left, taking with me LeMerle's fine horse as well as the money and provisions I found in its saddlebags.

I found Fleur waiting for me in our agreed place, the orphan look gone from her face—had it ever even been there?—and we fled across the causeway, chased all the way by the tide, arriving at Pornic three hours later.

I do not imagine they looked for me very far. The Bishop already had his man, and it would not have benefited him to blazon his Isabelle's disgrace any further. I think he let me lose myself rather than face the story I might tell, and in any case I had the tide between us and the island, with an eleven-hour wait for the next safe passage across the strand.

Travelling with LeMerle had taught me to value caution. I sold his horse as I had Giordano's mule so long ago, and with the proceeds bought myself a caravan and a mule to pull it. We lived well from our gold, Fleur and I, stopping for supplies in market towns but keeping to the smaller roads at other times for fear of the Bishop's men. Close by Perpignan we fell in with a group of gypsies who, when they heard my tale, welcomed us as their own. We had been travelling with them for almost three months when we met an Italian theatre troupe who agreed to take us both.

Since then, we have toured provincial towns all over the district. The *commedia dell'arte* begins to gain in popularity as the Italianate fashions return, and, masked, I need have no fear of being recognized as the Winged One of old. We are happy, Fleur and I, with our new friends: Fiorello who plays Scaramouche, and Domenico, who plays Arlequin. Fleur plays the drum and dances, and I play piety once more with Isabelle. That I should be given that part—that name—always fills me with a kind of laughter so close to tears that sometimes I can hardly tell them apart. The mask hides my smiles—and the rest—and Beltrame, who leads the troupe, tells me he has never seen such a spirited Isabelle.

And yet there are times—many times this past winter—when I ask myself whether it is not time to have done with it all. A floor of boards is not so sturdy as one of earth, and the thought of a piece of earth of my own returns to haunt me even in my present happiness. Fleur needs a safe place, a home. A cottage by a village, a hearth, some ducks and a goat, a vegetable garden . . . Maybe my life at the abbey has lost me my taste for the wandering life, or maybe I begin to feel the approach of winter. I count my gold with more than greed in my heart and promise myself that before the winter comes I will have my cottage, my hearth . . . Fleur bangs her drum, laughing.

Over a year has passed since I left the abbey. I still dream of it sometimes, of the friends I left there, of my sweet Perette—how I wish I could have taken her with us! In some ways I miss the abbey life; I miss my herb garden, the companionship of the chapterhouse, the library, the Latin lessons, the long walks across the flats to the sea. But we are free here. Fleur's nightmares have long since stopped, and this year has seen her grow taller, her hair darkened to russet but still bleached at the ends by the island's sun, and though the knowledge sometimes saddens me that minute by minute she grows away from me into the young girl—the adult—she will one day become, she is still the same sweet Fleur, wilful yet trusting and filled with open wonder at the world.

Last week a messenger, travelling with a group of players from the north, brought me a packet. It was addressed to *Juliett Ser Auguste, Dancer*, in a round hand that I did not recognize, and it bore signs of having been carried for many months before the players came to me by chance. There was no address upon the packet, but my messenger told me it had been given him by a nun from Brittany some five months ago.

I opened it. The packet contained a leaf of thick paper, close written in the same unfamiliar round hand, plus two printed news sheets. As I unfolded them something fell out from between the papers and rang upon the ground. I stooped to pick it up. It was a small enamelled medallion that I knew well: on it was Christina Mirabilis, the miracle worker, floating arms outstretched within a ring of orange flame.

I read the letter. Here it is:

Dear Auguste,
I hope this Letter findes You, as I Praye every Daye thatt itt will. I think of You and Remembere You in my Prayers, You and Flore. I have kept Your Garden here, and Soeur Perpétue, who is very Kinde to Me, teaches me how to Tende itt and the Fowles which are My Duty. Margerit is the new Abbesse now, and does Well enough. Itt is the Abbaye of Marie-de-la-Mer Once Again, and I am Gladde of itt. I am

366

Learning to Read and Write with the Help of Soeur Perpétue. She is Very Patiente, and minds nott thatt I am Slow. This is the First Letter I have ever Writ, and I Pray You will Excuse My Mistakes. I will Send itt with the Players at Mardi Gras. I love You Juliette, and Little Flore. I Send You Newes too of Père Colombin. I hope itt is nott a Sinne to be Gladde of Whatt has Past. I wish You Happinesse Both,
   Your Perett

Printed Text, dated September 1610,
Rennes Roundhouse.

Marvellous and Most Dreadful Tale of Witchcrafte!

On This, Twenty-First Daye of August, at the Abbey of Sainte-Marie Mère was Apprehended a most Fell Sorceror, Accused, Tried and Found Guilty of Various Offences against God and the Holy Church. Purporting to be a Holy Cleric, the Accused, Guy LeMerle named The Blackbird, Was Found to be in League with the Forces of Darknesse, to Consort with Familiars in the Guise of Birdes and to Conjure Satan, Bewitching to Death Several Holy Sisters of the Abbey by Foulest Means, and Guilty of Various Poisonings and Acts of Foule Desecration in the Abbey. When Questioned the Wretch Confesst Most Wholeheartedly to the Crimes of which he was Accused, showing a Most Damnable Pride in his Actions and Refusing to Recant his Allegiance to the Prince of Evil, even under Interrogation. Guards left to Ensure the Prisoner's Safety reported most Marvellous and Fearful Sights during that fateful Eve, whereby Familiars, taking Several Forms of Birde or Beaste, did Visit him in his cell and did Speak with him throughout the Nighte, Entreating him to fly with them from the Place, but to no Avail. The Prisoner was Kept Secure, the cell Being Blest by His Holiness the Bishop of Evreux, and Barred Thrice with Steele. On the Day of September Ninth Justice Will be Done in the Market Place in the Presence of the Bishop, of Judge René Durant and of the People of the Town. In the Name of God and of His Majesty, Louis Dieudonné.

Second Printed Text, dated September 1610, Rennes.

Most Monstrous and Damnable Tale of a Visitation.

On this, the Seventh Day of September in Rennes, the Criminal and Convicted Sorcerer Guy The Blackbird Effected a Daring and most Monstrous Escape from Confinement in the Round House of this Town, Being in league with the Spirits and Forces of Witchcraft. At midnight Guards set to at the Gate to Keep Close Watch upon the Prisoner were Approached by a Cloak'd Female bearing a Lantern, who did warn them to Stand Backe, if they did value their Souls.

Then Guards, Philippe Legros and Armand Nuillot, did request the Name of the Strange Visitor, and were at once render'd Powerless by Witchcrafte, and despite Prayers and Brave Resistance did fall as if Drugg'd upon the Grounde.

Whereby Trembling with Righteous Fear they Observed the Female enter the Round House by Demonic Means and in the Companie of Various Imps and Familiars, and though not Rendered quite Insensible, were by this Strange and Hellish Magicke Prevented from all Interference.

The Female left the Round House some short Time Later, followed by a Cloak'd Figure, closely Wrapt about, which did then Reveal itself as Guy LeMerle, throwing off its Disguise with Laughter and much Manifestation of Joy. The Witch then bestrode him a Pitchforke which had been left lying beside the Hay Stall and did Flye into the Air upon it, with many Mocking Cries to the Unfortunates Below, who did perceive various Spirits and Familiars in the guise of Birdes, Battes and Owles, which did Join Him in his Flighte. Monsiegneur the Bishop of Evreux will have it Known that Any Man with Knowledge of this Fellow, or of his Associates, should with all Speed Divulge this Knowledge, or any Suspicion which may be Had of his Whereabouts, that this Witch may be Brought to the Justice of God and the Church. A Reward of Fifty Louis is offered for any Such Information.

*   *   *

Well, I recall no familiars. Nor the mad flight upon the pitchfork. Doubtless the guards invented the rest to escape punishment. As for my part—yes, Perette, I was the Female with the Lantern—I cannot explain it. And yet, like you, I feel a reluctant gladness to know that he escaped. A vestige, perhaps, of my early loyalty, or a desire for an end to this long, long dream.

I had always known Giordano's alchemies would serve me some day. The roundhouse, with its thick walls and barred windows, was far from certain, even for your explosive powders, but well placed, and with a fuse made from a length of powder twine leading to a central bolus, I felt sure it would serve my purpose. I approached the guards first, offered them ale and companionship, and picked their pockets neatly in the process. I could have cut their throats—the old Juliette might have done just that—but I wanted to avoid it if I could; I have seen too many cruelties to add to the number. As it was, the guards ran away the minute the powder blew, and my assessment of their cowardice led me to hope for at least two minutes before they returned.

LeMerle was still half asleep when I came into the cell, curled upon the straw with his ragged cloak around him. Better not to look at him, I told myself. Simply leave the lantern and the keys and let him make his own way if he could. I saw him twitch like a wakening cat and turned to go, afraid perhaps that if I did not, I might never find the courage to leave him again. But it was too late; he murmured something indistinct and held up his arm to shield his face, and, like Orpheus, I looked back.

Of course he had been tortured; I had expected it. I know what happens during interrogation. Even a full confession only counts under torture. His face, half turned into the light, was a mask of filth and bruises. His raised hand was a talon, every finger broken.

'Juliette?' It was barely a whisper; barely a voice. 'My God, what dream is this?'

370

I could not reply. Instead I looked at him on the floor of the Roundhouse and I saw myself—in the cell in Epinal, and the cellarium of the abbey—and remembered how I had sworn eternal revenge, sworn I'd see him suffer. I felt a pang of surprise that the thought of his suffering did not satisfy me as once I had imagined it would.

'It's no dream. Hurry, if you want to be free.'

'Juliette?' He was more alert now in spite of the ravages done to him. 'By God, is it in very truth witchcraft?'

I would not reply, I told myself.

'My Winged One.' Now I could have sworn there was laughter in the tone. 'I knew it couldn't end this way. After everything we were to each other—'

'No.' I said. 'You were born to be hanged, not burned. This is destiny.'

He laughed aloud at that. They might have clipped his wings, I thought, but my Blackbird still sang. I was startled to realize how much the thought pleased me.

'Why do you delay?' My voice was sharp. 'Are you so comfortable here?'

Silently he held his chained wrists to the light. I threw him the bunch of keys.

'I can't. My hands.'

Haste made me clumsy, and I must have hurt him as I unlocked the irons. But his eyes held me still, bright and mocking as ever. 'It could be as it was, you know,' he said, grinning with the anticipation of triumphs imagined. 'I have money hidden away. We could start again. L'Ailée could fly once more. Forget carnival, forget market-day venues—that trick of yours in the tower was worth gold . . .'

'You're mad.' I thought so, too. Torture, imprisonment, ruin, failure, disgrace . . . Nothing had yet touched that arrogant assurance of his. That look of not-to-be-denied. He never gave a thought to the possibility of refusal, of rejection. I picked up the lantern, ready to go.

'You know you'd love it,' he said.

'No.' I was turning already towards the door. We had seconds, at best, before the guards returned. And perhaps the harm was already done, that last glimpse of his face in the soft glow of the lamp printed in fire and forever onto my heart.

'Please, Juliette.' At least now he was on his feet, following me to safety. 'All those years I was travelling roads, trying to find my way, and I never knew where until now. All those times I worked towards something I thought I wanted, which turned out to be nothing more than a passing whim on the hunt for some other rainbow's end; all those women I lusted for and trifled with and ultimately punished for being too short, or too soft, or too young, or too pretty—'

'We don't have time for this,' I said. I shook his hand from my shoulder, but he could not be stopped, every word he spoke a new refinement of pain.

'Come on, admit it. Why else would you have come back for me? It was you, Juliette. Always you. It didn't matter whether you loved or hated me, we're two parts of the same. We fit together. Complete each other.'

Without looking at him, and with a terrible effort, I began to walk away.

'Stubborn! Haven't I chased you long enough?' I could hear anger now, and a kind of desperation.

372

My step quickened. I could see the half-open door of the roundhouse in the torchlight. I ran out into the cool air. I could still hear LeMerle behind me, losing his footing, cursing in the dark. My shadow ran before me like a wild thing.

'You fool!' He was shouting now, heedless of whom he might alert. 'Don't you understand? Juliette! Must I say it in as many words?'

I could not hear it. I would not hear it. I ran forwards into the night, a rushing silence in my ears, though beneath the pressing of my palms I fancied I still heard him, a ghost of him, an echo of desire.

I fled fast and reckless out of Rennes. Only I knew that it was two hunters I fled. And Perette, if it is a sin to be glad, then we are sinners both, for the thought of a world without LeMerle in it somewhere seems to me to be no world at all. I will write to you, sweetheart, and send the letter on with next season's travellers. Tend my herbs well, but grow no morning glories among them. Chamomile brings sweet dreams, and lavender sweet thoughts. I wish you both, my Perette, and with them all the love you deserve.

EPILOGUE

It ends, as it begins, with the players. For a second, looking out into the sun at the scarlet caravan drawing close to my own, I could almost believe they were the same troupe who came to us that day. Lazarillo's World Players, Tragedy and Comedy, Beasts and Marvels. I tell myself I have seen enough of all of these. But the sun on their costumes, the sequins, the furs, the lace and scarlet and gold and emerald and madder and dusty rose, the piping of flute and beating drums, the masks and stilts and dancers all in greasepaint and road grime rang so sweet and so true in my heart that I opened my caravan window a crack to listen.

Fleur was with them, her blue dress flying bravely in the breeze, her dusty feet bare. She squealed and clapped as the fire-eater spat flame at the sun, the acrobats somersaulted from each other's shoulders, Géronte leering at demure Isabelle, Arlequin and Scaramouche duelling with wooden swords bedecked with multicoloured ribbons.

Fleur saw me watching. She waved at me and I saw something white in one hand, a handkerchief, perhaps, or a scrap of paper. I saw her speak to Scaramouche—a tall Scaramouche with a limp in the left leg and hair tied back with a ribbon—and he whispered in her ear and seemed to smile beneath the long-nosed mask. Fleur listened, nodded, began to run towards me, the white object—I saw now that it was indeed a piece of paper—waving in one hand. She pushed aside the brocade curtain that serves as a door in summer. '*Maman*, the masked man said to give you this.'

Another letter? I reached for the sheet, warmed by the sun and slightly crumpled from Fleur's clutching hand, and saw that it was not a letter, but a playbill. I read:

Le Théâtre du Phénix presents:
La Belle Harpie
A Play in Five Acts

Beneath the cursive lettering was the drawing of a winged woman, hair flying wildly, standing atop a tower whilst a crowd of onlookers stared up at her in amazement. Above the design was a crest depicting a burning bird above a fleur-de-lys and a printed motto, which I looked at for a long, long time:

My song endureth.

Then, a little breathlessly, I began to laugh. Who was to doubt it? The Phoenix above the fleur-de-lys, no Blackbird now, but a bird reborn from fire . . . His audacity knew no bounds, his arrogance no limits!

Fleur looked at me in some anxiety. 'Are you crying, *Maman*?' she whispered. 'Are you sad?'

'It's nothing,' I said, wiping my eyes. 'The sun on this paper, that's all. It stings.'

'The masked man said to give it to you,' she continued, reassured. 'He said he'd wait for an answer.'

An answer? I moved slowly to the window. Looking very closely I could see the crest, painted in gold upon the panels of the caravan opposite: *Théâtre du Phénix*. The players were still at their performance, colours flying, flame, purple, emerald and crimson. Only Scaramouche was still, plain in his black doublet, looking towards my window, eyes unreadable behind the mask.

'He said he'd go away if you told him to,' said Fleur from behind me. Then, as I still did not reply: 'Why don't you ask him in, at least? He says he's come a long way, hundreds of leagues, to talk to you. It wouldn't be polite, would it, to send him away?'

A pause, long as for ever. Fleur looked at me with enquiring, innocent eyes.

'No,' I said at last. 'I suppose it wouldn't.'

My heart has joined the drumming of the tabor. My breath quickens. I see the small blue figure run across the grass towards the players. Scaramouche bends to hear her message, folds her quickly in his arms and lifts her. Far away I hear her squeal of delight. Setting her gently back on the grass he turns again, pointing to his caravan, to the velvet-clad dwarf sitting on the steps with a monkey upon his knee . . . Then his eyes turn back to me, invisible behind the mask but unbearably bright nevertheless.

I feel a desperate urge to run to meet him, and an equally desperate longing to run far away in the opposite direction. I do not move. I am trembling a little, my stomach tightening with a dizziness I never felt when I walked the high rope.

Slowly, almost casually, the masked figure makes his way towards me. Halfway across the sward he takes off his doublet and throws it across his shoulder. The sun catches a mark, high up on his left arm, which shines silvery in the light. Then he puts out his hand, a tiny smile on his lips, in a gesture both tender and mocking.

From my window it almost looks like an invitation to dance.

ACKNOWLEDGEMENTS

Many thanks to all those who have given so generously of their time, effort and encouragement to make this book possible. To Serafina, Warrior Princess; to Jennifer, Overseas Warrior; to my terrific editor, Francesca, and all my friends at Transworld; to Louise Page, for services far beyond the call of duty; to Stuart Haygarth, for another gorgeous jacket; to Anne Reeve, for the gift of organization; and to my family and friends, especially Christopher Fowler, Charles de Lint and Juliet McKenna, for keeping me on track. Finally, my thanks to the sales representatives, booksellers and distributors who continue to work so hard behind the scenes to ensure that my books make it to the shelves.

HOLY FOOLS

For   by circumstance to seek refuge with Fleur,
her   ng daughter, in the remote abbey of Sainte
Ma   e-la-mer, actress Juliette reinvents herself
as   Auguste under the tutelage of the kindly
Ab   But times are changing: the murder of
He   IV becomes the catalyst for massive
uph   in France. A new Abbess is appointed,
and   ette's comfortable life begins to unravel.
Fo   the new Abbess is Isabelle, the eleven-year-
old   of a corrupt and noble family. Worse,
Iab   as brought with her a ghost from Juliette's
pas   querading as a cleric, a man she has every
rea   fear . . .